And don't miss these other Kay Hooper collections . . .

ENCHANTED

Includes *Kissed by Magic, Belonging to Taylor,*
and *Eye of the Beholder*

ELUSIVE

Includes *Elusive Dawn, On Her Doorstep,*
and *Return Engagement*

Kay Hooper

The Real Thing

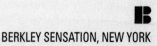

BERKLEY SENSATION, NEW YORK

THE BERKLEY PUBLISHING GROUP
Published by the Penguin Group
Penguin Group (USA) Inc.
375 Hudson Street, New York, New York 10014, USA
Penguin Group (Canada), 10 Alcorn Avenue, Toronto, Ontario M4V 3B2, Canada
(a division of Pearson Penguin Canada Inc.)
Penguin Books Ltd., 80 Strand, London WC2R 0RL, England
Penguin Group Ireland, 25 St. Stephen's Green, Dublin 2, Ireland
(a division of Penguin Books Ltd.)
Penguin Group (Australia), 250 Camberwell Road, Camberwell, Victoria 3124, Australia
(a division of Pearson Australia Group Pty Ltd.)
Penguin Books India Pvt. Ltd, 11 Community Centre, Panchsheel Park,
New Delhi–110 017, India
Penguin Group (NZ), Cnr. Airborne and Rosedale Roads, Albany, Auckland 1310,
New Zealand (a division of Pearson New Zealand Ltd.)
Penguin Books (South Africa) (Pty.) Ltd., 24 Sturdee Avenue, Rosebank,
Johannesburg 2196, South Africa

Penguin Books Ltd., Registered Offices: 80 Strand, London WC2R 0RL, England

This is a work of fiction. Names, characters, places, and incidents either are the product of the author's imagination or are used fictitiously, and any resemblance to actual persons, living or dead, business establishments, events, or locales is entirely coincidental.

PRINTING HISTORY
Berkley Sensation trade paperback edition / November 2004
Enemy Mine: published 1990 in Great Britain by Mills & Boon Ltd.; 1992 by Silhouette Books
The Haviland Touch: published 1991 by Silhouette Books

Library of Congress Cataloging-in-Publication Data

Hooper, Kay.
 [Enemy mine.]
 The real thing / Kay Hooper.
   p. cm.
 Contents: Enemy mine — The Haviland touch.
 ISBN 0-425-19833-2
 1. Love stories, American. I. Hooper, Kay. Haviland touch. II. Title.

PS3558.O587E54 2004
813'.54—dc22   2004046879

PRINTED IN THE UNITED STATES OF AMERICA

10 9 8 7 6 5 4 3 2 1

contents

The Real Thing

ENEMY MINE

To Leslie,
Who waited very patiently for this,
And for Eileen,
Who never wailed at me,
even though I'm sure she wanted to

chapter one

"*PENDLETON!* OH, GREAT, that's just great. It had to be you!"

"Nice seeing you again, too, Tyler. Damn it, will you get your foot off my—"

Tyler found a bit of purchase against his upper thigh and managed to boost herself higher. "Go to hell!" she snapped, holding on to an all too narrow ledge.

"We're both likely to get there any minute now," he told her, a little winded but entirely his normal insouciant self. His left hand groped and discovered a murderously narrow crack in the rock about two feet below her shoulders; wedging his long fingers into that, he hung by one hand long enough to remove her foot from his thigh and place it on an almost nonexistent ledge she couldn't see.

Tyler would have choked thanking him, but she felt more secure.

Kane Pendleton worked his other hand into the crevice and

pulled himself higher, the strain bunching powerful muscles beneath his khaki shirt and cording his forearms. Rock splintered a scant few inches from his shoulder, but he paid no attention even when the crack of the rifle echoed down the ravine.

His boots scrabbled for a foothold, discovering one finally, and he was hanging on to the same ledge, showing her white teeth as his tanned face split in a grin. "Fancy meeting you here," he said cheerfully.

Tyler ducked instinctively as another rifle shot chipped rock above her head, but her voice was as steady as it was fierce. "What're you doing here, Kane?"

"The same as you, I'd bet. Work your way along the ledge; the one you're standing on gets wider a couple of feet to your left. Come on, honey, move—that guy can't keep missing us forever."

"Don't call me honey!" she muttered, but began moving cautiously to her left. The ledge beneath her feet was soon wide enough to lend considerable security, and her tense fingers eased somewhat, no longer forced to bear most of her weight.

Since Kane was occupying himself in finding a more secure perch, she risked a glance at him. She didn't know whether to be relieved or annoyed to see that he had changed not at all in the several months since their last encounter. Only his face, throat, and forearms were bared to her sight, and she could see no scars, no recent marks on his flesh.

He was, as always, darkly tanned, his big, broad-shouldered body unnervingly powerful, those beautiful long-fingered hands of his still filled with their amazing strength. He wore no hat despite the heat, and his thick, shining black hair was, as always, a little long and somewhat shaggy.

A black-maned lion, she had always thought, proud and strong in the summer of his life.

Annoyed with herself, Tyler returned her full attention to the task of moving along the ledge, seeking some shelter from the sporadic gunfire far below them. She sent mental advice to the part of her that wanted to look at him, reminding herself that nothing would be different this time, nothing at all.

They were after the same thing—again—and neither would stop until the chalice was found and claimed. By one of them.

It had been a beaten gold necklace last time, she remembered, working her way along the ledge slowly and carefully. And before that—What had it been before that? Oh, yes . . . An uncatalogued Rembrandt offered for sale by a private collector in France.

Three years since their first meeting under the burning sun of Egypt, where they had met and fought for a golden figurine. And during those years they had clashed a dozen times all over the world. Mexico, Budapest, Hamburg, Madrid, the Sudan, Athens, Venezuela, Madagascar. To date, she thought wryly, the honors were evenly split. In twelve face-to-face confrontations, she had come away with the prize six times—and so had Kane.

Tyler found it incredible that she and Kane worked for bitter rivals, two indecently wealthy men who thought nothing of sending their representatives halfway around the world in a hurried and often dangerous search for certain carefully chosen rare art objects, antiquities and artifacts. She still found it hard to believe that those two men enjoyed a mutual bitter delight in their games of one-upmanship, each spending vast amounts of money to get the objects each coveted—and to get them first.

She could hardly complain that her own part in the games had not been both exciting, adventurous and profitable—all three being reasons she had taken the job in the first place. Her employer had found her in a small antique store in London, where her reputation for possessing an unerring instinct for detecting genuine antiquities over faked ones had grown so that even some museums kept her on a retainer.

Robert Sayers had introduced himself, talked to her for less than an hour and then offered her a job. Tyler had been twenty-three and restless; she had spent most of her life in following her archaeologist father into some of the most remote parts of the world, and her settled life since his death had taught her nothing if not that the gypsy in her was still strong.

She had been ripe for Sayers's offer.

Her mind in the past, Tyler stepped off the ledge and into thin air. Her fingers scrabbled for a hold and she felt Kane's hard arm lock around her waist.

"I'd hate to lose you now," he remarked, his deep voice showing none of the strain he must have felt; he was leaning outward from the cliff face to support her, one hand jammed in a crevice above them—and she was not a little woman.

She managed to regain her fingertip hold on the ledge and get her feet beneath her again. "You can't lose what you've never had!" she snapped, turning her head to glare at him. "And I thought you said the ledge widened."

His remarkably vivid green eyes were amused. Ignoring her second comment, he responded to the first. "Now that's a provocative thing to say. A challenge, no less." His arm tightened around her waist before releasing her. "One of these days—when we have time—we really should explore that. I wonder if I *would* lose you once I had you."

Tyler showed him a smile that was all teeth and no humor. "Don't hold your breath, pal," she advised.

Kane laughed softly. "Right. The ledge *did* widen by the way, and it widens again, on the other side of this spur. But we'll have to go around the tip."

She looked in the opposite direction and winced, grateful that he couldn't see her expression. Unnoticed by her, the ledge they'd traversed had swung outward to follow the spur that protruded into the ravine like some granite giant's elbow. They couldn't climb higher since the cliff face was sheet-smooth, and they certainly couldn't descend into the ravine where that gunman waited with his trusty rifle. They had to go on.

"Great," she muttered.

"Give me your hand," he instructed, "and stay pressed against the cliff. Try to stretch your foot around to the other side; the ledge should be within reach."

Tyler usually trusted Kane Pendleton about as far as she could throw a bull elephant, but she didn't hesitate to give him her hand and follow his orders. If she had learned nothing else of him during their past encounters, she had learned to trust him in times of danger. He might well pull every trick he could think of in order to beat her to whatever they both sought, but he would no more abandon a bitter enemy in trouble than he would his best friend.

She fell somewhere between.

And the strength of his big hand was comforting as she braced one foot on the ledge and stretched the other around the spur, keeping her body pressed to the rock. She searched blindly with that extended foot, holding her breath, feeling the rock dig into her painfully. She was no mountain climber, but this wasn't the first time she'd been forced to broaden her horizons out of the need to escape something or someone. The survival instinct, Tyler had learned, was a great motivator.

Her foot finally located the ledge, and she was pinned there momentarily while her hand searched for something to hold. Then she was sliding cautiously around the point of the spur, knowing that Kane wouldn't let go until she felt secure.

"Got it," she called breathlessly, all of her once more on one side of the spur. She moved along the ledge, pausing once she was a couple of feet away from the point to watch Kane work his way

around. Within seconds, he appeared, moving far more easily than
she. But then, he *was* a mountain climber. Among other things.

Securely on her side of the spur, he nodded toward what
looked like nothing more than a crooked gash in the face of the
cliff. "There's a cave, and it's invisible from the bottom of the
ravine; if we get inside fast enough, our friend with the gun may
lose us."

Tyler didn't waste time in working her way toward the cave,
but she wondered silently how Kane could possibly know of it.
Still, she didn't doubt his knowledge. Kane, damn his black-hearted
soul, was always right. *Always*. It was enough to give a woman a
complex.

She slid into the narrow opening of the cave easily and stood
staring, discovering that he could still surprise her.

"Hey, you're blocking the door."

Casting an irritated glance over her shoulder, Tyler moved
farther into the cave, muttering to herself. Obviously he hadn't
planned to be absent long, because he'd left a lantern on. The welcome scent of coffee filled the small cave, and Tyler's jaundiced
eye took in the creature comforts that Kane always—somehow—
managed to scrounge from what anyone else would consider bar-
ren wilderness.

A double-sized, double-thick sleeping bag was unrolled wel-
comingly a short distance from a small fire burning brightly in the
center of the roughly ten-by-twelve-foot cave. A backpack leaned
against the wall near a rifle, with two plastic jugs of water close by.
A camp chair was set up on the other side of the fire, and it was
here Tyler sat, frowning at the lantern.

It shouldn't have surprised her, she thought. Kane had an absolute genius of making himself comfortable wherever fate happened to drop him. He would, she knew, abandon most of his stuff
before he moved on, but he'd find more later when he got tired of

roughing it. He always did. She had once seen him find the only sleeping bag within two hundred miles. And he'd made it look *easy*.

"Coffee?" he asked, folding gracefully into a cross-legged position before the fire.

Even though she was thirsty, Tyler was in no mood for pleasantries. "What're you doing here?" she asked tautly.

Kane poured coffee into a gaily decorated ceramic mug and sipped, gazing at her with thoughtful, shuttered green eyes. "The chalice, of course," he said, calm. "You didn't come way the hell out here without a rifle, did you?"

Tyler gritted her teeth. "*No*, I didn't come here without a rifle. I dropped it in the ravine when that maniac started shooting!"

Kane shook his head pityingly. "That was hardly the best time to lose your only means of defense," he pointed out.

"You didn't have your rifle, either. You left it in here like the rawest tenderfoot."

"Touché," he murmured.

She saw the hidden smile and realized he had sidetracked her—again. It was a favorite ploy of his, and one she was ridiculously prone to accept. Determinedly she reclaimed her major grievance. "You won't get the chalice. *I* talked to the man who found the cache, and he—"

"Told you he'd give you the chalice if you brought the rest of the stuff back to him," Kane finished smoothly. He smiled a little as surprise and rage widened her fine amber eyes. His had been a guess, but her reaction was proof enough; they'd both been suckered. "Funny. He told me the same thing."

Kane sipped his coffee and watched her while she absorbed the implications. Tyler St. James was nothing if not quick, and Kane enjoyed the play of emotions across her delicate, expressive face. He remembered those tense moments on the cliff face and kept a grin off his own face with an effort. How many women, he wondered, could have spit curses at a man while dangling from a cliff from her fingertips? With someone shooting at her?

Not many.

She was one in a million, Tyler was. A strong, intelligent woman with the beauty to launch ships and the courage to follow them into battle. Kane could recall a number of past occasions when he'd been glad to have her at his side when things had gotten sticky. Tyler never waited for the cavalry to come charging to the rescue, but instead grabbed a big stick and started swinging.

She'd very nearly brained him once or twice.

That memory helped alter admiration to uneasiness. Apparently history was about to repeat itself yet again, and the duration promised to be bothersome. A hunter by choice and by nature, Kane certainly had no objections to Tyler's company on this particular hunt—in theory, that is. He wouldn't have minded another opportunity to discover what made the lady tick, for one thing. And, as partners went, she was far better than most at this sort of thing, and unlikely to panic if things got rough—and they almost always did at some point.

The trick, he thought, would be to come to some sort of understanding with her. They were rivals, after all, both after the chalice and both determined to have it. Still, with unknown dangers lying ahead of them and the gunman—who might or might not be after the cache, as well—possibly tagging along, two stood a better chance than one of making it.

Kane met that amber gaze, reflecting that he'd never met another woman who hid her thoughts so well. She made no secret of her emotions, but the thoughts behind them remained enigmatic. One in a million.

Her musical, deceptively gentle voice was even. "We both have the same information. The same directions to where the cache is hidden. So it's a race."

"Is it?" Kane freshened his coffee, frowning a bit. Apparently going off on a tangent, he said, "I was out reconnoitering when I saw you coming along the ravine. Then that shooter chased you up on the cliff face. Since you and I were obviously both after the chalice, I thought it'd be smarter if we teamed up."

"Really?"

Kane kept his gaze on the coffee; he wasn't sure that his ability to hide his thoughts was as good as hers. "Why not? We make a good team. When we aren't trying to con each other six ways from Sunday, that is. This clearly isn't going to be a piece of cake, not with a trigger-happy unknown likely dogging our steps and after the same thing."

"How do you know he is?"

"I don't," Kane replied promptly. "But I think we'd better assume he is. We're in the middle of nowhere with no reason to draw gunfire, unless you consider a hidden cache of antiquities. So what else could he be after? And since our cagey friend back in Panama obviously decided to hedge his bets by sending two of us after the cache, it's probably safe to assume we'll run into trouble somewhere along the line."

"Trouble that a team would stand a better chance of surviving than either of us alone?" she asked dryly.

"Stands to reason."

"And when we find the cache—assuming we do—and get it back to Panama—assuming we do? And assuming that our *friend* Tomas holds up his end of the bargain and gives us what he promises? Who gets the chalice, Kane?"

He ran a thumb along his jaw, half frowning and half smiling. "We draw straws? Flip a coin? Arm wrestle? Split the thing down the middle? I'm open to suggestions, Ty."

"I've told you not to call me that," she said, more or less automatically.

He looked vague. "Did you? I don't remember."

Tyler gave him one of the looks reserved especially for him, a combination of intense suspicion and total mistrust; Kane was, she knew, about as vague as a defense computer. And about as likely to raise the flag of surrender. He was up to something.

"Well? Look, Ty, we can waste time and energy in racing each other to the cache, or we can team up until we get the stuff back to Panama. Then, when we're on solid and relatively safe ground, we can decide about the chalice. Maybe we could even make like Solomon and call our respective bosses, asking which would prefer to hand the chalice over to the enemy rather than get only half."

Gloomily Tyler said, "They'd both say split it, you know they would. And neither of us could do that."

Kane was a little surprised that she knew that about him, but obscurely pleased as well. "We'll come up with something."

Tyler studied his face, keeping her own expressionless. All things considered, she'd rather he was within sight until the chalice was found and carried safely out of Colombia; it was simply *safer* to know what Kane was doing whenever possible. And if there was danger to be faced, he was the next best thing to a loaded gun and a mean dog to have at her side.

She smiled despite herself at the comparison, and saw Kane's green eyes drop to her mouth. And that slight flicker of his gaze brought home to her vividly the danger of spending any amount of time at all with him. Risky as it was to count him a partner for the duration, it was nothing less than insanity to place them both in the peculiar intimacy of a situation where they would be forced to depend on each other, possibly for their very survival.

Their past encounters had consisted of a series of brief meetings between fiercely competitive surges of independent action as they'd each fought to claim the coveted prize first. All told, they'd spent little time together—being mostly occupied with finding ways to trick each other—but even that had been taut with a tension that was far more intense than mere rivalry could have accounted for.

She could, Tyler thought, barely keep him in line now; what would happen if they turned *that* corner? And how did she feel about the possibility?

"Ty?"

For a moment she couldn't seem to breathe, but then her mind had neatly assigned Kane his proper place in her life. He was a rival. Usually an enemy. Sometimes a partner. Occasionally the strong arm that would prevent her careless dive off a cliff. Nothing more.

Her breathing resumed, steady and even. "I don't see a choice myself," she said calmly. "It looks like we're partners—for the duration." She ignored her mind's gentle siren song. *Seduce an enemy and earn his loyalty.* No. Not Kane. Seducing Kane for the wrong reasons would mean more than playing with fire; it would mean a blithe trek into a live volcano just to see what molten rock looked like.

"Then we've agreed," he said in a brisk tone. He glanced down at the broad watch on his wrist. "Nearly sunset. Our friendly gunman out there can't get close without alerting us, so we'll stay in here tonight and get an early start tomorrow. That okay with you?"

"Fine."

"When did you lose your backpack?"

If Tyler's teeth gritted again, at least it was a silent indication of annoyance. "When I lost the rifle."

Kane didn't seem disposed to make sarcastic comments on her ineptitude. Perhaps he was mellowing.

"Well, my sleeping bag's big enough for two." He met her gaze, his own mild. "Unless you object?"

There was, Tyler decided, a middle ground strewn with land

mines between assertive feminine independence and the coming decidedly chilly night. She swallowed her instinctive objection, determined to be rational about things. "Fine."

Kane seemed not to notice her struggle. He poured more coffee into his mug and handed it to her. "Have some. I haven't eaten yet; how about you?"

"Not since this morning."

He reached for his backpack and opened it, digging in and producing a wide array of packaged and canned foodstuffs. Tyler watched him retrieve his Swiss Army knife from his pocket, and when he looked quizzically at her, responded haughtily.

"Caviar, of course."

Kane grinned, but opened the can and arranged crackers on a tin plate. "Ought to taste good with coffee," he murmured.

"You mean you don't have champagne?" she demanded, offended.

He reached into the backpack and produced a bottle.

Tyler's mouth fell open. "Damn. And I thought I had you."

"I like champagne," he responded simply.

Annoyed by her inclination to giggle, Tyler set her mug aside and watched him neatly open the champagne and pour the foaming liquid into two tin cups. (For some obscure reason she'd never had the nerve to question, Kane always carried a variety of plates, cups, and utensils rather than just enough for himself. As if he always expected a party, no matter how unlikely.) She accepted a cup from him, wondering if he would propose a toast. Being Kane, he did.

"To our partnership."

She tapped her cup against his, a wry smile curving her lips. "Right. And let's hope we don't kill each other."

"I'll buy that," he murmured.

Silence fell as they sipped champagne and munched caviar and crackers. Tyler avoided looking at him, asking herself fiercely why on earth she had agreed to this. If asked to name the ten people she trusted least, she would put Kane Pendleton's name at the top of the list, underscored and in bold print. In fact, his name would probably occupy the first three places on that list. It was insane to agree to even a temporary partnership.

She could grudgingly admit that the man had a basic core of integrity, some kind of private code of honor he adhered to, but she knew nothing much else about him. Oh, she knew he'd garnered survival training somewhere in his past, and that he was a sharp-shooter with any handgun or rifle. That he was physically power-ful and blessed with singular endurance. That he had a quick temper and quick humor. That he was smart, tough and ruthless when he had to be. That he loved antiquities even as she did, and possessed a certain rare, intuitive "feel" for them, even as she did.

From their past encounters, she knew he was not cruel even to enemies, but did not hesitate to employ rough tactics if informa-tion was needed or if escape or survival depended on quick action. She knew he slept like an animal with every sense alert and that he was cool to the point of iciness under stress.

But what did she *really* know about the man? He might well have sprung full-blown into life, there on the sands of Egypt, for she knew nothing of his background. She had no idea of where he lived or what he did between assignments.

The silence was bothering her. In a casual tone, she said, "Tomas has a buyer for the cache, don't you think?"

Kane nodded. "I'd say so. As a matter of fact, I think he'd lined up more than one buyer, and that he's beginning to feel the pres-sure. He was jumpy as hell when I talked to him."

"Drugs," Tyler offered.

"No, I think his vice is gambling. I got the feeling he needed a lot of money very quickly. Maybe that's why he sent the both of us after the cache; he figured one of us was bound to make it."

A silence fell again.

Tyler glanced across the fire at him, studying him beneath her lashes. Her interest in Tomas was fleeting; she couldn't keep her mind off Kane. There was in him, she thought, something just barely tame, a cloak of civilization hiding what lay beneath, and women always seemed to sense that; Kane drew women like a magnet drew ore. And he was attractive, possessing aside from his rough good looks a sexual aura that was almost a tactile thing. Her stomach tightened, and Tyler ordered her body to ignore that. Not that it did. He was the most physically compelling man she'd ever encountered, and in a world where various types of liberation sought to overhaul the male nature, she found his toughness of spirit and blatant sexuality more than a little attractive.

Damn it.

In the past she'd found her thoughts turning speculatively to him because of that. In another age he would have been a warrior, a conqueror, even a king if there had been kingdoms to be won; in this day and time he appeared on the surface to be just that slight degree out of step with the times. A throwback to a more dangerous age. And yet he never treated Tyler as if her sex made her weaker than he, as if she needed his protection.

The man was an enigma.

"Ready for bed?"

She blinked and stared at him. "What? Oh—right."

"We should move out of here before dawn if we want to lose our trigger-happy friend," he observed mildly. "So we'd better get some sleep."

"Uh-huh." She shook off the uncharacteristic passivity, adding with spirit, "I hope you don't snore."

"I don't. How about you?"

Tyler gave him a look, set her cup aside and went over to the sleeping bag. She sat down and hauled her boots off, muttering to herself, then wiggled into the bag and tried to get as far over to one side as possible. Conscious of his watching gaze, she kept her face expressionless and hoped the heat she felt suffusing her skin wasn't visible to him. Turning her back to him, she resolutely closed her eyes, wishing she could have removed her bra; she hated sleeping in it. She listened to the faint sounds of Kane's movements, stiffening when she felt him slide into the sleeping bag beside her. He was a big man, and even the double bag was cramped with both of them inside it.

She felt a weakness in her limbs when his hard body brushed hers, her breath catching despite herself. Zipped into the bag, she felt trapped, helpless, and her own vulnerability shocked her as a wave of panic swept over her. How could she defend herself? She could barely move—

A hard hand grasped her shoulder, turning her over onto her back, and Kane's head blocked out the flickering firelight when his lips found hers unerringly. His kiss was rough, overpowering in its male demand, and Tyler pushed against his chest fiercely in a panicky rejection that was mental rather than physical. The banked heat inside her flared at the touch, and she almost moaned aloud in frustrated anger when she realized her mouth was opening to him, responding to him in the face of all reason and despite the cold mental panic. Her fingers curled, digging into his chest, and a dizzying wave of raw desire swept over her.

Abruptly Kane broke the kiss and turned away from her. "All right," he said dryly, "I've made my move. The attempted ravishment you were worried about. Now we can go to sleep. Good night, Ty."

Tyler nearly smothered trying to hide her ragged breathing, staring at him uncomprehendingly. And this time when her fingers curled, it required a supreme effort of will to keep herself from raking her nails down his back. Mentally calling him every violent thing she could think of, she turned her back to his. "Good night, Kane," she managed evenly. She thought she heard a faint chuckle from him, and spent a good ten minutes silently plotting to get even. Soon.

FAR BELOW THEM in the ravine, the watching man saw only a dim flicker of light at the cave entrance. He stood undecided for a moment, then shrugged to himself and moved silently away. Some distance down the ravine he found the woman's backpack and rifle, and gathered them thoughtfully. He made camp out of sight and hearing of the cave, eating and then settling down to sleep. His powerful body relaxed totally in sleep, but like his quarry he slept like an animal with every sense alert.

He didn't stir until nearly dawn.

TYLER HAD PECULIAR dreams. She was in a straitjacket and moved irritably to free herself, muttering in disgust at the feeling of confinement. The straps were cutting into her back and beneath her breasts, and her shoulders were chafed. She complained about the matter to her shadowy companion, whispering her grievance in annoyance. Then she felt one of the straps give and sighed in relief as the ones on her shoulders were smoothed away. Her arms were constricted for a moment as the elastic straps were worked free of them, and then there was an odd tickling feeling of something sliding away beneath her shirt, leaving her breasts free. Content, she murmured wordlessly and snuggled down in the warm pocket surrounding her, barely aware of something hard and warm at her side. The dream faded away.

The delicious scent of coffee woke her, and Tyler stretched luxuriously before opening her eyes. The rough ceiling of a cave met her startled gaze, and it was several confused moments before she remembered where she was. And whom she was with. Sitting up abruptly, she remembered her dream. But it hadn't entirely been a dream, she realized, because she was definitely—

"Where the hell's my bra?" she demanded, glaring across a cheerful fire at a man with quizzically raised brows.

Kane gestured toward a small mound of folded material lying near the sleeping bag. "There. I took it off," he explained casually. "You weren't comfortable, and you wanted it off."

"How do you know?"

"You told me in your sleep."

She stared at him, trying to remember. No, she didn't think he'd removed her khaki shirt to get the bra off. Had he? She was wearing it now, buttoned correctly. Granted, it was short-sleeved. And it was entirely possible to remove a bra without first taking off a shirt, as long as the straps were elastic; she had done it often when she'd wanted the thing off but hadn't been ready to change her outer clothing. But she certainly didn't remember asking him for help. Had he—?

"I didn't see anything, if that's what's worrying you," he murmured.

Glaring at him, Tyler reached out and snagged her bra, then slid down a bit so that the material of the sleeping bag hid her chest from his steady, faintly amused gaze. Given a choice—and another companion—she would have gone braless, but she was full-busted and preferred to wear support when she was active. The trick, however, was getting her bra back on without removing her shirt or otherwise giving Kane an eyeful.

Putting a bra *on* under a shirt was a bit more difficult than taking one off.

She wasn't overly modest, and her own behavior in Kane's company bothered her; why didn't she just turn her back to the man and wrestle the bra into place? Somehow she couldn't respond to the awkward situation with simple directness.

She had to remain sitting in order to get her bra back on, but the flap of the sleeping bag kept dropping to her waist. Finally, annoyed by the ridiculous picture she knew she was presenting, she gripped the material in her teeth and glared at Kane, daring him to say a word, while she managed to slip her arms from the sleeves of her shirt and get the bra on beneath it.

He watched her quite steadily, but in silence, and if he was amused he hid it well.

Decently attired at last, she scrambled from the bag and got to her feet, tucking her shirttail into the snug waistband of her jeans. Her long hair, having come free of its braid during the night—it always did—swung about her shoulders and persisted in falling forward over her face. Muttering, she pushed it back, only then noticing the comb Kane held out to her.

For only an instant Tyler hovered between stubbornness and need, then sighed and accepted the offering, sinking back down onto the sleeping bag to begin the task of restoring some order to her unruly hair.

Kane set the ceramic mug filled with coffee near her, then sipped coffee from his own tin cup while he watched her. Silence never bothered him, not even the prickly silence generally to be found in her company, and he enjoyed watching her tame her long, thick mass of red-gold hair. She was concentrating entirely on what she was doing, and Kane found his gaze dropping to her full breasts when her lifted arms drew the khaki material taut across them.

He should have tossed the bra into the fire.

chapter two

THE SHOOTER WAS nowhere in sight, and no gunfire greeted their cautious exit from the cave. Kane suggested that they climb rather than descend just to be on the safe side, and much as she wanted to, Tyler couldn't really disagree. The ravine below was narrow and appeared miles long, meaning that it was a dandy place from which to be ambushed, should their friend with the gun have that in mind. The cliff face above them, Kane pointed out, was climbable.

Tyler stood outside the cave on the narrow ledge and gazed upward, controlling a shiver. Tearing her eyes from the fifty-foot expanse of jagged rock rising above her head, she watched Kane crouch on the ledge and dig a long nylon rope from his backpack. He had, as she'd expected, abandoned most of his equipment, settling on the backpack and sleeping bag, two canteens, and his rifle.

Tyler carried one of the canteens, the strap slung bandolier-fashion across her chest; Kane had arranged the rest for himself to carry, but now he piled the gear on the narrow ledge.

Kane slung the rope over one shoulder and across his chest, then stood gazing upward with narrowed, measuring eyes. Then he sat down on the ledge and, unperturbed by the sheer drop below him, began unlacing his boots. "I'll go up first," he told her, "and drop a line for you and the backpack. Tie the pack securely. Keep the rifle with you, and when you're ready to come up, *don't use the rope to climb*. Just hold on and I'll pull you up slowly. All right?"

"I— Yes." Tyler watched him stow his boots in the backpack, and felt her throat tighten when he rose to his feet. "I know you've done this before. You *have* done this before?"

"Sure."

"So you're just going to climb using nothing but your fingers and toes. Right?"

"That's the plan."

"I thought this was a democratic partnership."

Kane looked at her, half guarded and half amused. "It is—as much as possible."

She ignored the qualification. "Then I vote we go down into the ravine. The shooter's gone."

"And maybe waiting up ahead for us. It's an easy climb, Ty, and we need to move to higher ground anyway. We should climb toward the coast and then head south."

Tyler didn't have to ask if Kane knew what he was talking about; he did. He probably had a map of Colombia imprinted on his brain, and she knew he spoke Spanish like a native. But Tyler wasn't exactly ignorant of the geography herself, never mind that she knew little Spanish. "Why the coast? It'll be murder traveling through those swamps and forests. Why not stick to the mountains and just head south?"

He studied her for a moment. "I get the feeling you're arguing the way a kid whistles in a graveyard—just to hear yourself."

His perception annoyed her. It also disturbed her in a way she didn't want to think about. She fought a brief silent battle with her pride and lost. "I'm not very good with sheer drops, that's all." She looked at him defiantly, daring him to make some smart crack about her phobias.

Kane glanced down at the drop below them, then back at her. "You hide it well, I must say."

In a put-upon tone, she said reasonably, "I'm standing on a ledge of rock; it may not be much, but it's solid. You expect me to dangle at the end of a rope. I don't like ropes. I don't trust them."

Matching her tone, he said, "Look, Ty, if we go down, we'll have to either take our chances there isn't an ambush ahead, or else follow the ravine about eight miles north before we can get to higher ground the easy way. In this terrain, that'll cost us a day at least. You really want that?"

After a moment Tyler sighed, picked up the rifle and held it ready for anything, and then leaned back against the rock. "All right, damn it. Climb."

He winked at her, solemn, then began climbing.

The morning air was chilly; Tyler told herself that was why she shivered as she watched him scale the cliff with the ease of a mountain goat. He never seemed to put a foot wrong, testing the placement of each finger and toehold with exquisite care before allowing his weight—and his life—to depend on it. He obviously knew what he was doing. And Tyler watched, her head tilted back against rock, her eyes fixed on him always.

Her mouth was dry and her heart seemed to have lodged in her throat, choking her with its pounding. She wasn't worried about him, she assured herself fiercely. After all, he thought too much of his own hide to risk it unnecessarily; he wouldn't have begun climbing if there had been any great danger. No, it was just that it was getting lighter, and they didn't know where their friendly gunman was.

It was eerily quiet, as it always was in the dawn hours, and Tyler's anxious sense of urgency grew as the light strengthened. Even in his khaki shirt and jeans Kane was obvious against the cliff, she thought, his thick black hair shining in alien darkness against the light-colored rock. If the shooter was still around, and chanced to look up . . .

She jerked her gaze from Kane and began searching the ravine, eyeing each jumble of rock suspiciously. Nothing moved, and there was no sign of anyone save themselves. It didn't reassure her particularly. The ravine was deep and wide. Rocks, brush. There were so many places someone could hide—

A rock nearly as big as her head bounded downward suddenly, striking the ledge not a foot from where she stood. Forgetting the gunman, she looked swiftly up to find that Kane had nearly reached the top; he seemed to be having no difficulty at all, but the khaki shirt showed damp patches indicating his task wasn't nearly as easy as it appeared.

Tyler felt dizzy as she watched him pull himself up over the top, realizing only then that she had held her breath, and her lungs were aching. She allowed herself to breathe normally now, faintly irritated by her reaction to his danger. She certainly wasn't worried about the man, it was just that this was a lonely area and it was nice to have someone to talk to, even if the someone was Kane. If he hadn't made it, she would have been forced to talk to herself.

But once she got up there . . . It occurred to her only then that she herself would be a dandy target while he pulled her up—and that neither of them would be able to hold the rifle ready to return any gunfire.

The nylon line snaked downward, and she knelt to tie the

backpack securely, her mouth twisting ruefully as she remembered who had taught her to tie a decent knot. Kane. In North Africa during their first meeting—and first clash.

She watched the backpack ascend, then slung the rifle across her back as the line dropped down again. She tied the end around her waist loosely, making certain not to use a slipknot, then waved to Kane to signal she was ready. The line tightened immediately, and she kept her feet braced against the cliff, "walking" upward as he pulled the rope. She didn't look down. She didn't look at anything at all, in fact, and realized that only when Kane hauled her over the top and spoke.

"You can open your eyes now."

He was laughing, and all Tyler's misgivings about the situation suddenly exploded within her. Her reaction, she knew, was excessive, but knowing that did nothing to lessen it. She dropped the rope and swung at him furiously and accurately, missing his jaw only because he ducked with a fighter's lightning reflex.

"Damn it, woman—"

Tyler lunged at him, both fists doubled and her legs tangling with the rope trailing from her waist. She told herself that rope gave him the advantage, told herself it was because of that Kane was able to wrestle her to the ground. Her pride wouldn't admit how pathetically easy it seemed to him.

He didn't make the mistake of allowing her to get a knee anywhere near him; she had used that trick before. Roughly pinning her hands to the ground above her head, he threw a leg across her and sat astride her hips, his two hundred pounds easily holding her still despite her best efforts to throw him off.

And she tried, bucking beneath him furiously, her impotent rage and sudden panic growing because he was holding her down and she felt smothered, helpless. She never wanted to feel like that again. Never. "Damn you, you son of a—"

"*Tyler!*" He glared down at her, his handsome face less humorous than she'd ever seen it, his mouth hard. "Just what the hell is wrong with you?"

"You laughed at me!" she practically screamed, panic clawing at her mind. "I hate that, I hate being laughed at!"

His flying brows drew together. "And that's why you attacked me like a wildcat? For God's sake, Ty, I wasn't laughing *at* you. You might have been scared to death, but you climbed the damned cliff. I happen to think that took a hell of a lot of courage."

"You laughed," she insisted between gritted teeth, fighting to hold the anxiety at bay.

He was still frowning. "Honey, I was laughing because I admired your guts."

She didn't want to believe that, but his steady green eyes were honest. And she believed him. Her rage drained away, leaving her shaking and oddly bereft.

With anger gone, there was nothing left to insulate her from those other disturbing feelings. He was sitting on her and she was more helpless than she could bear, but the clawing panic was fading with astonishing speed. The rifle beneath her jabbed into her back, but she hardly felt it. Instead she felt the warmth of him, the heavy weight of him, and he was leaning down so close she could see his oddly expanding pupils blocking out the green, and smell the musky male scent of his big body. Her wrists were held together by one of his hands, while the other lay on her shoulder just inches from her breast, warm and heavy.

The abrupt urge to feel that big hand close over her breast washed over her in a dizzying wave, and she could feel the tight prickling of her nipples in response to the astonishing burst of desire. Her belly knotted, and beneath his heavy weight something flamed inside her, heating her loins.

Her own response shocked her, not the least because helplessness had always been a fear and she knew only too well that sexual helplessness was the greatest fear of all. How could he make
her feel this way? *How?*

She almost moaned aloud, and her teeth gritted while she tried
frantically to control the insane impulse of her body. Dangerous.
Dear God, it was dangerous!

"All right," she said in a small, husky voice. "I believe you.
Now let me up."

"I'm not sure if that's a good idea," he said whimsically, his
eyes darkening even more. "You're an unpredictable lady, Tyler St.
James. And I've had cause to be sure of that. I remember it well.
After North Africa—and Budapest—I ached for days."

Tyler could feel heat sweep up her throat, and with an effort
she kept her gaze on his face. "That was your fault. You tricked me.
You made me furious; I struck out without thinking. And I could
have done worse."

"I suppose you could have used that knife you carried. Instead
of being bruised and sick, I would have been a total eunuch. I've
heard about places in the world where a woman does that to her
man in revenge for betrayal."

"You're not my man. Get off me!"

"I'm comfortable," he murmured wickedly. "I may make a day
of it. D'you still carry that knife, by the way? You didn't have it on
you last night when I took your bra off."

Tyler gritted her teeth in helpless rage, welcoming the return
of anger because it overwhelmed those other feelings. "Maybe I'm
just hiding it more carefully these days!" she snapped.

"Shall I search you and find out?" he asked softly.

She watched his gaze move considerably over her chest, where
khaki material was pulled taut by her position and the rifle and
canteen straps cut diagonally between her breasts. The khaki was

thin, like the silk of her bra, and neither hid the jutting response of her nipples.

A different kind of panic swept over her. In a desperate, mindless need to stop this before something irrevocable happened, she fed her anger wildly, and a snarl tangled in the back of her throat. In such a situation as this, unable to match his strength, she knew that only words could serve as her weapons. And Tyler had learned in a number of very hard and dangerous situations to use every weapon available to her.

Keeping her voice low and even, she said, "Is this the way you get your kicks, Kane? The old macho domination routine? Well, you weigh nearly twice what I do and you're strong even for your size, so I'm defeated from the start. I can't possibly win. Satisfied? Or d'you want me to cry and beg? I'm not very good at begging, Kane, but if that's your game, I'll play. Because I'm *very* good at surviving." And the flat, fierce truth of that was in her voice like a knife pulled from its sheath to gleam starkly in the sunlight.

Curiously blank green eyes met her wild amber gaze, and Kane was still and silent for a long moment. His mouth was hard again, his face expressionless. Without a word, he freed her wrists and lifted his weight off her, leaving himself vulnerable to an avenging knee for just an instant.

Tyler didn't take advantage of that. She sat up and untied the rope at her waist with shaking fingers, then got to her feet as he coiled the line and returned it to the backpack. He didn't look at her as he sat down on a boulder to put his socks and boots back on. Then he shrugged into the pack, his face stony, and started moving east into the forest.

Tyler followed. Her breasts felt heavy and achy, and she could still feel the imprint of him against her lower stomach and hips. She could feel his hand on her wrists, and looked at them vaguely, wondering why there were no marks. There should have been marks. Absently she adjusted the rifle so that she carried the strap on one shoulder. She had the feeling that Kane had deliberately allowed her to keep the gun. To make a point? She didn't know.

Her legs felt shaky and she had the curious urge to cry. Her eyes were hot, and she thought something had torn loose inside her. She didn't know what it was. Gazing steadfastly at the middle of Kane's broad back, she trudged along behind him.

HIS MOOD DIDN'T bother her at first, but Tyler soon discovered that Kane's silence was inexorably stretching all her nerves as taut as bowstrings, and she wasn't a nervous person. It would take days for them to find the cache even if there was no trouble; the thought of days filled with his brand of silence was enough to make her forget the childish determination not to be the first to break the deadlock.

"How far to the coast?" She addressed his back, since he was still leading the way.

Kane said nothing.

"He's obviously mad at me," Tyler told the surrounding forest, keeping her voice light. "I must have bruised his pride." No reaction from Kane. She gripped the rifle's carrying strap more tightly. "So now I'm getting the silent treatment." Nothing. Tyler began to feel seriously alarmed. She hadn't realized it until then, but in the days it had taken her to get this far, she had missed the sounds of human companionship.

Even the voice of an enemy was welcome, she told herself miserably.

Falling silent, she stared at his back and thought about their confrontation. So he resented what she'd said? Because she'd hit too close to home, or because what she'd said had been an insult to him? Curiously enough, she thought it was the latter. Kane wasn't the type to sulk because his ego was bruised.

No, his reaction was something else. Did he believe she had

meant what she'd said? Had his perception failed him this once so that he hadn't realized she had said the most hurtful thing she could think of—

She felt an odd jolt. The most hurtful thing? Had she been that certain of him? Some men would have taken her own words and used them to taunt her, proving their truth. But not Kane. *And she had known that.*

She wondered then, uneasily, if that was why her usual panic at being helpless had been brief. Had she known instinctively that her fears would always be groundless where Kane was concerned? Was she sure of him in a way she had never been sure of any man for ten years? She didn't want to think about that, didn't want to consider what it might mean.

Swallowing hard, she said, "I'm sorry, Kane. I didn't mean— I knew you weren't trying to dominate me."

Kane paused for a moment, consulting the compass that was a part of his multifunction watch. Then he continued. Silently.

Tyler bit her lip and followed.

By midday they were descending, leaving the mountains behind as they moved toward the coast. The forest grew more dense, slowing them; at times they had to force their way through underbrush. Kane halted at last near a narrow stream, and Tyler sank thankfully onto the trunk of a fallen tree. She took the rifle from her shoulder and leaned it against the tree, watching him shrug off the backpack.

"We're moving again in half an hour," he said flatly.

At least he said we. Sighing, Tyler moved to the stream and followed it a little way until she was out of sight. She knelt on the bank and pulled a big linen handkerchief from her pocket, wetting the cloth and wringing it out before washing her face and neck. It was when she was wiping her hands thoroughly that she noticed the *KP* monogram on one corner. She stared at it for a moment, shaking her head unconsciously. His. *His*, and she hadn't realized she had it?

She stood up, waving the handkerchief gently to dry it. It was hotter now; they were closer to sea level, nearer to the hot, flat land of the eastern plains. The linen dried quickly, and she watched it, bothered by the small indication of his persistent presence in her life.

But—no. That was nonsense, of course. She just happened to have his handkerchief, and she'd kept it and carried it only because it looked like one of her own large linen squares. Would he laugh, she wondered vaguely, if she were to confess that she carried large handkerchiefs always because of an old and popular movie? Would he think it amusing that a thirteen-year-old girl had gazed at a huge screen and listened to the hero tell the heroine that never in any crisis of her life had she had a handkerchief while he dried her tears with his own?

Odd the things one remembered. Tyler loved *Gone with the Wind* now, but then she had only despised Scarlett because she hadn't had a handkerchief and hated Rhett because he'd shot the pony.

And she was determined to always dry her own tears.

Shaking her head again, Tyler folded the dried linen square neatly and returned it to her pocket. Then she headed back to Kane. Back to her silent enemy.

He was sitting cross-legged on the ground, eating from a package of trail mix. He tossed another package to Tyler, watching her with unreadable eyes. She sat on the fallen tree again and began eating, enjoying the mixture of granola, dried fruit, and nuts partly because she was hungry and partly because she liked the stuff. She returned his steady gaze as long as she could, then looked away.

"Damn it, Kane, I apologize! How much longer will I get the silent treatment?"

"Sorry." He didn't sound it.

She took a deep breath and released it slowly. Without looking at him, she said, "Doing the kind of work we do, I've run into plenty of men who used muscle as a—a sexual weapon. If you had been that kind of man, you would have loved my recognition of that. It would have been a turn-on. But you aren't that sort of man, Kane. And I knew that. So I used it as a weapon, because I felt helpless and vulnerable. It's—it's almost a phobia with me, feeling like that. I can't take it, and I strike out. Do you understand?"

After a moment he said, "Yes. I just hope you really believe I wouldn't do that, Ty."

She almost slumped with relief at the shortened version of her name. "I—I do." She managed a twisted smile, looking at him finally. "And I won't be able to use that as a weapon again, will I? You'll know it for what it is—a bluff."

"There's always your knee," he murmured.

Tyler matched his tentative smile, but her heart sank momentarily when his face abruptly went hard. Within a few seconds, though, she heard the faint sounds that had alerted him.

"Take the rifle," he said softly, rising. "Move about twenty yards downstream and wait for me. If that's our gun-happy friend, he's going to stop right here."

She rose, as well. "But, you'll need—"

"Move, Ty! Go on. I'll be fine."

There was no time to argue; the sounds were getting closer. She snatched up the rifle and moved swiftly and silently downstream, tense and worried.

Alone, Kane dropped the backpack behind the fallen tree, annoyed with himself because he hadn't thought to have Tyler take it with her. He wore a hunting knife on his hip, and loosened it in its sheath now as he moved across the tiny clearing and got behind a shielding thicket of low-growing bushes. He could just barely see the clearing, and fixed his eyes at the point where he expected to see their visitor emerge.

But what burst through the underbrush a few moments later was hardly what he expected to see. It was a woman, her long black hair flying around her face in wild tangles, her brightly colored peasant blouse torn and her jeans filthy. She looked absolutely terrified, and Kane moved almost instinctively toward her, drawn by the helpless fear in her big black eyes.

For once, all his survival instincts failed him.

She was babbling incoherently in Spanish, her eyes widening even more when she saw him, and though Kane understood the language he couldn't get a word of hers. He stepped toward her, making soothing noises, removing his hand from the haft of his knife when she backed away shakily. He wanted to reassure her that he meant her no harm. But then, in the blink of an eye, a curious transformation took place. She straightened, smiling, and the fear in her eyes became a sultry wickedness.

Bemused, Kane's instincts were just that fraction of a second slow in reacting. And that was all it took. The cold male voice came from behind him, speaking steadily in all-too-understandable English.

"No sudden moves, señor. I have a gun."

Kane turned very slowly, hoping that someone besides Tyler was well-versed in the art of bluff. The hope died a small, resigned death. It was no bluff.

TYLER WAITED FOR ten minutes, tense and uneasy. She had heard voices, at least one of them speaking Spanish—a feminine voice. It had definitely been a man shooting at them yesterday, she knew. She hesitated, worrying. Then, silently marshaling arguments in case Kane got mad, she crept back upstream until she reached the clearing. The deserted clearing. She found the backpack, but no Kane.

She had taught herself years before never to give in to panic in a crisis. There was, after all, time for that once the crisis was past. So she didn't panic now.

Her mind went still for an instant, then began working coolly. She searched the clearing, foot by foot, her eyes trained on the ground. There was little to see, few signs available. But Tyler had learned to follow tracks as a child, and she knew what to look for. It took nearly half an hour, but she was finally able to distinguish a faint trail leading from the clearing.

North.

KANE VERY NEARLY found the situation amusing. He'd been caught off guard, pure and simple, and both the woman, Valonia, and the man, Silvio, were delighted that their trick had worked. Kane was almost amused because a pair of black eyes might well have sealed his fate.

They talked freely as Silvio's gun nudged Kane through the woods to higher ground. They were bandits, they explained, hiding in the hills after their last raid in Bogotá. And boredom had nearly driven them mad. Happily they had heard Kane passing not far from their shack and had followed him. Clearly they hadn't realized he was not alone.

This ingenuous explanation might have disarmed another man, but Kane wasn't about to let his guard down twice in one day. The gun in his back was damned real, and Silvio had the lifeless eyes of a shark. And if Kane was any judge, Valonia was a woman who would definitely castrate a man who had betrayed her. Or even one who had annoyed her.

Kane had heard of recent raids in Bogotá and other areas, and those accounts came back to him as he was herded through the forest. There was no romantic Robin Hood myth clinging to these bandits; reportedly they were educated and well-off, and simply raided because they enjoyed it. They didn't bother to spout political or social rhetoric; they merely attacked in cities, towns and remote villages, destroying property, stealing whatever they fancied and killing anyone who got in their way.

Comforting thoughts.

This wasn't the first tough situation Kane had found himself in and, as always, his mind was working, seeking a solution. He had an ace up his sleeve in the shape of Tyler; he doubted she'd abandon him to his fate. She was adept at tracking, and would likely be able to follow them. What worried him was that Tyler was apt to jump into danger with both feet and damn the consequences.

He had to get himself out of this before Tyler could act. The thought of what cruel men could—would—do to her didn't bear thinking of. But he did think of it, of course, and his guts clenched in a tight knot of fear for her. It never occurred to him to think along those same lines regarding himself, but other possibilities did present themselves.

Torture. They'd maybe torture him just for fun. Or curiosity. See how much the guy can take. What'll make him scream? How do you break a strong man?

Something like that had happened to him once before, and he still bore the scars to remind him. If he'd needed reminding. He didn't. Bile rose in his throat as he remembered. Still, he had survived. It was something to keep in mind.

When they emerged from the forest, Kane realized that these bandits had been here for a while. Three crude shacks had been thrown together and looked it. In front of one, three men were restlessly playing cards on a rickety table, and all looked up with brightening faces when Kane and his escorts approached.

Kane kept his own face immobile, his eyes roving constantly as he measured his opponents and looked for a means of escape. He barely listened as Valonia and Silvio explained how they had captured him, the laughter of the men rolling off him easily because he didn't give a sweet damn what they thought. But when they began discussing ways and means of enjoying their captive, he paid a bit more attention. An argument broke out over the subject, one man holding out for slow torture while another was determined on more exotic pursuits.

Stalling for time and only dimly hoping for success, Kane told them in fluent Spanish that he was on the trail of a vast cache of treasure, and if they'd only come with him—

It didn't work. He hadn't really expected it to. These bandits didn't give a damn about riches even if they had believed his tale. They just wanted to have fun.

"I want him," Valonia told the men.

It seemed the lady was the leader of these bandits, for her statement instantly halted the arguments. Even Silvio, his shark eyes blank, nodded obedience.

Recklessly Kane directed a few exquisitely polite and choice obscenities toward the woman. Spanish was such a wonderfully fluid language, filled with lots of pretty flowers—and lots of sharp thorns. He was clubbed beneath an ear for his trouble, and there was red-hot pain for an instant before blessed darkness claimed him.

He woke with an aching head to find himself tied securely to a narrow cot. He was alone, and he lay there for long moments just trying to clear his sluggish mind. Once that had been accomplished, he attempted to free himself and found it impossible. He was tied with leather thongs and the cot's frame was stronger than it looked. Flat on his back, he couldn't get enough leverage to wrench himself free. He was trapped and helpless. For the first time he truly understood what Tyler had done earlier in the day, and why. It was an unnerving feeling, helplessness, and one he wasn't familiar with.

He wondered, then, if she *would* come after him. Why should

she, after all? She wanted the chalice, and "losing" him would remove at least one rival for it. Certainly Tyler wasn't afraid of possible trouble; she didn't need a man for protection. The lady could
take care of herself, in all honesty. And she'd survived twenty-
some-odd years without his help. Of course, North Africa might
well have ended her career if he hadn't been there. But if he *hadn't*
been there, she never would have fallen into that pit while trying
to steal the figurine back from him.

She didn't need him.

It was a curious, unwelcome shock. Not that she didn't need
him, but that he minded. Kane avoided emotional baggage in his
life, and his thoughts of Tyler looked suspiciously like just that.
But it was absurd, of course. He was only thinking about her, regretting that he'd never see her again in all likelihood, because she
had never, however briefly, belonged to him.

During the past occasions when they'd fought each other for
antiquities, he had been always conscious of her as a woman. He
would have had to be blind and senseless to have not been conscious of her that way. Kane was neither. And he had wanted her.
In the midst of bitter arguments, he had wanted her. In the midst
of trickery, he had wanted her. In triumph and defeat, he had
wanted her. But Tyler was . . . Tyler. Different from any woman he
had ever known. Somehow beyond his reach. And desire was all
the more strong and bittersweet because of that.

Last night in the sleeping bag, he had ached with wanting
her. And unfastening her bra, slipping it off beneath her shirt
while she had murmured pleasurably, he had very nearly gone
out of his mind.

But she was Tyler. Sometimes enemy, sometimes partner and
even friend. A fiery hellion who would fight at his side or guard
his back with that intriguing explosive determination of hers. A
woman who *was* a woman, one hundred percent feminine; yet she

had a bedrock-solid core of strength and clearly felt no need to prove herself to anyone, man or woman.

Tyler. He wanted to see her again.

It grew dark as hours passed, and Kane bore the passing time stoically. He blanked his mind and waited, knowing that they would come for him. But when a lantern was carried into the one-room shack, he saw that Valonia held it.

He had been told, by a number of ladies in various parts of the world, that he had a charming smile and charming ways. He had been told he possessed the gift of being able to persuade a woman even against her own nature. But when he looked into Valonia's black eyes, he felt a primitive shock tingle down his spine. Because there was nobody there. And on the beautiful face that housed that soullessness was a smile never meant to be worn by a woman. A smile never meant to be worn by anything human. A smile of pure evil.

"You have a name?" Her voice was soft, gentle, her Spanish investing the question with a curiously erotic sound.

"Kane." She had cleaned herself up, he saw, and was wearing only a man's shirt that reached halfway down her thighs.

She set the lamp on an upended crate that served as a table, then turned to face him with her hands on her rounded hips. "Kane. Have you ever been at the mercy of a woman, Kane?" She laughed when he was silent. "No, I see you have not." She approached the bed and bent down, beginning to unbutton his shirt. Her own shirt gaped away from her breasts, giving him a view all the way to her navel.

He moved suddenly in resistance, realizing what she had in mind. And his mind balked violently. She was right; he'd never been at a woman's mercy before. Not like this, not physically. Not even emotionally. He didn't know if she planned to tease him sexually or simply torture him, but given her scanty outfit he thought the former was most likely. And the excitement gleaming in her eyes was purely sensual. She intended to . . . But he couldn't believe she meant to—

"A man can be raped," she purred, running a hand down his chest and curling her fingers under his belt. "But I want your full cooperation, lover." Laughing, she backed away from him and began moving slowly, sensuously, in a dance expressly designed to arouse a man. She unbuttoned the shirt, dropping it teasingly off one shoulder, then the other, her hips moving in a rhythmic gyration. Twirling on bare, light feet, she danced close to the cot and then away, her hair flying, the material of her shirt baring and then concealing golden flesh.

In all his varied adventures, Kane had never before had a woman dance to arouse him. He wondered if he could be aroused totally against his will. Somehow, he didn't think it would happen. Not this time, at least. His mind was blank, his body chilled. Valonia literally radiated sex, but it was a hungry, grasping thing. Like a black widow, she would consume her mate once his duty was done, whether or not he performed to her satisfaction. And though everything male in Kane acknowledged her beauty and sensuality, his instincts icily rejected the attraction and a hard inner core of self-preservation kept a wary guard on his senses.

Even when she danced close enough to stroke his chest and teasingly unbuckle his belt, Kane felt only a deep, cold distaste, a grinding revulsion so strong he could hardly keep it out of his expression. Her flesh was hot, burning, the red-painted nails curved like the talons of a bird of prey.

He watched her dance, his face immobile, his eyes detached and dispassionate. He wondered what kind of rage her failure would unleash.

TYLER HAD BEEN forced to bide her time after trailing Kane and his captors to their camp. Reckless in some ways she certainly was, but she wasn't fool enough to storm a camp containing four armed men and a woman who, unless Tyler didn't know her own sex at all, was more dangerous than the rest together.

It was dark when she managed to move closer to the shacks. She flitted silently from one patch of darkness to another, using cover wherever possible, careful to remain downwind. Peering cautiously between the warped boards of the shacks, she managed to place all four of the men in one; they were sitting around a fire talking, laughing. One was jabbering away in his own language and making graphically obscene gestures as he talked.

Tyler was glad her Spanish was almost nonexistent; she really didn't want to know what that one was saying.

Slipping away, she headed for the third and last shack. It stood apart from the others and seemed in better shape structurally. It was lighted from inside, and Tyler was cautious as she circled it far enough to find a few warped boards. She looked inside. For a long moment she remained frozen. Then, moving silently back, she searched until she found a piece of wood a little over a foot long and fairly heavy. Hefting it, she started around the shack toward the door.

KANE FOUND HIMSELF looking up into black eyes holding nothing but mindless, animal fury. His entire body grew taut, expecting that anger to explode into action. Deadly action. She was hissing obscenities as she whirled toward the door, groping almost blindly for his hunting knife where she'd left it on the upended crate.

As she turned back toward him, jerking the knife from its sheath, the door opened silently behind her. She barely had time to step toward him, arm raised to begin the vicious downward plunge, when a thick board cracked across the back of her head. She went down instantly.

Tyler eyed her for a wary moment, then knelt to check her pulse. Muttering to herself and completely ignoring Kane, she methodically shredded Valonia's abandoned shirt, bound the naked woman and gagged her. She picked up his knife then rose to her feet and looked at him expressionlessly.

"I thought you were probably having fun, but the lady seemed a mite upset. If you'd rather, though, I can untie her and come back later—"

"Just untie me, if you don't mind," Kane managed. "I got tired of the party a long time ago." Like Tyler, he kept his voice soft.

She used his knife to cut the thongs binding his hands, then sliced the ones at his ankles while he sat up and buttoned his shirt. Still expressionless, she said, "Well, I owed you one. You saved my skin last time in Hong Kong. And just like this—from a fate worse than death. *Would* it have been a fate worse than death? I'm just curious, you understand."

Kane grabbed her arm and pulled her down across his lap, holding her tightly and completely ignoring the knife she still held. He kissed her quickly, hard, and said in a rough voice, "Yes, it would have been—except that *that* lady didn't turn me on and *this* lady tracks better than Daniel Boone. Let's get the hell out of here."

"Sounds good to me," she murmured.

chapter three

THEY RETRIEVED THE backpack from where Tyler had hidden it, and within half an hour they were back at the clearing by the stream. Kane led the way from there, moving downstream swiftly to put as much distance as possible between them and the bandits. Around 2:00 A.M. they left the stream, heading due west. The night air was warm and sticky, and the forest grew even more dense.

By 4:00 A.M. Tyler decided that enough was enough. "Hey, let's stop, okay? I knocked that she wolf silly, and from the look of them, the men weren't about to interrupt her little games. We've got hours before they even know you're gone."

There was no moon visible, and it was almost pitch black in the forest. Tyler had been walking directly behind Kane, at his very heels, in fact, and when he stopped she banged into him. She grabbed at his shoulders to keep her balance, but almost instantly rebounded away from him nervously. Damn it, *why* did she react to just *touching* the man? She hadn't been aware of it before this encounter.

Kane spoke calmly, apparently not noticing her reaction. "If I know where we are, there's another stream about twenty minutes' walk from here. You game?"

"You've been here before?"

"No. I once met a man who'd traveled all through this part of the country."

It figured; Kane had a phenomenal memory. She sighed. "All right, but walk a little more slowly, will you? My night vision is practically nil."

Kane took her hand in a firm grasp and began walking again. She was beside him, a little behind, and didn't want to admit to herself that she felt more secure with her hand lost in his. Nor did she admit to the tingling warmth of his touch; what lay behind that was too frightening and dangerous to think about.

But she found herself comparing this adventure to the ones that preceded it. This was different not only because they were wary partners almost from the moment of encountering each other, but also because their surroundings were completely unlike the others. In North Africa they had maneuvered in baking cities and tumbled ruins, outguessing and outfoxing each other half a dozen times before temporarily joining forces to outwit a sophisticated gang of art thieves. Most of their other clashes had been equally harried and brief, with little time available to dwell on anything other than the goals they had shared, and they had rarely been alone together.

In Hong Kong, their most recent adventure several months before, it had been an all-out race for an elusive necklace. In that extremely crowded, overpopulated city, they had each won and lost the necklace, tricking each other a number of times before teaming up to smoothly con an expatriate American of Chinese descent who had a nifty racket going in stolen antiquities.

Kane *had* saved her from a fate worse than death on that occasion. He'd had the necklace and could have just left her to the tender mercies of the Tong leader. But he had come back for her, bursting in mere hours before she would have been shipped to parts unknown where her new life promised to take place inside a house with a red light at the door.

Dangerous circumstances, those. And even Tyler's innate craving for adventure had wavered from time to time. Still, she had found a fierce enjoyment in sparring with Kane, and her anger at his various tricks and betrayals had contained more than a nugget of reluctant and somewhat rueful admiration for his cunning. She had missed his presence on the few occasions that one or the other of them had located what they sought first and departed; as galling as it had been for her to admit he had beaten her to something, she'd found little pleasure in winning herself—unless it had been a face-to-face contest with both of them on the scene.

And their sparring in the past had been just that: a contest, a game with both working to win. Always on the move and generally surrounded by other people, with foes to outwit alone or together, foes they both recognized.

Now, this. The surroundings were curiously elemental, the circumstances new ones. They had teamed up for the duration. And there was a mutual enemy or two—they thought. The bandits had been unexpected, but fought successfully. The gunman lay behind them or before them, and they didn't know his face or his reasons for being involved in this.

They were virtually alone, moving cautiously through a lonely wilderness that was ever changing. First the cool grandeur of the mountains, and now the sticky, cloying heat of the approaching lowlands. The dense forest was gradually becoming marshy, the ground giving spongily beneath their feet.

"Wait here." He released her hand.

"Kane?" The question was instinctively uttered before she could get her bearings. She saw they had reached the stream; it was little more than a glittering ribbon of darkness whispering softly.

He touched her shoulder lightly. "I'm just going to check out the area. Stay put."

Tyler remained there, absently pulling the material of her shirt away from her skin. She was uncomfortable. It was hot and misty, and she felt dirty. She could tolerate any amount of dust, but the sticky dampness of heat and high humidity combined was something she hated. But not even that distraction could pull her mind from thoughts of this strange new relationship with Kane.

They could sharpen their wits on each other, face-to-face, both wary and a bit uncomfortable with this new arrangement. Like stray dogs they circled each other uneasily, both just on the point of lunging but holding back because territorial rights were maddeningly undefined. They had declared themselves partners, but their background was not such as to lend certainty or trust to the partnership.

And there was that other thing, that sexual awareness between them. It hovered just beneath the surface of words and looks and touches, as much mistrusted as their ability to depend on each other. And as likely to explode in some confrontation neither was ready for.

Tyler realized then that her misgivings about the situation had little to do with her ability to trust Kane; she hadn't trusted him before, yet they had been able to work together at the need. What had disturbed her instinctively was the intimacy inherent in a partnership in this place and time. They were too alone, too much together in surroundings that would spark primitive emotions between a man and woman.

Even if the seeds of those emotions had not been sown thousands of miles away and many months in the past.

She started when she felt him beside her again; she'd expected him to move silently, but was nonetheless unprepared for his lithe soundlessness. In a city he could move like a shadow; here in the forest, he moved like a jungle cat.

"We'll stay here," he told her. "I'll start a fire." He faded away again, and very faint noises indicated he was gathering wood nearby.

Tyler stood still until she saw the flickering of his lighter, then stepped toward him. The firelight shadowed and highlighted his lean face, and with his head bent as it was he looked curiously savage. His flying brows and hooded eyes gave him a devilish appearance, and the broad shoulders looked even more massive than they actually were. Tyler thought then that it would be easy to be afraid of him, and wondered why she wasn't.

He glanced up at her as she approached the fire, then reached to dig into the backpack he had laid aside. "How d'you feel about creepy-crawlies?"

Tyler shrugged a little. "Well, I don't like them. But I'm not deathly afraid of them, either."

"How about snakes?"

"The same."

Kane pulled a bundle of material from the backpack; it appeared to be a woolen blanket. "This is a ruana," he told her, indicating the slit in the middle of the blanket. "Put your head through here, and then you can belt it around your waist."

She glanced toward the stream, realizing what he had in mind.

"I'm going to build a lean-to," he continued, producing a plastic-wrapped bar of soap from the pack, "because it'll likely rain by dawn. If you want to rinse out your things, they'll probably be dry by then."

Tyler accepted the ruana and the soap, but stood her ground. "Why'd you ask about snakes and creepy-crawlies?"

"We're on the edge of the swamp, can't you smell it? Fair warning, Ty; you may share your bath with a snake. But this is a mountain stream, so maybe not. There's a deeper pool just around that bend; it looks pretty good. It's up to you."

She hesitated, then said, "We'll turn south when we head out again, won't we? Through the swamp?"

"Around it, if possible. But this may be your last chance for a decent bath for a couple of days. Is that what you wanted to know?"

"That's what I wanted to know." She turned away, then glanced at him over her shoulder. "If I yell, it *won't* be because the water's cold!"

"Gotcha," he murmured, smiling a little.

Tyler found the pool, discovering that the forest thinned out here and that dim light was able to show her the way. She eyed the peaceful water suspiciously, but laid the ruana on a rock and sat down to pull off her boots and socks. Her jeans felt stiff and damp, and she had to roll them over her hips and down her legs. The shirt, too, was damp, and her bra and panties had to almost be peeled away from her flesh.

She hesitated for a moment, feeling ridiculously like a wood nymph standing there naked. A glance over her shoulder showed her that she could barely see the campfire, and she could faintly hear Kane at work building the lean-to. She freed her hair from the braid, slipping the rubber band around her wrist since it was her last one, then unwrapped the soap and fished the handkerchief from the pocket of her jeans.

Stepping cautiously into the water, she shivered at the delicious coolness. The pool was waist-deep in the middle, the water moving sluggishly, and the bottom was sandy and fairly firm.

Tyler ducked completely under the surface, straightening with a gasp and blinking away water. It seemed lighter suddenly, and she looked up to find that the moon had peered through a break in the clouds.

She held the handkerchief in her teeth and worked up a lather with the soap, washing her hair quickly but as thoroughly as possible. When it was clean and rinsed, she moved toward the bank until the water reached her knees, then soaped the handkerchief and left the bar on a rock while she washed every inch of her skin.

There was still no sign of a snake, but Tyler wasn't anxious to push her luck. After a brief debate, she washed out her shirt, socks and underthings, reasoning that they would be the most likely to dry before she needed them again. The jeans were damp, but fairly clean, and too heavy to dry quickly if she attempted to wash them.

She returned the soap to its plastic and pulled the ruana over her head, realizing only then that she had nothing to belt it with; she never wore a belt with jeans. The light woolen material hung in folds to the middle of her thighs, and felt faintly scratchy against her flesh; it wasn't an uncomfortable sensation.

Shrugging, Tyler gathered her jeans and wet clothing together, picked up the soap and her boots and headed back for the campfire. The small clearing was deserted, but the lean-to had been completed and a small tin pot filled with some kind of stew simmered over the fire beside another pot of coffee. The lean-to was built near the fire, and she hung her wet things and the jeans over the line Kane had strung with his rope just beneath it.

Where was he? Bathing himself downstream? She looked at the soap she still held, then went to the stream's bank and called softly, "Kane? If you need the soap—"

"Downstream," he called back immediately.

Tyler followed the stream, seeing him just a couple of minutes later. He was submerged to his waist, and his chest and shoulders gleamed in the faint moonlight. He looked like something pagan, a part of the forest. A part of the wilderness. She glanced down at the pile of his clothing at her feet and swallowed hard.

"If this is our only bar of soap, do I dare throw it to you?" she asked him, striving for lightness.

Unlike Tyler's, Kane's night vision was excellent; in fact, it was too good at the moment. He could see her all too clearly, especially since the ruana she wore wasn't belted and tended to gape open at the sides. The darkness had stolen the fiery color from her hair, and it hung about her shoulders gleaming wetly and curling as though it were living. And despite her shapeless garment, the thrusting mounds of her firm breasts were as obvious to him as though she were naked.

He cleared his throat softly and tried not to think about her naked. "I don't think I should come out and get it," he returned, managing to keep his voice equally light.

After a moment Tyler stepped into the water and waded out until she was knee-deep. "Catch." She tossed the bar carefully, relieved when he caught it.

"Thanks, Ty."

"Sure." She retreated to the bank. "Oh, d'you mind if I use a piece of that rope? I don't have a belt for this thing."

"I noticed," he murmured. "Help yourself."

Tyler realized then that she hadn't exactly been holding the poncho securely; it covered front and back completely, but the sides were open. She wrapped it about her and headed hastily for the camp, further unsettled. Once there, it took several minutes' work with the rope to get herself decently covered, and even then she reminded herself not to bend over or move suddenly. She found his comb and used it to untangle her wet hair, then returned it to the backpack.

She unrolled the sleeping bag and used it as a cushion to sit on, then scrabbled in the backpack until she found the mug. She poured some coffee, wrinkling her nose at the first hot, strong sip. Black, and strong enough to raise the dead—she hated it that way. But she'd learned to drink it in the past, and since Kane always drank it like that, he wouldn't bring sugar or milk along as one of his little luxuries.

Kane returned to the camp a few minutes later, wearing only his jeans and carrying his wet shirt. His hair was wet, gleaming, and the thick mat of hair on his chest drew her eyes like a magnet. She looked away, angry with herself. What was *wrong* with her? She was too aware of him, too conscious of his every movement, and too apt to watch.

He hung the shirt on the line beside her things, and she glanced at him again without being able to stop herself, her gaze fastening on to the faint scars on his back. How had he got those? She'd seen them before but had never asked him about them. She wondered if he'd tell her if she did ask. Then she saw him finger the handkerchief with his monogram.

"I didn't know you still had this," he murmured.

Tyler could feel herself flushing, and looked hastily back to her coffee. "I don't remember how I came to have it," she said casually.

"Don't you?" He sank down beside her, cross-legged, reaching to dig into the pack for another cup and to return the bar of soap. "North Africa. The figurine was wrapped in it the first time you stole it from me."

Tyler could feel her hackles rising. It took a supreme effort of will to keep her eyes off him, and she was deeply disturbed by that. Anger was safe, and she allowed it to build. "You mean when I *rightfully* took it back after you tricked me to get it in the first place?"

"I suppose that's one way of looking at it." He sipped his coffee meditatively. "And it doesn't matter now, does it?" He was all too aware of her warmth beside him, and his eyes were drawn again and again to the bare length of her golden legs. Hard to think of the past—hard to think of anything at all when he looked at her.

"Maybe it doesn't matter," she was saying tightly. "Maybe I should keep it in mind. You've tricked me before; you'll trick me again. I can't trust you out of my sight, can I, Kane?"

He frowned a little, staring into the fire. "You'll have to make up your mind about that. There's nothing I could say to convince you."

"Is your word any good?" she asked bitterly.

Kane had the certain feeling that she was whistling in a graveyard again, deliberately starting an argument to divert herself—or him—from something else. But even with that feeling, he was aware of a slow, curiously bitter anger coiling inside him, tangling with the hot, building desire he felt for her. She always got under his skin. Somehow, she always got under his skin.

"Is yours?" he snapped back. He could feel her stiffen, feel the tentatively open doors between them slamming shut.

"I don't lie," she said shakily. "*You* made up the rules in this little game of ours—anything goes. I should have left you to the mercies of the she wolf and gone after the damned chalice alone!"

"Then why'd you come after me?" He gave a small, hard laugh. "The she wolf, as you call her, would have cut my throat in another few seconds. You would have been rid of me for good. So why'd you come after me, Ty?"

She swung around on the sleeping bag, her eyes glittering at him. "Beats the hell out of me!"

Kane didn't know whether to laugh or goad her until they both found out just why she'd gone after him. He wasn't given the chance to decide, however, because her fierce scowl faded abruptly and quick concern darkened her amber eyes.

"What happened?" She reached out, her fingers brushing aside his hair and lightly touching the bruised swelling just behind and below his left ear.

Bemused, Kane stared at her, highly conscious of her cool, gentle touch on his aching flesh. "One of the bandits." He cleared his throat. "I said something nasty to her majesty and one of her boys conked me."

Tyler set her mug aside and scrambled up in a flash of golden legs; she snagged the handkerchief from the line, going over to the stream and wetting it in the cool water. Returning, she knelt beside him and applied the folded pad to his head. "You should have said something," she told him irritably. "You must have a horrible headache."

Kane was gazing down at her upper thighs where the ruana had ridden up, and he barely felt the tin cup give a little under his tightening grasp. He closed his eyes briefly, then yanked his gaze upward. And that was a mistake, because the woolen material of the ruana had molded itself lovingly to her full breasts. Her nipples showed plainly, either because of the cold mountain stream or the friction of woolen cloth, and Kane couldn't take his eyes away. God, she was beautiful. . . . He could almost feel her against his fingers, his palms, feel her satiny flesh swell and harden to his touch.

The throbbing in his head spread slowly throughout his body and his loins ached with the hot surge of desire for her. It was a fire inside him, blazing rapidly out of control. He wanted to push her back on the sleeping bag and rip away the woolen material hiding her body from his. He wanted to look at her, touch her and taste her until she held no secrets, until he knew her body as well as he knew his own. He wanted to settle himself between her long, beautiful golden legs and fuse his body with hers, lose himself in her until he shattered with the pleasure of it.

He could feel her hand on his shoulder as she steadied herself, and was only dimly aware of the cool cloth pressed to his head. His gaze skimmed upward slowly, pausing to watch the pulse beating in her throat then lifting to examine the flawless pale golden flesh, the delicate features of her face. Her amber eyes were intent on her task, frowning slightly, and she was biting her lower lip with small white teeth.

God, that really got to him. It always had. It was a habit of hers whenever she was concentrating, and he thought it was the most provocative gesture he'd ever seen. He'd never noticed another woman doing it, just Ty. And it never failed to send a sharp jolt of desire through him.

Under his skin. Damn her, she was under his skin, like a thorn buried too deeply to get at. What would it take to get at that maddening thorn, to get her out of his mind, what would exorcise memories of her that had haunted him since the first time her amber eyes had blazed at him in a wild temper?

Always before, physical possession of a woman who attracted him had been enough. The first sexual excitement satisfied, boredom or restlessness had crept in. And it would again, he decided. If he took Tyler, she would no longer have the power to haunt his dreams. It was just desire, and the unusual circumstances of their past meetings had kept that desire simmering.

Unfortunately he couldn't believe that Tyler would make it easy for him. He was reasonably sure she felt an attraction to him, but there was something . . . stubborn in Tyler, something guarded and aloof.

And she wouldn't lie down with an enemy, except to reluctantly and warily sleep.

Tyler became conscious of the silence then, and when her eyes met the heat of his something turned over inside her. The skin of his shoulder burned her hand suddenly, and she drew away, almost dropping the folded linen of his handkerchief. "If—if we had some ice or something . . ."

"I'm fine," he said in an oddly still voice. "Thank you for saving my life, Ty."

It seemed a strange thing for him to say, not because he didn't owe her gratitude, but because there was little of that between them. Just acceptance or rejection, with few words about the matter. And his thanks bothered her, because his eyes were still hot.

She cleared her throat. "Don't mention it." She looked away from him, and when her eyes fell on the pot of stew her stomach growled audibly. She laughed unsteadily. "Somebody just rang the dinner bell. Is that stuff ready?"

"It's ready." He was casual again, digging into the backpack for tin plates and forks. He dished out the stew and handed her a plate, then began eating himself.

They had avoided it. Tyler was dismayed and unsettled when that thought occurred to her, because she couldn't avoid the realization that both of them were all too aware of the fact that there was a point of danger, a point of no return, and that they had retreated from it again with wary care. But what disturbed her more than anything else was that it was happening more often, this electric sensual awareness.

Enemy, she reminded herself with a surge of bitterness she was hardly conscious of. *He'll trick me if he can. When this partnership no longer suits him. He'll trick me again. Maybe he's tricking me now.*

And she had to be on guard against that.

Halfway through the meal, Tyler realized that she was exhausted. It came over her suddenly, in a wave, leaving her feeling decidedly shaky. Trailing Kane and his captors, and then waiting tensely for an opportunity to get him out of there, she'd felt no tiredness even though they had been on the move since dawn. And while they were putting distance between themselves and the bandits she'd been conscious of nothing but relief that the episode had ended in their triumph.

But now she was utterly tired, her eyes heavy. Dawn had lightened the sky and a few birds greeted the day merrily, but thunder rumbled a soft warning in the distance. She thought about that muzzily, remembering how much she liked to sleep when it was raining. And she started when Kane reached to take her empty plate away from her.

"Time for bed," he told her, unusually gentle. "Let's get the sleeping bag back under the lean-to."

Tyler moved off the cushioning softness, yawning uncontrollably, and the moment Kane had the bag positioned she was crawling into it. The lean-to provided a canopy of branches and leaves above her head, and she gazed upward sleepily while she listened to Kane moving about the camp. He was cleaning up, she realized, washing the pots and things, packing them away again.

Ready to be on the move again, instantly, at the need.

Tired as she was, she couldn't fall asleep until he joined her, and she was too sleepy to think about that. She waited, yawning, listening to him. The first patter of raindrops came before he did, but then he was sliding into the bag beside her. Tyler felt the rough material of his jeans brushing against her bare legs, pleasurably scratchy, and wondered vaguely if the ruana had ridden up to her waist the way it felt as if it had. Probably. Not that she cared.

"Will this thing leak?" she asked drowsily.

"Let's hope not. Get some sleep, Ty."

She fell asleep with the suddenness of a child, while Kane lay awake and stared at the branches overhead and listened to the rain. She had left her hair unbraided; he could feel strands of the silky stuff beneath his shoulder. And his mind taunted him with visions of what he would see if he were to throw back the top layer of the sleeping bag; he knew damned well her woolen garment had been pushed up to her waist when she'd slid into the bag.

She hadn't turned her back to him this time, and he could feel her warm curves pressed against his side. He wondered what she'd do if he began kissing her, touching her. Respond, probably, and there was no vanity in that thought. Tyler sleepy and tired was sweet and vague and vulnerable; he'd noticed that about her before. She never got cranky because of weariness, and all her prickly barriers came crashing down.

He was tired himself, and inclined to be reckless with the throbbing need of his body to taunt him, but he couldn't take advantage of her vulnerability.

He'd be just what she thought he was.

And why did that bother him? Why did he care, as long as the end result was achieved; she'd be out of his system then, out of his head, and the tormenting desire would be sated. He could take her now, right now, drive her as crazy as she drove him and watch her face as passion made of it something elementally beautiful. He could feel her warmth sheathe him, push his body and his senses to the edge of madness and beyond. He could steal an interlude of pleasure from her, just as he'd stolen a golden figurine and a few other antiquities. With trickery and treachery.

She'd hate him afterward. Hate him because it would be stealing, allowing her no chance to give. Hate him for a basic dishonesty that had nothing to do with their "anything goes" games. But she'd be out of his system then. Wouldn't she? The partnership would be null and void, and there would be no Tyler to ever again fight at his side.

Kane linked his hands together behind his neck, moving carefully so as not to disturb her. The rain was beating steadily against the branches of the lean-to and thunder rumbled, but Kane was listening to his own thoughts.

He should have been thinking about the chalice and the hefty fee Joshua Phillips would pay him to bring it back to New York. That fee would make the last payment on the ranch, and the place was self-sustaining now; he could retire. Could he do that? Yes, he thought he could. He'd spent ten years roaming the world, and it was getting harder now to leave home.

How did Tyler feel about ranches? Could she ride? She could ride a camel, he remembered, and smiled despite himself as he recalled that occasion. But his smile faded.

What in God's name was wrong with him? Thinking of Tyler on his ranch . . . that was absurd. And only moments before he had thought about stealing from her because it didn't seem possible she would give to him . . . not that. Not Tyler.

She moved then, murmuring in her sleep, turning to snuggle close to him, her cheek on his chest, one hand sliding upward to touch his neck, warm and boneless. Kane felt everything in him go still for an instant, and then he lowered his arm until it curved around her shoulders, and rested his chin in the fragrant silk of her hair.

Something inside her trusted him, even if she didn't know it consciously. And he couldn't take advantage of that.

The rain droned steadily on, and it was growing hotter and more humid, but Kane didn't notice. Tension seeped from his muscles as he held her, felt her soft breath, and he fell asleep without even realizing he was going to.

TYLER FELT VAGUELY bothered, and she realized only gradually that it was because of the rain. Or, more precisely, because the rain had stopped. The steady sounds, the pattering and the splashing, had helped to make her sleep deep and dreamless. But now the sounds were only faint and sporadic, an occasional splash, a minute thud, and she felt she should awake.

She moved restlessly, and the faint, pleasant scratching of something against her cheek woke her fully. Bewildered, she opened her eyes to see a thick pelt of curling black hair. She stared for a moment, then jerked her head off Kane's chest. She felt his arm around her then, and heat suffused her face as her eyes met his wide-awake gaze.

"You sleep like a cat," he murmured, his free hand lifting to smooth a strand of her hair back. "A trusting cat. Utterly boneless. Maybe you trust me more than you know."

She couldn't read his face. What was he thinking? Why was he talking to her like this? She wanted to push away from him and quickly get out of the bag with what grace and dignity she could muster, but another part of her was conscious of a suspended waiting, a deep, churning uncertainty.

The point of danger. Again, the point of danger. She could feel herself quivering like some wild thing scenting peril. But she couldn't find the strength or the will to draw back.

Kane's free hand slipped over her back to her waist, rubbing lightly. "You weren't bothered by the bra this time. You sleep in the buff when you're alone, don't you, Ty?"

"That's—none of your business." But she was shaken because he'd guessed right.

"I suppose not." The hand at her shoulder moved, his fingers curling around her neck beneath the heavy weight of her hair and drawing her slowly downward. He took his time, giving her the opportunity to pull away if she wanted. But Tyler stared into his eyes, her own startled and wavering, and though the nape of her neck was tense, she didn't resist him.

He had kissed her twice before, once roughly and half in anger because she had expected him to try, once very briefly in relief and thanks because she had saved his life when she could have left him to shift for himself. This time, Kane intended to leave her with a memory. He might never be granted this opportunity again, and he meant to make certain that Tyler faced the fact that there was something between them, something more than rivalry and mistrust.

He molded his lips to hers, guiding her head firmly, watching until her lids fluttered and then closed. Her mouth was cool and stiff beneath his for a long moment, but his tongue glided insistently between her lips and a helpless shiver went through her. He could feel her fingers curl against his chest suddenly, the oval nails digging into his skin, and then her mouth warmed, opened to him.

The wet heat of her mouth sent shudders through Kane's big body, but he concentrated only on the fusion of the kiss. His tongue touched hers silkily, demanding a response, receiving it instantly but tentatively. His hands roved to her waist, where he could feel the bunched material of the ruana, and the thought of the scant covering over her nakedness maddened him. The material had slid apart at her sides during the night, and his thumbs found the sensitive satin flesh, stroked it.

Tyler felt that touch as if it were fire, and when dizziness swept over her she didn't even try to fight it. He was taking her mouth, she realized dimly, possessing it and branding it his own, and she had never felt anything like that before. The roughness of his morning beard was a heady caress, and her skin tingled with the contact. He was seducing her, slowly and inexorably, kindling a fire where none had ever before blazed. She was hardly conscious that her hands had curled around his neck, barely aware that she had drawn one leg up over his, frustrated by denim when she wanted to feel his flesh against her own.

Then he was moving her, lifting her with his easy strength until she lay fully on him, the close confines of the sleeping bag pressing her tightly against his big, hard body. Her legs parted instinctively to lie on either side of his, and her body responded wildly to the swelling response she could feel from him. The denim between them was a rough caress and a curse, and his every faint movement was a searing jolt to her senses.

She felt no panic, no smothering sensation of helplessness and vulnerability. There was no hard shadow over her, blocking out the light and holding her down. There was only heat and a building tension that was restless and a strange, unfamiliar combination of pleasure and pain.

Kane hadn't meant for this to go so far; he hadn't expected such a total response from her. But her response was total, and his hunger for her had burst out of control. She was soft and warm as she lay on him, her breasts pressed to his chest, and he was drunk with the feel of her, the taste of her, the heady feminine smell of her. His hands slipped down over her hips until the firm mounds of her buttocks filled them, and he moved beneath her, driven, feeling he'd explode if he didn't take her, didn't roll over and bury himself in the warmth of her body.

But it was then that some ever-vigilant sense warned him of danger, and Kane forced his eyes to open and his lips to leave hers. Instantly, without thought, his hands jerked from beneath the quilted bag and shot upward, bracing the heavy branches of the lean-to a scant few seconds before the structure would have collapsed on them both.

Tyler was unaware of it at first. She was trembling, her breathing shallow and her body aching with an emptiness she'd never felt before. His chest rose and fell raggedly beneath her breasts, and she felt a blind, mad urge to find his mouth again because she desperately needed that heated touch.

But sanity penetrated the veils of her emotions, and her dazed eyes finally absorbed the rigid posture of his strong arms. Logic told her then that the rain had soaked an already marshy ground,

causing the lean-to's support posts to sink, and that the structure was heavy enough to have given them a nasty jolt.

Tyler moved without thinking about it, her actions dictated by some rational corner of her bewildered mind. She twisted, reaching for the zipper of the sleeping bag, trying frantically to ignore the screamingly aware nerves of her body as well as the rough sound he made as she moved on top of him. She could feel her face flaming. Unzipping the bag, she managed to squirm off Kane and get out, yanking the ruana down as she scrambled to her feet.

"Can you hold it a minute?" she asked him huskily.

"I can hold it." His voice was harsh, and his green eyes were blazing.

Ten feet away, Tyler found a sturdy limb with a forked end. She brought it back and kneeled to jam it under the crosspiece of the lean-to, bracing the other end firmly against the ground. The structure wobbled a bit, but it held.

Silently Kane crawled from the sleeping bag.

Tyler was holding the limb with both hands, staring at her fingers with a baffled expression. Then she looked at him, and the perplexity in her amber eyes was almost pain. "Another trick, Kane?"

He didn't pretend to misunderstand. Yanking his shirt from the line, he shrugged into it and growled, "You know damned well it wasn't. And you could have stopped me with a word, Ty. Think about that."

She was still frowning, trying to fit the action to the man she thought she knew, unwilling to examine her own participation. "You must have had a reason," she murmured almost to herself. "Something to gain by it."

He stared at her for a long moment, truly recognizing only then the gulf that lay between them. "Oh, I had a reason," he told

her bitterly. "I wanted you, Tyler, pure and simple. And you wanted me, whether you'll admit it or not. But we're just enemies under a flag of truce, aren't we? I should have remembered that." Turning abruptly, he strode off through the woods.

Tyler stared blankly after him.

chapter four

SEDUCE AN ENEMY and earn his—her—trust?

Had that thought occurred to Kane as well as to her? It was the only reason that made sense, and Tyler accepted it with a flash of pain that surprised her. She still refused to think about her own participation. Fiercely she reminded herself that he was adept at trickery, and ruthless. She didn't doubt his desire, but told herself that he was an innately sexual man; other men had found her attractive, and Kane apparently did, as well.

Physically at least.

She ignored the pain that she didn't understand, concentrating instead on this situation. Partners. Fine, then. Partners for the duration. And she wouldn't be seduced, wouldn't allow this insane attraction she felt for him to lower her guard.

By the time he returned to their camp nearly an hour later,

Tyler was dressed, her hair braided, her control and her guard firmly in place. The sleeping bag had been rolled up and tied to his backpack. She had made coffee, and had unearthed, from that rather amazing pack of his, pancake mix and canned milk. A stack of golden cakes was piled on a tin plate, and she was paying strict attention to the task of fixing more when he approached.

"If you had told me there was canned milk," she said mildly without looking up, "I would have put some in my coffee last night."

"You didn't ask."

His voice was calm and guarded, she reflected, like hers had been. It seemed they had both decided to ignore what had almost happened between them. It was safer that way, she reminded herself. Much safer. But she felt cheated somehow, and a part of her recognized that both she and Kane were fighters, that it was unnatural for them and totally out of character to ignore this particular battle.

But this battle, she also recognized, was too dangerous to be fought. Not here. Not now. And not between the two of them. No matter who won or lost, the scars would mark them both for life.

She stole glances at him as they both ate breakfast silently. He had shaved, and she couldn't help but think of how sensual his morning beard had felt against her skin. Realizing where her thoughts had gone, she tried desperately to redirect them. But it was impossible.

Was it only the situation that was different this time, the fact that they were too alone here, too intimate? Or had their relationship, sporadic though it was, always been heading toward this point? Was it possible, she suddenly asked herself, to feel so many strong emotions for a man, even though most of them were negative ones, without feeling also a primitive attraction?

They were alike, and she recognized that now. She and Kane

were very alike, cut from the same stubborn mold. Adventurous, humorous, reckless, tough when they had to be, independent. They both loved artifacts, and both were, conversely, capable of great honor and integrity as well as great deviousness.

Tyler pushed the realization violently away. Alike they may be, she thought grimly, but they were still enemies, rivals. Infusing her voice with a mildly speculative tone, she said, "That shooter. Who do you suppose he is?" They had hardly had time to discuss the matter before now, and she grasped the subject as something safe and relatively unthreatening.

"I didn't get a good look at him." Kane was paying attention to his meal. "Did you see him clearly?'

"I was too busy diving for cover." He didn't offer her a smile or make a sardonic comment, and Tyler sighed to herself. She didn't like this mine field they were so warily crossing; at least in the past they'd been too busy snapping at each other and being sneaky to worry about mines beneath their feet.

"He's after the cache," Kane said.

"How can you be so sure of that?" she asked, even though she agreed with him.

"Because nothing else makes sense." He took his plate to the stream and began cleaning it. Over his shoulder, he said, "I caught a glimpse of blond hair, so it's doubtful he's native to these parts. As far as I could find out, the only likely valuables in the area would be the cache Rolfe smuggled out of Germany during the war and hid—for Tomas to find more than forty years later. Maybe Tomas talked too freely back in Panama about his discovery. Odds are, our trigger-happy friend is after exactly what we're after."

Tyler ate the last of her breakfast as she thought about it. Like many of the valuables their employers sent them after, the chalice's rightful ownership was a matter of speculation; it occupied a kind of legal no-man's-land. During World War II, much of Europe had been looted of its valuables, and many items had simply vanished, never to be found.

During the final days of the war, a number of men had taken what they could and jumped Hitler's sinking ship. Some of those men had hidden their treasures in various parts of the world, and for more than forty years items had surfaced from time to time, appearing on the black market or just changing hands privately. Interpol had traced many art objects and antiquities and returned them to their proper owners, but lists were incomplete and often contained inspired guesswork because too many records had been destroyed during the war.

The chalice that she and Kane were after now was one such homeless artifact. Ownership couldn't be proven legally because of the gaps in various records and, indeed, Tyler knew very little about it except that her employer was hell-bent to get it in his hands. Its intrinsic value was hard to estimate; it was believed to have been in the possession of a very old church in Italy a hundred and fifty years before, but was reportedly lost long before the church itself was destroyed.

Then the war had happened, and somewhere along the way the chalice had ended up in a cache of valuables hidden in the wilderness of Colombia. And their slippery friend Tomas had discovered it while—he *said*—visiting his family in the area, and had left it there until he could find buyers. He hadn't dared return for it himself, he'd told Tyler with a wide, artless smile. He hadn't explained why, and Tyler had been in too much of a hurry to ask.

Absently Tyler said, "Sayers didn't tell me how he'd heard about the chalice. Did your boss?" Kane's boss was Joshua Phillips, who lived in London as did his enemy Sayers.

"No."

She looked at him curiously as he returned and began packing his plate and fork away. "What do you know about it?"

"I know it's supposed to be cursed," Kane answered mildly.

Tyler didn't react with scorn or disbelief. She knew enough history to be aware of the reality of curses. Not that she believed inanimate objects could contain a malevolent spirit, but she *did* believe that events were sometimes tied to objects, connected in a sense, and that because antiquities had such a long and colorful history unlucky events were certain to have occurred near them and to have been connected in one way or another.

"I haven't heard of that," she said now, getting up and going to the stream to clean her own plate. "Tell me."

Somewhat surprisingly, Kane didn't seem to be in a hurry. He waited until she returned to the fire, then focused his eyes on the flames and spoke slowly.

"Most of what I know is pretty much speculative. Ironically enough, I stumbled across a reference to the chalice and the legend in an unpublished private journal years ago. Never thought I'd have the chance to hold the thing in my hand."

Tyler understood what he meant. One of the reasons she enjoyed this job so much was that it gave her the opportunity to see and touch objects whose existence was, in terms of history, almost mythical. She nodded now, and watched his profile as he gazed into the fire.

"It all started," Kane said, "with Alexander."

Tyler blinked. "Alexander the Great? But you're going back more than two thousand years! The chalice can't be that old."

"There's some confusion about that. Very little documentation has survived, what with various wars and all. There's probably little hope that the chalice we're after is the same one in this story. But you never know." He glanced at her, something both quizzical and oddly intent in his green eyes. "Sure you want to hear it?"

She was a little puzzled, but curious. "Of course. All I know about the chalice is that it disappeared from the church in Florence about a hundred years ago. And that there were supposedly two of them originally. Your story sounds more interesting than that. So tell me. It started with Alexander?"

Kane was gazing into the fire again. "Alexander. You may remember that he was barely twenty when his father was assassinated, and that he rounded up a number of suspects whom he very quickly had executed. All of them had claims to the throne. He also gave his mother the honor of dispatching his father's young wife and newborn son."

"I remember." Tyler grimaced faintly. "They sort of glossed over that part when I was in school, but my father told me what the books left out."

"Your father?"

"He was an archaeologist. Go on with the story." She felt a little disturbed at having made a personal reference; she and Kane never did that. The past they shared had begun three years ago after a confrontation in North Africa, and neither had ever looked further back than that.

Kane half nodded. "So Alexander became king, and an arrogant one at that. He got busy conquering the world. He also made two marriages, both political, to Asian princesses. One of those wives was the daughter of the king of Persia."

"King Darius. I remember," Tyler said.

"You may also remember that Alexander conquered Persia, and that Darius was killed, supposedly by one of his own generals."

"Yes."

"What his daughter felt about that is a matter for speculation, since it was more or less Alexander's fault." Kane shook his head. "But in any case, it's likely she found out that being politically married to a king who was continually off conquering the world wasn't much fun."

"I can imagine," Tyler murmured.

"Her name was Statira," Kane said. "And whatever she felt for her husband, she seems to have kept to herself. However, somewhere around 323 B.C. Statira and Alexander's other political wife jointly commissioned a pair of golden cups—chalices—to be fashioned in his honor. They sent the chalices to him, together in one package, with a message assuring him of their loyalty. He was busy making preparations to invade Arabia at the time."

"And?" Tyler prompted when he fell silent.

"And he was at the palace in Babylon when the package arrived. There was a celebration of sorts going on, lots of drinking and partying. Alexander opened the package and promptly used one of the cups to toast his loyal wives. He handed the second cup to his closest general, who also made a toast."

Tyler half winced. "Poison?"

"According to history," Kane said, "it was likely malaria. In any case, within a few hours of drinking from the chalice, Alexander fell ill. He was dead within three days. The general who had drunk from the second cup was fine. There was much talk, according to the legend, about which of the two wives had tried to poison Alexander. But the chalices vanished, and with Alexander's empire coming apart nobody bothered to try to find out if he had indeed been poisoned."

"But the chalices were believed to be cursed?"

"Not just because of that. In 1478, Giuliano de' Medici was stabbed to death during mass by the Pazzi family. He was drinking from a gold chalice when he was stabbed; according to descriptions, it exactly matched one of the pair given to Alexander. And in 1791, when Louis XVI was captured at Varennes, two chalices were found in his coach—again, matching the description of Alexander's gold cups."

Tyler was frowning a little. "There are some big gaps in time in your legend. Where were the chalices?"

Kane shrugged. "There are just vague mentions of bad luck following the chalices, always connected in some way to betrayal and death."

"Is there a more recent history?"

"Just what you've heard. That one chalice was in the possession of a church in Florence around a hundred years ago and then vanished; there's no mention in existing records of the second one after about 1800."

After a moment Tyler said slowly, "The chalice we're after is just a piece of the loot Hitler collected; there's no record of where it was taken from, or any information about its history. What makes you think it's one of Alexander's?"

Kane shrugged again. "The description. According to what my boss gave me, the chalice we're after is the spitting image of Alexander's." A bit dryly, he added, "And Joshua Phillips, at least, is so excited about it that he was almost stuttering when he sent me after it. The bonus, assuming I bring it back, is nothing short of staggering."

Tyler stared at him. She couldn't read his expression, but all her doubts about her ability to trust him were uppermost in her mind. The stakes this time were high. "My boss promised me a—staggering bonus," she confessed somewhat warily.

Kane suddenly rose and began making preparations to leave, pouring the last of the coffee in the fire and packing up everything. Casually he said, "Obviously neither of us was told all our employers know about the chalice; I think they both believe it was Alexander's. Or else why the secrecy? We've both known exactly what we were after before. Didn't you wonder why you weren't told more this time?"

Tyler had automatically followed suit in getting ready to leave, and stood, absently adjusting the strap of a canteen over her shoulder as she gazed at Kane. "Maybe I was blinded by dollar signs," she suggested. If she had meant it to be a pointed reference—and she wasn't sure about that—Kane either missed it or ignored it.

He slung the backpack over one shoulder, picked up the rifle, and studied her deliberately. "No. You like the money, but that isn't the reason you do this. You do it for kicks, Ty. You do it because you love antiquities. And you do it because, for some reason I haven't figured out yet, you're driven to put yourself in danger."

She stood staring at him, conscious of her heart pounding suddenly, of confusion clouding her mind. How could he have guessed that? *How?* And why did she abruptly feel vulnerable as she never had before? With an effort she curved her lips in a sardonic smile. "You don't say." It wasn't much as comebacks go, but Tyler knew him too well to arouse his hunting instincts by going overboard on the side of denial.

His smile was every bit as sardonic as hers. "Don't you ever get tired of it?"

"Tired of what?"

"Holding your guard up with me?"

Before she could stop herself, her gaze flickered toward the wobbly lean-to. Without waiting for him to comment on that tiny betrayal, she said sweetly, "It's just a matter of common sense, Kane. You should always carry a whip and chair when you walk into a lion's cage. And you should never turn your back to that breed of cat."

"Even one raised in captivity?" he asked in a light tone.

"Especially that one." She could hear the stony note of absolute certainty in her voice. "He knows how to purr. He even knows how to jump through a hoop when he has to. But he never forgets where the cage door is."

Kane looked at her for a long moment, then nodded almost imperceptibly. Softly he said, "But you won't stay out of the cage,

Tyler. Think about that. Nobody forced you to step into it. You just won't stay out of the cage."

She followed as he left the camp, her movements automatic. That strange, disturbing feeling of suspension was with her again, and the curiously stark analogy of lion and cage clung to her mind stubbornly. Kane was right; she couldn't stay out of the cage, even though nobody forced her to go in. Even knowing the danger of the lion.

The slight sounds they made as they went on covered her soft gasp, and she was grateful that he hadn't heard the evidence of her own shock.

Danger. *Danger*. Was that why she was so violently attracted to Kane, why she relished their rivalry? He was the strongest, most dangerous man she had ever known, and when she was with him the encounters demanded every ounce of her own strength and will. She had to push herself beyond her self-defined limits in his company, physically, mentally—and emotionally.

Could it be that simple?

Did some part of her fiercely enjoy their rivalry because he was the lion she needed to tame, the danger she needed to face and attempt to control? Three years before, she had accepted Robert Sayers's job offer out of boredom and curiosity, but on encountering Kane a couple of months later her determination to best him had been instant and implacable, and that ambition had never since wavered. And on each succeeding assignment, she had looked eagerly for him.

Tyler followed along behind Kane in silence as the hours passed, wrapped up in her own disturbing thoughts. When he finally called a halt in the late afternoon, she put the canteen aside and gazed around her in vague surprise. They had been circumventing the swamp for some hours, but she was only now aware of the rich, ripe scents and eerie sounds of the marshlands.

"We'll start back inland in another hour or so," Kane said, and tossed her a packet of trail mix. "We should make higher ground before dark."

She nodded, eating because she should and not because she was hungry. Her mind started ahead to the coming night, and she frowned at her own chaotic thoughts. She felt hot and sticky, and decidedly unnerved by the uncertainty she felt regarding the motives behind Kane's earlier desire for her.

Kane watched her, very aware of her silence and of the troubled frown on her delicate face. He had shocked her, he knew, by observing that she fought him by choice; he had been more than a little surprised himself at the realization. He thought he was beginning to understand her, at least more than ever before, and with that tentative knowledge had come something he had hardly been prepared for.

Want was such a mild word, or always had been, but now it was something alive and clawing at him. All day, he had been starkly conscious of her almost silent movements behind him, and he had glanced back often to see her bright hair and preoccupied face. And every glance had sharpened the ache of desire that was centered deeper than his loins, somewhere in his very bones.

He wanted her with a strength he had never felt before.

And not just physically. He wanted to understand her. Always before, he had observed the enigma of her with interest and vague curiosity, with little time granted to him for probing. But this time he had caught several glimpses of what lay beneath her guard, either because of her own words or because he was looking harder. And what he had seen fascinated him.

He knew she mistrusted him, mistrusted even his desire for her. Maybe *especially* his desire. She suspected a trick, an attempt to get beneath her guard. He understood that; it was a reasonable suspicion given their past encounters. But what he was beginning to see was that Tyler herself was unconvinced by her own suspicions. She was wavering, looking at him one moment as an enemy and the next with puzzled uneasiness.

The question was, did her uncertainty argue well for a change in their relationship?

"We should reach the cave by tomorrow," he said now, casually, as he watched her. She looked at him almost blindly for a moment, but then her eyes focused and there was something in those amber depths he'd seen once before in the eyes of a doe, something wary and perplexed.

"Good," she responded in a taut voice.

"Assuming the cache is where it's supposed to be, we should be on our way right after that. We can head northeast to Bogotá and find transport out of the country. And since we have to get the cache to Tomas in Panama, our best chance of getting back to Europe is probably by ship from there. Agreed?"

Getting in and out of various countries with antiquities whose rightful ownership couldn't be determined wasn't exactly illegal, but both Tyler and Kane had learned not to call undue attention to themselves in the process; both were usually pressed for time, and also wished to avoid possible thieves and other interested parties. So they tended to bypass airports with their terrorist-spawned and highly efficient security in favor of land or water transportation, where their accommodations were generally several notches below tourist class.

Tyler had often found it ironic that she traveled with an unlimited expense account and could also draw from banks in any major city in the world, and yet usually went from place to place in rackety buses or the cargo holds of leaky ships. Still, she was seeing the world from a unique perspective in this jet age, and wouldn't have traded even her most uncomfortable experiences for first-class travel all the way.

But she was thinking about that now, thinking of a long sea voyage in Kane's company. Presumably they would have the chalice in their possession. At least one of them would. There was still no solution for the problem of dividing one old, golden chalice for two separate employers.

"Ty?"

She drew a deep breath. "Agreed. Who gets the chalice, Kane?"

He reached for his canteen and unscrewed the cap, frowning just a little but not looking at her. "We don't have to make that decision for a while yet," he noted neutrally.

"And when *do* we decide? When we dock at Portsmouth or Liverpool, or wherever? When we get to London?"

"You think I'm going to try and give you the slip in Panama," he said after taking a leisurely drink from his canteen. He was looking at her now, steady and faintly amused.

"You've done it before," she reminded him evenly. "In Madagascar, you managed to have me detained by the police, and in Cairo you left me making arrangements for a ship while you hightailed it across the desert."

Kane grinned suddenly as a memory surfaced. "You got even, at least in North Africa," he offered. "Telling those Bedouins I stole one of their camels was a sneaky trick, Ty. By the way, what was the last offer from that sheik?"

She glared at him for a moment, but her sense of humor couldn't remain submerged for long and a reluctant gleam lit her eyes. "Once I told him I had an employer who valued me, he started sending his proposals to Robert. I told Robert I didn't want to know what the offers were, but he says he's keeping a file in case I ever change my mind."

"Or he ever needs a big favor from the sheik," Kane said somewhat abruptly. And when she stiffened visibly, he added, "Sorry. Didn't mean that."

Tyler's glare was back, this time holding a chill light. "I don't give a damn what you think," she said in a voice that shook slightly. "But I'll tell you this, Kane. Not everything's for sale. Even to the highest bidder."

Kane had gone too far, and he knew it. He didn't know why he had implied that Sayers would—or could—use Tyler's sexual favor as a bargaining chip, and was more than a little surprised at both his implication and the savage emotions it had inspired in him. His gaze fell before hers. "I know. I'm sorry, Tyler, really. I suppose I was thinking about how ruthless Sayers and Phillips are in this feud of theirs."

She got to her feet stiffly. "We'd better move on if we want to make higher ground by dark."

As he rose as well, Kane reflected wryly that this encounter between them was running true to form in one way; a verbal see-saw with each of them besting the other occasionally but neither getting the upper hand for long.

He led the way in silence as they circled the last of the swamp. They had made better time than he'd expected, partially because the swamp was smaller than he'd been told, and also because they'd been moving quickly. The sun was sinking behind them as they left the swamp and began making their way through the thickening undergrowth of a dense forest. They were heading east now, gradually climbing into the Andes, and the temperature was already falling.

There was still plenty of light when the rain began falling steadily, and Kane glanced back to see Tyler look upward with more resignation than annoyance.

"We're lucky the rain held off this long," he said over his shoulder.

Tyler accepted the olive branch, though her voice was a bit stiff. "I know. But since we're almost into the dry season, I'd been hoping . . ."

"We usually have better luck," he agreed, turning to offer a hand to help her up a slippery granite outcrop. She came up beside him easily and without fuss, and remembering some of the feats demanded of them both in the past made him ask curiously as they went on, "Were you an athlete?"

She was silent for a moment as she followed him, then said, "If you mean in school, no. My father raised me, and since he spent at least six months of every year on a dig somewhere, I was lucky to just make decent grades."

"You went with him?"

"Yes."

He smiled a little at the brief answer. "So that's where you developed your strength and balance, climbing around ruins?"

There was another silence, and then she said, "Partly, I suppose. And, until I was sixteen, ballet."

Kane stopped on a rise to check the compass then looked at her with more than a little surprise. "Ballet?"

She smiled very faintly. "When I was fifteen, I was five-two and weighed eighty-five pounds. Between that birthday and the next, I grew five inches, gained thirty pounds, and, um—"

"Bloomed?" he suggested with a grin.

Tyler shrugged, unconsciously drawing his more intent scrutiny to the "blooming" that had turned her ballerina's slenderness into the rich curves of a woman. "Let's just say my possibilities as a prima ballerina went down the tubes," she said wryly.

"Any regrets?" he asked, trying to keep his eyes on her face as the steady rain plastered her shirt to the ripe breasts beneath it.

She adjusted the strap of the canteen on her shoulder, returning his gaze with the same wary look in her eyes that had been present since this morning. Not the suspicion of a rival; it looked like the misgivings of a woman risking more than defeat in a contest.

It was really beginning to bother him.

"No," she said finally. "I was getting interested in antiquities by then and . . ."

"And?"

She fiddled with the strap on her shoulder again. "And shouldn't we be going?"

Kane frowned a little. She was unnerved, and he didn't know why. What had she been going to say about the year of physical changes that had altered her life? He was curious, but reluctant to disturb the fragile calm between them. So he went on, automatically choosing the easiest path as they continued to climb into the mountains.

It was still raining steadily, and the last of the light vanished as though a switch had been thrown. The footing was slippery in places, and Kane was beginning to look around for a place to hole up for the night when Tyler fell.

"Damn," she muttered irritably as he knelt beside her. "Of all the stupid—"

"Are you hurt?" he asked briskly.

"My leg." She shifted her weight slightly, then batted his hand away from her upper thigh. "Not that high, damn it."

"It's dark," he murmured, knowing by the sound of her voice that she wasn't in much pain.

"And you have eyes like an owl. My ankle—the left one. Just twisted a little; the boot protected it. If you'll give me a hand up, I can—" She gasped as Kane slipped one arm beneath her knees, the other around her back, and rose easily to his feet holding her against his chest. "Kane!"

Reasonably he said, "You shouldn't put any weight on that ankle until we can take a look at it, which is impossible here. There should be a level place at the top of this slope where we can build a fire." He was moving steadily up the slope, apparently untroubled by either the slippery footing or his burden.

Tyler knew very well that his backpack weighed every ounce of fifty pounds since she'd carried it herself while tracking him and the bandits the day before. He was also carrying a canteen and rifle by their shoulder straps. And carrying her. Up a slippery slope. In pitch darkness.

She had put her arms around his neck automatically as he'd lifted her, and now made a determined effort not to think about strong arms holding her. Clearing her throat, she said, "So much for my balance."

Kane chuckled softly.

That ambiguous response made her say aggrievedly, "I didn't fall on purpose, you know."

"You're whistling again," he said calmly.

Tyler frowned into the darkness, wondering when she had suddenly become so obvious to him. "I am not," she denied, even though she knew she'd been doing just that, just making noise to distract them both from unexpected closeness.

"Of course you are." His voice showed no strain. "We've always been a man and woman, Ty, but you're just beginning to realize it. And you're shying away like a timid deer."

She couldn't trust him, that's why she didn't want this! But she couldn't tell him that. So, as always, she worked up a flare of anger. "Don't flatter yourself!"

Ignoring that, Kane said, "I've been thinking about it most of the day. I know you don't trust me. Fair enough. To be perfectly honest, sweetheart, I don't trust you, either." He reached the top of the slope and stood gazing around for a moment.

Tyler, who couldn't see a thing except him even though her eyes had adjusted as much as they could to the darkness, stared at his arrogant profile and opened her mouth to spit the angry words still forming in her mind.

Kane turned his head suddenly, and his grin was a flash of white in the darkness. "But I want you," he said.

She closed her mouth, then said, "Put me down."

"Sure." He carried her several steps, then ducked slightly to clear what was apparently an overhang and knelt to set her gently on dry ground. "Back in a minute," he said, shrugging off his pack and leaving it beside her. "I'll see if I can find some dry wood for a fire."

Tyler sat exactly as he'd left her, staring blankly into darkness. She was vaguely aware of hard rock at her back and dry dirt underneath her, and senses other than sight told her that a granite cliff curved protectively out above her. It couldn't be called a cave, but Kane had managed to find shelter.

She lifted a hand that shook and slowly wiped moisture from her face. She was wet and chilled, but she knew that the trembling she could feel in her body had little to do with either condition.

I want you.

She had heard the words, the implicit demand before, but not from Kane. When Kane said it, it was no overture, no testing of the waters before a relationship could take a next logical step. When Kane said it, it wasn't a simple statement of desire. When Kane said it, it was a challenge, a battle line drawn in the dirt between them.

After thinking it through, Kane wasn't willing to ignore this battle. He didn't trust her, or she him, but there was desire between them, and for Kane that was enough. He wouldn't pretend they were no longer enemies, that their rivalry was past. He wouldn't pretend to care about her.

Or at least, she hoped not. Bedroom lies were the one variety of deceit she would never be able to bear from him.

Tyler knew then that she wasn't ready for this particular battle. She shifted position in the darkness and began unlacing her left boot, trying to think clearly and finding it almost impossible. All she could bring to mind were memories of the tight, warm enclosure of the sleeping bag and Kane's hard body pressed so intimately to hers.

God, she couldn't let this happen. Her own body's response to him told her that not even her panicky feelings of helplessness and vulnerability could erect a guard between them, and with her mind in turmoil she had to doubt her intellectual will to resist him. It didn't matter that she didn't trust him, because her body didn't care about trust, and she doubted her mind's ability to control her body. Kane could make her want him, and he knew that as surely as she did herself.

She felt more than heard him return, but said nothing as he began building a small fire a couple of feet from her. The overhang provided a dry space four or five feet deep and about ten feet long, and he had placed the fire out near the edge of the hollow to give them as much room as possible.

"There isn't much dry wood out there," he said casually, "but I got what I could."

She watched the fire flicker as he fed it with sticks and then broke a couple of larger branches with his hands and one knee. The sharp cracking of the wood sounded loud in the silence.

"How's the ankle?" he asked, sitting back on his heels and brushing his hands together as he looked across the fire at her.

"All right." Her voice was steady. "Not even swollen."

He came around the fire, hunched a bit because he couldn't stand upright in the confined space, and knelt beside her. His khaki shirt was soaked and plastered to his muscular chest and shoulders, his shaggy hair was wet, and his face glistened. She had removed her boot, and he took her foot in his hand and stripped off the thick sock, his long fingers probing her ankle carefully. He frowned suddenly. "Your skin's ice-cold."

Tyler wasn't surprised. "Give the fire time to work."

His frown lingered as he swept her still body with a searching gaze. "The temperature's dropped a good twenty degrees, and you're soaked to the skin. We have to get you out of those wet clothes before you catch your death."

"No," Tyler said in a brittle voice.

Kane's eyes narrowed. "Don't be a little fool," he said roughly. He half turned away to begin digging in his pack, opening a section she hadn't noticed before, then dropped a bundle of clothing into her lap. In a flat tone that didn't invite her to argue with him, he said, "Get out of your wet things and into those. Don't worry, you'll be decently covered. Then climb into the sleeping bag. I'm going to get some water and some wood."

Tyler stared after him as he picked up the pot he used to make coffee and vanished out into the rainy darkness. She wanted to resist him on this, if only because she needed to feel in control of the situation again, but she was too cold and wet to feel like putting up much of a fight.

He had left her a flannel shirt and a pair of sweatpants, and she took a moment to speculate on his reasons for giving her the ruana instead of these last night. She didn't have to speculate very hard. She removed her right boot and set both of them aside with her socks draped over them, then got gingerly to her feet. Her left ankle twinged, but it was more of a grumble than a pain and she ignored it.

Minutes later she was draping her wet shirt and underclothes over a rock at one end of the shelter, having scrambled into the dry things very quickly, when it occurred to her that the fire lit her dressing room up very nicely for anyone watching from the darkness outside.

The shirt was ridiculously large; she had to roll up the sleeves to make them reach her wrists. And if the sweatpants hadn't boasted a drawstring waist and elastic at the ankles, she wouldn't have been able to keep them on.

Dry and warming rapidly, she unrolled the sleeping bag and sat on it with her back against the wall. Her hair was still wet, but she didn't have the energy to unbraid it. Granted this interlude without Kane's disturbing presence, she needed very badly to think.

chapter five

HE RETURNED TO the hollow a few minutes later carrying an armful of wood and the water. He put the wood down and arranged the pot over the fire on a hook device he carried in his pack, then sat down a couple of feet away from Tyler and began getting out of his boots.

"Kane—" she began, but broke off when she realized how strained her voice sounded even to herself.

As if his earlier statement hadn't been followed by an interruption for other things, Kane said, "I meant what I said, Ty." He set his boots and socks aside, then sent her a glance that was both intense and faintly amused as he began unbuttoning his shirt. "But not here. And not now."

She was too curious not to ask. "Why?"

Kane looked at her again, hesitating for the first time. She looked very small and fragile, swallowed in his clothing, the fire-light flickering in her wide amber eyes. After a moment he said, "We have company."

It was the last thing Tyler had expected. "What?"

"Our friend the shooter."

She stared at him, her mind scrambling to make the shift from personal to professional. "He's been following us?"

"All day."

"How long have you known?"

Kane stripped his shirt off, exposing the broad, hair-roughened expanse of his chest. He tossed the shirt to lie across a large rock at his end of the hollow, and half turned to face her. Keeping his voice low, he replied, "When you fell. As I turned back toward you, I caught a glimpse of him." His mouth quirked suddenly. "Why do you think I charged out into the rain while you changed clothes? If we'd been alone, I would have stripped you myself."

Tyler decided to let that pass, although her face felt hot at the image his words evoked. "So you were protecting my modesty?" She managed to make her voice dry.

"Let's just say I made sure he couldn't get close enough to see anything."

Her eyes flickered as she glanced out beyond the fire. "He's out there now?"

"Yeah." Kane answered her next question before she could voice it. "I'm a little curious about our friend. Doesn't it strike you as a bit odd that he wasted all that ammunition in the ravine and didn't hit either of us? That kind of lousy marksmanship generally happens only in B movies."

Tyler felt slightly sheepish that she hadn't thought of that sooner, but chalked it up to having been unsettled since encountering Kane. "You're right. So why would he be trying *not* to hit us?"

Kane reached into the pack between them and pulled out a second pair of sweatpants, muttering, "God, I hate being wet." He rose to his feet in the confined space and began unfastening his jeans. "I have a theory," he added.

"Oh?" Tyler was searching through the pack for the coffee, keeping her eyes fixed carefully downward while he stripped off his jeans and changed into the sweatpants. She concentrated on swearing at herself silently for having used up all the canned milk for pancakes, now she'd have to drink her coffee black and she *hated* that, she really did. . . .

"You can look now," Kane said in amusement as he sat down again and cast his damp jeans over the rock where his shirt lay.

With an effort, she stopped herself from throwing the bag of coffee at him. Handing it to him with utter control, she watched as he dumped some into the can of hot water. "No wonder that stuff's strong enough to raise the dead," she said, because she wanted to say something she could sound annoyed about. "Don't you ever measure?"

"Only when it counts," Kane said.

Tyler drew her knees up and wrapped her arms around them, scowling faintly as she stared at him. "What's your theory?"

Kane matched her pose and answered amiably. "Obviously the man is after the cache. Also obviously, he doesn't know where it is. Which is why he's following us. As to why he shot at us the other day . . . Maybe to hurry us along?"

"He isn't shooting now," she noted.

"We have to rest sometime."

Tyler shifted her gaze to the fire as she frowned in thought. Then she looked back at Kane, her eyes intent. "He's out there with a gun, and you aren't worried about it. Why not?"

She had been chewing on her lip again. Kane forced himself to be coherent. "I think I know who he is. If I'm right, it wouldn't do either of us much good to worry about him."

After a moment Tyler's mouth twisted and she said irritably, "Will you stop making me ask *why* every few seconds and just tell me what you know?"

"You're just so cute when you're in a snit," he explained solemnly.

"Kane . . ."

"Okay, okay. If I'm right—and that's a pretty big *if* since I hardly got a good look at him—our shooter is Drew Haviland. And you should know his name."

She blinked. "I think— Damn! He's a collector, isn't he? But he goes after antiquities himself."

"He certainly does. And he's beaten both of us more than once. Remember that jade necklace about eighteen months ago? He got it."

"I thought you did," Tyler said, remembering her own disappointment at having missed both the necklace and Kane.

"No. As near as I could figure, Haviland got to Shanghai about two hours before I did. I was a step behind him for about twelve hours, then lost his trail."

A bit ruefully, Tyler said, "The trail was cold by the time I got there. I just assumed you got the necklace because I knew you'd been there." She sighed, then said, "So this time he's planning to let us lead him to the cache."

"Seems likely."

"So what're we going to do about it?"

Kane dug the tin cups out of his pack and poured coffee, handing one cup to her. Sipping the dark, strong brew, he said slowly, "We won't shake him off, that's a given. We could—" He broke off suddenly, his big body going taut like an animal sensing imminent danger.

"You could offer me coffee," a new voice commented helpfully.

Tyler heard herself gasp, and stared across the hollow as a patch of darkness moved in out of the rain and joined them.

He was wearing an enveloping slicker and carrying a rifle. He was a handsome man about Kane's age—mid-thirties—but where Kane was rugged Drew Haviland possessed the finely drawn yet hawklike good looks of an aristocrat. His vivid blue eyes were mild and perpetually amused, as if he found the world to be an excellent joke, and his voice was deep and calm. British by birth, American by inclination, he had no accent, but his voice carried the slight lilt of the cosmopolitan.

Without a word Kane dug into the pack again, pulled out the ceramic mug and poured coffee into it. He handed it to Haviland as the other man hunkered down by the fire on his left. It was the visitor who spoke first after sipping the coffee, his gaze flickering from Kane's expressionless face to Tyler's startled one.

"I thought it might be smarter if we teamed up," he said.

"Why?" Kane asked, his voice mildly curious.

"You two left that lady bandit in a hell of a bad mood," he told them. "She and her boys are a few hours behind us. They seem to know the area fairly well, so they may not have stopped for the night."

"I assume they're armed," Kane said politely.

"Heavily. And not inclined to discuss the matter, I think. It might be best if we moved on pretty soon."

"No doubt," Kane agreed.

Tyler was getting a little annoyed by this civilized discussion. Staring at Haviland and ruthlessly changing the subject, she demanded, "What are you after?"

Pleasantly Haviland replied, "The cache, of course. By the way, I have your backpack and rifle, Miss St. James; I left them outside, against the cliff. Sorry I caused you to lose them. That wasn't what I'd intended."

"Why did you shoot at us?" Kane was still being polite.

Haviland reached over casually to lean his rifle against the rock wall as an amused smile curved his mouth. "Curiosity, mostly," he admitted in a dry voice. "I wanted to see if you two would team up. Your partnerships in the past have been interesting to observe."

"You could have killed us," Tyler reminded him.

Coolly he said, "No, I think not. I'm a very good shot. And though there was certainly some danger of one or both of you falling, I had complete faith in your uncanny survival instincts— to say nothing of your abilities."

Tyler stared at him speechlessly for a moment, vaguely aware of Kane's low chuckle. "Rats in a maze," she muttered angrily, disliking the idea of having been under observation.

"I didn't build the maze," Haviland told her. "I just watch. During your past . . . encounters, I was only slightly interested in the antiquities you were after; it was much more enjoyable to tag along and try to guess what you'd do next. In case you weren't aware of it, Miss St. James—"

"Call her Tyler," Kane grunted.

Haviland nodded his thanks as if Tyler had given him permission herself. "Tyler, then. Ours is a relatively small community, and among those interested in acquiring antiquities the two of you have gained quite a reputation. Your . . . antics in trying to best each other are becoming legendary."

Tyler stared at him. "Mr. Haviland—"

"Drew," he insisted courteously.

A laugh sputtered abruptly from Tyler as her sense of humor overcame anger. "This is ridiculous. This is a ridiculous situation. We're *rivals,* all three of us, and neither of you seem to give a damn!"

Haviland chuckled softly. "Not as bad as that, Tyler. You and

Kane are after, I believe, a gold chalice. I was promised the other valuables in the cache. I'm the buyer Tomas had found."

"Then why aren't you waiting in Panama?" Kane asked. "Is it us you don't trust, or Tomas?"

"I knew that whichever of you returned with the cache would keep your word to Tomas," Haviland said. "But I also know that Tomas was very nervous and needed money badly because of gambling debts, so I decided to keep an eye on him. Only hours after the two of you were sent on your way, he was killed."

"Because of the cache?" Tyler asked quickly.

"No. A senseless brawl in a bar. He was too quick to pull his knife—and not quick enough to use it." Haviland shrugged. "So I set out after you two."

He could have been lying, but Tyler believed him. Like both herself and Kane, Drew Haviland had the reputation of being honest in his dealings with others in the small "community" of people interested in art objects and antiquities.

"So you want the cache, but not the chalice?" she asked him intently.

"I'd like the chalice, as well," he said frankly with a faint smile. "But since you two want only that, I'll settle for the rest. There are supposed to be several good bits of jewelry and at least two figurines that might be Egyptian. With any luck, at least a piece or two will lack rightful owners."

Tyler had heard that Haviland was more scrupulous than some collectors, choosing to return any traceable items to museums or universities in the countries that claimed them. Like Kane and her, he refused to participate in the worldwide black market of antiquities.

In the beginning of her relationship with Robert Sayers, Tyler had twice refused to go after artifacts whose ownership was legally established; after that, he had always taken pains to assure her that whatever he wished her to find for him was legally "available" to a private collector. She never took his word for that, a fact that she made no secret of and he was ruefully amused by.

On giving her this particular assignment, Sayers had been, as Kane had described his own employer, almost stuttering with excitement. Tyler, restless because it had been a few months since her last task, had checked her sources at Interpol and various museums very quickly, and had found no mention of a gold chalice that had been stolen from its country of origin or otherwise wasn't where it was supposed to be. Her Interpol contact had merely said, "If it's part of the loot Hitler raided, Tyler, God knows if it belongs to anyone. Let me know."

And she would. She wanted to believe that Kane would also relinquish the chalice if it turned out that some country or family could rightly lay claim to it. She thought he would.

Kane was digging in his pack again. "Well, I think we should have a quick meal and then get out of here. If Valonia wants my blood, she's going to have to work for it."

Unable to stop herself, Tyler murmured, "It isn't your blood she's after."

"I know what she's after," Kane returned politely but with a gleam of amusement in his eyes. "However, if she got close enough to use a knife, she'd get blood, as well. And I still say she's going to have to work for it."

REUNITED WITH HER backpack and rifle, Tyler was able to change into dry clothing that belonged to her. The men politely turned their backs while she changed, and she silently turned hers while Kane, grumbling, got back into his damp jeans. She had a slicker tied to her pack, and Drew produced an extra one for Kane, who, for some unfathomable reason, never carried one himself despite his dislike of getting wet.

"How's the ankle?" Kane asked her.

"No problem."

"That isn't what I asked," Kane said, staring at her. "You'd walk on it if it were broken. How is it?"

She returned his stare, ignoring Drew. "Fine, Kane. There's no swelling, and not even a twinge. Satisfied?"

He wasn't. With Drew an amused observer, Tyler irritably submitted to having her ankle thoroughly examined and then wrapped tightly in an elastic bandage which was, according to Kane, "Just to be on the safe side."

Within an hour they abandoned the hollow and continued on. Tyler walked between the two men, with Kane in the lead. They were climbing steadily through the rain and darkness, and the temperature dropped as they moved higher into the mountains. A bit ruefully, Tyler found herself grateful for the elastic binding her ankle; it had begun to throb dully not ten minutes after they moved out, and she knew the extra support was needed.

Kane was always right. It was annoying as hell.

They moved in silence, with only an occasional comment or direction such as, "Watch that branch," or "Careful, the rock's slippery here." Most of the comments were from Kane.

Dawn found them well into the mountains. The rain had finally stopped, leaving a cool mist behind it, and they encountered fewer obstructions as the forest thinned out. All three of them were experienced hikers and were blessed with the strong endurance that came from active lives, so their pace was steady. They halted once, briefly, for a quick breakfast, but didn't linger.

By 10:00 A.M. Kane was moving more slowly, his keen eyes picking out landmarks as he began searching for the cave where Tomas had promised the cache to be. Their position was about a hundred miles southwest of Bogotá.

Tyler almost bumped into Kane when he stopped suddenly.

She sidestepped to peer around him, and instantly recognized the area from Tomas's description. They were standing on the edge of a narrow, inhospitable valley, the floor of which was thickly covered with tangled shrubs that had crept partway up the steep slopes. Kane double-checked his compass, sighting across the valley to a high peak recognizable for its odd shape, then looked at the others and nodded.

"This is it. The cave should be on the north slope, low down with the entrance hidden behind a boulder."

Tyler studied the north slope intently, then shook her head. "All I can see are bushes." With a sleepless night and hours of hard travel behind them, she was tired, but she also knew that she would press on as long as necessary. Still, an unconscious sigh escaped her as she eased the straps of her backpack and flexed her shoulders.

Kane looked at her steadily. "All right?"

"Fine. Let's go."

She was aware of Drew behind her as they moved cautiously down into the valley, but most of her attention was focused on Kane. He shouldered his way through the chest-high tangle of shrubs, making a path for the two behind him, moving steadily. They had all removed their slickers once the rain stopped because the gleaming black garments had made them too visible, and she fixed her gaze on Kane's khaki backpack and shining black hair.

To her surprise and vague uneasiness, she felt little excitement about being so near the chalice. Granted, they didn't have it in their hands yet and, granted, there was still a long way to go before they were safely out of Colombia, and quite a trip after that back to England. But she didn't think that was why she felt this way. She felt . . . suspended, a part of her detached and waiting, another part disturbed and uncertain.

But not here. And not now.

That was it. Kane wanted her, and if she knew anything at all about him it was that he was a fighter. What he wanted, he went after with all the strength and will in his big, hard body and tough mind. The very thought of that kind of fight between them made her legs feel wobbly.

"Watch it." Drew caught her arm firmly from behind as she stumbled.

"Thanks." She didn't look back at him, afraid of giving her thoughts away even to a stranger. This was absolutely ridiculous, she told herself fiercely. Bandits bent on murder or something worse behind them, harsh terrain all around them, a hideous trip ahead of them, her very *life* in danger, and she was worried about being seduced.

She told herself to stop worrying about ridiculous things. Five minutes later, she told herself again.

It wasn't working.

NEARLY AN HOUR passed before they were able to reach the north slope of the valley. The cave entrance itself was easy to find once they fought their way through the bushes. What Tomas had called a "rock" guarding the opening was actually a slab of granite that might have fallen from above hundreds or thousands of years before and now leaned back against the outcropping at the base of the slope. It was possible to enter the cave from only one side of the slab, where a space about three feet wide and six feet high was provided by the slant of the granite.

"No wonder this place stayed hidden so long," Tyler ventured, studying the granite door and the profuse greenery that made even it invisible from any distance.

"A nice hiding place," Drew agreed. "If Tomas hadn't stumbled onto it, God knows when it would have been found."

Kane tossed a stone into the cave, and they all listened for a few moments to make certain no animal inhabitants would be waiting inside to greet them. They shrugged off backpacks and each produced a flashlight, then Kane led the way inside.

The cave was surprisingly dry, the humidity decreasing as they moved away from the entrance. The shaft slanted upward into the hillside, but it was a gradual rise, and they had plenty of room to stand upright since the ceiling remained consistently several feet above even Kane's head. The floor was dry and sandy underfoot, and there was no indication that there had ever been a cave-in.

She wasn't claustrophobic, but Tyler was no more fond of dark caves than she was of heights. Gripping her flashlight a bit more tightly, she asked, "Didn't Tomas say this shaft was about sixty feet deep? We've gone that far already."

Kane shone his flashlight in a wide arc before them as he walked steadily forward, and responded to her over one shoulder. "Not much more than that. I think— There."

Three more steps brought them to the back of the cave, and they shone their lights on a jumble of boulders among which an iron box sat with the firm air of having been there awhile. It was about two feet square and a foot deep, and there was a heavy hasp closure; about a foot away from the box lay a battered, rusted padlock half buried in the sand.

"Let's get it outside," Kane said calmly.

Tyler remained silent while the men each grasped a handle on the side of the box and lifted it, then followed them back toward the cave entrance. She had felt the first real jolt of excitement upon seeing the box, and even though her common sense warned that there could still be disappointment in store for them, she didn't listen to it. That particular caution wasn't very strong, because Tyler was coping with an unfamiliar and disquieting sensation in addition to her excitement.

There was still the trip out of Colombia, still the journey back to England, but if the box contained the chalice then there would be nothing left for her and Kane except to decide which of their employers would get it. It wasn't a decision she looked forward to, but even less did she anticipate a return to London. Because then they'd part again.

They reached the cave entrance before she could explore that unnerving realization, and Tyler was grateful for the small mercy. She joined the two men in kneeling beside the box, and it was she who flipped up the hasp and lifted the heavy lid.

Tomas hadn't lied to them. Inside the iron box were a number of bundles wrapped thickly in burlap. Tyler unwrapped them one by one, revealing two necklaces of sapphire and ruby, a diamond-encrusted gold bangle, several intricate gold chains, three golden figurines—two of which were obviously Egyptian with the third possibly Spanish—and a chalice.

Drew examined the other artifacts one by one, but Tyler and Kane had eyes only for the chalice. It was about ten inches high from its heavy pedestal base to the lip of the cup, and wrought of solid gold. The metal had been crafted with exquisite skill and astonishing delicacy, and gleamed dully. It had obviously been handled a great deal over its life, because the warrior-figures worked so skillfully around the bowl of the cup no longer stood out in stark relief as they must once have done, as if many hands and polishing cloths had gradually worn them almost smooth. The chalice had no handles, and was very heavy.

Tyler knew the moment her hands touched the cool gold that this cup was many centuries old. She didn't recognize the style of the figures, although her instincts said they were Persian; she could barely discern at least two chariot-borne warriors, and the methods used to form those figures held a curious mixture of Greek and Egyptian styles.

She drew a deep breath and handed the chalice to Kane, saying steadily, "I'm not sure. What do you think?"

Kane turned the cup in his big hands for a moment, then upended it and studied the base of the pedestal. "Hell," he muttered.

Tyler was quick to catch the note of disappointment in his voice. "It isn't—" she began, then glanced aside at Drew a bit uncertainly.

"Don't mind me," he said without looking up from his scrutiny of the ruby necklace.

Kane said to the other man, "You know what we were hoping." And it wasn't a question.

"That it's Alexander's chalice?"

"Yes."

"I recognized it," Drew said simply.

Tyler exchanged a quick glance with Kane, then said, "What do you mean?"

Drew wrapped the necklace and put it in his backpack with the other bundles, then held out a hand. "May I?" He accepted the cup from Kane and turned it in his hands slowly, his eyes narrowed as he examined it. "The figures could be Egyptian, but there's clearly a Greek influence, as well . . . common with Persian art. And this small figure here"—he indicated one of the chariot warriors on the bowl—"is bearing a royal standard. The size and design match the descriptions I've found."

"You've searched for it before?" Tyler asked quickly.

"Paper search. The two chalices weren't always together, so it was difficult." As Kane had done, he upended the cup and studied the bottom. "It doesn't have Alexander's seal, but then, only one of the pair did."

"His seal?" Tyler was puzzled.

Kane accepted the chalice again as Drew handed it over, frowning slightly. "According to legend," he told Tyler slowly, "Alexander himself suspected poison. He wanted to mark the cup that he'd drunk from, so he had his manservant heat the base of the pedestal in the fire until the gold softened and then pressed his signet ring into it."

"You didn't tell me that," Tyler accused.

Kane shrugged. "It doesn't matter. This cup doesn't have a sign of any tampering with the base. It could still be one of the pair, of course, but I was hoping for indisputable proof."

Casually Drew suggested, "Then find the other one."

Tyler felt a surge of excitement greater than any she'd felt today. "If we could do that—"

"Where do we look?" Kane said dryly. "Considering how far this one's come from Babylon—assuming it's Alexander's—the other one could have ended up anywhere in the world, even if it still exists."

"Venice," Drew said, still casual. "Or thereabouts." He was stared at, and returned the stares with a flicker of amusement. "That paper search I mentioned. I started with the last known whereabouts of at least one of the cups, in Florence, and since records after that were destroyed I backtracked. About two hundred years ago, one chalice was in the possession of a wealthy Venetian family by the name of Montegro. Maybe theirs was the chalice that ended up in Florence. Or maybe not. I was . . . distracted by other matters at that point, so I'm not even sure if the family survives today. But if they do, it wouldn't be a bad idea to check them out. You never know, after all."

"What's your interest?" Tyler asked him slowly.

He smiled at her. "The same as always. I'd love to own both chalices. If you two do go after the other one, and do by chance find it and are able to acquire it, keep me in mind. I could probably match what your respective employers are paying, and it would be a shame to split the chalices up again."

Kane was slowly wrapping the chalice in its burlap, frowning. Tyler glanced at him, then looked at Drew as the other man got to his feet and shrugged into the backpack. "Montegro, you said?"

He nodded at her. "Worth a try." He glanced off toward the end of the valley they had entered, and said musingly, "We've probably got about six hours on the bandits. If you two head north, you should run into a road within a few miles to take you into Bogotá. I think I'll head west for a few hours; with any luck, the bandits will have to decide which of us to follow. It might delay them. But I wouldn't waste any time in leaving Colombia."

Tyler gazed at him a moment, then said bemusedly, "Why do I feel an absurd impulse to thank you after you shot at us?"

"I have no idea. But I'm sure we'll meet again." Drew grinned faintly, saluted them both casually, and struck out across the valley heading west. Within minutes he was out of hearing, and was soon lost to sight.

"We should move out, as well," Kane said almost absently. "Drew was right about that road being a few miles north. If we find some transport, a truck or jeep—hell, even a couple of burros—we could reach Bogotá by tomorrow afternoon."

Tyler took a deep breath. "And then?"

Kane looked at her a moment in silence. "You want to carry this, or you want me to?" He lifted the burlap-wrapped chalice slightly.

"And then?" Tyler repeated steadily.

He half shrugged, then said somewhat tersely, "We could go to Venice."

She hadn't wanted to be the one to suggest it herself, but Tyler felt relief sweep over her. "Do you think we have a chance of finding the other chalice?"

"Probably not. But I'm willing to try."

Tyler got to her feet and shrugged into her backpack, tacitly agreeing that he should carry the chalice and watching as he put it into his own pack. She felt a return of her earlier weariness but squashed it determinedly; they had a long way to go yet, and she'd be lucky if she rested at all during the next twenty-four hours or so, much less slept.

She told herself it was that dull weariness that made her suddenly more conscious of his every movement as he stood and slung his pack onto his back, and an anguished little voice in her mind asked her what on earth she was doing even considering spending as much as weeks more in Kane's company.

She was out of her mind. . . .

Kane took two steps to reach her, and lifted one hand to push her chin up slightly. "Nobody loses if we find the other chalice, right, Ty?"

She gazed into his vivid green eyes and felt her heart lurch painfully. "Right," she managed.

His almost caressing tone became suddenly sardonic. "But we still don't trust each other. Because even if we do find the other chalice, the two of them together are worth more than anything we've ever gone after before, right, sweetheart? Think of the bonus if one of us returns to an employer with both of Alexander's legendary chalices."

Tyler felt sudden tears sting her eyes, and blinked them away. It was just rage, she told herself, rage because he took endearments like sweetheart and honey and made them sardonic or flippant, and she *hated* that.

"Right," she agreed flatly. She meant to jerk free of his grasp in a gesture of scorn and anger, but before she could move Kane lowered his head abruptly and covered her lips with his.

Shock held Tyler still beneath the onslaught, but it wasn't

caused by his action. She was shocked because the first touch of his warm, hard mouth sent every last vestige of her anger spinning away like something shattered beyond repair. She was vaguely aware of a soft whimper of stark pleasure in the back of her throat as her lips parted beneath the insistent pressure of his, and when his tongue explored her mouth with hot need she swayed toward him with another mindless sound of delight.

Kane's hands dropped to her waist, sliding beneath the bottom of her backpack to hold her firmly as he pulled her hard against him. Her arms crept upward, her hands tangling in his thick hair, and she felt her body come alive wildly as it pressed against his. Her breasts ached heavily as the hardness of his chest flattened them, and she could feel the pounding of her heart and his. Instinctively her lower body molded itself to his, and even through the thick bulk of their jeans she was starkly aware of his throbbing response.

He lifted his head at last with a reluctant slowness more eloquent than words could ever be. His eyes were darkened and hot, his face taut, and when he spoke it was in a rough, harsh tone hardly louder than a whisper.

"But trust doesn't come into it, does it, sweetheart?"

For a full minute Tyler didn't know what he was talking about. She was still pressed against him, her fingers moving helplessly in his hair, her entire body aching and weak and heated, and she could only stare up at him in bewilderment. Her breath came rapidly between her parted lips, and she couldn't have spoken in those first few seconds even if she had been able to string words together coherently.

Want. It was in her mind, a seductive whisper, and in her body it was incessant demand, like a fire burning her. But then his flat words sank into her dazed brain, and shock ran cold through her again—because he was right. Trust didn't come into it, because she still didn't trust him and . . . it didn't matter.

"Damn you," she whispered raggedly.

Kane gave an odd, low laugh and released her as her hands fell away from him. "Sure you want to go to Venice?" he mocked.

Tyler turned away from him to get her rifle where it leaned near the cave entrance, and held it firmly pointed downward despite her impulses. She couldn't control what he made her feel and that terrified her, and yet, as always, faced with a choice between running and fighting, she fiercely, even unreasonably, chose to fight. She wouldn't run from this, couldn't, even though every primitive instinct she could lay claim to told her that Kane and the emotions he evoked would always be beyond her control.

"Lead on, Macduff," she mocked in return.

A gleam showed itself briefly in his eyes, but whether it was annoyance or admiration she couldn't tell. He got his own rifle and started off across the valley, heading north.

As he pushed his way through the tangle of shrubs, highly conscious of her behind him, Kane silently cursed the bandits on their trail. He would have given much to have been able to remain in the valley with Tyler for another day or so. Or, hell, even a few hours. Her instant response had both surprised and delighted him, and even though he knew the mental and emotional battles remained to be thrashed out, he also knew that physically Tyler had more or less surrendered.

Strangely enough—and Kane found his own obstinacy baffling—it wasn't enough. Tyler was a beautiful, desirable woman, but he wanted more than just a female body responding to his in passion. He wanted that stubborn, aloof part of her to respond to him, as well, wanted her totally involved mentally and emotionally as well as physically. And he wanted her trust.

Stupid. A snowball had better chances in hell.

But at least there was more time now. He had thrown down the gauntlet and Tyler had picked it up with a flash of stubborn fire in her eyes. And he felt more than a glimmer of admiration for her when he remembered that fire. She had courage and spirit and strength—and too much of all three to run from him or from anyone else.

Anyone else . . . For the first time he wondered about the men in Tyler's past. There had to be at least a few; with her fiery beauty, she drew men effortlessly. He knew that from their past encounters. The sheik in North Africa, so fascinated by Tyler that he'd even tried to literally steal her one night—he had been philosophical about the broken nose Kane had given him, saying only that he would have fought for her, and that it was perfectly understandable Kane had done just that.

And others, all over the world, men who had tried wooing, threats, bribery, and outright kidnapping. Tyler always seemed surprised, and always disinterested. But there had to be men in her private life, Kane thought.

Had some other man discovered the same fire and courage in Tyler? Was her wariness now based purely on her mistrust of him, or had some other man hurt her? Walls came from hurt, Kane knew that, and she quite definitely had walls.

He felt something inside him tighten, and recognized the sensation for the first time even though he had felt it before without understanding it. He had felt it in Hong Kong when Tyler had been held captive, and he had felt it in North Africa when she had been in danger. And in all the places in between, whenever she had been in peril. He had felt like this, his chest tight and a hot rage coiling inside him, and had acted instantly and instinctively to help her.

He didn't want Tyler to be hurt, not in any way. He didn't even like to think about some man in her past hurting her, yet the question was in his mind now and eating at him. And he knew he'd get the answer eventually.

THEY STOPPED ONLY briefly through the remainder of the day, and since they had found the road as predicted the going was much easier and faster than it had been until then. It was dark by the time they neared a small town. Kane found a shelter in the tumbled remains of a deserted barn.

Shrugging out of his backpack, he said, "You wait here with the packs. Keep your rifle ready."

"Where are you going?" Tyler asked, trying to keep the weariness out of her voice.

"I'm going to look for a truck or something. We could make Bogotá by noon with some wheels."

Tyler dropped her pack to the hard dirt floor and glanced upward at the stars shining through what was left of the roof. Flexing her shoulders, she said dryly, "Try and find us a hot meal, will you?"

"I'll do my best."

They were both wearing jackets now, and Tyler drew hers tighter around her as she sat down and leaned back against one of the barn's two remaining walls. She was bone-tired, chilled and hungry, and as she looked up at the tall shadowy figure that was Kane she felt a flash of longing for the hard warmth of his arms holding her and his body against hers.

"Don't go to sleep," Kane warned.

She found a flare of spirit from somewhere. "Have I *ever* gone to sleep when I shouldn't have?" she demanded.

He chuckled. "No. I'll be back as soon as I can, Ty."

"I'll be here," she said with a sigh.

*   *   *

TWO HOURS LATER he returned to the barn. He had found—and bought—a rackety truck with a missing muffler and four bald tires. And, with his peculiar talent for acquiring the little luxuries of life, he had also purchased, from a bewildered family on a nearby farm, a pot of stew.

chapter six

WHEN TYLER CLIMBED out of the truck just after noon the following day in the sprawling city of Bogotá, she had only one thing
to say to Kane.

"Shoot it. Put it out of its misery."

Kane grinned at her, and managed somehow to look sexy despite a heavy growth of beard and eyes reddened with weariness as
he patted the rusting hood of the truck. "Don't say mean things
about Trigger," he told her solemnly.

She paused a moment before dragging her backpack out to rub
her abused posterior. The truck had no shocks whatsoever, and the
seat's springs had a habit of poking whatever sat upon it. "I refuse
to ride Trigger to the coast," she said flatly. "We can get a train or
a plane out of here."

"Shouldn't be a problem," Kane agreed, abandoning Trigger

without a backward glance as they moved by tacit consent down the street toward a hotel that looked as if it might be able to accommodate two weary travelers with the pesos to pay for a couple of rooms. "In fact, I have a friend here with a plane. And he owes me a favor."

In a reasonable tone Tyler said, "Even if the bandits *do* trail us to Bogotá, they aren't likely to catch up with us anytime soon, not in a city of this size. So I vote we spend the night here and head for the coast in the morning. I want a bath, and then I want to sleep for about twelve hours."

Amiably Kane said, "Fine with me. But I'd like to go ahead and make arrangements for the trip. Why don't you get us a couple of rooms, and I'll see you back here in a few hours." Before she could speak, he handed her his backpack and added, "You keep the chalice."

Tyler hadn't even been thinking about that, which surprised her more than a little. But she was exhausted, and she chalked up her unusual trust to that. Because she had to say something, she said, "We're just going to leave the rifles in the truck?"

"Better that way. We don't want to attract unusual notice by carrying guns here."

"Okay."

"Got enough money for the rooms?" He grinned a little. "No offense meant, but the way you look, any desk clerk's bound to demand the money up front."

Tyler eyed him, but decided a retort wasn't worth the effort. "I have enough."

He nodded. "Try to get connecting rooms, and leave your side open, will you? I'll need to get my stuff later, and you'll probably be asleep."

She hesitated on the point of turning away from him and toward the hotel. Connecting rooms . . . and the doors left open.

A bit roughly Kane said, "Take the damned chalice out of my pack and put it under your pillow."

Again Tyler coped silently with her own lack of mistrust where Kane and the chalice were concerned. She had been thinking along entirely different lines. I'm very tired, she reminded herself reassuringly. "Fine," she said mildly.

He stared at her for a moment, his mouth a little tight, then muttered an oath under his breath and strode away.

AN HOUR LATER Tyler stood under the lukewarm spray of a shower and mused happily about how living rough made one appreciate the simple things in life. Like showers. She washed her hair thoroughly with an herbal-scented shampoo she'd bought in the gift shop off the lobby, then soaped her body luxuriously with a soap bearing the same scent.

She remained in the shower until her skin started to wrinkle, then got out and dried off, dressing in the thick terry robe which the gift shop had also provided. She had sent every stitch of clothing she had with her to the laundry, stripping naked in the bedroom and reaching around the partly opened door to hand the stuffed laundry bag and a handful of pesos to a bemused bellman waiting patiently in the hallway.

Now she wandered back out into the bedroom towel-drying her hair, and eyed the connecting door warily. As instructed, she'd opened her side a few inches, and Kane's pack reposed on a chair near the door. The chalice was still inside. She had idly considered taking it out, but common sense told her that Kane could find it easily if he was so inclined, no matter where she hid it. Besides, she was just too tired and sleepy to worry about it.

Still drying her hair, she went over to the window and pulled back the curtains, gazing out from the tenth-floor room at the sprawling city of Bogotá. In this basin high in the Andes, the temperature maintained an average of just under sixty degrees, so Tyler wasn't tempted to open the window. She looked out for a few moments, picking out, in the distance, the cable cars that carried tourists higher into the mountains for a bird's-eye view of the city.

Finally, too tired to think, she tossed her towel toward the bathroom, brushed her damp, tangled hair off her face with her fingers and climbed into the double bed. She had already hung out her Do Not Disturb sign, bolted her door and put on the night latch.

The last thing she remembered was pulling the covers up to her chin and sinking down into a too soft bed that felt wonderful.

KANE MANAGED TO make arrangements for their transport to the coast and get back to the hotel within two hours. He thought Tyler's plans for the remainder of the day had sounded dandy, and he meant to get cleaned up and fall into bed himself. He got his key from the desk clerk and went up to the tenth floor after requesting that a bellman come up to get his laundry. Like Tyler, Kane had learned to take advantage of the amenities offered by hotels, especially when there was still a great deal of hard traveling ahead of him with accommodations of the find-a-corner-and-roll-out-your-sleeping-bag variety.

The room was the usual sort, with practical furniture and uninspiring prints framed neatly on the walls and everything small enough to carry off bolted down, and he barely took notice of it. He went immediately to the connecting door and opened his side. She had left her side open, with his backpack in plain view of the door. He stepped into her room silently.

She was no more than a slender mound under the covers, and from this angle all he could see was a shimmering curtain of red-gold hair spread out on the pillow. He lifted his pack from the chair, and knew instantly by the weight that the chalice was still inside.

Not, he acknowledged to himself, that it meant anything, because she had been tired, and being tired made her sweet, and vague, and vulnerable.

He stood there for a moment longer, tired and dirty and beard-stubbled, gazing at her and wishing he could crawl into bed with her. Memories of her soft, slender body against his made his loins tighten and begin throbbing, but he shook his head and retreated silently back into his own room.

The spirit was certainly willing, but the body badly needed the rest more than the recreation.

He stripped and stuffed his clothes into a laundry bag, leaving out only a clean pair of sweatpants—actually the pair Tyler had briefly worn. The same bemused bellman again accepted a laundry bag and a handful of pesos held out to him by a disembodied arm, and went away muttering to himself.

Kane found the energy to shower, but decided to shave when he woke up, and barely took the time to dry off before crawling into his own bed naked and falling asleep instantly.

When he woke to a dark room, his internal clock told him at least six hours had passed, and he felt rested and hungry. Tyler would no doubt be hungry, as well, and they could always go back to bed in a few hours; it wasn't much past ten o'clock. He turned on the lamp by his bed and then reached for the phone, calling room service and ordering enough food for a small army, along with milk and coffee.

Tyler liked milk with her coffee. Not cream. Milk.

Room service informed him it would be at least half an hour, and Kane accepted that amiably. He got out of bed and took another shower, then shaved and dressed in the sweatpants. Then he went into Tyler's room, moving silently in the darkness until he could turn on her bedside lamp.

She had moved only to push one arm out from under the covers, which had fallen down below her shoulders. She was lying on her back, dressed in a white terry robe, and the lapels had slipped open to reveal the creamy inner curves of her breasts.

He felt a rush of desire so sudden and fierce it was as if he shuddered under some unexpected blow. He could almost feel her full, firm breasts filling his hands, her slender thighs cradling him between them, her silky warmth surrounding him. His body hardened in an instantaneous arousal that made sweat break out on his brow, and he could hardly breathe.

God, how much longer could he wait for her?

Kane sat down slowly on the edge of the bed, his eyes moving from the beckoning curves of her body to the vulnerable curve of her lips and the satiny skin of her delicate face. Her long lashes made dark crescents against the softly flushed cheeks, and beneath her eyelids were faint flickers of movement as she dreamed. Around her small face, fiery hair tumbled in unruly curls, like sunshine trapped in the dimness of the room.

She drew a sudden, shuddering breath, her breasts lifting jerkily, and her mouth quivered as a soft sound escaped. It was a strange sound, like a jolt of pain so deep and dreadful it could only be voiced in a whimper. Like a shriek muffled behind locked teeth. A primitive sound, as if it came from a wounded animal.

Kane frowned, holding an iron rein on his desire as he leaned over her so that his shadow fell on her face. "Ty?" he murmured softly. "Wake up, baby."

Her reaction as his quiet, husky voice shattered the silence was instant, unexpected—and violent. The dark lashes lifted to reveal wide eyes that were blank for an instant and, focusing on the big silhouette above her blocking out the lamplight, those amber eyes dilated with sheer terror. Her face went deathly white, and her lips drew back in a soundless scream as her shaking hands jerked up, palms out, in a mindless, pathetic attempt to shield her face. She seemed to sink into the bed, as if her very terror lent her slender body weight, as if that could provide some escape for her.

"Tyler!" Kane spoke with unconscious harshness, so shaken by her response that for a moment he could hardly think. This was no nightmare, no phantom conjured by the dark, this was something all too dreadfully real . . . And then, in that flashing instant, he remembered the lightly spoken words that had seemed to mean very little—then.

"*. . . I felt helpless and vulnerable. It's—it's almost a phobia with me, feeling like that. I can't take it. . . .*"

Quickly Kane straightened so that he was no longer blocking the light, so that she could see his face. And even as the answer to his earlier mental question jarred through him, he was speaking softly again, reassuringly. "It's just me, baby. Kane. You were having a nightmare."

For another endless moment the anguished, stricken eyes stared at him between her fingers, before her hands turned to cover her face and a shudder racked her. Hesitating only an instant, Kane drew her up into his arms, holding her gently but firmly against him. She was stiff at first, and he could almost literally feel her withdrawing mentally and emotionally, but gradually her body relaxed.

She didn't cry, didn't make a sound or shed a tear, and for some reason that hurt Kane more than anything else.

Pushing back away from him finally, she lifted one shaking hand to push the tumbled hair off her face and the other to draw the robe together over her breasts. Her eyes wouldn't meet his. "Some nightmare," she said shakily.

Kane opened his mouth, but a soft knock from the door in his room stopped him from saying what he wanted to. Instead he said, "I've ordered some food. It's only a little after ten, so we can go back to bed later. Hungry?"

"Starved," she answered, her voice more steady now.

"I'll have the cart left in my room. Come on in when you're ready." He rose from her bed and went into his own room to let the room service waiter in.

Tyler threw back the covers and got up, making her way into the bathroom on trembling legs. The last dark claws of terror and pain lingered in her mind, pricking now instead of raking, and the face that gazed back at her from the mirror was white and taut. She tried to control her breathing as she struggled for composure, and the sick, helpless fear gradually faded.

Dear God, it had been so long since that nightmare had tormented her sleep. Years. And its return reminded her of what the counselor had warned her when she had said that it would probably always be with her, that it would be likely to resurface with stress or other kinds of fear.

Stress. She'd been exhausted, and the changing relationship between her and Kane had unnerved her. The latter, of course, was bound to trigger the fears that her rational mind could deal with but her subconscious shied violently from confronting. Then she had awakened abruptly, and the starkly male silhouette above her had made the nightmare seem all too terribly real.

Tyler splashed cold water on her face and dried it. The face in the mirror was still pale, made more so by the riotous flame of her hair and her darkened eyes, but it was less tense. She finger-combed her hair and tightened the belt of her robe, then took a deep breath and went to join Kane in his room.

"Coffee?" he asked as she entered. "Or would milk be a better idea?"

Tyler managed a smile, her gaze fixed on the meal awaiting them. He had brought the chair from her room so they could both sit at the table, and she did so. "Milk, I think," she agreed. She had long passed the stage of being afraid to go back to sleep after the nightmare, having learned that it seldom occurred more than once in a single night.

Kane sat down across from her. "I tried to avoid the more spicy dishes. The *ajiaco* should be good." He indicated the bowls of thick soup with potatoes, chicken and corn. "Eat, Ty."

He said nothing else while they began eating, and Tyler made no attempt to break the silence. Conscious that he was merely waiting, that he intended to ask questions, she was engaged in a silent battle with herself.

It did no good for her rational mind to be certain she should feel neither shame nor guilt; the emotions lingered even after all these years and despite all reason. It was always the response, she knew, but knowing did nothing to lessen the feelings. There were still remnants of helpless rage and disbelief inside her. And, if that weren't enough, she had never talked about it to a man since it happened, not once. The doctors and counselors had all been women, even the police had provided a gentle female officer to take her statement, and the grinding shame she had felt had prevented her from talking to her father, despite all his loving attempts.

And now . . . to talk about it to Kane . . .

"Who did it, Ty?"

She started slightly, but kept her eyes fixed on her plate. "I don't want to talk about it, Kane. Not to you."

That hurt him. "Tyler . . ."

Don't cross the line, she wanted to plead, but it was too late for that, they had already crossed the line between professional and personal. And if she told Kane about this, if she exposed her pain to him, nothing would ever be the same between them. If she trusted him with her pain, the only thing left to her was honesty, and that left her terribly vulnerable.

"Goddamn it, tell me."

She looked up jerkily from her almost untouched food, and

once she met his eyes she couldn't look away. His voice had been very quiet, but there was something in his eyes she'd never seen before, something hard and fierce and implacable.

"Who raped you?"

Tyler put her spoon down with infinite care and sat back in her chair. In an automatic, instinctive gesture, she crossed her arms over her breasts, almost hugging herself as his stark question evoked burning waves of shame and guilt and anger. And she didn't want to tell him, not Kane, but . . .

"I don't know his name." She heard the words emerge jerkily in a low, rapid tone. "They never caught him."

A rough sigh escaped Kane. "Tell me, honey."

Some part of her mind noted and wondered at the change in that endearment—because it *was* an endearment. Not sardonic or flippant. She vaguely remembered that he'd called her baby before, in a soft voice so unfamiliar that she had hardly recognized it.

"There isn't much to tell." The words were pulled from her by the determination in his eyes, by the taut waiting in his big body, like something primitive tugging at her. "I was on my way home from school, crossing a park. It was raining, that's why there was no one except . . . except him in the park."

"How old were you?"

"Sixteen."

Kane almost jerked, feeling that stark answer like a blow. Sixteen, just a girl who had blossomed during the previous year, probably still bewildered by the changes in her body and shy at the male glances that had grown more intent. He felt a hard, hot rage tighten around something in his chest, wishing savagely that he could get his hands on that soulless bastard for just five minutes, that's all it would take, just five minutes to break every bone in his miserable carcass.

Then he heard Tyler's low, toneless voice going on, and another nameless bastard joined the list.

"I had a boyfriend, we were going steady. When I—when I went back to school, he asked me to give his class ring back. He said his friends were saying I must have asked for it . . . and that I was . . . damaged goods."

"You know that isn't true," Kane said, his voice rasping over the words.

"My mind knows. Maybe it even knew then. But the feelings . . . wouldn't go away. There were doctors and counselors to talk to me and try to help. They kept telling me rape was an act of violence, not of . . . of passion. That I'd done nothing to provoke him and I shouldn't feel guilty or ashamed." Her brows drew together in a childlike frown of distaste. "But it was a long time before I felt clean again."

Kane sat very still, watching her pale face, the distant, unfocused eyes. She looked almost frail, like something ethereal, and the wild mass of her bright hair, freed from its usual severe style, made her white face seem very small and very young. But her eyes weren't young. Her eyes were far too old. She had been cruelly wrenched out of childhood, hurt in a way no woman should ever be hurt, and the scars would be with her for the rest of her life. Even now . . .

"No wonder you can't stand feeling helpless," he said roughly.

She looked at him, focused on him. "It's been ten years. The nightmare is—rare now. There were years of therapy before I learned to deal with what happened. The fear of being helpless, that one lingered. I learned to defend myself because I never wanted to feel helpless again." Then her mouth twisted with a touch of bitter humor. "But nature didn't balance the scales, and muscle and size *do* make a difference; so I learned to carry a knife, and to handle guns."

"And to build walls. Since then, you've never let a man get close, have you, Ty?"

Just one man. But the words remained unsaid; he knew he had gotten close, he had to know, so she ignored that question. She felt driven to make him understand something else, perhaps because so much of their past had involved deception. "There was a sense of grief for a long time. Something was . . . stolen from me, in violence and pain and fear. Not just virginity, but my dominion over my own body. I was pinned in the mud and brutalized—and I couldn't stop it. *He* stopped it when he—when he was through. And left me in the mud."

"Honey . . ."

She glared across the table at his white face. "You asked, Kane. You wanted to know." Her voice was fierce.

He half nodded, an odd spasm of pain tightening his features briefly.

Tyler drew a short breath. "They say the physical healing is quickest and easiest. For me, it could have been worse. The doctors told me that. I had three broken ribs, a fractured arm, assorted bruises and cuts and—tears. I healed. As good as new. Almost. But he took something I can never get back. *My choice.* It should have been my choice. In the back seat of a boy's car, or in a bed, or behind the bushes at some party—it should have been my choice." She heard her voice thicken with grief and rage, staring across the table at Kane's face through a shimmering veil of tears she couldn't shed.

Before he could speak she drew another breath, this one longer and deeper, and her voice steadied. "I had no control over what happened to me. For months afterward I couldn't bear to be alone, not even for a moment, and I felt helpless about everything in my life. I hated that, hated what he'd done to me. It was like putting myself back together one piece at a time. It took me years to feel like a whole person again."

After a long moment Kane said slowly, "And now you—court danger. Try to control it."

Tyler shrugged a little, a weary gesture. "I don't know. Maybe. Maybe I need to face all the fears he left me with. I've learned to fight."

"And now you're fighting me." Kane leaned forward a little, his very posture insisting on an answer. "But *what* are you fighting in me, Ty? When I hold you and touch you, you aren't afraid. You want me as much as I want you. So it isn't sex. What? What are you fighting in me?"

She felt painfully vulnerable in that moment, and if she had not taught herself to be a fighter she would have run from his question because sure safety lay only in that response. But she was a fighter. And these last days had given her the truth of her violent response to Kane, a truth she could no longer avoid. Honesty was all she had left, and how ironic that honesty was her last defense against Kane.

"Tyler . . ."

With a twisted smile, she said, "He stole something I can never get back, Kane."

Kane's face hardened and his mouth went grim. "And you believe I'll do the same?"

"You have before." She held up a hand when he would have responded, and said, "Oh, I know those things we went after weren't really important. It was a game, and we both played by the rules. Rivals, enemies. But it's different this time, and we both know why. This . . . between us, it's personal, not business. Somewhere along the way, we crossed over the line, and the rules have been shot all to hell."

"Trust," Kane said flatly. "That's what it comes down to. We can be enemies without it, partners. We can even have sex without it, because we sure as hell have the desire. But we can't be lovers."

Tyler hesitated, then met his eyes with all the steadiness she could muster. "Maybe you don't want a lover, just the sex. No emotions, no . . . connections. But I can't risk that, Kane. Not for myself. I can't risk seeing myself in pieces again because the choice was stolen from me. It has to be an emotional choice, not a physical one."

Kane found it ironic that Tyler was just now confronting the knowledge he had faced days ago. Physically he could arouse her past the point of no return, and they both knew that. But he had also known, days ago, that the choice had to be Tyler's, that he couldn't steal what she wasn't willing to give.

A little harshly he said, "I want more than sex, Ty. I can buy sex on a street corner. I want you."

She felt her body respond to his grating voice and the demand of his desire, and a tremor shook her. Very softly she said, "I don't want an enemy in my bed, Kane. Or a rival. I'm not even sure I— I want a lover. But we both know I can't control what you make me feel. If I give in to those feelings without making a conscious choice to do that, it'll be as destructive to me as it was to give in to that man because I wasn't strong enough to fight him."

"No," Kane said. "It's different."

"Not to me. It's the truth, and what I feel."

Kane felt as if he hadn't drawn a deep breath in hours, but he did now because his chest was hurting. He leaned back in his chair and let the breath out slowly, but the dull ache wouldn't go away. There was something wrong with this, something that didn't fit, but he couldn't make it come clear in his mind. He believed that *she* believed what she was saying, but his instincts told him it was wrong somehow.

After a moment he stirred and said with deliberate dryness, "So you need to make a clear, rational, logical decision to take a lover."

Tyler felt heat flood her cheeks, although she couldn't have said why. "It isn't as cold-blooded as you make it sound," she objected.

"That's just what it is. Tyler, by its very definition, physical desire is something we don't control—it controls us. It's a drive, an instinct millions of years old, it isn't a logical thing." Keeping his voice deliberate, he went on, "So what happens if you coolly decide at some future date that you're ready to take a lover—and the desire isn't there? Will you just find some likely candidate because you'd rather betray your body than your mind?"

The flush drained from Tyler's face, and she stared at him. "No! I'd never . . ."

Kane went on as if she hadn't spoken. "We've got—what?—a few weeks ahead of us at best? Then we go our separate ways, with or without the second chalice. You back to London, me back to the States. And maybe we'll run into each other six months or a year from now. Or maybe not."

"So it's now or never, is that what you're saying?" Her amber eyes had begun to glitter with anger. "Lust today, for tomorrow we may die?"

He didn't have to force his grin. As always, he had found the quickest and surest way of angering her. This was the Tyler who would fight him on a level where he stood a chance, and he felt no remorse at needling her. Her guarded posture had altered to become stiff annoyance; rage had chased the shadows from her eyes and she looked like a cat about to hiss and claw at him.

In a mild voice he said, "You're the one who has to make a choice, Ty. It's up to you. I was just pointing out one of your options."

Her glare narrowed. "Well, you made the point."

"Good." He nodded briskly. "Then why don't we finish eating and get some more sleep. Tonio wants to leave before nine in the morning."

Tyler blinked, then picked her spoon back up and began eating the cool soup. He had shaken her off balance again, damn him. Determined to keep that knowledge to herself, she managed to hold her voice calm and steady. "Tonio? Your friend with the plane, I assume."

"Right. He's going to fly us to Santa Marta. Where, you'll be interested to hear, there's a cargo ship now loading. Her destination is Greece."

She stared at him as an uneasy suspicion prickled in her mind. "Don't tell me."

"Afraid so. Dimitri's ship." Kane smiled a little, but said, "Sorry, Ty, but it's the only ship heading in the right direction, and it *will* take us all the way to Italy."

Tyler lost her appetite. She put down her spoon again and took a drink of her milk. "Great. That's just great. I'll have to spend days on a ship that should have sunk from sheer age a decade ago, being leered at by a crew of pirates, and listen to Dimitri try and entice me away from you—because of course I'll be pretending to be your woman again."

They—actually, Kane—had created that particular fiction on their previous trip aboard Dimitri's infamous ship, after Kane had caught one of the crew trying to creep into Tyler's sleeping bag in the middle of the night. Kane had thrown the sailor overboard, which might have been a little drastic except that he could swim and Dimitri stopped long enough to fish him out of the Mediterranean. After which, Kane made a brief trip from bow to stern, telling every man on board with a chillingly mild smile that the next one who dared to touch his woman would be dead before he hit the water. And he made the promise in fluent Greek, to avoid future misunderstandings.

"It worked the last time," Kane murmured.

Tyler admitted that silently. The leers had continued—out of Kane's sight—and Captain Dimitri had tried his hand at verbal persuasion, but she hadn't been forced to defend herself. She had been somewhat amused at the time, and realistic enough to have shrugged an acceptance of Kane's protection; she disliked having to depend on any man for anything, but the cloak of Kane's fictional possession had allowed her to sleep nights, and at that point the rest had more than made up for the blow to her pride.

Besides that, Kane had an odd habit of defending her honor, something that had at first enraged her and, later, bemused her somewhat. And no matter how many times she'd told him to let her get herself out of sticky situations prompted by unwanted male attentions, he had never listened to her. After a while she had resignedly accepted his actions, attributing them to his occasionally primitive instincts; she had never stopped to wonder why he was so protective of her, and she didn't want to wonder about it now.

"Unless you have a better idea?" Kane added.

"No." She sighed. "This will be a much longer trip than before, and I don't fancy sleeping with a loaded gun and one eye open." She drank the last of her milk and pushed her chair back. Getting up, she said, "What time are we leaving here?"

"I'll order breakfast for seven. That okay?"

"Fine." She went toward her room, but paused in the doorway as Kane asked a quiet question.

"Will you be all right?"

He meant the nightmare, she realized, and nodded. "I'll be fine. Good night, Kane."

"Good night, Ty."

She went into her room, leaving the connecting door open a few inches, and crawled back into bed. She turned off the lamp on her nightstand and lay in the dark room listening as Kane pushed the room service cart out into the hallway and then returned to bed himself.

Tyler couldn't fall asleep immediately, even though the nightmare had disturbed her sleep before and left her feeling something less than rested. She was still tired, but couldn't seem to close her eyes. Thoughts met and tangled in her mind, snatched at by emotions so that nothing made sense.

She didn't regret her honesty with Kane, because he seemed to have understood. But he had also, quite mildly, made it plain that if he were going to be the lover she "chose" she'd better be making up her mind about it. And even though she had known she was raising a last defense against the desire between them, his mild acceptance had disturbed, and even hurt her. Not because she didn't trust him not to push her—she did, oddly enough. But because . . .

Because he didn't seem to care terribly about the matter. He wanted her, yes. That was obvious, and he certainly made no secret of it. Or at least he had made no secret of it up to now. But then he had spoken of the distinct possibility of not seeing her again for six months, a year—ever—without so much as a flicker of emotion in his voice or on his face. Nor had he even implied that if they were to become lovers they wouldn't, afterward, go their separate ways.

That seeming indifference and total lack of a commitment of any kind should have shored up her resistance to him, but instead, angrily conscious of an echo of shame, she couldn't help but wonder if Kane was another man with no taste for . . . damaged goods. He wouldn't have expected her to be a virgin, but a sexual history that consisted entirely of a single brutal memory might well present a hurdle he wasn't eager to attempt.

Tyler felt a throb of pain, and even as it ebbed dully she refused to examine the cause. She told herself fiercely that it would be best if Kane lost interest, best for them both. They could cross back over that stupid line and be rivals again, and know the rules. The safe rules.

It was almost dawn when she crept from her bed and went into the bathroom. She closed the door and turned on the light, then shed her robe and turned on the shower. The water was hot, and she stood under it for a long time, soaping and rinsing her tense body over and over again.

IT WAS JUST over an hour later when Kane pushed open the connecting door to find Tyler fully dressed in jeans and a flannel shirt and sitting on the bed as she braided her hair into its accustomed neat style.

"Breakfast is on its way," he offered, then noticed the plastic-wrapped clothing lying over the dresser by the door.

"They brought your clothes up as well when I called down for mine," Tyler explained.

Kane looked at her for a moment, then picked up the clothing and said, "Let room service in if they come before I'm out of the shower, will you?"

"Sure." She wasn't looking at him.

He retreated, frowning a little. She was aloof this morning, and he didn't like it. Was she regretting, now, a painful confession sparked by a nightmare? He had forced himself to be deliberately low-keyed, even though he had ached to hold her in his arms and comfort her, to wipe away the remembered anguish. But she had been on the thin edge of control, and he hadn't dared take advantage of that. So he had needled her instead, and her own temper had steadied her.

He had lain awake long into the night thinking, studying the germ of a realization. But he didn't know quite how to handle the conclusion he was left with. It *was* Tyler's choice, whether they became lovers, it had to be after what she'd gone through. And yet the terrible experience that made that choice so vital was blinding her, he thought, to the reasons for her own reluctance to take that step.

He had to make her see—and he couldn't afford a mistake in doing that. She had stubbornly and courageously taught herself to face all her fears except one. But that one was the most devastating, and it sickened him to think of an act of violence so terrible that it remained an open wound on her spirit even after ten years.

Kane saw the irony of it. If he hadn't begun as Tyler's enemy, there would never have been a question of a personal relationship between them. On the personal level, she was far too guarded, too aware of attempts to get close to her. If he had met her simply as a man attracted to her, she would have run—and rationalized her reasons. But they had met in a dangerous situation, immediately rivals and even enemies, and having neatly assigned him that place in her life Tyler had felt safe.

Until this encounter. Until awareness as heated as the steamy jungle had surrounded them. And, too late, she had realized that her enemy was a man, and that he had gotten too close. She couldn't run; she wouldn't let herself fight, not the way she needed to fight.

"Hey, breakfast." The announcement was accompanied by a rap on the bathroom door.

"Coming." Kane finished shaving, then got an iron grip on his patience and went out to join her.

chapter seven

THREE DAYS LATER Tyler leaned somewhat gingerly against a rusted railing and gazed off across a dull gray expanse of ocean, her loose hair blown back from her face by the steady breeze. The sun was hidden somewhere behind the clouds, not yet below the horizon. It was just a lull in the storm, she knew, but she had taken the opportunity to go up on deck and get some fresh air.

The cabin she and Kane occupied was hardly worthy of the name, having been stripped of all its fixtures years before, but it was the only empty cabin, and held the added advantage of being on the opposite end of the ship from the crew's quarters.

With an eye to the main chance, Dimitri had long ago converted the cabins to storage space and carried, in addition to his legitimate cargo, a number of crates and boxes that would never pass through customs. In any case, since Dimitri never smuggled drugs or guns, officials tended to more or less ignore him. And he rarely carried passengers. When allowed on board at all, they were expected to make the best of scanty accommodations.

Kane had done his best, and with his scrounging talents his best wasn't bad at all. He had firmly taken possession of the small cabin before Dimitri could stuff it full of cargo, and had managed to bring aboard a thick mattress to provide extra cushioning against the steel-plated deck. With their sleeping bags laid atop the mattress, the bed was reasonably comfortable.

They actually had a small bathroom with a tiny shower to themselves, and if the mattress took up most of the floor space in the cabin and there was no porthole, at least they had privacy and a door with a working lock.

The crew remembered them, but Kane nonetheless repeated his announcement of so long ago. He had also been extremely possessive of Tyler, remaining close to her almost all the time and offering the crew few opportunities to leer. And Captain Dimitri wore a disgruntled expression on his florid face after Kane had several times frustrated his attempts to entice Tyler.

As for the only woman on the ship, she was all too aware of ragged nerves and a pain she didn't want to explore. Kane had returned to his old mocking self when they were alone, and that coupled with his public possessiveness—blatantly for show—had served to steadily reinforce her belief that there was no longer a choice for her to make. Kane had made it himself.

Tyler might have salvaged something, self-respect or pride, but their enforced intimacy left her trapped with him. They slept in separate sleeping bags, but shoulder to shoulder on the mattress, and the body he had awakened ached long into the night.

She wasn't looking forward to the coming night, because they had hit rough seas for the first time and, though it was calm now, the forecast promised more rough weather within hours. Tyler was a good sailor, but the thought of her being tossed into Kane's reluctant arms while the ship heaved beneath them was one that made her feel sick.

"Where's the watchdog, missy?" Dimitri's voice was jovial, but there was a touch of wariness, as well.

Tyler straightened from the rail and turned to him, thinking for the tenth time that the captain of this heavily laden vessel looked more like a young Santa Claus than a smuggler. His tightly curling hair and beard were black, his dark eyes gleamed merrily, and his cheeks were like polished apples. He was portly, though surprisingly light on his feet, and his accentless voice was caressing when he spoke to her, bland when he addressed Kane, and a bullhorn bellow when he was ordering his crew.

Replying to his question, Tyler said dryly, "Where you should be, Captain. On your bridge. He went to check on the weather up ahead."

Dimitri gestured expansively. "We won't be into the rough until after midnight, missy. It's just a low-pressure system, nothing to worry your pretty head about."

Tyler didn't bother to point out that hurricanes originated in low-pressure systems, and she ignored the caressing tone. He was far more dangerous than he looked or sounded, but she wasn't afraid of him. Then she saw Dimitri's eyes widen fractionally as he gazed past her toward his bridge, and wasn't surprised to hear Kane's mild tones.

"Hello, Captain. Taking in the scenery?"

Dimitri smiled widely at him, murmured something about a course change coming up, and sidled around the much larger man as he made his escape.

"I can handle him, Kane," Tyler said, turning to face him. "I'm not afraid of him."

Kane's face, so impassive these last days, tightened suddenly. "Yeah, I know. You aren't afraid of any of them, are you, Ty? Just me."

She automatically grasped the rail for balance as the ship wallowed heavily between one trough and another, staring up at Kane. "I'm not afraid of you!" she flared.

"No?" He laughed harshly. "Every time I get within two feet of you I can see you stiffen. What's that if it isn't fear?"

The ship rolled again, and Tyler used the movement as an excuse to turn away from him. "I'm going below. I feel queasy."

"You don't get seasick," Kane retorted, following as she made her way through the jumble of crates Dimitri had chosen to lash to his decks.

"I might this time," she muttered, moving through an open hatch that would be bolted shut if the weather worsened. The hallway was narrow, and worn iron steps led down into the dimness of the cabin area. Tyler found her way more by memory than sight, since Dimitri had removed most of the lights along the hallway.

The light was on in their cabin; it was a large hurricane lamp that Kane had brought on board, and not subject to Dimitri's habit of turning off electrical lights to save power. Tyler took a step toward the mattress, and the door thudded shut behind her as hard hands grasped her shoulders and turned her around abruptly.

"I can't take any more of this, Ty. We have to talk. I'm not going to let you bury your nose in one of those books you bought before we left port, not this time."

Tyler was holding on to her control with every last ragged shred of her pride, and the strain was obvious in her thin voice. "There's nothing to talk about, Kane." She lifted her chin and managed a bright smile. "You've made your choice, and that's fine. Sorry you have to be penned up here with me, but—"

"What?" He stared down at her, frowning. For an instant he had no idea what she was talking about, but then it hit him. Struggling with his own worry about how to handle her fear, he hadn't stopped to consider that she might view his careful distance as a rejection. But she obviously had, and he realized now that he couldn't have picked a worse time to draw back no matter what his reasons were.

She had told him about being raped, about a boyfriend who had considered her "damaged goods," and Kane had withdrawn from her physically. God, he should have held her then, comforted her the way he'd wanted to.

"I don't blame you," she said in a light tone that didn't hide the stark control. "Really. I—"

"Hell," Kane growled, and abruptly slid his hands down her back to her hips. He yanked her against him, widening his legs and holding her against him so she could feel the hard ridge of desire. "Does that feel like I don't want you anymore?" he demanded roughly, ignoring the hands that were braced against his chest. "You've been driving me crazy since the day we met, and nothing's changed that."

Tyler caught her breath as he moved against her and heat bloomed deep inside her. She was staring up at him, at the vibrant green fire in his eyes, and the fierce need she saw there made her body tremble with desire and relief. But even then, she was fighting the feelings, holding her upper body away from him and struggling to control the wild sensations inside her.

She opened her mouth to voice a desperate protest, but Kane's head bent and his lips covered hers. And this time he took her mouth, possessed it with deliberation, his tongue invading with an utter certainty of her response. She couldn't smother the moan as pleasure jolted through her, or prevent her hands from sliding up to grip his shoulders convulsively.

The protest was still there, in her mind, but the response of her body to him was overwhelming and she was helpless against it.

When he finally lifted his head, she was trembling, shaken, her breath coming swiftly.

Kane drew a deep breath, and for an instant held her even more tightly against him. Then he drew away and guided her to sink down on the mattress. He saw her eyes widen, but he made no effort to press her back onto the sleeping bag, to continue what he'd started. Instead he sat down and leaned back against the bulkhead, saying nothing until his own breathing steadied and he could speak in a careful, even voice.

"You have to face it, Tyler."

She drew her knees up and wrapped her arms around them, staring at him. She felt baffled and uneasy. "Face what?"

"Your fear."

Her chin lifted. "I told you before—I'm not afraid of you! I hate that, I hate being afraid—"

"I know." His voice remained steady. "That's why you can't admit it to yourself. It's the one fear you've never been able to fight. Even to face."

Only vaguely conscious of a flicker of panic, she snapped, "It isn't fear. I just don't trust you, that's all."

"You do trust me, Ty, when it counts. When it matters. You've slept in my arms, trusting as a child, and unconscious certainty is the deepest kind. All the tricks in the past, they were part of a game we both played, and that *didn't* matter."

"Kane—"

He went on inexorably. "Then we crossed that line you were talking about, and the games were over. I'd gotten too close, and it was too late for you to run. You found out you couldn't control your need for me, and it scared the hell out of you. So you decided that you didn't trust me, and didn't want an enemy in your bed. A defense, Ty. A mental defense against something you couldn't physically control."

"I was telling the truth!" she cried.

"You tricked yourself," he said flatly. "Don't you see? It isn't mistrust. It's what happened to you ten years ago. Your body's forgotten the pain, but your mind hasn't. And you can't make the choice you *need* to make—until you face the reality that you're terrified of sex."

Tyler felt as if he'd hit her. She drew in a breath sharply, staring at him. "No. No, you said that wasn't it. You said the way I— the way I responded to you meant that wasn't it."

"I was wrong." His voice had softened. "The body heals and forgets pain, but the mind never does, Ty. It never forgets pain or fear unless it's taught to." He sighed roughly. "Honey, you've taught your mind to fight everything else that bastard left you with. You've learned to defend yourself, to face danger coolly, to overcome all the fears—except one."

"It was an act of violence." She was very cold, and her voice shook. "Not sex. I know the difference."

"How can you?"

The soft question was stark in the quiet of the cabin, and the motion of the ship was slight. There was no excuse she could grasp now, no distraction to avoid facing this—truth. She sat stiffly, her eyes burning with the tears that had never been shed, and his low voice was shattering the last, deepest defense, the one she hadn't even been consciously aware of.

"Ten years, Tyler. You're a beautiful, desirable woman, and in ten years you've never let a man close enough to touch you."

"You," she whispered.

"I was an enemy, not a man." His lips quirked in an odd smile. "I was . . . safe."

To label Kane "safe" was the most absurd thing she'd ever heard, but Tyler understood what he meant. All the violently negative emotions he'd stirred in her had blinded her to the reality that he stirred positive ones inside her, as well. Until it was too late. Until the needs of her body and her emotional confusion had made escape impossible.

And now . . .

Kane hesitated, hurt by the frozen whiteness of her face, the blank desolation in her eyes. Primitive terrors were the most deeply buried, corroding fears of all, and after ten years Tyler was confronting the worst, most primal fear a woman could ever face. She had been so young, so vulnerable in her shyly awakening womanhood, and an act of violence had changed her life forever.

She stirred suddenly, her face still frozen, and began very methodically removing the rubber-soled shoes she'd bought in Santa Marta. In a queerly conversational tone, she said, "I think I'll go to bed." She tossed the shoes aside, her eyes flickering around the tiny cabin as if she were looking at it for the first time. "It's going to storm again anyway. Get off my sleeping bag, will you, please? I want to—"

Kane reached out and grasped her shoulders, making her look at him. "Tyler . . ." he said gently.

She stared at him, and her shoulders moved under his hands as her steady breathing became ragged. The blind look in her eyes became something else as they filled with tears, and when the tears spilled, her frozen mask shattered.

"He hurt me." Her voice was little more than a whisper, but it held both the uncomprehending anguish of a child and the dreadful agony of a woman. "He hurt me . . ."

Kane pulled her into his arms and held her cradled across his lap. He stroked her soft hair and murmured a wordless comfort, even though she couldn't have heard him over the raw sobs jerking her body. The sounds seemed to claw their way out of her like something alive and vicious, muffled against his chest, and she clutched his shirt as if that were her only lifeline.

When she was finally drained and limp, he found his hand-kerchief and gently raised her chin. She was silent as he dried the last of her tears, her eyes fixed on his face with some emotion he couldn't read lurking in the amber depths.

"Why did you do that?" she whispered huskily. He had dried her tears, she thought vaguely. She had sworn no one else would ever do that for her, but he had.

"What?" He smiled a little.

She drew a shaky breath. "Make me . . . face that."

He was silent for a moment, still holding her across his lap and fighting a growing consciousness of her soft weight. Then, a bit roughly, he said, "You were cheating both of us, Ty. Running instead of fighting." One big, warm hand surrounded her face, and he held her eyes intently with his own. "And it's my fight, too. I earned the right."

Something inside her acknowledged that, accepted it. They had fought so often and in so many ways, sparring, snapping, mocking, competing with each other; together they had fought outside threats, back-to-back and side-by-side. They had fought fairly and with trickery, loudly and in silence. They had fought, finally, to this point. All the years of therapy and counsel had failed to uncover her deepest fear, yet Kane had fought his way past all the barriers she had desperately flung up, and had found it.

She swallowed hard. "I—I don't know if I can."

He stroked her cheek gently. "You can. The only question is if you trust me enough. I won't hurt you, Tyler. But you have to trust me not to."

She managed a shaky laugh. "I think this is where I came in."

He smiled, but his eyes remained intent. "No. This is different."

She knew that, and if she hadn't the look on his face would have told her. He wanted her, but he was waiting, leaving the choice up to her. Very deliberately, he was putting control of the situation in her hands, asking for her trust but not demanding it. And it was the basic kind of trust between a man and a woman, the kind that was all that really counted in the end.

Her enemy . . . Suddenly, as if it had always been there, she made the distinction. She had never trusted Kane as a rival, and possibly never would, but she trusted him as a man. Trusted him enough to put her life in his hands on more than one occasion, enough to sleep in his arms without a qualm. She trusted him enough to tell him what she had never told a man before, to share her pain and shed tears no one else had ever seen. But she didn't know if that trust was strong enough or deep enough to conquer a primitive fear.

"Tyler?"

She wondered, vaguely, if there had ever been a choice to make. It wasn't logical or rational or reasonable. It probably wasn't even sane. But for the first time in her life she wanted a man, and that desire was the only possible means of fighting her fear.

"I want you," she whispered.

His eyes darkened in an instant response, and the hard arm under her shoulders raised her until he could kiss her. His mouth was warm, the small possession of his tongue slow and gentle. He seemed totally absorbed in kissing her, taking his time, exploring her mouth while his fingers stroked her cheek lightly.

Tyler felt her body heat and begin to tremble, and there was no fear in her mind, just a vague uneasiness. There was no threat, not now, just slow waves of pleasure. Tentatively her tongue touched his, her mouth opening wider for him, and the heat built inside her. She felt him lift her, still kissing her, and her arms went around his neck as he eased her back onto their bed.

She drew a shuddering breath when he finally lifted his head, her eyes flickering open dazedly as she looked at him. He was lying beside her, raised on an elbow, flaming eyes fixed on her face. His other arm lay heavily across her middle for a moment and then shifted as he slowly began unbuttoning her shirt.

A flare of panic made her gasp. "Kane—"

"Shh." He kissed her again, deeply, and again until pleasure drowned the panic. Her shirt was opened, and when he raised her gently she helped him by automatically pulling her arms out of the sleeves. He unfastened her bra as he eased her back down, slipping it off and tossing it aside before she could react.

He had been concentrating fiercely on moving slowly, but when the scrap of lace covering her breasts was gone it was all he could do to hang on to his resolve. She was beautiful, just as he'd known she would be, and the sight of her round, firm breasts, the coral nipples tight and hard sent a shaft of pure flame through him. He bent his head and drew one hard bud into his mouth while his hand moved to surround the other breast, his thumb rasping gently over the nipple beneath it.

Tyler gasped again, this time wordlessly, as her body arched in a helpless response. The burning pleasure was instant, spreading outward in ripples of sensation that stole her breath and clouded her mind. All her consciousness seemed focused only on what he was doing to her. The erotic suction of his mouth was a caress like nothing she'd ever known before, and her body responded to it with a wildness she couldn't begin to control. She was on fire and couldn't be still, her head moving restlessly, her legs shifting, pressing together in a mindless attempt to ease the throbbing ache that kept getting worse, stronger, until she thought she'd go mad with the awful tension.

She was so wrapped up in the sensations, so totally involved in her awakened body, that it seemed perfectly natural to lift her hips when he unfastened her jeans and pulled them and her panties off. But her eyes opened wide suddenly, and an inarticulate cry of alarm escaped her when his warm, heavy hand began to ease her legs apart.

"Easy, baby," Kane murmured huskily. He shifted his hand to her quivering stomach and rubbed gently while his mouth caressed her breasts, and gradually he felt the stiffness ebb. His hand slid lower, settling over the soft red-gold curls, then remained there, unmoving, waiting.

Tyler's frightened memories of cruel hands and brutal force faded, even as the burning need of her body intensified wildly. He was so close . . . so close. . . . Instinct demanded that she open herself to him, and with a shudder her body obeyed as her legs parted. She felt a burst of raw pleasure as he stroked her gently, and a moan jerked from her throat. The inferno inside her burned out of control and she couldn't be still, couldn't think, couldn't do anything except give in to the blind, primitive drive toward release.

It seemed to last an eternity, tension spiraling until she could hardly bear it, and then her senses shattered, her body shaking and throbbing violently in a powerful wave of ecstasy.

Tyler was hardly aware of the gasping sobs that escaped her as she lay trembling in the stunned aftermath of that explosion. Her eyes opened slowly, finding Kane as he rapidly stripped off his clothes and tossed them aside, and her breath caught when he returned to her. She hadn't expected—somehow she hadn't known he would be so beautiful. But not all the beauty of rippling muscles and easy grace could hide the raw power of his big body, the male strength she could never match.

"I won't hurt you, Ty." His voice was low and a little rough, but the hands stroking her body were gentle, and despite the burning hunger in his eyes he was clearly in control.

"I know." She heard herself whisper that, and didn't question the truth of it. Still, she struggled to overcome the panic when he widened her legs gently and eased between them, when his big body rose above her. Helpless . . . God, there was no other position that left a woman so utterly vulnerable, pinned in place by a strength she couldn't fight.

Kane braced himself away from her, responding to the fear in her eyes even though his need for her was tearing him apart. His entire body ached, rigid with the effort of control, and her body was ready for him, moist and warm, waiting to accept what her mind feared. She was unconsciously holding him off, her hands trembling against his chest while her breasts rose and fell with the jerky gasps of panic.

He lowered his head and kissed her deeply again and again, murmuring, "It's all right, baby . . . it's all right." Carefully, he eased into her, giving her time to accept him, watching her face as her body's willingness and his own care fought against her fear. Her eyes were wide, but the fixed look slowly disappeared as her body accepted him without pain. Desire was stirring again in the amber depths, and her hands stopped holding him away as they slid up to his neck.

"Kane," she murmured, as if assuring herself that it was him, that she had nothing to be afraid of.

He murmured her name in return, assuring her that she was no nameless victim but a woman desired. Slowly he let her feel more of his weight, but braced himself on his elbows. She responded by lifting her hips slightly, tentatively, her eyes drifting half shut as the mat of hair on his chest rasped her sensitive breasts and her body accepted him completely. Her breathing was steadier now, deep and slow.

The silky heat of her was tight around him, and Kane gritted his teeth as a hoarse groan rumbled in his throat. His control was threadbare, and only the fierce need to make certain of her pleasure allowed him to move slowly and cautiously. He fixed all his will on arousing her to the peak she had reached only once before, kissing her, stroking her body as he thrust gently.

And the intense satisfaction he felt as she came alive beneath him made the strain worthwhile. Her soft little cries and throaty moans deepened his own taut pleasure, holding him on the ragged edge of exploding until purely sensual shivers like nothing he'd ever felt before feathered along his spine.

He was deep inside her when the hot inner contractions of her pleasure caught him wildly, and he heard her wordless whimper even as a rasping groan tore free of him and his own tension snapped with a fury that shuddered through him.

When he could think again, Kane didn't want to leave her, but he knew he was heavy and wasn't about to risk a return of her instinctive panic. He raised himself slightly to look down at her, then gently kissed the lips that were curved in a wondering, bemused smile. Her eyes were closed, her face softly flushed. Her eyes opened slowly to gaze up at him, and glowing in the amber like something trapped in resin for eons was the sensual exhaustion of female satisfaction.

"You're beautiful," he murmured, his own eyes gleaming with the dual pleasure of an equally satisfied male body and a somewhat arrogant male mind.

Sleepy humor widened her smile as she saw and recognized that look for what it was, and a ghost of a laugh escaped her. "If you start crowing," she murmured in a warning tone, "I'm going to start carrying my knife again."

He couldn't help but grin down at her. "A gentleman never crows," he told her, wounded.

A mock frown drew her brows together. "What's that got to do with you?"

"Cat." Kane kissed her again, then gently withdrew from her. She didn't try to hold him, but willingly returned to his arms when he got them both into his sleeping bag. He reached out with a long arm to turn down the lamp still burning a foot or so from the mattress, and the tiny cabin was lit only by a dim glow.

He hadn't noticed the motion of the ship until then, but realized that it had grown a bit rougher; the storm was building outside. It didn't disturb him, since he and Tyler were both good sailors. They'd probably sleep through the worst of it, he thought, unless the ship sank. And it wasn't likely to sink, not with cargo aboard; Dimitri wouldn't allow that.

He felt a little sigh escape Tyler, and his arms tightened around her; she was already asleep, he knew, her slender body boneless in that way that never failed to make something inside him turn over with a lurch. He thought back to the first days of this trip, when he had wondered if taking her would be enough, if he could afterward forget her. He had thought it unlikely even then; now he knew that he would never be able to forget Tyler.

And he was uneasily aware that after this there was just no predicting her attitude toward him. She was staunchly independent, and the rueful conversation of minutes before had told him only that she intended to be matter-of-fact about this new turn in their relationship.

He knew only too well the risk he had run in forcing her to confront her fear, and the question lingered in his mind now. Tyler had chosen this, but had she done so out of desire and deeper feelings for him—or simply because she was a fighter and it had been the only means to conquer her fear?

He didn't know. But as sleep tugged at him, his arms remained firmly around her and his last conscious thought was a grim resolve he didn't examine very closely because it simply *was*.

The fiction had become fact. She was his woman now. Partner, rival, enemy . . . lover. And he meant to make certain she recognized that as well as he did.

TYLER HADN'T SLEPT well the last few nights, but that night she slept deeply and dreamlessly until past dawn. She didn't know another day had begun when she woke in the cabin that boasted only artificial light, but she thought she'd slept for a long time. The cabin was stuffy enough so that Kane had left the sleeping bag unzipped, and she slipped away from him cautiously.

How on earth had she ended up on top of him? Bemused, not quite certain what she was feeling about all this, she concentrated on not waking him, and a glimpse at the luminous dial of his watch told her it was nearly seven. In the morning. He didn't stir when she left him, which surprised her since he usually slept with the lightness of a cat. Still, he was no doubt tired. . . .

Tyler felt herself flushing. Swearing silently, she collected the clothes that had been flung all over the floor. She put yesterday's shirt and underwear aside, then dug into her pack for a clean shirt and panties, and the small zippered pouch that contained her toothbrush and a few other items. The bathroom was tiny; her elbow was brushing the musty shower curtain when she closed the door behind her. An experimental flick of the light switch caused a dim bulb to flicker awake.

She didn't look at herself in the cracked mirror over the tiny basin, but quickly put her hair up with the big barrette she kept in the pouch, and then took a hasty shower. She tried not to think about the difference in her body this morning, but it wasn't really something she could ignore. There was a faint soreness in her muscles and deep in her body, and her very flesh felt sensitized, as if all the nerve endings were closer to the surface.

When she finally faced her reflection in the mirror, she saw that her lips were fuller, redder, even now, hours after his hungry kisses. She saw her eyes go distant at the memory, and muttered to herself as she got her toothbrush from the pouch. She brushed her teeth, and put the brush away, then pulled a small plastic case from the pouch and stared at it.

Kane had been right in his belief that she had never let a man get close in ten years, but both Tyler and her doctor had been practical in considering her unusual lifestyle, and she had been on the pill for the last few years. Since Kane was always careful to give her as much privacy as possible, she'd been able to keep to her schedule without his noticing. But there had been a couple of days without her pack. . . .

Well, there was nothing she could do now but wait. Her periods were irregular, not even the pill had changed that, but she thought another couple of weeks would provide the answer.

The carefully matter-of-fact thought shattered suddenly, and Tyler realized dismally that it wasn't going to work. She couldn't be bland about this, couldn't accept with casual ease the fact that she had a lover. She could pretend with Kane, but not with herself. It wasn't casual, not to her.

Kane was her lover. And the single inescapable reason he was her lover was that she loved him.

Automatically Tyler finished in the bathroom and then crept out into the cabin. He was still asleep. She put her things away, then eased out into the hallway and headed for the ship's galley, more to be moving than because she was hungry. On deck she paused, drawn to the rail by the clear sparkle of an ocean washed clean by the storm she had slept through.

When had it happened? she wondered vaguely as she stared out over the water. She knew things about him that only dangerous situations could reveal, things the average person could learn about a lover only after a lifetime, if then. Yet she didn't know the simplest facts of his life, his background. He could make her angrier than any man she'd ever met, yet he had been the one who had put the last broken piece of herself back into place and healed what another man had done to her.

Tyler drew a deep breath and turned away from the rail, heading once more for the galley. It didn't matter when it had happened. Or where, or how. It didn't even matter why, because it was nothing she could change. She was in love with Kane.

WHEN SHE ENTERED their cabin an hour later, Kane was just coming out of the bathroom. He was wearing jeans but was bare-chested, and had obviously just shaved.

"You're supposed to leave a note on the pillow," he growled.

Tyler set a thick mug on the upended crate wedged into a corner; they'd been using the crate as an occasional table. "I'll remember next time," she responded calmly. "I brought you some coffee, but I thought you'd rather go to the galley for breakfast. Nikos is a surprisingly good cook, but he doesn't deliver and I hate carrying trays."

Kane took a step and pulled her into his arms, kissing her hungrily. Her hands slid over his chest and up around his neck as she melted against him, and when he raised his head at last to stare down at her she was heavy-eyed and a little breathless. He moved his hands down to her hips, curved them around her firm buttocks as he held her hard against him, letting her feel his desire for something other than breakfast.

She cleared her throat in an uncertain little sound, and said with a stab at lightness, "This is going to sound like a ridiculous question, but you're not married, are you? I mean, I draw the line at getting involved with married men."

His lips quirked slightly even as his hands shifted to begin unbuttoning her blouse. "No, I'm not married."

"A girl in every port, I suppose?" She was trying to keep her voice steady and having little luck. He opened her blouse to bare her naked breasts, and when his hands closed over them gently all the strength drained out of her legs.

"Only the ports where I found you, baby," he murmured.

Tyler lost interest in the conversation for the time being. The response of her body to him no longer shocked her, but the swiftness of it, the instant need for him, disturbed her on a deep level, and she knew why. Because it was casual for him, an appetite to be satisfied, and if he displayed the control and skill to make certain she was with him all the way, well, that was only the mark of an experienced, unselfish lover.

But right now she didn't care about that, she didn't care about anything but the touch of his big hands, his mouth on her, his body hard against hers. She was dimly aware of clothing falling away from them, her desire escalating so rapidly that she was whimpering when he lowered her to their bed. And when he gently spread her legs and settled between them, her panic was only an echo shunted aside instantly by need.

She wanted him now, wanted him with a burning hunger that was a starving thing because she loved him and this was all she could have of him. Her arms wreathed around his neck and she moaned when she felt the slow, throbbing push inside her. Wildfire was burning her nerves, her senses, he was filling her with himself and it was more than she could bear. Her legs lifted to wrap around his hips and she writhed suddenly with a strangled cry as her pleasure peaked in a stunning explosion of sensation.

Kane held her tightly while she shuddered, astonished and delighted by her capacity to enjoy what she had feared for so long, her wild response driving his own desire higher. The tight, hot clasp of her body shattered his control, and he slid his hands beneath her, lifting her to meet each deep thrust. He barely heard himself groaning hoarsely as she held him with her slender legs, her arms. He could feel the ebbing tension inside her begin to build again as she instinctively matched his rhythm, so attuned to him that she was rushing toward the peak again. And this time they reached it together, hurling over the rim of something that was almost insanity.

*   *   *

IT WAS A long time later when Kane raised himself on an elbow beside her and gazed down at her. Her eyes were closed and one of her hands rested on the arm lying heavily beneath her breasts, her body totally relaxed. God, she was incredible. He had considered it something of a miracle that she had trusted him enough to accept him as a lover, both because of her fears and their stormy past relationship; her total response to him, abandoned and uninhibited, was nothing short of staggering.

The satisfaction he found himself was unlike anything he'd ever known before, yet the moment he caught his breath and looked at her, he wanted her again. And it was more each time, deeper and stronger, something that edged into savagery.

"What are you thinking?" she murmured without opening her eyes.

He drew a deep breath and somehow managed to make his voice light. "I'm wondering how much Nikos would charge to deliver," he said. "Otherwise, we're going to starve."

Her mouth curved, but before she could laugh Kane covered her lips with his.

chapter eight

A CITY FOR lovers. From the balcony of their hotel room, Kane could see the bell tower in St. Mark's Square and, beyond, the mouth of the Grand Canal. Venice was lovely, the weather clear and cool, and for two days he and Tyler had enjoyed a rare taste of first-class accommodations while they performed the necessary research to chase down Drew Haviland's paper search to the second chalice.

Kane went back into their room and settled into a comfortable chair by the bed, watching Tyler. She was lying on her stomach, maps and notes and papers spread out across the wide bed, propped on her elbows as she frowned down at the open book between them. Her hair flowed around her shoulders like wildfire, glowing in the late morning sunlight that came in through the open balcony doors.

"Interesting family," she commented absently. "And the name dies with the present contessa. It's a pity."

They had indeed found a surviving member of the Montegro family, but only by marriage; the contessa, in her sixties, had been American-born and had married Stefano Montegro thirty years before. She had been a widow raising a young stepson, but had never borne a child of her own. To all intents and purposes, the Montegro name had died with Stefano ten years ago.

"There's the villa," Kane reminded her. "According to our information, it's been in the family hundreds of years, and she inherited it."

Tyler looked across at him suddenly, her amber eyes bright with interest and speculation. "It says here that when Hitler's goons looted the area, they were mad as hell to find just a few trinkets in the villa. Think the family hid their valuables?"

"I would have."

"A secret room?" she suggested.

"Maybe. But the chance of it still being stuffed with the family silver are slight. It's been more than forty years, and the family hasn't been what you'd call rich for the last twenty. Stefano may have been a hell of a guy, but he was a rotten businessman. If the contessa wasn't a stubborn woman, she would have sold the villa years ago."

Tyler returned her gaze to the book. "I don't know; how many people could afford to buy Palladian villas these days? A hotel chain, maybe, or a crazy billionaire."

Kane didn't offer a response, but merely watched her absorbed face. He had found himself doing that often since they'd become lovers a week ago. He had seen the slow change in her, the gradual blooming of a woman accepting and finding pleasure in her own womanhood. And it had been a slow thing, despite, or perhaps because of, her instant response to him physically. In his arms she was a deeply sensual woman, but she was only now accepting his presence as a lover; she was no longer self-conscious while dressing or undressing around him, no longer tentative about touching him, or elusive after waking in bed with him.

He was delighted with the changes in her, but he was also aware that she was still matter-of-fact about their relationship, and clearly considered it one without ties or promises. When he had belatedly brought up the subject of birth control, she had assured him calmly that there was no problem, she was on the pill. And when he had casually asked if she'd thought about moving back to the States, she had merely replied that she enjoyed London and felt no inclination to move.

He thought of his ranch, thought of returning there alone, without Tyler, and he didn't like the hollow feeling it left him with. Maybe it was unfair to want her to give up her life in London and live with him, but, hell, there were museums in the States where she could work as a consultant if she wanted to work, and it would be easier to move her out of a flat than it would be to abandon a ranch he'd worked ten years to build. She was *his,* damn it, he felt that certainty in his bones, and he had no intention of letting her get away from him.

"It says here," she said in that absent tone, "that the contessa's involved in historical preservation. I wonder . . ."

Kane wasn't thinking of the chalice, or of the contessa or her villa, or anything but Tyler. She was lying there on her belly, wearing one of his shirts that just barely covered the seductive rise of her bottom, kicking her bare feet in the air slowly, and he was coming apart just looking at her. God, he was worse than a horny teenager with sweaty hands, always wanting to touch her, to grab and hold on tight.

He rose from the chair before he was even aware of it, taking two steps to the bed. He used one arm to sweep the clutter of notes and books and maps carelessly to the floor, then turned her onto her back in a single motion. Tyler looked up at him with eyes that were briefly startled, but they held no panic now, there had been no panic for days. The surprise vanishing, her arms slipped up around his neck, and her legs moved to cradle him as his weight settled on her.

"I thought we were going to have lunch in St. Mark's Square," she murmured.

"Later," he growled.

THEY MISSED LUNCH, but Kane promised her dinner in the Square instead, which was fine with Tyler. They shared a shower, and then she left him shaving in the bathroom while she sat on the tumbled bed wrapped in one towel and drying her hair with another one. She listened to the sound of water running, her absent gaze moving to the phone, settling there.

Think of the chalice. It was something she reminded herself of often, using that businesslike focus to keep her balance and avoid any suggestion of clinging to Kane. It had become a virtual litany by now, a toneless exhortation aimed at the part of herself that ached to cry out her love and hold on to him with all her might. Because she couldn't do that, couldn't cling to him. Couldn't tell him she loved him.

He'd said nothing to indicate she was anything more than an enjoyable bedmate, and if there was a new look of satisfied masculine possessiveness in his green eyes, it was doubtless only because this conquest hadn't been easy and the male animal was always triumphant after such a chase. His passion would burn itself out, probably soon, because a fire so hot had to be refueled eventually by emotions deeper than desire.

And then he'd say goodbye or, as in their past encounters, simply vanish out of her life.

Dear God . . .

How many women had loved him? She could imagine, but tried not to because the images evoked feelings so primitive she could barely hide them from him. He was a consummate lover, virile and skillful, arousing her to a degree she'd never believed possible, satisfying her utterly. She didn't want to believe it was a normal thing to him, an average thing. That other nameless women had seen his vivid eyes blaze with hunger, felt his hands tremble, his body shudder in pleasure, heard that electrifying raspy sound of stark need in his low voice.

Think of the chalice.

She lost herself in him, and it was growing harder and harder to make herself separate from him afterward. The feeling of oneness was so overwhelming it was as if her flesh, her very bones, became a part of him. No longer only a brief but intense sensation during his lovemaking, that affinity caught her unawares at odd moments, stealing her breath as she looked at him or felt him moving out of her sight.

Think of—

The water was turned off in the bathroom, and Kane came into the bedroom buttoning his shirt. "A gondola ride," he said.

"What?" She was proud of her tone, a little blank, slightly amused.

"You've been here before. Ever taken a gondola ride along the Grand Canal?"

"No," she admitted, tossing her second towel aside and finger-combing her damp hair.

"Good. After dinner, we'll take one." He eyed her with a slight lift of one brow, which managed to convey a world of exaggerated masculine patience. "And since you're not ready yet, I'll go arrange everything and come back for you."

Tyler returned his gaze for a moment, then took the bait

mildly. "You men have been using words to that effect for far too long; it's high time you stopped getting away with it. I would have been ready ages ago, but *you* got my hair wet."

He grinned. "So I did." He bent and kissed her with slow thoroughness, then said, "I'll be back in a few minutes, baby," and left their room, whistling softly.

She stared at the closed door almost blindly until her breathing steadied. Baby. Caressing, not sardonic or flippant. But he probably called all his women baby, and—

Damn it, think of the chalice!

Tyler fixed her gaze on the phone and made herself think safe, painless professional thoughts. The only way to visit a private villa, she mused, was to be a guest. An invited guest. Which was a bit difficult when you were a stranger. Unless, of course, you were able to produce impeccable references and had a good reason for wanting to visit the villa, a reason of which a contessa interested in historical preservation might approve.

She didn't hesitate, but immediately picked up the phone.

"I WANT YOU."

The words were low, barely above a whisper, but the sound of them went through Tyler like an electrical current. Her head tipped back against his arm as she looked at him, and the current was pulsing, beating with hot blood, roaring inside her. Not here, she wanted to say, because the gondolier was so close and they were in an old gondola floating quietly along an older canal, and even though it was dark, they weren't alone.

She couldn't say it, couldn't make a single protest. It didn't matter where they were, because the searing force of the current was lashing her. She stared into his eyes, helpless, burning, mindless, his. She wanted to plead with him not to do this to her, not to leave her with nothing, and in the same breath beg him to take her until she was drained, empty, until there was nothing left.

Kane's glittering eyes dropped briefly to her trembling lips, then lifted again, trapped her, mesmerized her.

"Say it," he whispered.

She knew what he wanted, knew he wanted her to admit that he could take her here and now, that she wouldn't be able to stop him. That she couldn't control this need he had created in her, it was like a drug she couldn't do without. She was lost and they both knew it, rudderless, adrift. She held on to him, trembling, because there was nothing else.

"Say it." The demand again, whispered, raw.

"Yes." It was almost a sob, a sound of defeat and triumph, an admission she had to make. And if that admission sent pain piercing through her, it was only because it meant so much more to her than it did to him. To him it was simply an affirmation of his power over her, the sexual prowess that left her totally helpless in his arms; to her it was an acceptance of a truth that freed her from ten years in an emotional prison.

She had battled fiercely to control her life after what had happened to her, swearing that she would never again be powerless because she wasn't strong enough or fast enough or brave enough to fight when she had to. She had fought Kane with all she had, layer after layer of herself, with every ounce of strength and will she could command—and she had lost. But in her defeat, she gained something she hadn't expected. One man had taught her the bitter anguish of defeat, and with that had changed her life; Kane had taught her the proud glory of surrender, and with that had freed her spirit.

"Yes," she whispered again, her shaking body pliant against the hardness of his.

Kane's lips touched hers with the lightness of a sigh, and then he silently drew her head to his shoulder and just held her. But she could feel the heat of his big body, the faint tremors of something held so tightly it shook with strain. Beneath her hand on his chest, she felt the hammering of his heart, as if he'd run some endless, dreadful race.

Had it meant that much to him? Could simple desire so powerfully affect an experienced man like Kane? Tyler was blind to the old buildings rearing on either side of the canal, and she didn't notice the dark, musty scent of a city like no other in the world, a city built on water. She was nourishing a tiny spark of hope, a longing so deep in her heart it was wordless.

Neither of them said anything, and Kane didn't let go of her in the gondola or in the motor launch that returned them to their hotel. And as soon as they were in their lamplit room, still without a word, he stripped her clothes off with the single-minded determination of a male animal intent on possession. Tyler was so shaken with desire that she couldn't help him rid them of the clothing, couldn't move at all except when he moved her.

For the first time he was a little rough with her, hasty, almost wild, as if waiting even seconds was more than he could stand. She didn't care. As always, she was instantly ready for him, desperate for him, clinging to his shoulders as he kneed her legs apart and entered her with a powerful thrust. Tyler arched beneath him with a moan, wrapping her legs around his hard hips, her nails digging into the muscles cording his shoulders.

Kane dug his fingers into her hair, holding her head still as he kissed her hungrily, taking her mouth with the same primitive urgency with which he took her body. It was a mating, quick, primal, their bodies relentless in the blind drive for satisfaction.

AN UNEASINESS PRODDED Kane, and he responded to it by raising himself on his elbows and beginning to ease away from

Tyler. He was heavy, pinning her, and he was still reluctant to risk any return of her panic in that. Always before, she had made no protest when he left her, but this time her legs tightened around him.

"No." Her voice was husky. "Stay with me."

He could feel the ebbing tremors of her body, faint aftershocks in her flesh. He lowered his head to kiss her swollen lips, the flushed curve of her cheek. God, she was so beautiful, her face glowing, the eyes that opened slowly holding a luminous amber fire. And secrets. He could rouse her to passion, even to surrender, hurl her into the same frenzy that gripped him, but her thoughts were still a mystery to him.

"What are you thinking?" he muttered, because he was going crazy trying to find a way across the distance between them.

"Nothing. I'm not thinking at all." Her hands moved over his back slowly, her nails scratching lightly in a tickling caress.

"Think about me," he ordered, conscious of a wry smile tugging at his lips.

Her long lashes veiled the amber eyes even more. "I'm feeling you," she murmured. "Isn't that enough?"

No. But he didn't say it. Instead he began kissing her again, wanting her again with a hunger that grew and grew until it was a living thing inside him, clawing, desperate. It was a long time later when he finally got them both under the covers and reached to turn out the lamp.

TYLER WAS AWARE of two things when a buzzing disturbed her sleep; that they'd left the balcony doors open last night, and that Kane's shoulder was wonderfully comfortable. She murmured a complaint when her pillow moved, then worked an elbow beneath her and levered herself up slightly as his voice woke her fully and she realized he had answered the telephone.

"Just a minute." He took the receiver away from his ear and looked at her, his mussed, shaggy hair and morning beard making him look unbelievably sexy. "For you. Keith Dutton?"

Tyler stared at him blankly for a moment, then remembered. "Oh. Right." She sat up, shivering as the chill of the room struck her naked flesh, and snatched the sheet up to cover her breasts as she took the phone from him. "Keith?"

"I gather," he said politely, "that I just woke up Kane Pendleton."

She felt herself flushing, which was ridiculous. "I told you he was with me," she muttered.

"You didn't tell me he was in your bed." Before she could respond, Keith's tone became plaintive. "And after North Africa—to say nothing of your other encounters these last years—you swore you'd kill the man if he ever crossed your path again. Over and over, you kept swearing that. I distinctly remember you mentioning slow torture or, failing that, both barrels of a shotgun."

"Yes, well. Things change," she offered lamely.

"Obviously. I guess it was bound to happen, though. When you rub two flints together, you've got to expect a fire sooner or later. You picked the right city for it; it can only burn down to the waterline."

"Very funny."

His voice lost part of the mockery and became at least halfway serious. "Watch out that you don't get your fingers burned, Tyler. The scars last a long time."

"I will." That warning, she thought, had come far too late. She didn't look at Kane, but was very conscious of him lying beside her.

"Sorry, but I feel a certain responsibility, kiddo. After all, I dandled you on my knee."

"You did not," she said indignantly. "Cut it out, will you? Do you have any news for me?"

"As a matter of fact, I do—"

Kane watched Tyler's face as the quick flush faded and her expression became absorbed. She was just listening now, giving away no clue to the conversation. Who was Keith Dutton, and how the hell had he known how to contact Tyler? Was he here in Venice, or back in England? How long had he known Tyler?

Kane knew there had been no other man in her bed, but that certainly did nothing to ease the sudden, fierce stab of pain he felt. That note of easy familiarity in her voice when she had spoken to Dutton told him this man was close to her, perhaps in a way that he himself could never be, a mental or emotional closeness. Did Dutton know the enigmatic part of Tyler, the secrets in her eyes? Had he fought with her? Had he loved her helplessly for years just like—

Kane looked at her, at the morning light bathing her in gold as she sat in the bed with the sheet held to her breasts, the smooth flesh of her back bare to his gaze. Her glorious hair tumbled around her shoulders in silky curls, a gleaming mass of living fire. He saw the clean, delicate bone structure of her profile, the graceful line of throat, the stubborn chin, the slender, seemingly fragile body. And suddenly he couldn't breathe, suddenly she was so beautiful it broke his heart.

He reached out a hand slowly, touching her warm back with just the tips of his fingers because he needed to touch her, tracing the straight, deceptively fragile line of her spine upward. She moved under his touch, a sensuous ripple like a cat being stroked, unthinking, instinctive pleasure.

He loved her. He had always loved her. Under the stifling sun of Cairo, he had met—no, clashed—with a woman of caged fire. In that ancient, dusty city, she had glared at him, her bright eyes spitting fury, her magnificent body stiff, and he had been lost from that moment.

Had he sensed then that she was wounded, that she would

have clawed and bitten like a cornered animal if he had tried to step closer? He wasn't sure. Maybe. Or maybe it had been his own unconscious resistance to the emotions she'd roused in him that had made him willingly accept the role of enemy and not look beyond that for so long.

She was talking, now, to that man on the phone, her voice quick and eager, but Kane didn't take in the words. She was his physically, a passionate bond of the flesh that she willingly accepted, yet her heart and her thoughts, those secret thoughts, she wouldn't allow him. He didn't know how to reach her there, in her solitary places. But he had to find a way, somehow, because if he lost her now it would kill him.

"Kane—we're in!" She leaned across him to cradle the receiver, and his arms kept her there. She squirmed a bit, yanking the covers up over her shoulders. "I didn't know Venice was so cold in October," she muttered. "Kane—"

"Who's Keith Dutton?" he asked, feeling his pulse quicken with instant desire as her hard nipples, chilled and tight, rubbed against his chest.

She snuggled into his warmth, but her voice was rapid and businesslike. "He's worked for museums all over the world—the Palazzo Ducale this year—and I thought—"

"Who is he?" Kane repeated.

Tyler pursed her lips at him, not quite a pout, clearly impatient. "I've known him for years; he worked with my father on several digs. The point is that I thought he might know the contessa, so I called him—"

"When?"

"While you were arranging for the gondola ride." Her voice quavered just a bit when she remembered that electrifying trip along the canal, then steadied. "He *does* know her, and he's fixed it up so we've been invited to spend a few days at the villa. Isn't that great?"

Whatever reaction she'd expected from Kane, it certainly wasn't the one she got. She could feel his body stiffen, and watched in bewilderment as his eyes narrowed.

In a grim tone, he said, "In a hurry, Ty?"

"We've learned all we can here," she pointed out, wondering what in the world was wrong with him. "We have to get inside the villa, and it isn't open to the public."

"What's the plan?" His voice was still hard.

Tyler was completely off balance by then, and getting mad about it. "Keith and I decided that the best way"—she broke off as he sort of growled, then went on defiantly—"to get invited by the contessa was to use our own credentials. I can have references telexed from half a dozen museums, and since you have two separate degrees in archaeology—" She interrupted herself this time to say sweetly, "So *nice* to hear that from Keith, by the way."

"You never asked," Kane muttered.

She glared at him. "The contessa thinks we're researching some of the old Venetian families, and the Montegro library is stuffed with family books and papers. Keith says she's wanted to get somebody in there to catalog everything for years, but her stepson always talked her out of it. Anyway, he's out of town for a few days, so the timing couldn't be better."

"We aren't going to catalog her library," Kane said flatly.

"Of course we aren't." Tyler jerked away from him and sat up. "We'll try to find some mention of the chalice and we'll snoop around the villa. What the hell's wrong with you, Kane?"

"Nothing." He flung the covers back and got out of bed. Their clothing was scattered across the room, and he muttered to himself as he found his briefs and jeans, and stepped into them.

"I get it," she snapped angrily. "It was *my* idea, that's why you're rumbling like a thundercloud."

"You know better than that," he growled, zipping his jeans.

"Then, what?" Tyler had forgotten the chill of the room in the heat of her baffled fury. She was kneeling in the middle of the tumbled bed, gloriously naked, and held her hands wide in a gesture of bewilderment. "If you want to fight, that's great. Glad to oblige. Just tell me what we're fighting *about* so I can gather my ammunition!"

Kane turned to stare at her, and a sudden rueful grin pulled at his lips. "Baby, your ammunition would stop an army in its tracks."

Tyler glanced down at herself, then jerked her furious gaze back to his. "Damn you, Kane—"

"Here." He tossed her his shirt. "Put that on."

She shrugged into the shirt, fastened a couple of the buttons, then looked at him. In a tone of absolute astonishment, she said, "Are you mad about Keith?"

Kane wondered which would be the safest admission: that the other man's very name made him grind his teeth together, or that it hurt him to see her so eager to complete the "business" ostensibly keeping them in Venice—and together. After a moment he went to the bed and sat down, eyeing her. "Tell me he's sixty-five and doddering."

Her anger gone, still gazing at him in surprise, Tyler cleared her throat and murmured, "No. Thirty-five or so. Plays tennis."

"Damn," Kane said.

"You weren't jealous?" she ventured.

He looked reflective. "Well, I could be wrong, but I think that's what it was. Is."

"Why?"

"He knew you before I did," Kane said simply.

Tyler didn't quite know what to make of that. Jealousy didn't necessarily indicate caring, not in a man as innately possessive as Kane seemed to be. But she could hope, even though she wasn't willing to let him see that wistfulness.

"Oh." She cleared her throat again and made her voice cool and dry. "Dog in a manger, Kane? Well, never mind, it isn't important."

"Isn't it?" His voice was silky. He watched a baffled frown draw her brows together, but it was a fleeting expression and she shrugged.

"No reason it should be. Look, don't you agree that we have to get inside the villa? We have to check out the family history and see if there's mention of the chalice. Because even if we don't find the second one . . ."

"We may discover that our chalice legally belongs to the Montegro family," Kane finished. He would have been wishing both chalices in hell by now except that the first one had brought Tyler and him together, and the possible existence of the second one, he was beginning to believe, was the only thing keeping her with him now. How much time did he have before she left him?

"We have to make sure," she said. "The chalices have been split up so many times, only one of them may have been in the family. But which one? Keith says that the Montegro library has family journals at least two or three hundred years old; if we can't find the answer there, we won't find it."

Kane leaned back on the bed, resting on his elbow. "Agreed. And you got us invited to the villa."

"Keith did."

If Kane hadn't known his jealousy had made no impression on her, he would have suspected her of deliberately needling him. But there was no guile in her clear amber eyes, and her tone had been absent.

"And," she went on briskly, "we're expected sometime this afternoon. We have to go shopping, both of us."

He knew what she meant, but he wasn't in the mood to be reasonable about this. "Why? We're supposed to be researchers; the contessa won't expect us to show up in designer clothes."

Tyler raised her eyebrows at him. "She won't expect us to show up with backpacks, either. And I don't know about you, but I'm ready for something other than boots and denim."

"Your vanity's showing, Ty."

She stared at him for a moment, her face completely expressionless, and then slid off the bed gracefully. With the total calm that generally heralded a storm, and a very sweet smile, she said, "Either you badly need a cup of coffee, or else you're determined to pick a fight. As I said before, glad to oblige if you want to fight, but you'll have to tell me what we're fighting about. In the meantime, I'm going to take a shower and go shopping."

Kane remained where he was until he heard the shower, then pushed himself up off the bed. What he felt for Tyler, the helpless love and fiery desire as well as the grinding uncertainty, was making him as edgy as a bear fresh out of hibernation; all his senses were quivering, and he was hungry, impatient. He *wanted*. He wanted Tyler, all of her, and the only hold he had on her was so damnably unsure it was driving him crazy.

He shed his pants and briefs, then joined her in the shower. She turned to him, her eyes glittering, and as he pulled her wet body into his arms she might have whispered, "Bastard." Kane didn't care what she called him, because her arms were around him, her hard-tipped breasts rubbing against his chest, her soft belly and loins yielding. He didn't care what she called him because his mind was fixed on the compulsion to make her his so utterly that she could never leave him.

TYLER WAS STILL feeling a bit shaken by the interlude in the shower late that afternoon as their rented car left Venice behind. Shaken and confused, and fighting not to hope too much. If Kane's desire for her was going to burn itself out, she thought, it would have to do so with the fury of a nova, because it certainly hadn't diminished. In fact, with every day that passed he seemed to want her more, his hunger urgent and unhidden.

But he was . . . different. Always before, Kane's temper had been fierce but, like a storm, soon over and forgotten. He'd never been a man to brood, and if he was mad she always knew why. Yet for the last few days, he had been moody, unusually terse. And unusually volatile, cheerful one moment, inexplicably angry or darkly passionate the next.

She wanted to hope that his brittle temper meant something, but she was afraid that what it meant was that he was growing restless or uneasy. That despite all her efforts not to cling, he was beginning to feel trapped by her—and his own desire.

"You're very quiet," he said suddenly.

They were heading north where, about twenty miles away, lay the small town of Treviso and the Palladian villa belonging to the Montegro family.

"Just thinking," she responded. Tyler hadn't had much time to think since the morning. Shopping for clothes and the like had taken time, even though she and Kane had separated and met back at their hotel with their purchases.

"The contessa dresses for dinner," she'd warned him as they were about to split up.

"Black tie?" he'd muttered with all the reluctance of a man who viewed formal dress as the social equivalent of a straitjacket.

"There's no time to be fitted—and you'd have to be," she had said, eyeing his broad, powerful shoulders. Kane had given her a look she couldn't interpret to save her life, but had merely said that he'd meet her back at the hotel in two hours.

Now, watching his profile as he handled the car expertly, Tyler had the feeling that he'd managed to acquire a dinner jacket despite the scant time, just as she had expected. He had looked mildly satisfied with himself, and had been carrying a garment bag in addition to a large suitcase. Like Tyler, he had found and bought used bags, and like her he had packed everything as it had been purchased.

Remembering the shopkeepers that had bemusedly watched her filling her own garment bag and suitcase, Tyler found herself acknowledging, for the first time, that she and Kane were really somewhat unorthodox. They had wandered around Venice wearing denim and khaki, even in the best restaurants and their fine hotel, and neither of them had thought about it. Nor had they been denied entry anywhere at all, no matter what the dress code.

Tyler looked at Kane's big, powerful body, relaxed behind the wheel of the car, and wasn't terribly surprised that no snooty head waiter had challenged them. Even now, wearing dark slacks and a white shirt instead of the rougher attire she was accustomed to, Kane possessed an aura of primitive strength that didn't invite careless confrontations, especially over unimportant things like dress codes.

"How did the contessa strike you?" he asked suddenly, sounding restless. Tyler had called her just after lunch.

"Very American," she replied dryly.

Kane sent her a glance. "How do you mean?"

Tyler reflected for a moment. "Well, I know she's lived here in Italy for thirty years, but I'd swear she just left Alabama. Pure Southern drawl. Very gracious and welcoming. She said she was sure we'd find plenty of interesting information in her library, and that she hoped we could stay at least several days, longer if possible."

He glanced at her again, his eyes probing hers, intent. "Did you happen to mention to her that we wouldn't need separate bedrooms?"

"I didn't have to bring up the matter." Tyler couldn't help but laugh a little, even though all her senses were straining to read each nuance of his deep voice, searching for the meaning in every glance. "She was very brisk about it. 'Two bedrooms, my dear, or one?' I said one, and she said fine."

"Good," Kane said.

Tyler hesitated, and her own uncertainty made her blurt, "I wasn't really sure that's what you wanted, but—"

"What?" This time, his glance was very readable because it was utterly incredulous.

She shrugged defensively, controlling a leap of hope. "For all I know, you've got some stuffy job as a professor back in the States."

"What the hell does that have to do with anything?"

"Well, a hotel is one thing and a private home something else. The academic world tends to be fussy about the reputations of its professors. Maybe you wouldn't want it known that you were shacking up—"

Kane whipped the car violently onto the shoulder of the road and stopped, then turned in the seat to stare at her. His eyes were glittering dangerously, but his voice emerged very quietly. "I have a ranch, Ty. In Montana. I don't teach. And I don't give a sweet damn if the whole bloody world knows we're lovers. Understand?"

She nodded, a bit wary. She would have felt on safer ground if he'd yelled or snapped; that deadly quiet was unnerving. Holding her own voice steady and calm, she said, "I just didn't want you to feel . . . obligated. I didn't automatically assume you'd want to share a room, and I wanted you to know that."

"Assume it from now on."

Tyler couldn't discern any emotion in his voice, and so the command did nothing to ease her uncertainty. She managed another shrug. "Everything ends, Kane." She was trying to tell him she wouldn't cling, wouldn't hold on if he wanted to leave her.

When. When he wanted to leave her. She tore her eyes away from his hard, compelling face and stared through the windshield. "Shouldn't we be going? I said we'd be there by four, and—"

His fingers bit into her jaw as he turned her face back to him, and he caught her gasp as his lips covered hers. He kissed her with a slow, dark hunger, a stark possessiveness, sliding his tongue deeply into her mouth, his big hand moving down to hold her throat caressingly. His free hand grasped one of hers and carried it to his thigh, guiding her fingers until she felt the hard ridge straining beneath the fabric of his pants.

A stab of pure heat jolted through Tyler, her entire body reacting wildly to his desire, and she trembled under the force of it.

Kane lifted his head, staring down at her with glittering eyes while his hand held hers firmly against him. "God, you make me crazy," he muttered thickly, a savage bite in his voice. "Not everything ends, Ty. Some things last forever."

When he released her hand, she drew it slowly away from him, feeling feverish, fighting the driving urge to go on touching him. She watched dazedly as he pulled back onto the road, and when he hauled her to his side she didn't even try to resist.

For the first time she realized that Kane was caught as surely as she was; the anger in his voice had told her that. And she'd been right in thinking that his desire would burn itself out only with the fiery explosion of a nova.

The flame between them could very easily end in destruction.

chapter nine

THE VILLA ROSA had, astonishingly, survived the World War II
air raids that had badly damaged the town of Treviso. It perched on
a hill outside the town, with the Alps rising behind it, and the clas-
sical Roman temple design of its massive single porch made it look
like a place of rest for the gods at the foot of Olympus. It had a low
dome at the center of the roof, Roman statuary adorning the porch
and the corners of the house, and extensive grounds that were
lovely even in their unkempt state.

It was a ruin of a place, worn by its four centuries of existence
and yet still standing despite wars and pollution and the constant
erosion of nature.

Getting out of their car at the foot of the steps leading to the
templelike porch, Tyler studied the place, comparing the dignity of
this decaying grandeur with the bland modern glass-and-steel

highrises now sinking their impersonal roots into the earth and their snouts into the clouds. If any of those monotonous buildings stood in four centuries, she thought, who would care?

"It's a shame, isn't it?" Kane murmured, joining her as he shrugged into a dark jacket.

Tyler nodded, reaching up absently to straighten his collar. "I was just thinking how little original style is left in the world. It all seems to be old and falling into ruin."

"Not all of it," Kane said.

Tyler was about to ask him what buildings he was thinking of when the heavy front door opened and a somberly dressed old man peered out at them. Kane took her hand in his and they went up the steps to the door. The old man nodded at them, his blue eyes birdlike with interest but his lined face impassive, and when he spoke it was in the clear, precise tones of an English butler. The kind of butler, Tyler reflected, that, like the villa, was a product of a lost way of life.

"Miss St. James, Mr. Pendleton. Welcome to Villa Rosa. The contessa and Mrs. Grayson are waiting in the drawing room. This way, please." He stepped back and opened the door wider.

They entered the villa, and both Tyler and Kane felt as if they were stepping back in history. Marble floors worn by countless feet, Veronese frescoes cracked with age, the cool, musty smell of centuries and inexorable decay. Tyler felt Kane's hand tighten around hers, and again she was conscious of that deep sensation of affinity as they followed the butler past an impressive staircase and across the entrance hall to a set of double doors.

He opened the doors for them, and in the instant before he announced their names they heard a somewhat shrill voice raised in nervous complaint.

"But, *strangers*, Elizabeth! How you could have invited them here—"

"Miss St. James and Mr. Pendleton," the butler announced crisply.

A tiny, white-haired lady rose from a brocade chair and came toward them, her smile as welcoming as that other voice had been annoyed. Elizabeth Montegro wore a plain silk dress with such innate dignity and style that Tyler realized only later that it was ten years out of fashion. Her delicate face was almost unlined, her green eyes still beautiful, and her voice was the slow, rich sound of the American South.

"I'm so glad you both could come," she said, shaking hands briskly with each of them. "I'm Elizabeth Montegro." Her accent lent the surname a curious cadence that was pleasing.

"Thank you for inviting us, Contessa," Kane replied, his deep voice holding all the easy charm he could command when he chose to exert himself.

"My pleasure, believe me. Fraser, see that their bags are taken up, please."

"Immediately, Contessa," the butler replied before backing out of the room and closing the doors softly.

She smiled at them, then half turned to nod toward the other woman in the room. "My stepson's wife, Erica Grayson."

While they murmured polite noises at each other and sat down on old brocade chairs, Tyler studied the other woman and remembered Keith's swift summation.

The stepson is Simon Grayson; he's some kind of consultant, Tyler. His wife is a cold fish by the name of Erica. And for "fish" you can read piranha; the woman could devour a man boots, bones and all. They live with the contessa because—according to rumor—Erica enjoys living in style and Simon spends too much on her pretty baubles to be able to afford a mansion for her. Rumor also has it that she'd dump him in a heartbeat if she could find someone as easy to manage with money.

Tyler could believe it, even without seeing Simon Grayson. Erica was a dark woman somewhere in her thirties. She had a predatory gleam in her black eyes, rings encrusting almost every finger, and her ethereal slenderness was burdened with a heavy rope of pearls and at least three gold chains. Her silk dress, unlike the contessa's, was very much in style, her black hair worn in an elaborate and queenly coronet, and she was quite beautiful in a sulky way.

She had held out a languid hand to Kane, her eyes both speculative and openly hungry; after a single glance at Tyler's casual skirt, sweater and neat single braid, she had offered a dismissive hello and thereafter focused her sultry attention on Kane.

"Keith Dutton was quite enthusiastic about you two," the contessa told Tyler as they all sat down. "He said you were researching some of the old Venetian families?"

"Preliminary research, at the moment," Tyler replied, smiling at the older woman. "There aren't many private journals and family papers that haven't been published or at least cataloged, so we haven't decided what to focus on yet."

"What's your own area of interest?" the contessa asked curiously.

"Heirlooms," Tyler replied promptly. "You can visualize so much of daily family life, even centuries ago, when you study the valued possessions handed down from each generation to the next. They're often mentioned in journals, particularly if there's an interesting story or set of circumstances connected with the object."

Erica laughed softly, one thin hand playing with her pearls—brushing them and her fingers gently against her breasts—as she eyed Kane. "And your . . . interest, Mr. Pendleton? Do you enjoy dusty journals and interesting stories?" Her tone gave the seemingly innocent question several layers of a very different meaning.

"Certainly." His tone was lazy, his vivid eyes veiled as he

looked at her. "Although Tyler and I tend to be more active in our research than at present—climbing around ancient ruins rather than sitting in private libraries."

"All over the world, I imagine?" the contessa's voice was wistful.

"Most of it," Kane confessed, smiling at her.

"It sounds so exciting," she said.

Tyler said, "That's one word for it." She carefully avoided looking at Kane. "Vilely uncomfortable more often than not, but I wouldn't trade any of our adventures for tour guides and five-star hotels."

Erica stirred slightly, and her discontented mouth tightened. "Have you been together long?" she asked throatily, looking only at Kane from under her lashes.

"Years," he replied, returning her stare with nothing but polite attention.

The contessa sent her stepson's wife a quick look, then smiled almost apologetically at Tyler and said smoothly, "I'm sure you'd like time to unpack and settle in before dinner. We dine at six, and please don't feel you have to dress formally. I keep to the old ways, though Simon and Erica tell me I should be more casual and modern. . . ."

Tyler, who was developing an acute dislike for Erica, smiled back at the contessa. "We don't get many chances to dress up, and I'm looking forward to it." She and Kane rose as the contessa got up to pull an old tasseled bellrope by the marble fireplace.

"Fraser will show you to your room," the contessa said as the doors opened almost instantly and the butler stood waiting. "Please make yourselves at home."

"Thank you," both Tyler and Kane said, and then followed the butler out.

Five minutes later, alone with Kane in their room, Tyler stood gazing around slowly. The villa had been modernized a few decades back to provide adequate plumbing and other necessities, but it was relatively unchanged by modern conveniences. This room was huge and bright, and if the silk hangings of the four-poster bore the fine slits of age and the velvet draperies at the two big windows were faded from sunlight, it was still a splendid room.

The furniture was a blending of heavy bulk and ornate detailing, the woods holding the dull patina of age and care, and the rugs, though threadbare, were still beautiful in their muted colors and artistry. Paneled walls provided some insulation from the cold stone of the exterior, and a brisk fire burned in the grate.

Tyler opened one of the two big wardrobes and began to methodically unpack. "What do you think?" she asked Kane.

"I like the contessa."

"So do I. And I hate lying to her."

Kane glanced at her as he hung several shirts in the second wardrobe. "We aren't lying. We *are* researching an old Venetian family—the Montegros."

"We're looking for the chalice. Don't split hairs, Kane." She picked up the airline flight bag that he had found to carry the chalice in and set it in the bottom of the wardrobe. She was frowning.

Kane watched her for a moment in silence. He felt as if there were suddenly a wall between them, as if she were deliberately distancing herself from him—already. As if she saw the end of this "adventure" looming just ahead, and wasn't prepared to wait to begin saying goodbye to him. Even after the interlude in the car . . .

Was that it? he wondered suddenly. Was it less a matter-of-factness about their relationship than a determination on Tyler's part to remain fiercely independent? Had his passionate, almost desperate possessiveness in the car served only to make her feel smothered and trapped? She had been very silent afterward.

For one of the very few times in his life, Kane felt helpless and uncertain. He wanted to tell her that he loved her, that he needed her, that he wanted no more partings between them, but he was afraid of pushing her even further away from him. Afraid . . . God, he was scared to death of losing her.

"Kane?" She was staring at him, still frowning. "Are you all right?"

He took two steps to stand before her, one hand lifting to cup her cheek. He bent his head and kissed her lightly, then said, "We aren't hurting anyone, Ty. If anything, we have a chance of helping the contessa. If our chalice ends up belonging to her, she could sell the thing for enough to keep her in comfort for the rest of her life. We aren't planning to steal from her. Maybe the second chalice is here, but we aren't going to take it; we just want to find out if it still exists."

She was staring up at him, her amber eyes shadowed by some emotion he couldn't read. Her emotions had always been transparent to him, yet now she was hiding even in that way.

"Something else is bothering you. What is it?" he demanded, an unconscious tension in his voice.

Tyler couldn't tell him the truth; that Erica Grayson's blatant advances to him had awakened a demon of jealousy inside her and that it had made her all the more aware of the uncertainty of their relationship. She couldn't tell him that. So she fell back on another fear, one that had been virtually absent from her thoughts since they had become lovers.

"If we—if we end up with only one chalice . . ."

His eyes narrowed. "I thought we'd gotten past that, Ty," he said roughly. "Do you still believe I'd steal the thing from you, or trick you in some way? Even now?"

"I don't know." It was almost a whisper. "I don't know what I believe."

"You trust me, you have to." His voice was still harsh.

Tyler fumbled for an explanation that wouldn't sound as if she was being demanding or possessive. "I trust you to be honest with me—there," she managed, nodding toward the bed. "I trust you not to pretend, not to offer—bedroom lies. But that's only part of what we are, Kane."

"Rivals."

"Has that changed?" She looked at him, a wordless hope drowning inside her.

Kane hesitated, then grasped her shoulders gently. "Yes." His voice was quiet now, slow and almost tentative. "We crossed the line, Ty. You said it yourself, the rules are different now. And we can't use what we are now to play the games on the other side of that line."

"What are we now?" She needed to hear his answer.

"Lovers." It was instant, certain.

"And when we're not lovers anymore?" The question was impossible to contain. "Do we step back over the line? Do we go back to being enemies and rivals, and fight for the chalice then?"

Again, Kane hesitated, afraid of pushing too hard, of holding on to her too tightly. But she seemed to be asking for some kind of reassurance, and he had to risk it. He tried to make his voice calm, but he knew the strain showed through, knew that he sounded too intense. "Tyler, we won't stop being lovers just because we find—or don't find—the chalice. We won't stop being lovers because we leave Italy." His hands tightened gently on her shoulders.

She looked up at him and said in a small voice, "There's an ocean between us."

He hoped she was talking about the Atlantic. "We'll work it out. I want you in my life."

Tyler managed a shaky smile, the hope inside her alive again. "Sure about that?"

Kane followed her lead and deliberately lightened the conversation. "Definitely." He kissed her, adding in the same intentionally light tone, "I haven't spent all this time chasing you just to settle for a few weeks in your bed, you know."

She gave him a startled look, but quick amusement flashed in her eyes. "I seem to recall chasing you in a number of places, including North Africa—literally chasing you," she said in a dry voice.

"All right, so I'm a bit unorthodox." Kane disappeared briefly as he carried his shaving kit into the bathroom, then returned to the bedroom and grinned at her. "I knew you'd come after me then, and seeing you on a camel was worth the wait."

Tyler couldn't help but laugh, though her most vivid memory of that "chase" was the soreness she had felt for days afterward. Her earlier uncertainty had lessened; just knowing that Kane saw some future for them beyond their return to London was more than she had expected, and she was determined not to ask for more than he offered.

They worked in companionable silence for a few minutes to complete the unpacking, but she had to comment when she saw him hanging a black dinner jacket in his wardrobe.

"So you did get one after all," she murmured.

"It wasn't easy," he admitted with an obvious air of satisfaction. "The shop charged the earth for fitting—" He broke off suddenly and stared at her. Slowly, a gleam of rueful amusement showed in his eyes. "You little witch."

Tyler allowed a wicked smile to curve her own lips. "Well, you wouldn't have gotten one if I hadn't made it a challenge."

"How long have you been managing me?" he demanded.

Clearly he was more pleased than angry at the realization; that surprised Tyler somewhat, but she kept it light. "Only on occasion, and always for your own good," she said virtuously.

"Uh-huh." His eyes narrowed in a look of mock danger. "I'm going to have to pay more attention to your needling."

She kept her face innocent. "Worried, Kane?"

"Only for my immortal soul," he said dryly.

Almost an hour later, as he watched Tyler moving around the room getting dressed, Kane reflected that he wouldn't mind not calling his soul his own if Tyler claimed it. He was still feeling a bit sheepish over the realization that she had quite easily gotten him into a dinner jacket without in any way saying that she wanted him to wear one, and he couldn't help but wonder how many of his past actions owed their existence to her deft guidance.

Not that he cared.

In all the time he'd known her, Kane had never before seen Tyler in formal dress; he had never seen her wear jewelry other than a somewhat masculine watch and plain gold studs in her earlobes; he had never seen her wear makeup or arrange her glorious hair in anything but a neat, simple style.

Now, fascinated, he watched her. She was so accustomed to his presence by this time that she didn't seem to notice his attention; she wore the intent yet curiously detached expression of a woman performing the little feminine rituals so alien to most men, and Kane couldn't take his eyes off her. There was grace in every movement, from the tilt of her head as she replaced her simple earrings with heavy gold hoops to the way she lifted her arms to arrange her fiery hair in a sophisticated chignon.

Light, deft makeup had given her lovely face an exotic air that was intensified by her clear amber eyes and the faintly Oriental design of her earrings. She was wearing a sleeveless black gown that was high-necked in front and backless. A wide, softly glittering black belt accentuated her tiny waist and made the rich curves above and below it all the more eye-catching.

Kane could attest to the fact that she wore only a pair of brief black panties under the dress, and his own secret knowledge of the bare, creamy flesh demurely hidden by thin dark silk was driving him crazy.

She stepped into a pair of black pumps and slipped a heavy gold bangle over one delicate wrist, then surveyed herself briefly with a critical gaze in the dressing mirror in one corner of the bedroom before turning away with a faint, unaware shrug.

She didn't know, Kane realized dimly. She had no idea of how beautiful she was. It was incredible.

"We're going to be late," she said briskly. "Yes, I know it's my fault, so you don't have to say it."

"I wasn't," he protested as she picked up his dinner jacket from the bed and held it for him. He felt her fingers absently smooth the material over his shoulders as he shrugged into it, and that unconsciously familiar touch affected him like nothing he'd ever felt before. He turned and pulled her into his arms. "God, you're beautiful."

Tyler was a little startled, and a soft flush rose in her cheeks. "Thank you. You look pretty good yourself." *Pretty good?* she thought a bit wildly. The starkly formal black dinner jacket made him so sexy she could hardly keep her hands off him. He was so big and obviously powerful that no clothing could hide it and, if anything, the formality only increased her awareness of the hard, muscled body cloaked by civilization.

His hands moved slowly down her bare back and curved over her bottom, holding her against him. "I don't suppose we could skip dinner," he murmured.

She managed to keep her voice steady despite her weakening legs and the curl of heat his touch always evoked. "What would the contessa think? Um, we're going to be late."

Kane bent his head to kiss her, not lightly this time, and then released her. And when they rejoined the contessa and Erica

Grayson downstairs moments later, he held Tyler's hand firmly tucked into the crook of his arm.

It was a strange evening. Tyler, who had looked forward to talking with the contessa, found herself with ample opportunity since Erica attached herself to Kane with a blatant disregard for her marriage vows or his relationship with Tyler. It wasn't quite so apparent at dinner, but once they returned to the sitting room for coffee afterward, the dark woman made her designs on Kane flagrantly obvious.

The contessa was clearly upset by Erica's behavior, but it was distress rather than surprise; evidently it was Erica's habit to go after handsome men whenever her husband wasn't present—and possibly when he was. She had smoothly claimed a place beside Kane on a low sofa and talked to him in a husky voice, occasionally stroking his arm or lapel with her nervous fingers.

Tyler didn't hear what was said, since she kept her own attention fixed on the contessa, but the quiet murmur of the dark woman's voice quickly began grating on her nerves. She had the satisfaction of knowing that the attempted seduction was apparently having the opposite effect on Kane, since his mild smiles and veiled eyes were signs of temper rather than enjoyment, but Tyler could easily have slapped Erica for the distress she was causing the contessa.

It didn't really surprise her when the contessa commented on the situation; strong emotions tended to push aside the normal formality of virtual strangers, Tyler had found.

"I'm sorry about Erica, my dear," the contessa murmured with a somewhat strained smile. "Simon usually keeps her in line, but when he isn't here . . ."

Tyler smiled with genuine warmth at the fragile old lady. "Please don't let her upset you, Contessa." She suddenly remembered a female bandit intent on a more colorful seduction, and her smile turned wry. "Kane has a strong effect on most women, so I'm not really surprised." But she was, because Erica's determination was so obvious it was almost as if she were playing a role in which she had no clear idea of the limits. And to act the vamp, much less with such exaggerated intensity, under the eyes of her husband's step-mother was both ludicrous and insane, Tyler would have thought.

The contessa's smile became more natural. "I shouldn't think you'd have to worry about other women; he rarely takes his eyes off you."

Before Tyler could react to that surprising statement, the contessa continued.

"I'll try to keep Erica out of your way while the two of you work in the library, but if she does disturb you, please don't hesitate to tell her so. She usually sleeps late and spends much of her time in her room."

"Contessa—"

"Please, my dear, call me Elizabeth."

"If you'll return the favor."

The contessa chuckled. "Gladly, Tyler. Does anyone shorten that, by the way?"

"Only Kane. How about you?"

"My husband did." Her eyes turned misty. "My second husband, I should say. Stefano. He called me Beth. An odd diminutive for an Italian to use, isn't it?"

"I would have expected Liza or Lisa, something like that," Tyler agreed.

"Stefano was an unusual man. He loved America even before we met there, though he afterward said that was the reason for his affection for the States. But he was very proud to be Italian. He fought during the war—" She broke off and gave Tyler an apologetic smile. "I don't know why I'm boring you with these old facts."

"Please, I'm very interested." It wasn't a lie; Tyler was interested, both for the sake of the contessa, whom she liked very much, and for the sake of the reason they were here.

Still, as Elizabeth continued to gently and fondly tell Stefano Montegro's story, Tyler allowed it to sink into her mind without examining what she was being told. From the corner of her eye, she saw Erica's painted talons resting possessively on Kane's thigh, and it required all her self-control to avoid giving the dark woman a glare that would have skewered her.

She felt primitive, and the strength of those emotions shocked her somewhat. Jealousy and possessiveness were alien to her, or at least had been until now, and even though she was reasonably sure Kane wasn't susceptible to Erica's wiles, she couldn't master her own feelings. Despite his earlier words, the lack of a commitment between her and Kane made her uncertainty linger painfully, and those other alien emotions . . .

Get your claws off him! He's mine!

God, was that really her thinking like that? With all her independence, all her certainty in the belief that no one had the right to own another human being, she still couldn't bear the sight of that woman's predatory hands on her man.

And wasn't that, really, how she had always thought of him? With that small, possessive pronoun? My enemy. My rival. My lover. My man. Mine.

". . . his father had hidden away the valuables," Elizabeth was saying. "And, after the war, when Stefano came home, the town was all but destroyed; he was surprised to see Villa Rosa still standing and unharmed."

"He must have been pleased," Tyler said automatically.

"Oh, yes. But his father was on his deathbed, and the war had changed so much. There was little money then, for anyone, and so much rebuilding to be done. Stefano did what he could, but it was very difficult for him . . ."

What would Kane say if she told him she loved him? How would he feel about that? Trapped or smothered? Would his desire for her die? Would he, God forbid, pity her? One-sided love was a thing to be pitied, after all, a thing fit for compassion . . . And her love was that. It made her so rawly vulnerable that she wanted to scream with the anguish of it.

Tyler had felt strong emotions before, had flinched under the brutal force of them. She had known pain, bitterness, grief, rage, hatred. But all of those primitive feelings paled in comparison to what she felt now, what Kane had awakened in her. For the first time she understood what the poets had tried to say about love, about the madness of it.

Everything else in her life shrank to a dim insignificance and became terrifyingly unimportant.

"If you'd like, Tyler, I can show you the library now. Stefano made an effort to organize some kind of reference system, but I'm afraid it's very haphazard." Elizabeth sounded a bit distressed again.

Tyler glanced aside to find that Kane and Erica had left the room while she had been totally involved with her own miserable thoughts. She managed a smile for the contessa. "Thank you, I'd like that very much."

As they rose, Elizabeth said unhappily, "Erica probably offered to show him around the villa. I don't know what's gotten into her; she's never been like this before."

Tyler heard the ghost of a laugh escape her lips. "Don't worry about it, Elizabeth, please. Kane can take care of himself." And she never doubted that, of course. Kane Pendleton was the least help-less man she had ever known, and perfectly capable of remaining on his own feet.

Particularly since Erica had no henchmen to knock him out and tie him to a bed.

*   *   *

WHEN HE CAME into their room a couple of hours later, Kane was feeling puzzled, disgusted and definitely on edge. The first two emotions were due to Erica Grayson, who had hung all over him until he was certain his dinner jacket had been stamped with her musky scent. She had played the vamp with an almost shrill, desperate determination, and Kane couldn't believe it was because she'd been bowled over by him. He was neither that vain, nor that gullible. So what was the woman after?

He was on edge partly because of Erica and her murky motives, and partly because of Tyler. She had seemed completely fascinated by her conversation with the contessa, not looking at him even when he'd gotten up and left with Erica, and her lack of interest had hurt him more than he cared to admit.

Coming into their room now, he looked around swiftly and felt a surge of relief mixed with wryness when he saw her standing by one of the windows; obviously no pang of temper or jealousy had prompted her to pack her bags and move into another room.

Only the dim glow of a lamp on the nightstand lit the room, leaving the corners in shadow, and he couldn't read her expression. She had changed into something white and flowing, and taken her hair down, but she didn't move to meet him or speak.

So it was up to him. "Damn that woman," he muttered, jerking his tie off and flinging it toward a wardrobe. "She must have taken a bath in that perfume of hers. I probably smell like a cathouse."

"You do," she said dryly. "At least, I assume so. I can smell it from here." She sounded faintly amused and nothing more.

His jacket joined the tie on the floor. "I'm not wearing this again, Ty, not unless I can get it cleaned first." He crossed the room to the bathroom door and reached in to flick on the light. "And I'm definitely going to take a shower."

Tyler reached up to draw back the curtains, turning her head away from him and gazing out on the moonlit countryside with an abstracted air. "You should," she murmured. "That lipstick's the wrong shade for you."

It wasn't the words, but the faint quiver in her voice that caught Kane's eager attention. He wanted to go to her and yank her into his arms, because that slight tremor had sounded like unhappiness; he didn't want her to be unhappy, but the realization that she felt anything at all over Erica's pursuit delighted him.

"She wouldn't take no for an answer," he said somewhat gruffly, wanting to hold her but unwilling to do so while he smelled of another woman.

"Some women are like that," Tyler said quietly. "Go take your shower, Kane. It's late."

He hesitated, then went into the bathroom.

Tyler didn't move until she heard the shower running. She released her grip on the velvet drapes and looked at the crushed material bearing the imprint of her hand. Then, very deliberately and with utter calm, she left the bedroom.

Elizabeth had shown her briefly around the villa before they had parted to retire for the night, so Tyler knew where she was going. Her slippers made no sound on the smooth marble floors, and she didn't pause until she faced a closed door in a silent corridor of the west wing of the house. She knocked softly, and a sultry voice immediately invited her in.

Tyler felt her eyebrow lift with a kind of dry amusement. So Erica had expected Kane to seek her out here? She made a mental bet with herself as to the dark woman's probable position on the bed, then opened the door and went into the bedroom.

She lost her bet; not even her imagination could have conjured the theatrically seductive pose Erica had assumed. The woman was lying on her side on an artfully tumbled bed, her dark hair trailing over her shoulders and glistening in the light of a number of candles placed around the bed. She was wearing a black lace teddy, the wide, plunging V-neckline of which bared her breasts almost to the nipples and ended at the base of her belly. She was on her side, one leg drawn up and her head propped on a hand, and the smile on her face was pure feline.

The smile died quickly when she saw Tyler, and a tide of red swept up over her surprised face.

"Hello," Tyler said with gentle courtesy. "I thought we should talk a bit." Her soft voice, like Kane's mild smiles, didn't hide the pure steel underneath.

Erica flounced up on the bed, apparently undisturbed by the fact that one breast was in imminent danger of escaping from the teddy. Her voice was sulky when she said, "I don't believe we have anything to talk about."

Tyler shrugged. "Then I'll do the talking." She was beginning to feel puzzlement over Erica, an unwilling curiosity. "It's really very simple. Stay away from Kane. If your own marriage vows haven't the power to stop you—I have."

Erica's lips curled and her dark eyes flashed. "Power? You know nothing of power. And you have no hold on him. He needs a woman who will burn in his arms—" She broke off abruptly, obviously realizing how absurd that sounded in the face of Tyler's flaming red hair and brilliant amber eyes, both attributes denoting quite a bit of fire. Her flush deepened to an ugly, mottled scarlet.

Tyler stared at her in growing astonishment and not a little confusion. What on earth, she wondered, was *with* this woman? She acted like the prototypical vamp in bad B movies and sounded even worse. Tyler's simmering anger cooled as she tried to figure out what was going on. Because of her tumbled thoughts, her voice was almost absent when she spoke.

"Look, if you want to fight over him, I'm willing. But I'd better warn you that I get mean when I fight. And I know how to fight dirty."

Erica made a sound probably meant to indicate regal disgust; it was actually a snort, and not a very ladylike one at that. "I would never demean myself—"

"Demean yourself? Erica, you've already done that." Tyler hardly knew what to say to this absurd woman. It was the strangest encounter she'd ever had, and considering the past three years that was really saying something.

"I can take him away from you!" Erica flared.

"Why? I mean, what are you planning?" Tyler was honestly curious, and it was apparent in her voice. "Do you mean to divorce Simon? Kane wouldn't stomach being a gigolo, you can bet on that. And if you're just after a little slap and tickle while hubby's away, that won't work, either; Kane's too honorable to sleep with both of us under one roof." Tyler reflected for a moment, then added thoughtfully, "And even if he wasn't, he knows I'd start carrying my knife again."

Erica sputtered for a moment.

Tyler watched her curiously. She had come here with the angry intention of stopping Erica, but now she was intent mainly on discovering the motives of this woman. There *had* to be a motive somewhere.

"I enslave men!" Erica announced finally.

Feeling her eyebrow rise again, Tyler fought back a laugh. "You won't enslave Kane," she said, and then added consolingly, "Venus herself couldn't do that; he's too independent and too damned stubborn."

Erica would have stamped her foot in frustration if she'd been standing; since she was sitting on the bed, her foot made a stamping motion in midair.

Tyler laughed out loud that time, unable to help herself.

"Erica, this is ridiculous. Kane's in my bed, and you're married to another man. What do you think you're going to gain by all this?"

"I'll get him." Erica was breathing in jerky little pants, her black eyes almost wild. "I can turn a man to jelly in my arms, take him to heaven. I can . . ."

She went on in that vein for a few minutes, while Tyler watched her in fascination. The thought that she might be literally insane skittered through Tyler's mind, but she dismissed it; there was something else here, something . . . desperate. Erica was right on the edge, but the edge of what?

What the hell's going on here? she wondered.

"All right, I get the point," Tyler interrupted finally, seeing that the dark woman was working herself into a frenzy. "But you'd better get mine. Stay away from Kane."

Erica smiled a brittle smile. "I'll get him into my bed. Unless you take him away from here, I'll get him."

Tyler felt the hairs on the back of her neck stirring, and suddenly understood what Erica's motive was; she knew now what the other woman was trying to do, even if she didn't yet know why.

She kept her voice calm and even. "Oh, I never run from a fight, Erica. Ask Kane. He knows. And I learned to fight in places you couldn't imagine. Think about that." She turned and left the bedroom, closing the door softly behind her.

chapter ten

AS SHE ENTERED their bedroom, Kane swung around to face her with a scowl. "Where the hell have you been?" he demanded harshly.

It wasn't normal for her to meekly accept that sort of question, far less in that tone of voice and from Kane, but Tyler was so distracted by her encounter with Erica—and by the towel that was all Kane wore at the moment—that she hardly noticed. She had intended to be evasive if Kane finished his shower before she returned and discovered her missing but, again, she was so rattled that she answered with the truth.

"I went to see Erica," she murmured, wondering if she'd ever be able to look at him without feeling a shock of desire. No. Never. Especially when he was like this, half naked and beautiful. Had he been about to dress and hunt for her? One of the drawers in his wardrobe was open with clothes spilling out.

Kane went still, some of the anger draining visibly from his big frame. "Why?" he asked in a different voice.

She wanted to be evasive about *that*, but Tyler just couldn't lie to him. Even more, the various tensions and puzzlements of the day boiled up in her suddenly and escaped with a force she had no way of fighting. Her hands lifted to rest on her hips as she assumed an unconsciously challenging stance, and she faced him defiantly with no more than two feet separating them.

"You told me to assume you wanted to be in my bed, so that's what I assumed. I went to tell Erica to stay away from you unless she wanted to tangle with me. Satisfied?"

"No," he said somewhat thickly.

Tyler glared at him. "Great. I'll go tell her she can have you. I'll be *damned* if I'll fight for a man as stubborn and contrary as a Missouri mule!"

Kane laughed and took a quick step so he could pull her stiff body into his arms. "No," he repeated huskily, "I'm not satisfied. You make me hungry, and I can never get full."

She blinked, then caught her breath as her lower body instinctively molded itself to his and she felt the hardness of his arousal. Her flash of rage vanished as swiftly as it had come. Somewhat uncertainly, she said, "That wasn't what I meant."

Kane pushed the filmy white negligee off her shoulders and let it drop to the floor, his darkened eyes drawn to the creamy golden curves of her breasts. The white gown she wore was demurely high-necked, but since the bodice was fashioned of eyelet lace there was nothing chaste about it. He could feel her tightening nipples against his chest, feel her stiff anger vanish as her arms went up around his neck.

"Damn you," she murmured helplessly. "I was mad. What

happened to my mad?" She could feel his warm lips against her throat, feel his chuckle.

"I don't know, but on you even mad looks great."

His words reminded Tyler of Erica—on whom mad looked really awful—and she tried to focus her thoughts. It wasn't easy with his lips on her and his hands sliding down over her bottom, but she tried. "Kane . . . about Erica—"

"I don't give a damn about Erica. Do you realize this is the first time I've ever seen you in a sexy nightgown?"

"I hadn't really thought about it."

"Hadn't you?"

Tyler felt heat rise in her cheeks, and hoped to heaven a blush looked better on her than it did on Erica. "All right," she muttered as he lifted his head to look down at her. "I had thought about it. And *don't* tell me my vanity's showing!"

"Did you buy this for me?" He was smiling, a peculiarly masculine smile of enjoyment.

She was somewhat beyond evasion; the effect this man had on her was a little frightening. Eyeing him with a certain amount of bitter resentment, she said, "You really want your pound of flesh, don't you?"

His hands moved gently over her bottom, slow, intimate, holding her against him. "I want everything I can get from you, Ty, haven't you figured that out yet?" Before she could answer, he repeated, "Did you buy this sexy gown for me?"

He didn't sound like a man wary of feeling trapped or smothered by a woman, Tyler realized. She frowned a little as she gazed up at him, trying to ignore the sensations he was rousing in her body at least long enough to understand this. Stalling for time, she said, "You should have seen what Erica was wearing."

Kane's eyes narrowed. In a deliberate voice, he said, "I don't care if she was stark naked and built like Helen of Troy. Answer the question."

"Yes. All right? Yes, I bought it for you."

He kissed her angry mouth until it softened, until her lips parted for him and a murmur of pleasure purred in the back of her throat. When he lifted his head at last, her lips were faintly swollen, her eyes dazed with desire.

"Damn it," she whispered, dizzy with desire and the seesawing of her emotions.

Kane couldn't help but grin. She was still mad at him, or at least wanted to be; that fighting spirit of hers was something he'd never be able to conquer even if he wanted to, which he didn't. He had fallen in love with her when she first raged at him, her heart-breaking eyes blazing with fury, her magnificent breasts heaving angrily, and her fiery temper could still get to him faster than any other of her moods.

Still smiling, he said, "Getting any kind of admission out of you is like pulling teeth. You really love making me work for it, don't you, Ty?"

"Work for what?"

He kept his tone light. "I know you're crazy about me, but will you admit it? No."

Tyler smiled up at him very sweetly. "Crazy being the operative word." This kind of sparring, she thought, was safe. Light, humorous, ultimately without meaning. A kind of verbal sexual teasing in a lamplit room.

"You're a stubborn woman," he murmured. "A maddening woman." His fingers were moving against her bottom again, slowly gathering the silky material of her gown as he drew the hem up. "But I can make you want me. Even when you're furious."

She gasped as she felt his big, warm hands on her naked flesh, the heat inside her spreading wildly. A distant part of her wondered why she even bothered to deny her feelings to him; he was too experienced not to know that her desire was so swift and powerful only because deeper emotions fed the flames. He had to know. He had to.

"Can't I?" he demanded.

"Yes," she murmured unsteadily. She found the knot holding the towel around his lean waist and fumbled with it until the terry cloth slid to the floor. He had pulled her gown up to her waist, holding the material bunched in one hand at the small of her back, and she bit back a moan as his hardness pushed at her. Her forehead rested on his shoulder for a moment and her hands stroked compulsively over the solid muscles of his back, feeling them move under her touch.

God, she wanted him. It was like an addiction, a craving in her soul. Her mouth slid over his bronze skin, and she tasted his clean flesh, breathed in the tangy scent of soap. All her senses expanded with a rush that was almost painful, until she was so acutely aware of him it was as if there was nothing else in the world. His breath was coming roughly, like hers; his skin was heating from the fire inside it, like hers; and she could feel his heart hammering, his body shivering as she touched him.

Kane uttered a rough sound and abruptly stepped back, quickly pulling the gown up over her head. "Have I told you how exciting you are?" he asked in a rasping voice, lifting her naked body easily into his arms.

Tyler nudged her slippers off automatically, clinging to him as he lowered her onto the bed and joined her. "No," she breathed, staring up at his taut face, feeling a sense of wonder that she could make him want her like this.

"You are." His mouth trailed down between her breasts, brushing fire across her flushed, swollen curves. His hands were stroking her body slowly. "Wildly exciting. You looked like a queen tonight, so damned beautiful and sexy I could hardly keep my eyes off you. And my hands."

Tyler could feel her body begin to move against him, restless and wanting, her hands trembling as she held on to him with a rising desperation. "Kane . . ." He was torturing her with his slow caresses, his own body tensed and shaking, his expression fixed in a look of utter absorption, and she was on fire with needing him. "Kane, please . . ."

A chuckle that was more like a growl rumbled in his throat as he held her twisting body firmly and continued the maddening caresses. "Why do you think I left the sitting room when I did?" he demanded gutturally against her breast, his thumb rasping over one tight nipple while he tasted the other. "I couldn't be still, just like a turned-on kid with raging hormones and no control. I wanted to pull up that silky skirt and take you right there, no matter who was watching."

She moaned deeply and pulled at his shoulders, seduced by his words and his touch, wild to feel him inside her. He resisted her silent plea, teasing her aching breasts with tiny licks and hot nibbles, letting her feel his teeth and his tongue.

"Damn you," she whispered, and slid one hand down his hard stomach, closing her fingers around him. She felt him jerk, heard his breath catch with a hoarse sound, and her own excitement spiraled violently as she explored the throbbing power of him, hot and rigid in her hand. She stroked him slowly, watching his vivid eyes flicker, his face tighten with a pleasure that was almost agony.

"God, baby . . ." His control shattered. With a groan, he rose above her, spreading her legs and pulling them high around him, entering her with a strong thrust of urgent need. He thought he'd explode when her hot, moist flesh tightly surrounded him, and he drove deeper in a primitive craving to merge their bodies completely.

She returned his passionate force with a lithe strength of her own, her flushed, beautiful face taut, her half-closed eyes luminous with the fire he had ignited. It was like before, like always, desperate and uncontrolled, almost a battle, like two wild things mating to sate a need they hardly understood.

"YOU WERE JEALOUS," he murmured.

Tyler pushed herself up on an elbow and gazed down at his relaxed face. She started, absurdly, to deny it, but then remembered his own wry admission of jealousy. Keeping her tone dry, she said, "Well, I *knew* Erica wasn't sixty-five and doddering."

His mouth curved, and sleepy eyes opened to look up at her. "Good."

She made a face at him, but didn't resist when he hauled her closer. Absently fingering the pelt of black hair covering his chest, she said, "Kane . . . about Erica."

He yawned. "What about her?"

"She really went after you."

"Can I help it if I'm adorable?"

Tyler pulled at several hairs until he winced.

"Ouch." He eyed her somewhat ruefully.

In a reasonable tone, she said, "Look, I'll admit that you're sexy—"

"How sexy?"

She narrowed her eyes and glared at him. "Very sexy. But—"

"No buts. I don't want to hear buts."

"*But,*" she continued firmly, "Erica was just trying too damned hard. You're a stranger, she's married—and she didn't even try to spare Elizabeth's feelings. Or mine. She's hellbent to get you into her bed, and it's just—" She broke off abruptly and added, "What's more, she expected it to be you knocking on her door tonight instead of me."

"She got the wrong idea," Kane murmured.

"Oh, yes?" Tyler's voice was very polite.

He grinned a little. "Well, I told you the state I was in when we left the sitting room. Since she was rubbing up against me like a cat in heat, I imagine she noticed."

"And thought she was turning you on?" It made Erica's confidence in ensnaring him more understandable, Tyler reflected.

"Could be. She acted like it. But then, she acted like that all evening."

Tyler stared at his neck, even though no trace of the lipstick remained. She forced herself not to think about that. Except that her voice didn't obey her mind. "Did she miss your mouth, or was she *trying* to get lipstick all over you?" Damn! She sounded like a shrew.

"Shrew." But Kane was smiling. Then the smile faded and he said seriously, "You know, I think that's just what she was doing. It's hard to believe, but even as . . . as frantic as she seemed to be, it was sort of . . . bravado. Something she almost had to do."

"She was branding you. For me to see."

Kane frowned a little. "I don't get it."

"Neither did I, until I talked to her. What she more or less said was that as long as you were here, you wouldn't be safe from her, um, seductive wiles. I think she fully expected me to panic, grab you by the collar and hustle you out of here."

He gazed up at her, still frowning, one hand toying gently with her tumbled hair. "Are you saying that whole vamp bit was designed to make us leave the villa? Baby, that doesn't make sense."

"No, because we don't know why. But I think I'm right, Kane, I really do. Nothing about her was natural tonight; it was like she was playing a part—being *forced* to play it—and scared to death of not doing it right."

"Surely she could have found an easier way of getting rid of us," he objected.

Tyler chewed on her bottom lip as she thought about it, until Kane lifted a hand to cup her cheek and used his thumb to gently ease her lip free.

"Don't do that," he murmured. "It makes me crazy."

She had to laugh, but said, "I'm trying to think; stop distracting me."

"I can't think of anything but you right now," he retorted, and pulled her head down firmly.

The conversation ended for the time being, and both of them were too pleasantly exhausted to resume it. The lamp was turned off, and they fell asleep still entwined.

It was hours later when Tyler woke up, and she couldn't figure out why; dawn was no more than a faint gray light in their silent bedroom, the house quiet and peaceful. Then she heard a sound from outside, faint and muffled. She eased away from Kane and slipped from the bed, crossing to the window and shivering unconsciously at the cold floor beneath her feet.

The window was open just an inch or so, which explained how she'd managed to hear anything at all from outside. She pulled the drapes aside and gazed out. Nothing moved, and in the gray light she could see nothing unusual, nothing out of place.

But she felt tense, jumpy.

"Ty?" Kane's voice was sleepy, puzzled. "Baby, come back to bed."

With a shrug, Tyler abandoned the window and returned to him, sliding under the covers and cuddling up to his warm body as he pulled her close.

"Why'd you get up?" he murmured.

"I thought I heard something."

"What?"

"Just a noise; it woke me up, I guess. But I didn't see anything."

He murmured something wordless and pressed a kiss to her forehead, recapturing sleep with no effort. But Tyler lay awake for a long time, bothered. She felt uneasy, the way she had from time to time in the past when there had been puzzling undercurrents in a situation.

After experiencing stark, primitive fear herself, it was almost as if some barrier of civilization, some protective veil, had been ripped away from her. People who had known the physical and emotional trauma of violence, her father had said, were changed forever by it, left wary on the deepest levels of themselves. Instincts that most people never needed in their lives were born—or released—in violence.

Now, in the gray light of a silent dawn, Tyler felt those instincts stirring. Like an animal bristling at the stench of fear, she felt tense and anxious, her unconsciously straining ears listening for . . . something.

But the house was silent. Gradually Tyler forced herself to relax. The steady rise and fall of Kane's broad chest and the thud of his heart beneath her cheek lulled her senses, until finally she drifted back to sleep. She had strange dreams, remembering in the morning only that they had disturbed her, that she had been searching for someone whimpering in pain.

ALL THE NEXT morning Tyler and Kane worked in the big library. Despite their active adventures in the past, both were competent researchers, and it took them very little time to become familiar with the haphazard system Stefano Montegro had tried to impose on nearly four hundred years of chaos. They briskly decided that Kane would wade through the stack of household ledgers and inventories they had unearthed, while Tyler studied the available journals and diaries.

They had already agreed to explore the villa later in the afternoon; the contessa told them at breakfast that she always rested after lunch, and it seemed to be Erica's habit to do the same. The dark woman's pursuit of Kane was apparently reserved for evening hours, since she put in no appearance at breakfast and they saw no sign of her during the day.

They were working companionably in a silence broken from time to time as one or the other of them made a comment. Since he was dealing with the big, heavy ledgers, Kane sat at the mahogany desk while Tyler was curled up nearby in one of the reading chairs.

"Here's something," he said when they had been at work no more than an hour or so.

Tyler looked up from frowning over the faded ink and spidery writing in the journal on her lap. "What?"

"It's dated 1894. Household inventory." Steadily he read, "Item: one heavy cup, no handles, on a pedestal base; figures of Greek design, warriors and chariots, et cetera. Gift." He looked up at her with a wry frown. "It doesn't even say who the gift was from. Or when it was given. This entry could have been carried over from an earlier inventory that doesn't even exist anymore."

She stared at him. "No mention of its being made of gold?"

"No. But none of these entries bother to mention if any item is made of precious metals. Two lines above the cup, there's a terse entry concerning a dagger. From the description, you'd think it was just another knife, but I happen to know *it* was made of gold, the handle at least, and studded with rubies. It's in a museum now, and has been for the past fifty years. It's called the Rose Dagger."

Tyler accepted his certainty about that. "Then the cup could well be our chalice."

"Could be. And it doesn't help that there's no mention of a mark on the base of the pedestal. It could have been missed or ignored, or there might not have been one."

She sighed. "So we still don't know which chalice belonged to the church in Florence, and which one the Montegros owned."

Kane straightened in his chair and flexed his shoulders slightly. "Any luck at your end?"

"No. This is one of the oldest journals—a diary, really—dated from 1860. Unfortunately it belonged to a very silly girl named Melina."

Kane grinned at her. "Why's she silly?"

"I just read three pages describing her newest ball gown. It'd be bad enough in English, but in Italian it's hell. Stop laughing, or I'll make *you* read it!"

They paid no attention to the passing hours as they worked, and were disturbed only once as Fraser crept in with a tray of coffee and sandwiches sometime after noon. Tyler, immersed in the second of Melina's three diaries, thanked him absently in Italian. She hardly noticed when he left again.

"Come up for air," Kane requested, leaving the desk to pour coffee for both of them. "Are you still on Melina? I thought she was silly."

"She is. But it's a fascinating kind of silliness. She writes about *everything*. Fashion, what people talk about over dinner, the servants, her parents . . . a sexy stableboy."

"She didn't write that he was sexy, I imagine?" Kane set a cup of coffee on the table beside Tyler's chair, then leaned over her shoulder to gaze at the diary.

Tyler tilted her head back and looked up at him. "No, but she described their tryst in an empty stable for five pages. I think it's safe to assume he was sexy."

"Maybe I should read it, after all." He kissed her lightly before she could respond, then added, "Take a break. We'll have lunch and then go exploring. I don't know about you, but my eyes are beginning to cross."

Tyler had no fault to find with the suggestion, and after finishing the sandwiches and coffee they set out to explore the villa. They had both dressed casually for the day, choosing to wear jeans, and neither was disturbed by the dust they stirred up as they wandered among the closed rooms on the third floor. The contessa had told them that this floor was unused and had been for some time, but she had also invited them to look around and they took her at her word.

It was a lonely place in its disuse, a part of the house cut off from life. Heavy furniture under Holland covers, rugs rolled up along walls, some windows bare and some shuttered. An occasional dark painting hung on a stained wall, so covered with layers of varnish that there was no hope of guessing what subjects the unknown artists had depicted.

"It's so sad!" Tyler burst out as they headed back down the hall to the stairs. "A slow death. This place should go out in style, with laughter instead of this awful silence."

Kane took her hand and squeezed it slightly. "I know. But this house was built for a way of life that's gone, Ty. It can never be the kind of private home it was once."

Tyler sighed an agreement and tried to make her voice brisk. "Well, we can't do much poking around on the second floor; it's mostly taken up with suites for the family and servants and a few guest bedrooms like ours. Elizabeth has a suite in our wing; Erica and Simon have one in the other along with Fraser and his wife. She's a good cook, isn't she?"

"Mrs. Fraser? Very good."

They were moving down the stairs by then, and a glance at the cracked frescoes on the curving wall depressed Tyler all over again. Before she could say anything, however, they reached the second floor and found themselves facing a stranger.

"Good afternoon," he said cheerfully. "I'm Simon Grayson."

*   *   *

HE WAS A medium man. Medium height and weight, medium coloring, a voice in midrange. His smile was easy, his handshake firm and cool. He seemed polite and mild. And smooth.

"Are you finding everything you need in the library?" he asked as they continued down to the ground floor. "Mother told me about your research. It sounds fascinating."

Tyler responded almost at random. "The Montegro family is fascinating. Between the journals and the ledgers, there's a lot of information about them."

Simon smiled at her. "I'm afraid that I'd be defeated at the outset by all that spiky writing. You read Italian, then?"

She glanced at Kane, who was unaccountably silent, then nodded at Simon. "Yes, we do. I can claim only French and Italian; Kane probably has half a dozen languages." She knew, in fact, that he had at least that many.

Kane neither confirmed nor denied it; he had stopped at the closed library door and stood with one hand on the handle, and was looking at Simon with a kind of detached, vaguely polite attention. Despite his powerful size and rugged handsomeness, the abstracted air gave him the look of a scholar with his mind fixed on some weighty problem.

Tyler was baffled, since she'd never seen him look like that before, but some instinct alerted her to say nothing about it in the presence of Simon Grayson. Instead she said casually, "We'll probably work the rest of the afternoon. Will we see you and Erica at dinner?"

Simon took the polite dismissal with good grace. "Of course. Until this evening, then." He smiled and strolled off toward the stairs.

Kane opened the door for her, then followed her into the library. She leaned back against the door and watched as he began pacing restlessly.

"He didn't waste any time, did he?" Kane muttered.

She frowned a little. "You think he came back early from his trip because we're here?" She didn't bother to keep her voice low, since the thick stone walls and massive wooden door made the room virtually soundproof.

"I'll bet Erica called him as soon as the contessa told her about us. Elizabeth said he was in Brazil, didn't she? Last night at dinner?"

"Yes."

Kane grunted. "The hell he was. He came tearing back here to cover his ass, and it wasn't from Brazil; he couldn't have made it back so quickly."

Tyler pushed away from the door and moved across the room to sit on the arm of a chair. "Kane, what're you talking about?"

He stopped pacing and faced her. "Damn it, you were right. Erica was trying to get rid of us. I don't know if the method was her idea or his, but you can bet he told her to do it."

"He wouldn't have told his own wife to—" She broke off suddenly. "Simon wants us out of here? But, why? He doesn't even know us."

"He knows we're researching in here, reading the family journals and ledgers. Which means we could well stumble across information he'd much rather keep for himself. He must have nearly had a heart attack when Erica told him we were coming here and why. You said he'd always talked Elizabeth out of having this stuff cataloged; the last thing he wants is someone picking around in here, especially a couple of adventuring archaeologists. Who both speak and read Italian." Scowling, he added, "Damn it, we always start out with a simple goal, and end up tangling with crooks!"

Tyler had to laugh, but she was still bewildered. "Kane, will you start at the beginning, please? What do you know about Simon Grayson that I don't?"

Kane eyed her for a moment, then said, "Why don't we just

leave, now? I know you, Ty, you'll get fierce about the contessa and we'll both end up in trouble."

She didn't take the bait. "Tell me."

He swore softly but with exquisite creativity. "All right. Simon Grayson deals in the black market for art objects. He supplies them."

Her mouth fell open. "What?"

"Cute, isn't it? Interpol's had their eye on him for three or four years now, but they've never been able to nail him."

"Are you sure?"

"Positive. I never connected the name, but I recognized him. A friend with Interpol showed me a photo about a year ago. They wanted to know if I'd ever encountered Grayson. He's been driving them nuts by selling untraceable art objects into the black market. They believe he has a stash somewhere; they even got an agent in the villa once, but he couldn't find a thing."

Tyler felt limp. "Why haven't they arrested him?"

"You know how it is. They *know,* but they can't prove it in court. The middlemen he deals with are pros and not likely to even admit knowing him. It was just an unlucky chance that they got onto him at all; he made the mistake of using a ruby necklace to pay off a gambling debt—Erica's, I imagine. The necklace, appraised and cataloged around the turn of the century, was listed as having disappeared sometime during World War II; at that time, it belonged to another old Venetian family in this area. I forget the name. Anyway, the guy Simon bought off with the necklace tried to sell it, and Interpol was alerted."

"Couldn't he testify against Simon?"

"He could. Except for one thing. A few hours after he'd made an informal statement to the police, he ended up in the morgue. Hit and run."

"They think Simon did it."

"Thinking isn't proving. Simon was supposedly a hundred miles away at the time. With Erica."

Tyler chewed her bottom lip. "Damn."

"I told you not to do that," Kane growled.

It took her a moment to realize what he meant, and she was a little surprised by her ability to distract him. She stopped chewing her lip. "Sorry. Kane, we have to do something."

"I knew you were going to say that." He half closed his eyes.

She was surprised again. "When have you ever run from a fight?"

Kane started pacing again, reluctant to tell her that he wanted to run from this one because of her. The thought of Tyler in danger made him sick with fear—and she courted danger, she'd taught herself to face it. She'd rush in with that fiery spirit of hers, just the way she had in North Africa and Mexico and Budapest and the Sudan and Hamburg and Hong Kong, and all the other places their jobs had taken them. Matching her strength and her wits against crooks with nothing to lose and a taste for violence. Damn, damn, *damn*.

"Kane?"

He loved her courage, even the maddening independence revealed in every defiant lift of her chin, but he wanted her safe and that instinct was too primitive to be denied. He'd wrap her in cotton wool if she'd let him, but she wouldn't let him, he knew that only too well.

"He's dangerous, Ty," he said finally, evenly.

"All the more reason." She sounded puzzled. "Those art objects have to be the Montegros'; he has no right to them, no right at all. He's robbing Elizabeth."

"The ruby necklace wasn't the Montegros'." He was reaching for objections, and he knew it.

"I can't explain that," she admitted. "But the answer's here in the library, it must be. In the journals and diaries or the ledgers.

Whatever it is, he probably didn't dare take the chance of destroying anything in here for fear of Elizabeth finding out."

Kane knew he had lost. He should have kept his big mouth shut about Simon Grayson's little scam, but it was so natural to discuss it with Tyler that he hadn't stopped to think. All he could do now was work with her, be alert to those reckless actions of hers, and guard her back. He didn't intend to let her out of his sight as long as they remained at the villa.

"Kane?"

"All right," he said briskly, heading for the desk. "So now we're looking for two things. The chalice, and some indication of what was hidden, when it was hidden, and where."

Tyler gave a gasp suddenly and began searching through the pile of diaries and journals beside her chair. "Stefano's father," she muttered. "I know I saw a couple of his journals, and Elizabeth said he hid the valuables during the war."

Kane had seated himself at the desk, and now looked across at her with a frown. "Wouldn't Stefano have known about that?"

"I'm not sure. Damn, I wish I'd listened more closely." Tyler found the two leather-bound volumes and sat down in her chair with them. She looked at Kane. "Stefano's father, Vincente, was on his deathbed when his son returned at the end of the war; I don't know if he was even capable of talking. And this area had been damaged so heavily that Stefano could have assumed the valuables had been destroyed or looted."

"Elizabeth knew they'd been hidden," Kane observed.

"Yes. But I don't think she knew *where*. And if she didn't know, neither did Stefano. From what she said, I got the impression Stefano had assumed the stuff was hidden away from the villa . . . somewhere nearby, maybe. And he didn't spend a lot of time here as a child, he was away at school; he might not have known there was a hiding place in the villa."

"We don't know, either."

"No, but we can find out." Tyler opened the first of Vincente Montegro's journals, flipped through a few pages, and then sighed. "He didn't date the entries by year, only the day and month. I'll have to read every page."

Kane smiled a little. "Is it ever easy for us?"

"No." She looked up at him. "Do you really think Simon's dangerous?"

"I think we'd better assume he is. And since we won't know— until we find it—exactly what he's afraid of us finding, we'll have to be very cautious about talking to him." Kane looked at the stack of ledgers on the desk. "I'll go on looking through this stuff, but our best hope is probably the journals."

Tyler nodded in agreement, then bent her head over Vincente Montegro's first journal. His handwriting was clear, at least, and she was secure enough in her knowledge of Italian to be able to read it with fair ease. Vincente, however, had an annoying habit of sprinkling his entries with phrases in other languages. After asking, and receiving, translations from Kane of bits of entries in German and Latin, she finally looked up at him with a curious frown.

"How many languages *do* you have?"

He looked a bit sheepish. "Both my parents taught languages at the college level . . . and they were linguists. My brothers and I were multilingual almost from the time we could talk."

Distracted, she said, "How many brothers?"

"Two, both younger. Matt's a professor at Cal Tech, and Craig runs a computer business."

Tyler stared at him for a moment. "How many languages?"

"French, Spanish, Greek, Italian, German, some Latin, Arabic, a smattering of Japanese, Cantonese—"

"I'm sorry I asked," she said somewhat blankly.

Kane grinned at her. "Read your journal."

She returned to her study of the journal, thinking that Kane was the most surprising man she'd ever known. Two separate degrees in archaeology, a linguist, a mountain climber and a pilot—she hadn't known *that* until he'd taken the controls for a while during their flight from Bogotá to the coast. He was an expert with guns, a competent sailor, was adept with mechanical things like engines, and possessed an infallible sense of direction.

He was a Renaissance man.

chapter eleven

BY THE TIME the afternoon waned, Kane and Tyler were no closer to finding their answers. He had continued to wade through the ledgers and household accounts while she read Vincente Montegro's first journal. But neither of them found what they were looking for. When they went upstairs to dress for dinner, Tyler took with her Vincente's second journal and, with a shrug, Melina's final diary, as well.

"You never know," she told Kane. "And I'd rather not leave them down here tonight. Simon will probably want to find out exactly what we've been reading."

To Tyler's amusement and Kane's disgust, they found upon reaching their room that his dinner jacket had been cleaned and neatly rehung in his wardrobe.

"Fraser, I suppose," Kane said irritably. "You never see the man unless he's serving something, but he always makes his presence felt. Is there a maid? I haven't seen one."

"A girl from the town comes in daily, according to Elizabeth. But the jacket was probably Fraser's doing. I'll bet he's used to cleaning up after Erica."

"Cat," Kane said, and ducked into the bathroom to take his shower before she could throw something at him.

Sometime later, as she was dressing, Tyler said absently, "I wonder when Simon got here."

"Does it matter?" Kane asked, watching her.

"I don't know. He just appeared so suddenly." She was arranging her hair in a thick braid to hang down over one shoulder, a style that exactly suited her evening gown with its square-cut neckline, full sleeves, and snug bodice. The gown was a soft gold color, and the full skirt fell in graceful folds to her delicate ankles. Tyler was, as always, detached and critical of her appearance. "I look like a peasant girl," she muttered to herself, turning from the mirror.

"You look beautiful," Kane said deeply.

She gave him a startled look. "Thanks, but I wasn't fishing."

"I know that." He smiled a little. "Forget that dig I made at your vanity, Ty. You don't have an ounce of conceit."

A little uncomfortable, she shrugged. "I always wanted to be tiny and raven-haired. Instead I ended up tall, all legs and cursed with a shade of hair that clashes with practically everything."

Kane took her hand and tucked it in the crook of his arm as they left the bedroom. "Hair like fire," he murmured. "Eyes of pure gold. A mouth that drives me crazy. Long, beautiful legs that wrap around me like warm, strong silk . . ."

Tyler couldn't believe it. They were walking down the stairs, formally dressed, outwardly sedate, and he was seducing her. Her legs felt weak and shaky, her skin flushed and hot, and an ache of desire throbbed slowly inside her. She glanced up to see that his eyes held a hot flicker of desire, and amusement.

"Kane," she protested softly, wishing that she could feel angry at his obvious enjoyment; he knew exactly the effect he could have on her simply with words that evoked sensual images. She lifted her free hand to briefly touch her hot cheek, hoping that no one else could guess the state she was in.

"After dinner," he said, "we're going to go for a moonlit walk outside."

"We are?"

"In the best romantic tradition. I'm trying to sweep you off your feet, you see," he added conversationally.

Tyler couldn't respond to that with more than a startled look, because they reached the sitting room then and Kane led her inside. And, as the evening progressed, she didn't get much of a chance to think about it.

The contessa was her usual gentle self; Erica was dressed in royal blue and diamonds, and almost utterly silent; and Simon was playing Master of the Manor to the hilt.

She didn't know if it was her heightened senses or not, but Tyler was almost painfully aware of undercurrents the entire evening. It didn't take her long to realize that Simon was at the center of them; he was the stone dropped into a quiet pool, spreading ripples of unease. At first Tyler thought that only Elizabeth was unaffected, but she soon realized that the contessa was simply showing it less; there was strain in her lovely eyes, and the firmness of control held her lips steady.

Erica was jumpy, responding to her husband's occasional bland endearments in a smothered voice and hardly looking at anyone else; Simon was cool and dry and faintly superior. Kane was laconic, and Tyler wasn't sure what she was feeling.

"How's the work progressing?" Simon asked as they gathered in the sitting room for coffee after the meal.

Tyler looked at him. "Slowly." She mentally reviewed what she and Kane had decided they could tell Simon. "At this point, we're primarily organizing the ledgers and journals into some kind of order. You know, according to date and, in the case of the journals, author. We need to see what kind of time span we have, if there are any large gaps, like that."

"I imagine there will be a number of gaps," he said indifferently. "Aren't there usually, among family papers?"

"That depends on the family." Tyler smiled at him brightly. "The Montegros seem to have been a literary lot."

"Stefano said that," Elizabeth murmured. "His own father kept a journal, and he was encouraged to, as well. Have you found Vincente's journal, Tyler?"

They hadn't counted on the contessa's innocent questions, Tyler reflected wryly, and answered as best she could. "Yes, his is the most recent. We'll start with the oldest ones, though, and read forward."

"Read?" Erica's dark eyes looked haunted. "I didn't think— silly of me, I suppose—"

Simon interrupted the disjointed phrases coolly. "They both read Italian, darling. I thought I told you."

Erica's cup clattered unsteadily against its saucer. "Oh. Yes, of course," she murmured. The glance she sent her husband held a pathetic mixture of fear and entreaty.

Tyler, who suddenly saw and understood the reason behind Erica's heavier than usual makeup, felt herself stiffen. Beside her on the low sofa, Kane slipped an arm around her and grasped her shoulder warningly. So, she thought, he had seen, as well.

She kept her voice light and casual. "My Italian's a bit rusty, but I imagine I'll get by well enough."

"If not," Simon murmured, "you're welcome to ask me to translate. My Italian is fluent. So is Mother's, of course."

"Thank you." Tyler kept the smile on her lips, but Kane must have realized that she was on the raw edge of exploding, because he rose to his feet and pulled her gently to hers.

"I realize it's early," he told Elizabeth with his charming smile, "but I promised Ty a moonlit walk. Would you mind very much if we said good night now?"

She returned his smile, the tension around her mouth easing. "Of course not. The old gazebo is still standing, and the garden is quite lovely in the moonlight. Just please be careful of the uneven ground; we've had some flooding in the area. If you aren't back by the time we retire, I'll have Fraser leave the front door unlocked, and you can lock it when you come in."

"Thank you," Kane said, and led Tyler out before she could do more than repeat the thanks.

A few minutes later as the soft scents of the untended garden closed around them, Tyler said tensely, "Her face was swollen. He's been hitting her."

"I know."

She glanced up at him as his fingers tightened slightly around hers, and even though she couldn't see his expression clearly she recognized the flat sound of his voice. Kane was as angry as she was. "Elizabeth's afraid of him, too. You don't think . . ."

"That he's violent with his stepmother? No. Not physically, at least. She's too strong a woman to stand for that. But she may be at least partially dependent on him financially, and you can bet he uses what power he has against her."

They walked in silence for a few moments, moving farther from the villa, and then Tyler said, "No wonder Erica was trying so hard. And I think . . . God help her, I think she loves him."

"How could she?" Kane murmured.

"I don't know. I mean, I really don't understand how love can survive that kind of violence. But the way she looked at him . . . She's terrified, but . . . suppliant. She has the reputation of going after other men, but I'll bet Simon tells her to. For whatever distorted reasons of his own."

"Probably," Kane agreed. "She certainly doesn't enjoy doing it, yet, in a way . . ."

"In a way, she does. How do people get so twisted, Kane?"

She sounded a little lost, and Kane stopped them, turned her to face him. "I don't know, baby. But we can't untwist them."

Tyler slid her arms around his waist and rested her forehead against his broad chest for a moment. "I'm ruining your romantic moonlit walk," she murmured wryly.

He kissed the top of her head, then smiled at her as she looked up at him. "No. But try to remember there isn't a lot we can do about some things. If we can find what we're looking for, maybe we can put Simon out of circulation for a while and even help Elizabeth financially. But we can't fix all the broken things in their lives. We can't, Ty."

"I know." She sighed. "I'll stop thinking about it."

"Maybe I can persuade you to do that." He pulled her a bit closer. "Could you think about me instead?"

"Well, if you ask me nicely . . ."

THEY WALKED IN the garden for a long time. The air grew chilly, but neither of them noticed. Kane made her laugh by describing her as a "pagan maid in the moonlight" when she stood inside the small, Roman-templelike gazebo, then drove laughter out of her mind when he held and kissed her passionately.

He seemed bent on courting her, as if they weren't already lovers, murmuring words of desire that heated her blood and stole the strength from her legs. Touching her with a hunger that was potent and curiously moving. He made her feel incredibly desirable. He made her feel, for the first time in her life, really beautiful.

It was late when they finally started back toward the house, walking slowly. Tyler was almost reluctant to go back into the villa, her feelings about the people who lived there confused and painful and uneasy. But Kane held those feelings at bay, and she loved him more than ever because of that. He made her want him until nothing else mattered.

They had reached the foot of the wide steps leading up to the porch when she noticed a faint light about twenty yards off to the right. It took her a few seconds to recognize the interior light of their rental car, which was parked there.

"Kane," she murmured, keeping her voice low. "Someone's been in our car. The dome light's on."

His arm tightened around her and then, as always, he moved quickly to deal with the situation. "Wait here," he breathed, and glided away from her like a shadow.

Tyler half turned to watch him, wishing her eyes were as good as his in the dark. The area where the car was parked was in the murky shadows cast by the villa, and she could just barely see Kane as he neared the car. A moment later the car's interior light went out.

And, in that instant, Tyler felt the hairs on her nape stirring as a soft scraping sound reached her ears. She tensed like a deer alerted by the cocking of a gun, all her instincts shrieking a soundless warning inside her head.

"Tyler!"

Kane's hoarse shout galvanized her as nothing else could have done. She leaped instantly away from the steps toward him, a sudden understanding of what was happening lending her that extra measure of strength and quickness that had so often meant the difference between life and death. As it did this time. Behind her there was a thunderous crash, and she felt small shattered pieces of what had fallen pelt her legs.

And then Kane's arms were around her, holding her with a strength that was almost crushing, and she could feel his heart hammering violently.

"Ty . . . Baby, are you all right?" His voice was still hoarse, shaking. And the hands that framed her face as she looked up at him were trembling.

She nodded, finally found her own voice. "I—I think so." She felt cold with the shock of what had happened, but forced herself to think. "It was one of the statues, wasn't it?" she asked, not wanting to look behind her.

"That bastard. That murderous son of a bitch—"

Tyler was shaking her head. "It could have been an accident. The villa's four centuries old." And there was, she knew, easy access to the porch roof from at least four of the third-floor windows.

"For God's sake, Ty—"

"Think," she urged him quietly. "If it was Simon, he's already back in his room. Everyone else is in bed, and they wouldn't have heard a thing; all the bedrooms are on the other side of the house. And the villa *is* old. The statue had to be loose, or he could never have pushed it over. We don't have any proof, Kane."

"I don't need proof," he said.

Tyler could feel the rage in him, like a deadly inferno, and her awareness of that was the only thing holding her own calm shell in place. Kane was unarmed, and though she had no doubts of his ability to kill Simon with his bare hands, she also had no doubt that the other man would probably be waiting inside his bedroom with a loaded gun trained on the door.

"Please, Kane." She kept her voice soft. "If you go after him now, you'll end up in jail." *Or worse.*

After a long moment Kane drew a deep breath. His arms gradually relaxed, and he bent his head to kiss her gently. He didn't say
a word, as if he didn't trust himself to speak. He kept one arm
around her as he guided her around the mound of rubble at the
foot of the steps. They went into the silent house. A few faint lights
had been left burning for them. Kane locked the massive front
door behind them, but left the lights on as they went upstairs.

Their room awaited them as it had the night before, with the
lamp glowing softly and the covers of the wide bed turned back
invitingly. Kane locked the door. Tyler had begun to shiver with a
delayed reaction to the shock, and the sore places on her lower legs
where pieces of the statue had hit her warned that she'd have
bruises by morning; there would have been cuts if the material of
her long skirt hadn't protected her somewhat.

She knew Kane wouldn't like seeing those marks on her. And
he didn't, though he noticed the reddening marks, because he immediately ran a hot bath for her and put her in it, still utterly
silent. His face was white and still, his vivid eyes darker than she'd
ever seen them. Anger and what looked like pain tightened his
firm mouth when he saw the marks on her legs, but he handled her
very gently as he bathed her and then dried her warmed body with
a fluffy towel.

Then he carried her to bed. Tyler said nothing as she watched
him undress, but as he slid into the bed beside her, her anxiety over
his silence made her say his name hesitantly.

Kane leaned over her, gazing at her face with that odd, fixed
look in his eyes. He lifted a hand to touch her cheek very lightly,
and then kissed her. He was gentle at first, but there was something inside him clawing to get out, and the force of it shuddered
through his body and made his kisses grow rough and urgent, and
his hands hard with need.

"Kane?" she whispered as his lips left hers to burn their way down her throat. She was a little tense, uncertain. She wasn't afraid of him, but this dreadful silence was scaring her.

"I almost lost you," he muttered in a jerking voice half muffled against her skin. His hands were moving over her almost frantically, as if he were reassuring himself of her warmth and life. "Let me love you, baby . . . For God's sake, just let me love you. . . ."

Tyler's anxiety vanished as his rough words emerged, and her body came alive. Her response to his touch was as powerful as always, yet he was different and she was responding to that, as well. She could hardly believe what all her instincts were telling her, yet she had to believe even though he didn't say the words she needed to hear. He had been shaken by her narrow escape, too shaken to be able, now, to hide what he was feeling.

He loved her as though afraid of never again having the chance to hold and touch her, his hands trembling as he stroked her body, his own big frame shuddering almost convulsively with desire. He kissed her again and again, catching her soft sighs and whimpers in his mouth. He muttered rasping words against her skin, words that were stark, graceless, bluntly sexual.

Tyler was burning, dizzy. His desire ignited her own with a ferocity she'd never felt before, and even as her body went wild in his arms, it seemed as if some ultimate barrier inside her shattered. She had surrendered to him long ago, but now she wasn't simply giving way to something too strong to fight, she was giving herself fully and freely.

There was a need in him that was naked, intense, the sound of it raw in his voice and the look of it dark and haunted in his eyes. He desperately wanted something from her, something more than passion, and the very strength of his need compelled her to offer him everything she had to give.

It wasn't a reasoning decision on her part, or even a conscious one. She loved him, and he needed. She offered her body, accepting

his eagerly; she offered the wild fury of her desire for him, returning his urgent passion with nothing held back. But he needed
more, and she gave willingly.

"I love you," she moaned, crying a little, holding on to him
with all her strength because he needed that, too. He jerked at her
words, a low groan bursting from his throat, burying himself
deeper as if he were trying to fuse their bodies in the eternal instant when violent pleasure shuddered through them.

KANE LIFTED HIS head at last to gaze down at her softly flushed
face, her shimmering eyes. She was still holding him in a mute refusal to let him leave her, and there was a stark vulnerability in the
tremulous curve of her lips.

"Say it again," he murmured, needing to hear it.

Her lips quivered, but those beautiful, wet eyes met his gaze
steadily. "It was the one thing I never guarded," she whispered.
"The one thing I never expected you to steal from me. I love
you, Kane."

He half closed his eyes. "Thank God. Ty . . . Baby, I've loved
you since the day we met."

"What?" She stared at him numbly.

He couldn't help but smile at her total astonishment. "I didn't
know it for a long time. I just knew I couldn't get you out of my
mind." His hands lifted to frame her face, his thumbs brushing
gently at the silvery evidence of tears at the corners of her wide
eyes. "Your big gold eyes and flaming hair, your temper and the
cool way you faced trouble. Everything about you fascinated me—
even the habit you had of tricking me every chance you got."

Tyler drew a shaking breath. "I never realized . . ."

He kissed her. "I was afraid you were feeling trapped after we
became lovers. You're so damned independent."

"I thought *you* were feeling trapped."

"I am." He kissed her again. "Trapped in something I never want to escape. Lord, Ty . . . I love you so much it's like madness. When I . . . when I saw that statue falling tonight . . . I've never been so terrified in my life."

She threaded her fingers through his thick, silky hair and lifted her head off the pillow to kiss him. A bit ruefully, she said, "Maybe we should thank Simon for that. I was too scared of clinging to tell you I loved you. Until tonight."

"I wish you would cling a little," he said, matching her tone. "Damn it, I want to wrap you in cotton and spoil you to death."

Tyler gazed at him gravely. "I wouldn't mind being spoiled, at least some of the time. But, Kane—"

"I know." He grinned faintly. "Don't think I'm picturing a demure little hausfrau with a smudge of flour on her nose. You're a hellion, Ty, a fighter, and that's the woman I fell in love with. I have no doubt you'll scare the hell out of me at least once a week, because you just can't stay out of trouble—"

She raised her head to kiss him again. "Trouble?" Her amber eyes were innocent.

"You're a lightning rod for it," he said firmly.

"Look who's talking," she murmured. Slowly, provocatively, her even white teeth began worrying her lower lip.

Kane felt an instant jolt of desire, but eyed her somewhat warily. "You're doing that deliberately," he muttered. "To distract me. You're an evil woman." He had always suspected that if Tyler ever chose to be deliberately seductive, a man would be putty in her slender hands; he had been right.

"I love you, Kane," she said softly, her big eyes warm and shimmering.

He groaned and lowered his head to kiss her hungrily. So what if he was putty in her hands? Big deal.

*   *   *

SOMETIME LATER, TYLER sat up beside him. "I'm not sleepy," she announced.

He opened one eye to peer at her, then opened the other because she was glowing with happiness and incredibly beautiful. "It's after midnight," he murmured.

"Are you sleepy?"

"No."

"Good." She leaned over him to open the drawer of the nightstand, producing the two diaries. "Then I think we should read these tonight. Simon's obviously made up his mind to get rid of us, and if we give him time to pull another stunt like he did tonight, you're going to kill him."

Kane sat up and banked the pillows, then settled back against them. "I'd only be doing the world a favor, to say nothing of Erica and the contessa," he pointed out.

"Yes, but the Italian police might not see it that way. We have to get evidence against him, or at least find out where the art objects are."

He nodded a reluctant agreement. "Okay, but I don't want you out of my sight as long as we stay here. Please, Ty," he added as she looked at him gravely. "I know you tend to land on your feet just like a cat, but I don't think I can take another scare like tonight— at least not right away."

Tyler smiled at the last rueful words. "All right. It's no hardship, staying with you." Then, sternly, she said, "Just don't expect me to hide behind you. I'll guard your back, but I won't hide."

"I know that." A slow smile curved his lips. "And there's no one I'd rather have guarding my back."

"I'm glad." She settled beside him, turning over onto her belly as she handed him Vincente's journal. "You read Vincente; all those languages are impossible for me. I'll stick with Melina."

"You're fascinated by her," Kane noted in amusement.

"Well, since she writes about practically everything in her life, maybe something will ring a bell."

It was over an hour later when Kane said, "Ty."

She looked up at him quickly. "You've found something?"

"Listen to this. 'I fear the worst. Even now, the countryside shudders under enemy fire, and we have heard the stories of atrocities; burning and looting. It is said that the vile Hitler means to plunder Europe of its riches. Today, several of my neighbors came to me with a plan. They are still young men, unlike myself, and mean to fight for our country. They have sent their families to safety, and have asked me to store their valuables at Villa Rosa.' "

Kane read slowly, obviously being careful of correctly translating Vincente Montegro's multilingual writing. " 'Their families know nothing of this; we feel it safer that only the six of us know. We have drawn up a list of each family's possessions, so that the valuables may be returned to their surviving members once this hateful war is over. I have sworn a blood oath to do this.

" 'I sent the servants into town on errands, and my neighbors helped me to make all safe. Even if the walls of Villa Rosa fail to stand, I have no doubt the secret room—' " Kane looked up at her. "The rest of the page is missing."

"Damn," Tyler said softly. "So Simon was at least that careful."

Kane studied the journal on his lap. "I'm only about halfway through; maybe there'll be something else further on."

She nodded, but didn't hold out much hope. After a moment she said, "Stefano couldn't have known; he would have honored his father's blood oath. The necklace, Kane, the ruby necklace that Simon used to pay the gambling debt: it was never returned to the family that owned it. Those five men must have died during the war, and Vincente died before he could tell Stefano what they'd done with the valuables."

"He knew they'd been hidden," Kane agreed, "but he had no

idea where. Why didn't he read his father's journal when he got home after the war?"

"I don't know. Maybe we can ask Elizabeth about it." Tyler returned to Melina's diary, feeling depressed. She read almost without attention, a part of her mind trying to figure out where a "secret room" might be in the villa.

Absently Kane said, "So Simon had an added reason to keep this from Elizabeth. Not only because he wanted all the Montegro wealth for himself, but because he was selling items that didn't even belong to her. She wouldn't stand for that—"

"Kane!" Tyler gasped.

He looked at her. "Not Melina?"

Tyler drew a breath and began reading softly. " 'My cousins enjoy playing a game of search, and they are vilely bad tempered when they cannot find me. They beg Mama to tell them where I hide, but 'tis a Montegro secret, and she would not betray it. She scolded me for discovering it myself, saying I was too young and flighty to be trusted, but I will never reveal our secret! My cousins have searched the cellar again and again, coming so near me that I laughed to myself, knowing they would not think to press the stone hand of a pagan god.' "

"I'll be damned," Kane said blankly.

Lifting his eyes from the diary, Tyler looked bemused. "Melina. Silly Melina. The cellar . . . A *wine* cellar! Palladio designed some fancy ones, I know. There must be a statue or something of Dionysus. No, the Roman version. Bacchus. The god of wine."

"Guarding a hidden room," Kane murmured. "Clever."

"It's the middle of the night." Tyler's eyes were shining with excitement. "We could go and look now."

Kane hesitated, though he was as eager as she. "I don't know, Ty. I don't trust that bastard to be asleep in his bed."

"He's already tried—and failed—once tonight," she pointed

out reasonably. "He'll have to regroup and consider his options. Think it through."

"Yes, if he's being logical about it. But is he? Maybe we should wait until morning and talk to Elizabeth."

Tyler waited silently, watching him. She had known Kane before this adventure, but her love gave her even greater insight now, and she knew what he'd decide. Despite his newfound anxiety over seeing her in danger, he was something of a lightning rod himself and could no more choose the safe path than she could. They were two of a kind, and she gloried in that certainty.

"Hell," he said finally, his lips curving, vivid green eyes alight. "Let's do it."

Half an hour later, both dressed in dark sweaters, rubber-soled shoes and jeans, and armed with their flashlights, they made their way silently downstairs and toward the rear of the villa where the kitchen was located. They found the heavy wooden door leading to the cellar and went cautiously down, Kane leading the way.

There was a switch at the top of the stairs, which they had made use of, and a number of shaded lights hanging from the ceiling of the cellar provided adequate illumination. Three walls were lined with tall racks, sadly depleted so that few bottles remained, and the rest of the floor space was taken up with stacks of odd bits of broken furniture and old trunks.

Directly across from the foot of the stairs, standing upright and apparently a part of the wall itself, was a marble slab. Carved from the stone was the muscled figure of a naked and bearded man, a cup in one hand and the other upraised as if to halt anyone who approached.

As they crossed the room and stood before the life-sized sculpture of Bacchus, Tyler giggled as a sudden thought crossed her mind. When Kane looked at her questioningly, she murmured, "I wonder how many parts of his anatomy Melina fondled before she found the right one."

Kane grinned at her. "She does seem to have been a mite precocious." He looked at Bacchus, then said, "You do the honors, Ty. You're the one who stuck with Melina."

In spite of their light words, they were both tense, and Tyler's hand trembled just a little as she raised it and touched the cold stone of the god's hand. She pressed steadily, feeling it give beneath the pressure; there was a sharp click, and the marble slab swiveled easily on a central axis.

For an instant they both stood staring at the blackness of a doorway, then they exchanged looks. Kane flicked on his flashlight and aimed it into the opening.

The room was relatively small, no more than twelve feet square, the walls, floor and ceiling constructed of stone. And it was nearly half filled with wooden crates, iron strongboxes, and other containers. In the beam of the flashlight, the blackened gleam of tarnished silver was visible; at least three of the crates were filled with platters and cups and candelabras. Kane moved the beam of light slowly, revealing a number of very old jewel cases piled haphazardly atop one another, along with numerous paintings rolled up and propped against the walls.

"My God," Tyler said softly. "Some of the richest families in Italy lived in this area. Kane, most of this stuff has to be priceless." She was on the point of turning her own flashlight on and going into the room to explore more carefully, when some faint sound or her own instincts warned her. Kane whirled around even as she did, both of them staring at the wicked barrel of a pistol held in a steady hand.

"Quite priceless," Simon agreed coolly. "And people are always willing to pay for priceless things." He laughed a little, the sound like the dry rustling of leaves.

"You fool," Kane said flatly. "Do you really think we can disappear without questions being asked?"

"Oh, but you'll be found. Or, rather, your bodies will. Mother did warn you, after all, that the ground around the villa is treacherous. I'm afraid you're both going to lose your footing and fall. There's a certain place I know where you'll fall a very long way."

He was, Tyler thought with the clarity danger always lent her, talking too much. It was the classic blunder of villains, particularly amateurs like Simon Montegro. Her mind worked quickly. Her peripheral vision caught a slight flicker as Kane's flashlight twitched, and that motion was enough to alert her to what he had in mind. Rivals and enemies they might have been, but in three years dangerous situations such as this had welded them into an efficient—and decidedly original—team.

Tyler dropped into that accustomed role with total ease and even a surge of almost savage enjoyment. She laughed.

Simon jerked slightly, his cold eyes sending her a sharp glance as the unexpected and inappropriate sound pierced the silence. "What're you laughing at?" he demanded.

"You," she told him dryly. "Of all the melodramatic postures, yours is the worst, Simon." She had his attention now, and held it easily. "And you're so damned pathetic. Stealing from your stepmother, beating your wife. You're really a worm of a man, aren't you?" She could feel Kane tensing beside her, readying himself.

"Bitch," Simon muttered.

Tyler wanted to tell him that he really shouldn't have said that because he'd pay dearly for it later, but she didn't waste her breath warning him. She laughed again. "Do you really expect us to be herded along meekly and pushed over a cliff? Honestly, Simon, that's so—"

She never finished the sentence. In common with most polite people, Simon was waiting for her to finish it; that was a human trait she and Kane had learned to take advantage of in the past. They had also learned through experience that Tyler could throw an object and accurately hit a target within her reach.

Simon's hand was her target, and the flashlight she threw while she was still talking hit with her usual accuracy. The gun went flying, and Kane lunged with a growl.

Tyler went to get the gun, returning somewhat hastily when she heard agitated sounds from Simon. "Kane, stop choking him."

"I want to kill him." Kane's handsome face was wearing a fighting grin that held no humor and would have been familiar to a berserk Viking howling his way into battle.

Simon's well-made shoes were dangling off the floor, his fingers plucking at the iron hands encircling his throat, and the noises escaping him were growing desperate.

She knew Kane was honestly furious, not the least because Simon had nearly killed her. But she had seen him almost this angry in the past, and had learned to deal with his very rare but killing rages by being matter-of-fact and even humorous about the situation. It occurred to her only now that if she had stopped to consider her ability to calm him down in the past, she would have realized he had cared more about her than either of them had realized.

Tyler tucked the gun into the waistband of her jeans, brushed Simon's hands away and began prying Kane's fingers loose. "Well, you can't kill him."

"Why not?" Kane demanded fiercely.

"Because your friend with Interpol wants to arrest him," she replied calmly, still working his fingers loose. "And because I love you, and I don't want to have to bail you out of jail."

Kane looked at her for a moment, then dropped Simon onto the floor. He glanced down at the villain who seemed unable to do anything except cough and gasp, then returned his wistful gaze to Tyler.

"Can't I break at least one of his arms, Ty?"

"No, but you can tie his wrists together." She looked down at Simon thoughtfully. "Tightly."

Kane's chuckle started deep in his chest, emerging in a sound of utter delight. He pulled her into his arms and kissed her. "I love you," he said huskily. And added, "What's that poking my stomach?"

"The gun," she answered cheerfully.

He kissed her again. "Oh. Find a piece of rope or something, will you, baby?"

Simon didn't even struggle.

chapter   twelve

"HE WAS A good boy when he was small," Elizabeth Montegro said sadly. "But . . . unaffectionate. Cold. I could never get close to him. After his father died and I married Stefano, Simon chose to spend most of the year in a boarding school. Then he grew up and . . . I'd barely seen him in years when he married Erica and they moved in here. It was only a few months later that I realized he was still cold. And that he was cruel, as well."

They were in the sitting room, all tired after the long day behind them. Elizabeth, Tyler, and Kane. Erica was in bed and under a doctor's care, though her hysterics had worn themselves out hours before. Officers from Interpol had arrived late in the afternoon and had taken Simon away; two of them were still down in the cellar making an inventory of the valuables.

Vincente's list had been found in one of the jewel boxes and,

along with his journal, had provided the officers with the story behind Simon's activities on the black market. The contessa knew
now, and though she grieved, she was hardly surprised.

Tyler stirred slightly as she sat close behind Kane on the low
sofa. She was exhausted, but she wanted all the loose ends tied up.
"You let them stay here because of Erica, didn't you?" she asked
the old lady gently.

Elizabeth nodded. "By the time they moved in with me, I'd
already heard she . . . she was known to chase after other men.
But once they were living here, I realized that Simon was behind that. He used her, had her get information from other
men. Then he used that information. I'm sure there were stock
tips and advance warning of business mergers and the like. Perhaps even blackmail. I thought—I hoped—I could protect her, at
least a little."

"Why did Erica stay with him?" Tyler asked. "Love?"

"She wouldn't confide in me. But I thought that was her reason. She does love him, I think, but . . . I was blind to what was
really happening. The doctor told me this afternoon that she'd
been using drugs. Simon was giving them to her, I'm sure."

Quietly Kane said, "Don't blame yourself, Elizabeth."

The contessa managed to smile at him.

Tyler decided it was time to change the subject. "Elizabeth, I
remember you said that Stefano had known about the hidden
valuables. But if he didn't know where they were hidden . . ."

"He didn't." She seemed to welcome the change. "Vincente
was something of a tartar, according to Stefano, and he was very
secretive. I'm sure he intended to tell his son about the existence
of the room, but he died before he could. He'd written to Stefano
and said only that the family valuables were hidden on the
grounds of Villa Rosa. When Stefano returned here, his father was
in a coma. The entire area had been bombed heavily, and a number

of outbuildings here had been destroyed. Stefano assumed the valuables had been lost."

"Why didn't he read his father's journals?" Kane asked.

"He couldn't find them at first. The old devil—" She smiled quickly, honestly amused. "His description of his father. Vincente had hidden them away. Stefano found them years later when he was searching for something else; they were in a trunk in the attic along with other journals. He took one look at the jumble of half a dozen languages, and just put all the journals in the library."

Tyler looked at Kane. "Simple enough."

"Once you have the answers," he agreed. "Then Simon read the journals a few years ago. And found the valuables. All those art objects, virtually untraceable because they'd been missing since the war years. Most of the records had been destroyed; he knew that. As long as he disposed of them gradually and cautiously, he stood to make a fortune."

"Thank you," Elizabeth said suddenly. When they looked at her, she smiled gently. "Someone had to stop Simon and I—I didn't have the strength. I'm grateful the two of you did. Erica will be all right; I'll see to that. She'll get the help she needs."

"You'll be able to renovate the villa," Tyler said with an answering smile. "The majority of those things in the cellar are yours, Elizabeth. You'll have private collectors and museums beating a path to your door."

"The way the two of you did?" She laughed in genuine pleasure at their startled looks.

"You knew?" Tyler said blankly.

"That you were searching for something specific here? Yes, my dear, I knew. After I talked to Keith Dutton, I called a few of the friends I had made over the past few years—friends involved in historical preservation. They knew of both of you."

Kane winced. "Then I'm surprised you invited us here."

"On the contrary. I was told in no uncertain terms that you were scrupulously honest people." Elizabeth's green eyes were twinkling. "In addition to being fascinating to observe. I was told to expect fireworks of one kind or another."

Tyler laughed a little. "Lightning rods, both of us. But thank you for trusting us, Elizabeth."

"I am curious," the contessa admitted. "What brought you here?"

Kane and Tyler exchanged looks, both of them remembering the final bit of helpful information that silly Melina had provided in her diary; Tyler had discovered it just a few hours before.

Papa is so angry! That ugly cup he lent the church in Florence has come up missing. He has the other one, the one with the odd mark on its bottom, but he says it's worthless now. I think it's an ugly thing anyway, but he says Alexander was poisoned with one of them and that makes the pair valuable. And they were a gift to the family. . . .

Tyler leaned forward to open the flight bag on the floor by the sofa. Elizabeth, who had hardly noticed they'd come into the room with it, watched now as a heavy chalice was placed on the coffee table between them. She looked puzzled.

"This," Tyler said. Quickly she explained how she and Kane had come into possession of the chalice, and how Drew Haviland had put them on the trail that had led to Villa Rosa and the Montegro family. Then she explained what they'd found in Melina's diary, finishing with, "So it's yours, Elizabeth. We haven't had it authenticated, of course, and it'd be worth far more if we'd found the other chalice with the valuables, but Kane and I think it could be one of Alexander's. I suppose the mate was sold somewhere along the way, or—" She broke off, because Elizabeth was laughing weakly.

"Are you telling me that cup is priceless?"

"It's an antiquity," Kane said slowly, puzzled by her reaction. "Valuable for that, and the gold content. If it's Alexander's, it certainly is priceless. Elizabeth—"

The contessa rose to her feet, still smiling with an odd, rueful humor. "It's late, and we're all tired. But before we retire, I want to show you something. Kane, please bring the cup."

He obeyed, and they followed the contessa up to the second floor and to her suite of rooms. They were baffled, even more so when they stood in her sitting room and she faced them with a smile.

"Look around."

They did, still puzzled. It was a warm room, decorated in bright colors and modern furnishings. Sturdy shelves held books and framed photos and knickknacks; there were a few landscapes on the walls; wildflowers from the villa's garden were arranged in two chipped porcelain vases.

Elizabeth laughed softly at their bewilderment. "I don't feel so bad now," she said dryly. "If you two experts missed it." She pointed to one of the bookshelves silently.

Tyler saw it then, and gasped. It stood in the center of one of the shelves, books leaning against it on either side, and since no light fell directly on it, there was no way of guessing that it was made of solid gold.

Kane set their chalice down on a table near one of the chairs and went to lift the second one from its shelf. He turned it in his big hands for a moment, then upended it and studied the bottom of the pedestal base. Slowly his mouth curved. He carried the cup back to Tyler and silently showed her the faint but visible mark pressed into the base.

She touched the cool metal softly, thinking of a dying king trying to leave evidence of possible treachery. "It's Alexander's," she murmured, and she felt no doubt of that.

"Alexander's," Kane agreed. He placed the chalice beside its mate on the table.

Elizabeth shook her head ruefully. "I suppose I assumed it was made of brass. I never lifted it. It's been on that shelf as long as I can remember. How absurd . . ."

It was absurd, and Tyler started to laugh. Kane and Elizabeth both joined in, all of them thinking about a priceless chalice squatting peacefully on a shelf for years, a missing piece of history.

"Take it," Elizabeth said softly when their laughter had finally died. "Take them both. If the two of you hadn't come here . . . I owe you so much. Take the cups, please."

It was an incredibly generous offer. Kane looked at Tyler, then put his arm around her as she smiled up at him. He returned his gaze to the contessa. "Thank you, Elizabeth, but we can't. We brought them together—we won't be responsible for separating them again."

"I don't understand."

Quietly Tyler said, "If the cups were ours, Kane and I would be . . . honorbound to turn them over to our respective employers. Two men who are bitter rivals. The chalices deserve better than that." She smiled suddenly. "However, we *do* know of a man who would give them both a good home. And give you a good price for them."

HALF AN HOUR later as they got ready for bed in their room, Tyler said sleepily, "I don't know about you, but I'm in hock with my expense account. I'll have to pay Robert back. It's a good thing my bank account's healthy. I hate to think what he's going to say about losing the chalice."

Kane grinned a little. "I'm more interested in hearing what both of them say when they find out about us. Maybe we should accept Elizabeth's invitation to stay here for a few weeks, at least until they cool down."

"I'd like to stay here for a while," Tyler agreed, crawling into bed. "And we can help Elizabeth, run interference for her when the collectors and museums start calling."

Sliding into bed beside her, Kane said conversationally, "Just how many of these sexy nightgowns do you have?"

Tyler smiled up at him, her arms lifting to wreathe around his neck. "A few. I was hoping you wouldn't be too tired to take this one off me."

"Aren't you tired?" he murmured, nuzzling her neck.

"Not that tired."

"Good," Kane said huskily, and took the nightgown off.

KANE STOOD ON the balcony of their hotel room and gazed out over the city of Venice. After spending three weeks at the villa, they had returned here a few days ago; they both loved the city and had wanted this time to explore—and to be with each other. Kane found himself smiling as he remembered these last weeks, and wondered how he had ever survived without Tyler in his life and his bed.

Once they had each gotten over the fear of being thought too possessive by the other, everything had been just fine. In three years of battles they had learned to know each other with a depth and certainty that few lovers ever achieve, and with the barriers between them gone their love was absolute. Not peaceful, however; since they shared intense passions—about everything including each other—the fights had been as glorious as the loving.

And Kane knew it would always be that way. It wouldn't suit some people, but it suited them perfectly. They had promised each other that they'd never go to bed angry—which was something that seemed utterly impossible anyway—and that left them free to enjoy their fights.

"Are you still sulking?" she called out sweetly, and Kane grinned to himself as he turned to go back into their room.

Fights, indeed.

"Of course I'm not sulking," he told her as he came inside. "It's undignified."

"That's what I thought," she said with a nod. She was sitting cross-legged on the bed, bright-eyed and beautiful, and only wearing one of his shirts. "Besides, I said I was sorry."

Kane sat down on the edge of the bed and stared at her. "I heard you."

"I wasn't sure," she murmured. "You were yelling so loudly I thought you might not have heard me."

He laughed despite himself. "Damn it, Ty, next time will you just *tell* me before you go haring off?"

"Look, Drew was leaving Italy and wanted to talk to one of us, and you were gone off on some mysterious errand you wouldn't tell me about—"

"—I came back to find you gone, not even a note—"

"—and I wasn't away more than an hour—"

"—scared the hell out of me—"

"—you didn't give me a chance to explain—"

They both stopped and stared at each other.

"I'm sorry," she said meekly.

Kane, knowing only too well that his Tyler was about as meek as a star going nova, burst out laughing. "Sure you are."

Her amber eyes were dancing. "Cross my heart. I didn't mean to worry you, really. Forgive me?"

"Yes, damn it," he growled, and leaned over to kiss her.

"Good." She slipped her arms around his neck. "Now I can tell you what Drew said."

"He has the chalices?"

"Yes, he bought them. But that isn't it. He'd heard about Sayers and Phillips firing us, and then about them meeting by chance in Westminster and screaming at each other."

"How'd he hear that?" Kane asked curiously.

Tyler giggled. "It made the papers. Apparently they stood there toe-to-toe accusing each other of base treachery at the top of their voices, and a very confused reporter who happened to be there took notes. He wrote an article."

"God help the reporter," Kane murmured.

"I know. Anyway, Drew wants to hire us."

Kane stared at her. "He what?"

She nodded. "He says it's more fun to watch us than to do it himself. A funny little man in Calcutta sent him a message about a jade bull, and—"

"No," Kane said.

Her eyes were dancing again, but her voice remained solemn. "It sounds really fascinating."

"We're going to be busy," Kane said firmly.

"Doing what?"

"Making a baby. The winters in Montana are long and cold; we'll be spending a lot of time in bed."

Her laughter vanished, and she looked at him gravely. Her disappointment at learning that she wasn't pregnant had surprised her; until then she hadn't realized how much she wanted to carry Kane's child inside her.

He kissed her a bit roughly. "Damn it, look what you made me do," he muttered. "I was going to propose tonight in a gondola." He reached into his pocket and brought out a small black velvet case. Inside was a beautiful diamond solitaire.

"Kane . . ."

He slipped the ring gently on her finger, then held her hand against his cheek and gazed at her with warm, inexpressibly tender eyes. "You're a beautiful, maddening, vile-tempered woman, Tyler St. James, and I can't live without you. Marry me."

"Yes," she whispered. "Oh, yes." She went into his arms, her face glowing. "I love you, Kane."

"I love you, too, baby."

A LONG TIME later, the afternoon sun shone through the open balcony doors and onto a tumbled bed where two lovers lay in each other's arms, temporarily sated.

"Can you ride a horse?" he murmured drowsily.

She yawned and rubbed her cheek contentedly against his broad chest. "I can ride a camel," she reminded. "There can't be that much difference."

He chuckled, wondering what a horse would have to say about that vague statement. He rubbed his chin against her soft hair. Beautiful, wonderful Tyler. He'd have his hands full for the rest of his life, and he was looking forward to every second of it.

Drifting slightly, he was barely aware of saying, "A jade bull?"

"Mmm. Stolen from a temple, supposedly."

"In Calcutta?"

"Uh-huh."

"Odd."

"Yes, it is." Tyler smiled secretly and cuddled closer to his warm, muscled body. So what if their route to Montana took them east instead of west; the world was round, after all.

They'd get home eventually.

author's note

THE FACTS CONCERNING Alexander the Great's life and death are accurate. I have speculated that his death, believed to be caused by malaria, might instead have been due to poison; however, that is pure speculation on my part.

The two golden chalices exist only in my imagination, and in the pages of this book.

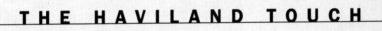

THE HAVILAND TOUCH

chapter one

THE MAN BEHIND the massive antique desk reached one elegant but curiously powerful hand into the chamois bag his visitor had just set before him and pulled out a heavy, ornate necklace. The instant light caught them, a half-dozen green stones threw shards of color in a glittering show of emerald fire.

"I told you it was something, didn't I? Thirty thousand, Haviland, and not a penny less."

Without commenting aloud, Drew Haviland produced a jeweler's lens and studied the necklace intently under the bright light of his desk lamp. The six large teardrop emeralds came under his scrutiny, as well as the numerous smaller diamonds and the craftsmanship of the gold work. Finally he raised his head, slipped the lens back into his pocket and looked at the other man. He was smiling slightly.

"Thirty thousand, Hanson?"

Hanson knew that smile, and his own was a bit uneasy. "You can't say it isn't worth it."

"Let me ask you," Drew said pleasantly. "Is it worth a decade or so in jail?"

"I *told* you it wasn't stolen, and it isn't," Hanson protested quickly.

The silence lengthened, and Drew's usually amused blue eyes were curiously flat as he stared across the desk at the other man. Finally he said in a very soft voice, "These are the Wyatt emeralds, Hanson."

A look of surprise crossed Hanson's face, swiftly followed by comprehension. "Hell," he muttered, "I'd forgotten that you'd probably know them."

"Yes, I know them."

Something about that level voice made Hanson rush on quickly, even nervously. "But not stolen, I swear. The—the lady came to me. She said she needed the money and couldn't sell the necklace on the open market. I didn't ask why."

Drew gazed at the chamois bag resting in the center of his neat blotter and asked mildly, "How much did you give her for it, Hanson?"

"That's not a fair question," Hanson muttered. He might have said more, but when those vivid, usually amused blue eyes lifted to meet his he decided not to bother. Several years' experience in dealing with the urbane and aristocratic Haviland had taught him that underneath that smooth exterior was an iron will, a rare but explosive temper and the kind of sheer physical strength it wasn't wise to provoke. Sighing, Hanson said, "Ten thousand."

"I'll give you fifteen."

"What? But—"

"That's five thousand for your trouble. And since your trouble consisted of hardly more than a few minutes' work, you shouldn't feel cheated."

"I could find another buyer."

"No, you couldn't." Drew smiled. "I'd see to that."

Hanson eyed him resentfully. "You would, too, damn you."

"Certainly I would. Is it a deal?"

"What choice do I have?"

Half an hour later, Drew stood at a large window of his study and stared out into the night. The room behind him was empty, the visitor having departed with fifteen thousand dollars in cash, and the chamois bag containing a costly necklace resting on the desk blotter. Drew hadn't looked at the necklace again after his first methodical examination, but if asked he could have described it in minute detail.

The Wyatt emeralds.

When had he first seen them? Eleven years ago? No, twelve. He couldn't even pretend to himself that he'd forgotten. It had been twelve years ago. The first time he had seen her. She had been a heartbreaker even then, Miss Spencer Wyatt, barely sixteen years old and already a belle of Washington, D.C., society. Her mother's death the year before had pushed her early into the position of her father's hostess, and she had claimed that responsibility with a grace and poise far beyond her years.

Drew could still remember, with disturbing clarity, the sight of her at one end of the long dining table. The promise of great beauty had shone in her flawless complexion and delicate bone structure, in the wide-spaced gray eyes that held intelligence and humor as well as an unusual sweetness. Her shining raven hair had been swept up in a sophisticated style, she'd worn very little makeup, albeit expertly applied, and the green of her dress had complemented the emeralds perfectly. Her figure had been trim but girlishly plump; within the next two years the puppy fat had vanished, leaving seductively womanly curves on a petite and slender frame.

Washington society regarded her as a woman long before the law agreed, and considering her father's preoccupation with his own affairs as well as his doting fondness of her, she might have been expected to run wild with a kind of freedom few teenagers in her position enjoyed. But she hadn't. She had clearly enjoyed the parties and other social events, yet had been at the top of her class in the private school she attended and had steadfastly refused to go out with any man other than her father alone until she turned eighteen.

Allan Wyatt was no one's idea of a stern father and, in fact, openly and proudly said that Spencer ran her own life. He would have granted her far more freedom than she accepted, particularly since he was by nature an indulgent man and openly adored his only child. Spencer hadn't taken advantage, at least not in that way. Drew had believed then that her poised social mask had hidden an innate shyness; she had sometimes seemed a little nervous and wary in his company.

Innocence, he had thought. For all her surface confidence and polish, she had been a very young woman who'd had a fairly sheltered upbringing, and more than once Drew had seen a look almost of dismay in her eyes whenever some eager swain had showered her with compliments or tried to get her alone. She had seemed more comfortable when those around her adhered to at least the surface courtesy that convention demanded, as if she felt safer when the rules were plainly marked.

Staring out the window and blind to the night landscape of the gracious Washington suburb where he kept a house, Drew moved slightly, restlessly, a frown crossing his face as the memories refused to leave him alone.

Would it have all been different, he wondered, if he had not chosen to play by those rules? If he had followed his instincts?

He'd wanted her from the first time he had set eyes on her, but she'd been too young then and he had known it. Two years of watching her, of feeding the hunger inside him with prosaic dinner-table conversations and sedate dances while he waited with what patience he could muster for her to grow up.

Apparently he waited too long. He could still remember, too vividly, his bitterness and anger, and pushed it aside with an effort. Ten years was a long time, he reminded himself. He was over that now, had been over it for years. He hadn't wasted a thought on Spencer Wyatt.

Drew turned away from the window and returned to his desk, sitting down in the chair and staring at the chamois bag on the blotter. Why had she sold the necklace? It had been in her family for generations, the famous Wyatt emeralds, and had been, he re-membered reluctantly, a personal favorite of hers. With all the Wyatt jewelry hers after her mother's death, she'd had her pick of a number of exquisite pieces, but the emeralds had been most often around her slender throat.

It wasn't his business, of course. If she wanted to sell every jewel she owned, it was entirely up to her. But why not sell it on the open market? She could have gotten fifty thousand easily, and likely more. Selling privately to someone like Hanson made the whole thing look . . . secretive and desperate.

Drew told himself again that it was none of his concern, but he reached for his phone anyway. He made several calls but managed to get only a few sketchy bits of information in answer to his dis-creet inquiries, none of which indicated that the Wyatts might be having financial problems. Not that it meant anything; it was quite possible for a prominent family to be a whisper away from broke without any of their friends or acquaintances being aware of it. Many an old and proud family had drained the last of their re-sources just trying to keep up appearances.

The Wyatts could have been in that situation but, if so, certainly showed no signs of it. In fact, six months ago while Drew had been in Europe and just before Allan Wyatt's stroke, Allan had bought his daughter a hideously expensive sports car—the latest in a long line of extravagant gifts.

Of course, Wyatt's illness meant medical expenses, probably enormous ones, but his finances had always been, on the surface at least, rock solid. Spencer had gone to the most expensive schools, worn the finest clothes and had owned a half-dozen thoroughbred hunters as well as two racehorses. The elder Wyatt had spent money lavishly on her, probably without much wheedling on her part since it wasn't necessary, and had himself been known as a man with expensive tastes. He wasn't a collector, like Drew, but he had more than once paid fantastic sums for a piece of artwork or some other trinket that had taken his fancy.

The more Drew thought about it, the more his curiosity grew. That was all it was, just the hell-bent curiosity that had gotten him into trouble in the past. He told himself that. Then he picked up the Wyatt emeralds and left his study.

Half an hour later he parked his car in the curving driveway of an elegant old Georgian mansion and approached the heavily paneled front doors. It was after nine o'clock in the evening and he had no certainty that she was even at home. He'd been out of the country for the better part of the past six months, since her father's stroke, and hadn't seen her at all in nearly a year. She could have been heavily involved with someone or still making the nightly rounds of glittering D.C. parties for all he knew.

He pushed the doorbell and waited. A couple of minutes later the door was opened by a formally attired butler who briefly lost his customary impassivity when he recognized the visitor.

"Mr. Haviland . . ."

"Hello, Tucker." Drew stepped inside the foyer, unwilling to wait and find out if he'd be invited in. "Is Miss Wyatt at home?"

"I believe so, sir." Tucker was back on balance, his elderly face bland once again. He had followed Allan Wyatt all over the world in their younger days, acting as a general factotum in an age when wealthy men had personal servants no matter what uncivilized corner of the globe their wandering footsteps crossed, and Drew had always thought that he could have told some incredible stories about those adventurous times if he'd wanted to.

But Tucker, who had been with Wyatt since the late nineteen thirties, was very much of the old school. He offered the kind of loyalty that came from an earlier age, the kind no amount of money could buy, and whatever he thought of his employer of more than fifty years he kept to himself. He also kept most other emotions to himself, but Drew heard the faint note of restraint in his otherwise toneless voice.

"But she may not be—receiving visitors?" he asked, deliberately mocking.

Tucker's expression didn't change. "If you would care to wait, sir, I'll inquire."

"I'll wait in the library." Drew hadn't set foot in this house for ten years, but turned unerringly toward the short hallway that led to the book-lined room at the rear of the house. He paused and looked back, however, before he left the foyer. "Tucker . . . I heard about Allan's illness. How is he?"

The butler, one foot on the bottom tread of the curving staircase, looked at him impassively. "Dying, sir," he said without inflection, and continued up the stairs.

Drew went on to the library, frowning a little, what he had noticed in the foyer and now along the hallway just touching the edge of his awareness because he was thinking of Allan Wyatt. He had barely seen Allan in the past ten years, but during the two years before that they had been close. They had in common a love of art and antiquities, and though forty years separated them in age they had found a great deal to talk about. While Drew was an amateur archaeologist with an instinctive feel for what was genuine, Allan had been trained in his youth by some of the most famous explorers and archaeologists in history, and he had enjoyed talking about those colorful days.

Drew had felt a great deal of respect for Allan, seeing in the older man one of the last of a dying breed. He'd been a true adventurer in his time, wandering all over the world in search of relics, and if his family's wealth had made his travels easier than they might have been, that took nothing away from his courage. Those days prior to and following the Second World War had been dangerous ones for any traveler.

He'd survived. He had survived the reckless adventuring of his youth and a war in which he'd been decorated for valor. He had settled down in his forties to marry and raise a child, becoming a well-known and respected figure around his nation's capital both for his past exploits and for his sheer charm. His young wife had died young. And now, at seventy-five, he was dying.

Drew went into the library, thinking about that. Allan Wyatt was truly the last of his kind. There might be others once humanity pushed out into space, but for now there was no real frontier left to explore.

He stood looking around the room, noticing a few things even as he remembered what he had seen in the foyer and hallway, adding it all together. Drawn across the spacious room to the old oak desk because of the working lamp glowing there, Drew stood looking down at the cluttered surface without really paying attention for a minute or so. Then his gaze sharpened, and he leaned forward to intently study the pages of several open books.

When the door opened a few minutes later he was standing

behind the desk, engrossed in reading pages of notes carefully printed on a legal pad.

"What are you doing here?"

Her voice was uniquely hers, low and a bit husky, still with that thread of sweetness in it that Drew knew better than to believe in now. He straightened, looking at her as she slowly moved across the room toward him. It was the first time in more than ten years they had met alone, face-to-face. For a moment, as she reached the other side of the desk and came into the bright glow of the lamp, what he felt most of all was anger, because she was still beautiful, damn her, and he still wanted her.

Only a few inches over five feet tall, Spencer Wyatt was petite, almost fragile in appearance, with small bones and delicate features. She was more slender than he remembered from the last time he'd seen her a year or so before, and the big, smoke-gray eyes seemed more opaque, almost completely unreadable. Her generous mouth was held firmly steady in a look of control, but her chin was up, Wyatt pride and confidence in the gesture he found disturbingly familiar. In that moment Drew was conscious of an almost savage urge to do something—anything—that would cause her to lose her unfailing composure.

"What are you doing here?" she repeated.

Quite deliberately, Drew looked her over with insolent thoroughness from the raven hair bound in an elegant chignon to the plain, high-heeled black pumps she wore. He allowed his gaze to linger on the firm mounds her breasts made beneath the green sweater, then trail slowly down to her narrow waist, and to the curved hips that were snugly encased in black slacks. He saw her small hands bunch suddenly into white-knuckled fists, and when he looked back at her face—angry heat rose in her cheeks, eyes glittering, bottom lip a bit unsteady now and her chin several degrees lower than before—he felt a jolt of almost brutal pleasure.

So her haughty poise could be disturbed, after all. He wondered what was underneath it, wondered what she would look like with the self-possessed mask at her feet in splinters. Would Wyatt pride keep her chin up and her voice soft even then? Or would the spoiled, calculating, ambitious bitch he believed was there finally show her treacherous face?

Perhaps that was what he needed to see, Drew thought. One glimpse of the Medusa, to cure him of her once and for all.

Leaving that thought where it lay, he reached into his pocket and pulled out the chamois bag, then tossed it to land on her side of the desk. Still a little flushed, she stepped forward stiffly and picked up the bag. Her fingers quivered just a bit as she opened it and drew the necklace partway out.

Without looking up at him she said evenly, "Where did you get this?"

"I bought it. From the man you sold it to." His own voice sounded normal, he thought, even casual.

Spencer pushed the necklace back into the bag and then tossed it to his side of the desk carelessly. "I hope you got it at a good price."

She was back on balance again, meeting his gaze with a direct, unreadable stare. A faint smile curved her lips, and her chin was back at its accustomed imperious angle.

"An excellent price—considering that it's worth about three times what I paid."

"Then you got a bargain."

"Why did you sell it, Spencer? And why to Hanson?"

"None of your business."

Drew picked up the bag and returned it to his pocket, then said, "I could ask Allan."

Something flickered in her eyes, some emotion that was restrained too quickly for him to be able to read it, but her expression didn't change and her voice remained calm. "He's sleeping right now. He sleeps most of the time. And I don't want you to upset him."

"Upset him? You mean if I tell him you sold the Wyatt emeralds secretly, he'd be upset?" Drew smiled, and wondered fleetingly how it looked to her, because it felt strangely unnatural. "He doesn't know, does he?"

"The necklace was mine to sell."

Very softly, Drew said, "Like the paintings that used to hang in the foyer and hallway, the ones you've replaced with prints? Like the Ming vase that was once on the mantel over there? And the ivory lions that should be on that shelf by the door? Were all those yours to sell, Spencer?"

She was a little pale now, but he couldn't tell if it was anger or something else. And she remained silent, staring at him as though frozen.

Drew laughed. "You finally did it, didn't you? Reece Cabot divorced you without a penny in settlement, so you came crawling home to daddy—and in a few short years you managed to go through a fortune it took the Wyatt family centuries to build. But that wasn't enough for you, was it? You couldn't wait to inherit what was left from Allan; you're selling everything off piecemeal before he's even in the ground."

Spencer heard him as if from a great distance, heard him saying things that were even more devastating because they were uttered in his cool, unemotional voice. She had always felt inadequate in his presence, miserably aware that while her gloss of elegance was only that, only a pretense to hide the shyness and uncertainty inside, his was innate and the genuine article. He was never rattled, never at a loss, never unsure of himself.

She had watched him cross crowded rooms and had seen other men give way to him as if by instinct, and she had seen women look at him in unconscious fascination because they recognized what Spencer had understood from the first time she had seen him. That he was different from most men, set apart from them somehow, like a thoroughbred stallion in a herd of mustangs.

He had awed her then, left her tongue-tied and nervous. Now those old feelings swept over her again, battering at her hard-won assurance until she wanted to find a dark corner somewhere and crawl into it. He had looked at her in a way he never had before, bringing tears of both pain and humiliation to her eyes. She'd felt as if he had stripped her naked and clinically assessed her body—and was contemptuous of the conclusions he had arrived at.

She had known what he must have thought of her all these years, but his distant politeness during their occasional public encounters in the past hadn't prepared her for that shattering appraisal or for this chilling attack.

How he must despise her!

"Nothing to say, Spencer?" His voice was smooth and yet, at the same time, indifferently cruel. "Not a word in your defense? Not even an attempt to shift the blame? That isn't like you, sweet. You always used to perform such a wonderfully innocent act of surprise and dismay whenever Allan gave you some expensive new trinket. But I suppose you've used up all your curtain calls over the years."

Shift the blame . . . With an effort she continued to meet his scornful gaze squarely. All she had left was pride, and she clung to that desperately because she couldn't let him destroy her. There was nothing she could say to change his opinion, his idea of what she was; that obviously was too deeply rooted to be affected by words. Accustomed most of her life to playing a part, Spencer numbly accepted the one he handed her simply because she was too exhausted to fight.

"What do you want, Drew?" she asked flatly.

"I want to hear you admit it. You have been selling off Allan's things, haven't you?"

"Yes." She was willing to say anything, if only he'd go away and leave her to find some kind of peace.

"He doesn't know."

It wasn't a question, but Spencer shook her head slightly, anyway. No, her father didn't know. Her father had no idea how bad things had gotten in the past months, and she had no intention of allowing him to find out.

"Do you have any jewelry left, or were the emeralds the last to go?"

If he was after his pound of flesh, she thought tiredly, he was certainly determined to get it all. "The last." It wasn't hard to make her voice cold; she felt frozen inside.

He laughed again, a sound that seemed honestly, if derisively, amused. "Every well has a bottom—what happens when you hit yours? Another besotted idiot like Cabot?"

Spencer lifted her chin another fraction of an inch and called on all the acting ability he had so mockingly referred to before. "Whatever it takes," she said deliberately.

He stared at her for a long moment, his classically handsome face completely expressionless, and then reached down and lifted a bulging file folder from the desk, holding it up between them. "But first this, I think," he said in a soft tone. "Do you plan to sell Allan's notes to the highest bidder, is that it? Just throw his life's ambition to the wolves and watch someone else finally locate the Hapsburg Cross?"

As if his slow movement and soft voice had hypnotized her, Spencer's gaze drifted to the folder and the lifetime's notes it contained. Notes on a holy relic that most historians and archaeologists denied the existence of, asserting that it was only myth. For fifty years those same experts had referred to the Hapsburg Cross as Wyatt's Holy Grail or, more commonly, Wyatt's Folly.

He had talked about it for all of her life, and searched for it all of his. In recent years he had called it merely a hobby, perhaps discouraged by the fruitless search, but he hadn't given up and Spencer knew it. Sifting through books, journals, diaries, poring over maps, endlessly speculating and piecing together the tiny bits of information he regarded as accurate, he had collected an impressive amount of data.

To think she would sell that . . . She wasn't capable of telling that lie, and answered involuntarily, "No, I won't sell the notes. I'm going to find the cross."

Drew laughed. He laughed as if the very idea of Spencer doing anything of the kind was utterly and completely ridiculous, and the contempt in that sound hurt her worse than anything else he had said. Already daunted by the task she had set herself and wretchedly aware of her lack of any formal training, his derision could have been enough to make her give up before she'd even tried. Could have been—but wasn't.

Spencer looked at him and found within herself a determination stronger than anything she had ever felt before. Now she had two overwhelming reasons to find the cross: to put it in her father's hands before he died, and to see the man in front of her shaken off his imperturbable balance just once.

"I'm glad you find it so amusing," she said icily. "I hope you're still laughing when you have to deal with me to add the cross to your splendid collection." Now why, she wondered with a pang of sudden dismay, had she said that? It was bound to make him think—

"Of course," Drew said in a tone of understanding, no longer laughing. "The things you've been selling can't begin to compare to the Hapsburg Cross. With that in your greedy little hands you could ask for millions—and get it."

He would never believe the truth, Spencer knew that. Never believe that all she wanted was to see her father's face when the dream of his life was put into his hands. Never believe that all she could give the father she adored in the last days of his life was the triumph of knowing that he had been right, and that his work had uncovered not a myth but a priceless relic.

Drew wouldn't believe that, no matter what she said. So Spencer clung to her pride and let him believe what he wanted, wishing only that his opinion didn't hurt so much.

"You'll never find it," he said flatly. "You don't know a damned thing about archaeology."

"I had the best teacher in the world—my father. He's forgotten more about archaeology than most of today's experts ever learn. And I have his notes."

For the first time, Drew showed some emotion other than scorn: incredulity. He looked at her as if she had lost her mind. "You think that's going to make it easy? These notes aren't step-by-step instructions, Spencer, and they don't contain a nice, neat little treasure map for your convenience."

She wouldn't allow herself to be withered under his ridicule, even though it cost her to continue to meet his eyes. "I know that. But the notes give me a place to start, and I—"

"A place to start? You mean Austria?" Drew put the file back on the desk, shaking his head. A pitying smile curved his lips. "That's a fine place to start. In fact, it's where legitimate archaeologists began searching a hundred years ago. Since the Hapsburgs supposedly owned the cross—and lived there—it only makes sense. Common sense, honey, of which you appear to have less than your share."

Though she badly wanted to convince him she wasn't the fool he thought her, she wasn't about to tell him that her father's notes narrowed the field considerably more—and to a place in Austria where no search for the cross had ever been conducted. No matter what Drew thought of her, the last thing on earth she would have done was give *him* a place to start.

Her father used to say that whatever formal training Drew lacked was more than made up for by an intuitive, almost instinctive sense of understanding. He had "the touch," an unerring ability to detect the genuine over the false, and a singular gift for finding artifacts, relics and ancient works of art that other more educated eyes had missed.

Until now, Spencer hadn't considered that someone else could beat her to the cross; since the experts maintained it didn't even exist, no one except her father had tried to find it in the past thirty years or so. But Drew, she realized with a sinking feeling of panic, could well decide to try his hand at the search. Given his obvious enmity toward her, he might even decide to do so just to teach her a lesson.

One of his elegant, powerful hands was resting on the file now, and she looked at it fixedly as she tried to regain control of her panic. Even if he had looked in the file, she assured herself desperately, he'd hardly had time to see the clues it had taken her months of intense study to find. From what he'd said, it was clear he believed she was planning to jaunt off to Austria without the least idea of any specific location.

That realization eased her anxiety, and she returned her gaze to his face. "I'm going to find the cross," she said, refusing to give him the satisfaction of listening to her try to defend herself. Since he so obviously thought her a stupid, greedy little gold digger, then so be it.

"You don't have a hope in hell."

Spencer managed to force a smile that she hoped was a mocking one. "Then you can gloat later, can't you?"

He stared at her for a long moment, then shook his head with a touch of impatience. "I'll deny myself that pleasure. Even if I decide not to go after the cross, I'd hate to see Allan's work lost—and you're bound to lose it between here and Austria. You'd better sell the notes to me."

He didn't even think she was bright enough to copy everything and leave the originals safely here, Spencer realized. She had no conscious intention of throwing down the gauntlet, but because he'd had the upper hand from the first moment she'd walked into the room and her own control was strained almost to the breaking point, her emotions got the better of her and she wasn't very surprised to hear the icy certainty in her own voice when she said softly, "Not if you were the last man left alive."

He stiffened, vivid eyes suddenly hard and curiously bleak, and his mouth a grim line. Spencer felt no pleasure from having successfully struck back at him, though she was vaguely surprised that she'd been able to. What she felt most of all was a bone-deep weariness, a raw pain like an open wound at the conviction that she had turned this man into an enemy, and an overwhelming knowledge that nothing in her life had prepared her to cope with any of this.

Drew removed his hand from the file and came around the desk toward her. She managed not to flinch away from him, and even turned to face him as he reached her, fighting the still-familiar apprehensive urge to back away. Too close. He was too close, forcing her to look up in order to meet his eyes. She felt smothered, backed into a corner by some primitive threat she couldn't even name and had no idea how to protect herself from. She had always felt that way whenever he was close to her—nervous, wary and terrifyingly inadequate.

Halting no more than an arm's length away, he reached for her hands and held them in his, turning them briefly as he stared down at her soft palms and slender fingers. Her nails were long and perfectly manicured, polished in glossy red. The pale gold flesh of her hands was smooth and unmarked by scars.

"You haven't done a day's work in your life," Drew said, his deep voice not cool now but curiously taut. "Even if you knew exactly where the cross was, do you really think it's just lying out in the open for you to pick up in your delicate hands?"

"I'm not stupid, whatever you think," she said, trying without success to draw her hands away. His touch was warm against her chilled skin, the slight roughness of his palms mute evidence that he had worked with his hands despite his elegant appearance. But it wasn't that which unnerved her. It was the strength she could feel in him, the almost tangible aura of sheer physical power.

He seemed larger than she remembered, his shoulders broader, his entire body more impressive and overwhelmingly masculine. She had the confused idea that she'd never really looked at him before, or that some part of himself always hidden beneath the cultivated exterior was closer to the surface now. She felt surrounded by him, trapped.

"What I think?" He seemed to lean down toward her, his features stony, eyes glittering. "I think you're a greedy, ruthless little fool. I think you broke that sick man upstairs, just like you'll break any man insane enough to love you."

chapter two

SHE WAS TRYING again to pull away from him, desperate to escape the knives of his words. She could feel the last of her control deserting her, rushing away just like the strength in her legs, and she knew she was going to afford him immense satisfaction by bursting into tears any minute now.

Then Drew released her hands, but before she could back away he was grasping both her shoulders and looking her up and down the way he had earlier, stripping her naked with insolent eyes and coolly weighing her charms.

"And it doesn't show at all," he said almost to himself. "That's the most dishonest thing about you, sweet, that beautiful, enticing package. It could easily blind a man until he'd believe he had struck gold instead of greed. But I know the truth, don't I?"

"Stop. Don't say any more." Every word she forced out hurt her tight throat. "Please, Drew—"

"Please, Drew," he repeated in a musing tone, his eyes on her face now and narrowed consideringly. "I like the sound of that. The surroundings could be better, though. A bedroom, I think, with you flat on your back between the sheets saying 'Please, Drew.' "

She made a smothered sound like the muted whimper of an animal in pain, both small hands lifting to push against his chest. Her mask was cracking, but he still couldn't read the depths of her darkened eyes. For all he could tell she was just furious.

He was furious, at himself as well as her. He *knew* she was a heartless bitch, and everything she'd said in this room only confirmed what he knew—but he still wanted her. The hunger he felt was so intense it had been gnawing at his control from the moment he'd looked up and seen her. Fighting that, he had needled and mocked her, trying savagely to make her reveal her true colors so that he could *see* the truth and be cured of this bitter craving for her.

But it hadn't worked. And once he had held her hands in his, the response of his body to just touching her had pushed aside everything except his painful struggle against it. He had forgotten her ludicrous plan to find the Hapsburg Cross and her frosty refusal to even consider selling him Allan's notes.

"Let go of me," she said huskily, pushing against his chest. "Get out of this house."

He laughed, the sound harsh in his ears. "You forgot to say please. And you, of all people, should know you're more apt to get what you want if you say please. I like hearing you plead with me, Spencer. It almost makes up for feeling like a fool when you jilted me."

She went still, gazing up at him with enormous smoky eyes he couldn't read. "That was ten years ago," she said, her voice still husky. "I'm sorry for what happened between us, but—"

"Between us? Nothing happened *between* us. You didn't even have the guts to face me once you'd made up your grasping little mind to run off with Cabot. I suppose I should have been grateful that you at least sent my ring back to me since it was a family heirloom, but I find it hard to forgive you for leaving Allan to break the news to me."

She flinched visibly, and he almost shook her because her look of pain and regret was so real he almost believed it. "I was only eighteen," she said with a tinge of despair in her voice. "I was afraid to face either of you."

"Afraid, hell. You just took the easy way out, honey, and left the mess for daddy to deal with. But you made a bad mistake, didn't you? Cabot might have been besotted, but his family's pure steel, and it didn't take them long to toss you out on your pretty bottom without a dime. I've often wondered—didn't you know then that I was the better catch? Or were you just convinced that he'd be easier to handle?"

Spencer stared up at him mutely, unable to deny that because it was partly true. Not that she'd wanted to handle Reece, but he had appeared simpler and less complicated than Drew, all his emotions on the surface—and his love had seemed so *real*. She had felt sure of herself with him, at least then, in the beginning. Reece's intense, passionate emotions had convinced her that to be loved so totally was far better and less painful than to love a man she didn't understand and was half afraid of.

Drew smiled cynically at her silence. "You should have married me, you know. I might have divorced you as quickly as Cabot did, but I probably would have paid for the privilege of being rid of you."

Under the hands gripping her shoulders, he felt her slump a little, and saw bloodless lips quiver in a starkly white face. Unblinking gray eyes were as blind as fog and held the same desolate chill.

"Lucky for you I did marry someone else," she whispered, her hands sliding away from his chest to hang loosely at her sides. "Think of all the money you saved."

The oddest sensation came over Drew as he stared down at her. It was a feeling he'd known before, countless times, but always and only when some object had been placed in his hands, its age or authentication in dispute. In every case he had felt the way he did now, as if a bell went off inside him, and the clear or discordant note of it told him what he needed to know. *Yes, it's the real thing.* Or no, it's a fake.

Now that bell was loud inside him, almost jangling, the harshly dissonant sensation too strong to ignore, and his recognition and understanding of it was completely involuntary. *She isn't what I think. Somehow, I've got it wrong.*

He had learned to trust his instincts when it came to objects, but he had never depended on that when it came to people. In fact, he couldn't remember ever experiencing the reaction to anything but inanimate objects. And he didn't trust it now. His mind and his emotions told him what she was, and he'd believed too long to let go of the certainty easily. His instinct for detecting the genuine, no more infallible than any other ability, had been deceived by her, that was all.

She was good, he acknowledged, staring down at that pale, beautiful face. She was so good that for a moment he had felt as if he'd kicked something defenseless and vulnerable. And she'd done it so easily, like turning on a switch that worked his emotions. It made him furious that he had let her get to him, if only for a moment. He wouldn't make that mistake again, he promised himself savagely.

He wouldn't let her make a fool of him twice.

But she had infected him years ago, her sweet, false smile lodging itself like a painful dart in some place deeper than his flesh, and for years he had let himself believe her betrayal had cured him of the hunger for her. Now he knew it wasn't true, knew that she'd have the ultimate triumph of destroying him unless he could rid himself of the poison of wanting her.

"I can't go back and change anything," she was saying now, her voice little more than a murmur.

"Very affecting," he drawled. "You should take to the stage if all else fails."

She shook her head a little, as if in bewilderment, then said tiredly, "Think what you like. If you've said what you came here to, I wish you'd leave. It's late. It's too late for any of this to matter."

"There's just one more thing," Drew told her, his hands tightening on her shoulders as he began pulling her toward him.

In the blankness of her eyes panic stirred, and her body tensed as she saw or sensed his intentions. "No—"

"I made the mistake of treating you like the innocent virgin you were supposed to be ten years ago," he said tautly, "and all I got for it was a slap in the face. You're treacherous and selfish and predatory, Spencer, but I didn't know that then and you got under my skin."

She felt like some small creature frozen in dread as it gazed at the hawk diving toward it, all her instincts shrieking for her to run, to get away, yet she was held immobile by something greater than terror. His hands were on her back now, relentless, and she gasped when he suddenly jerked her against him. His body was hard, and even through their clothing she could feel a heat that was almost feverish emanating from him. It seemed to seep into her flesh, her muscles, melting her resistance so that her body molded itself to his with instant, stunning compliance.

She was shaking her head unconsciously, and felt one of his hands slide up her back until his long fingers tangled in her hair.

His hand was rough and abrupt, scattering the pins restraining her thick hair so that it tumbled loosely around her shoulders, and then holding her head steady. He was staring at her fiercely, narrowed blue eyes burning so hot that she felt scorched by them, one hand pressing her lower body tightly to his until the unmistakable hardness of his arousal shocked her senses.

"I know what you are now," he muttered. "But it doesn't matter. Your tricks don't work on me anymore, and this time I'm calling the shots. You were promised to me years ago and I intend to collect the debt."

"What?" She could barely get the word out, so stunned by the ferocity she could see and feel in him that she could hardly think. If his cool sophistication had daunted her years ago, this strangely intense and implacable determination she saw burning in his eyes made her feel utterly helpless.

His laugh was short and harsh. "Oh, I don't want a wife, sweet, so don't think you've found another poor bastard you can try to bleed dry. All I want is you in my bed—for a while."

"No—" Her instant, whispered denial was cut off when his fingers tightened in her hair, drawing her head farther back. It wasn't painful, but she felt another queer shock when she realized that he could hurt her very easily. He was almost a foot taller and twice her weight, his arms steely around her—and he was angry, he was so angry.

"Yes," he said with flat certainty, his head beginning to lower toward hers.

Spencer closed her eyes as his hard features filled her field of vision and made her dizzy. She was quivering in his grasp like a trapped animal, her mind crying out silently against this. Both her arms were pinned to her sides, and she knew she wouldn't have been able to escape him even if they'd been free, because he was too strong to fight.

Then his mouth closed over hers, hard and hot, and it was like an electric jolt of pure raw sensuality. She had never in her life felt anything like this, and it was all the more shocking because she could feel it now with him. Everything else, all the confused, painful emotions, were submerged beneath waves and waves of sharp, heated pleasure. She couldn't fight the sensations any more than she could fight him, her mouth opening helplessly beneath the pressure of his. A convulsive shiver rippled through her when his tongue probed deeply, and she was suddenly very conscious of her breasts flattening against the hard planes of his chest as her body sank limply against him.

He had been gentle with her before, his kisses soft and his embraces light—careful, she realized now, of her inexperience and youth; at the time, she had seen detachment rather than restraint, and since he hadn't seemed to care deeply about her it had made her own unexpressed yearning feel somehow wrong.

Now there was no doubt of his desire, and even though Spencer knew that at least part of that passion was meant to punish her, she couldn't help but respond. When his hold on her shifted slightly, both her arms lifted as if by instinct to slide inside his suit jacket and around his lean waist.

He kissed her as if he were taking what belonged to him and demanding even more, the force of his hunger unrelenting and overwhelming. But he didn't hurt her. She was, on some dim level of awareness, surprised by that, because he could have hurt her so easily and because he seemed bent on doing just that.

Then, suddenly, Drew lifted his head, and his voice was little more than a hoarse rasp when he said, "Look at me."

Spencer forced her eyes to open, feeling dizzy and breathless. Her lips were throbbing, her whole body was throbbing, and she realized vaguely that she'd fall if he wasn't holding her so tightly against him.

"I could take you right now," he said. "I could pull you down to the floor, here, and in five minutes you'd be begging me to take you. I'm looking forward to that, sweet. I'll enjoy every minute of watching you go so crazy with wanting me that nothing else matters. When the time comes, you'll know what it feels like to be in thrall to someone else."

She couldn't even accuse him of arrogance or vanity in his certainty; her response had been instant and complete, and they both knew she couldn't fight it.

The heat inside her ebbed, leaving her chilled, and her arms dropped limply to her sides when he put his hands on her shoulders and set her brusquely away from him. She felt the edge of the desk behind her, and leaned against it because her legs were shaking so badly. He was looking at her, she thought, the way a cat would look at a mouse it intended to play with before killing.

"Don't run this time, Spencer," he warned almost lightly. "I'd only come after you."

She wanted to cry out. *It was only your pride I hurt, not your heart—why are you doing this?* But she was no longer so sure of that. What she felt in him was too intense to have its roots in wounded pride; hate came only when the cut went much deeper.

Unable to say a word, she watched him turn away from her and cross the room to the door. He was entirely himself again, the force that had washed over her numbingly now buried underneath his elegant, smoothly polished surface. Almost as if it had never existed. He didn't say goodbye or even look back at her; he simply left the room, closing the door behind him.

After a moment Spencer pushed herself away from the desk and went around it to the chair. She sat down, looking blindly at the clutter of books, maps and notes covering the blotter.

How did the saying go? That the road to hell was paved with good intentions? Her intentions had been good ten years ago. Selfish, perhaps, and in the end stupid, but not deliberately cruel, and motivated by the blind fears and confusions of an eighteen-year-old. She had been obsessed by Drew as only the very young can be, her emotions a painful tangle of love, fear, uncertainty, passionate hunger and a miserable sense of her own inadequacies.

Only seven years older than she, he had been far more mature, and people accorded him a respect that a much older man might have envied. British by birth but American by inclination, he had grown up all over the world. His father had been known for wanderlust, packing up his wife and son at least once a year for another move, often to the opposite side of the globe, so that Drew's schooling had been incredibly eclectic.

It occurred to Spencer now that the wanderer's life might also have been lonely, though Drew had never shown a sign of feeling deprived in any way. Still, it must have been at the very least disconcerting for a boy to be plucked out of a school in France and dropped into one in Hong Kong, or to start the year in Spain only to finish up in Italy. A close family life could have eased those strains, but from all Spencer had heard that hadn't been the case for Drew.

Despite the elder Haviland's penchant for taking his family along wherever he went, he was reputed to have been a reserved and even withdrawn man. A wealthy speculator with the Midas touch, he had built up his personal fortune to a level the old and aristocratic family hadn't seen in centuries. By all accounts, his wife had been a beautiful and languid woman, apparently content to follow her husband and with no ambition to assert herself in any way that ran contrary to his wishes.

At eighteen, Drew had left his parents somewhere in the Orient and had come to the States to enroll at Princeton; Spencer had no idea if he had done so for more emotional reasons than simply to remain in one place long enough to complete his education. In any case, he had stayed in America for the next four years, studying business as well as art, and becoming an honor student. Two months before his graduation, both his parents had been killed when their private plane crashed near London.

As far as Spencer could remember, he had never mentioned either his parents or anything about his childhood to her. She had found out what little she knew on her own, asking other people and reading newspaper and magazine accounts of the family. She hadn't asked Drew because she hadn't wanted to pry.

Pry! The man she had promised to marry, and she'd been so nervous around him that she hadn't felt comfortable asking about his family.

Her feelings about him then had been so confused. She had always felt too much, her emotions surging wildly from one extreme to the next all during her earliest childhood and into adolescence; it was as if there was a storm inside her, one she couldn't control. Then her mother had died, and at fifteen Spencer had faced the stark truth that the people one loved sometimes went away.

Like all of life's bitter truths, it changed her, but what might have been a maturing process became instead a kind of subterfuge that, once begun, turned into a prison. She had been wrenched from the self-preoccupations of adolescence, forced for the first time in her life to provide strength for someone else. Her father had been shattered, and it had been left to her to make all the arrangements that so swiftly and relentlessly follow a death. Burying her own wild grief, she had assumed a mask of quiet confidence and had set about trying to fill the place her mother had left in the family.

Spencer didn't regret that, but she knew now what it had cost her. She had pretended to be something she wasn't, hiding, even from her father, her lonely fears and insecurities. Because her mother's death had left such a gaping hole in her life, she always felt that she came up lacking in trying to be the poised, assured, gracious woman her mother had been.

And then Drew had stepped into her life, just at the moment her self-doubt was greatest. The first emotion she could remember feeling toward him was something very like wonder; at an age to worship blindly, she had taken one look into his amused blue eyes and tumbled headlong into love. He had seemed so . . . perfect. Tall, blond, classically handsome, his deep, slow voice holding the slight lilt of the cosmopolitan and his smile charming, he had appeared to Spencer like a god.

A girl could worship a god at sixteen. She could even, two years later, promise to marry one. But by then had come the confused questions and anxieties that had churned endlessly beneath her mask. What did he feel? Why did he want *her?* He said he loved her, but his voice was calm and matter-of-fact, with no hint of the frantic emotions she felt. And what was it she felt? Love, yes, but nervousness, too, and when he was close she felt uneasily threatened in some way she didn't understand.

In the end, she had run—as much away from Drew as toward Reece. With an adolescent's panicked confusion, she had thought that Reece's intense, passionate, all-consuming adoration would make her happier than Drew's restrained love.

Hindsight, as they say, is perfect. Spencer hadn't been emotionally mature enough to recognize that Reece's love had been as completely ephemeral as it had been violent. Like a child with a new toy, he had been devoted only until familiarity bred boredom and another new toy gleamed brightly with promise on the horizon.

She wondered now, with a sharp pang, if she would have found Drew's love to be everything she had wanted. Looking back, she could remember how he had watched her, how his voice had changed slightly when he talked to her, and how he had touched her often even if those touches had seemed impersonal. Not a detached man, she realized now, but a very private man whose emotions, though controlled, went deep.

Tonight he had lost control. Some part of her recognized that. She was older now, and if she was still uncertain of herself she had at least learned to see other people with more clarity. She didn't know why he had decided to come here tonight, why her selling of the emeralds had acted as a catalyst to finally release his bitterness and anger. All she knew was that his promise of physical possession had been no idle threat.

He wasn't a cruel man; she couldn't believe that of him even now. But he was angry and had—from his viewpoint, anyway—reason to believe she was a greedy, heartless bitch.

She hadn't been able to defend herself against that belief, partly because she was just too tired. The past few months, since her father's stroke, had been mentally and emotionally exhausting. The shock of his illness had been bad enough, but then to find out that he was uninsured and that they were heavily in debt had been almost more than she could handle.

It had been a nightmare, and one she had struggled through with a crushing feeling of hopelessness. Still, she had managed to at least hold back the floodwaters of defeat. She had learned to negotiate with creditors, from the bank that held the stiff mortgage on this house to the IRS—which had granted her a moratorium on back taxes. Forced to get a job doing the only thing she felt reasonably adept at in order to pay for the private nurse her father required, she had been slowly selling off everything she could for living expenses and to whittle away at the mountain of debt.

Her own things had gone first. Her car, the horses she owned, her jewelry. Her trust fund provided some income. She couldn't touch the principal—a bitter frustration—but the interest brought in at least enough to stall creditors while she struggled to pay them off.

She wasn't sure, even now, where all the money had gone. Her father was no businessman, but there had at one time been income from real estate property and stocks that were gone now. She couldn't even ask her father what had happened to it all, because she didn't want him to worry. His memory had been affected by the stroke, and if he had ever realized he was on the edge of financial ruin he didn't remember it now.

Spencer honestly didn't know what she would do when she reached the end of her dwindling resources. Virtually everything of value was gone, the house was not only heavily mortgaged but also had a tax lien against it, and despite the lesser expense of being at home with a private nurse, her father's medical bills were staggering.

And with all that weighing her down, she was determined to travel alone to Europe, for the first time in her life, and find a holy relic that had eluded experts for centuries.

"Miss Spencer?"

She looked up with a start, her racing heart slowing as she saw Tucker standing in the doorway. If he had knocked she'd been too lost in thought to hear it. "Oh—Tucker." She forced her mind away from the useless and numbing thoughts. "Is there something wrong?"

He crossed the room soundlessly, his face as usual impassive, and placed a chamois bag on the desk. "Mr. Haviland left this, miss. He said to give it to you. I would have brought it in sooner, but the nurse required my help."

"Is Dad all right?" Spencer asked automatically, her disbelieving gaze fixed on the bag.

"Yes," Tucker replied. "He insisted on changing his bed jacket, miss, as he does every night before you visit him."

It was her habit to spend an hour or so sitting by her father's bed each evening, talking to him cheerfully or reading to him, and the visits had become a ritual. But Spencer wasn't thinking about that right now. She was staring at the bag holding the emeralds she had sold.

Why had Drew left them? As a mocking gesture, made in the confident expectation that she would instantly sell them again? It had broken her heart to sell them once. . . . She drew a breath and lifted her gaze to Tucker's.

"I want the emeralds returned to Mr. Haviland first thing in the morning," she said evenly.

"Any message, miss?" Tucker inquired.

Her mouth twisted. " 'Go to hell' might be appropriate, but, no. No message."

Tucker picked up the bag, but hesitated. In his normal colorless voice, he said, "He could help you. With everything. It won't be easy, finding the cross."

Spencer had no secrets from Tucker, and he'd been an absolute godsend these past months. She had never viewed him as a servant, seeing him more as her father's friend and her own. If there was a rock of solid support and quiet understanding in her life, it was Tucker. He continued to run the house and to take care of her father as he'd always done, as well as quietly make her life as easy as he could. And though he was, and always had been, invariably formal in speech and behavior, he never hesitated to offer his opinion or advice when she asked. Or sometimes even when she didn't.

She half nodded in acknowledgment of what he'd said, and replied, "I know he could find the cross, but . . . I can't ask him to help me. Not him. Even if he'd agree to do it, which I doubt very much, I can't ask him. And I don't want him to know how bad things are."

"He noticed the missing paintings."

"Yes." She forced a rueful smile. "He had his own ideas about those, but it doesn't matter. All that matters is that I find the cross.

Dad's friend in Austria has talked to the authorities, and even though they don't believe I can do it, I have permission to bring the cross back here for Dad to see."

From what Drew had said, Spencer knew that he thought she was ignorant of international law and expected to be able to call the cross her own if she found it; why else would he make that remark about her selling it? Or else, she realized dismally, he thought her totally dishonest and believed she'd try to smuggle the relic out of Austria. But Spencer didn't consider the cross the answer to her financial problems, only a last gift to her father. And her biggest anxiety . . .

She looked at Tucker with unconsciously pleading eyes. "Dad will wait for me, won't he? He'll hang on long enough for me to find it and bring it back here?"

Tucker hesitated, then said quietly, "The doctors give him a few more months, but he's stronger now. Your plan to find the cross has given him a reason to fight."

It was all she could hope for—no guarantee, but at least a chance.

Spencer nodded and watched the old man turn back toward the door. Just before he left the room, she said, "Tucker? Have I thanked you?"

He looked back at her, the hint of a smile softening his stolid features. "Yes, miss," he said quietly.

She gazed at the closed door long after he'd gone, her own faint smile slowly dying. She was booked on a flight to Paris only a few days from now, and after that her journey would take her by train to Austria. She would arrive there virtually without money, driven to hurry because her father's health was precarious, and knowing no one there except an old friend of her father's who wouldn't even be in the area she had to search.

And if all that wasn't enough, now there was Drew. She had no doubt that he would make good on his promise to take her, a prospect that was both humiliating and painful but also something a longing part of her desperately wanted, if only . . . But she had thrown away his love once, and this was hardly a second chance for that. He meant to use her, to—what had he said?—hold her in thrall to him. And despite her knowledge of his motives, her ability to resist him sexually was nil. She'd gone to pieces when he kissed her, instantly mindless with pleasure and need, totally unable to resist what she had craved for so long.

And he knew. He knew she couldn't fight him. She wasn't smart enough to outthink him, or quick enough to outmaneuver him, or fast enough to outrun him. Her pride wouldn't let her surrender, yet her body already had, and she lacked his force, his will, his hatred. . . .

Spencer hated feeling inadequate. It was like her own personal nemesis, a sick, shamed feeling that dogged her steps constantly. She always seemed to be at the mercy of that painful emotion, and suddenly, knowing how easy it would be for Drew to destroy her, something snapped. All her weariness coalesced into a single, wildly fierce realization.

She was tired of it. Tired of feeling powerless and inept and somehow lacking. Tired of being afraid. And tired of being *tired*. All she could do was her best, and if that fell short of her own standards or someone else's, then so be it. She wasn't her mother. Elegance and assurance couldn't be borrowed or fashioned out of thin air—they had to be earned. She had her own strengths, and those would become apparent with time.

And if she couldn't fight Drew physically, she could at least struggle to have something left when he was through with her.

With that decided, Spencer felt strangely calm. No more pretense. She straightened in the chair, aware only then that she'd been slumping. One hand lifted to her hair, and she mentally pushed aside the unbidden image of Drew's hand there even as she wondered what Tucker had thought when he'd seen her. Probably, she realized, he had a very good idea of at least part of what had happened in this room, but he would, as usual, keep his thoughts to himself.

She got up and went around the desk, bending to collect the scattered hairpins. She left them among the cutter on the blotter, deciding not to try to put her hair back up. It was getting late and she wanted to sit with her father for a while before she went to bed. Tomorrow would be a long day, since her job began early in the morning; she was trying to put in as many hours as possible before she left.

She turned off the lights in the library and left the room, and for the first time she didn't notice the missing paintings in the foyer as she went steadily up the curving staircase.

"ARE YOU SURE he's ready?" Mike Bartlet asked the next morning as Spencer was leading her third mount of the day out into the big ring. "You've done wonders with him, but after that hellish fall he took, any jump higher than a foot makes him crazy with fear."

Spencer stroked the glossy chestnut neck of the young horse and smiled at his owner reassuringly. "He'll be fine. I want to take him over the jumps this week, and then we'll let him stay in his paddock until I get back. With no pressure and no show crowd to get on his nerves, he's already gotten a lot of his confidence back."

Bartlet smiled at her. It was almost impossible not to, because her smoky eyes and slow smiles were so direct and honest. She was such a little thing he'd initially objected to her handling his big, rawboned hunters, but the owner of this farm, where he boarded his horses, swore she had a special talent for gentling the ones that were bad tempered or that had picked up nasty tricks and habits. After several months of watching her work, Bartlet definitely agreed. She certainly knew what she was doing and the horses clearly loved her. Whether it was her soft, sweet voice or gentle touch, they responded to her in a way he'd never seen before.

A middle-aged man with a weather-beaten face and gruff manners, Bartlet found himself speaking softly around Spencer Wyatt. She had that effect, he'd noticed, on a lot of people. There was something very fragile about her despite the physical strength and endurance she showed with the horses, and people in her presence wanted to do things for her. Especially men. She could hardly lift a saddle without one of the grooms rushing over to help her, and even though she gently and firmly insisted on doing her own work, they kept right on trying.

She worked on a commission basis, being paid for each horse she handled. This farm was a large one with scores of boarders year-round, most of them hunters and many of them temperamental, and Spencer was easily the most popular trainer who worked here. She had a great deal of quiet confidence, and she was always even-tempered and friendly.

Bartlet liked her very much. And he worried about her. Though she never said much about herself and certainly never complained, he had the feeling that she was having a difficult time right now. Sometimes she arrived here with a look of strain around her fine eyes, and even though she seemed to forget her troubles while she worked with the horses, it bothered him.

Life should be good, he thought, for someone like Spencer. She was such a gentle lady. Sometimes he tried to make her laugh, just to hear the sweet sound and see her eyes light up.

"You be careful," Bartlet said now, unable to help himself.

She looked a little surprised, but nodded, and as he gave her a leg up into the saddle Bartlet reflected that she seemed to have no idea why people—especially men of all ages—wanted to watch over and protect her. He stood watching as she rode the big hunter

in an easy trot around the ring, then went back through the gate
to get out of her way and watch from outside the ring.

Spencer eased the hunter into his workout, allowing his muscles to warm and loosen in slow gaits and a series of limbering
turns. She spoke to him softly, watching his ears flick backward. At
first he hadn't wanted to pay attention to her, but after weeks of
rides he now responded as quickly to her voice as he did to her
knees and hands. Unlike many of her mounts, he had no vices; a
crashing fall in his first show had simply resulted in a bad case of
terror. It had taken her days to get him anywhere near a jump, but
her idea of turning him out into the jumping ring every night for
a week, alone and riderless, so that the fences could become familiar and unthreatening sights, had worked.

Now he trotted and cantered past imposing jumps with no sign
of fright, weaving in and out among them obedient to her guiding
touch, his gaits smooth. When she calmly put him to a very low
and simple jump, his ears pricked up and he took it in stride.

Praising him with her voice and a stroking hand, Spencer felt
a sense of heady accomplishment. She loved horses, and handling
them was the one thing she knew she did well. From the time her
father had set her atop her first pony twenty-five years earlier, it
had been a love affair. Until a few months ago she had never considered riding as work, but her position at this farm was one she
valued over and above the necessary earnings; she could be herself
here, with no need to pretend. Her abilities were genuine, and her
confidence in them secure.

For the next half hour she rode the powerful chestnut, gradually putting him to higher jumps—though she had mentally set a
limit of four feet. The only jump he seemed wary of was one re-
sembling the one he'd fallen at, an obstacle built to resemble a red
brick wall. Its height was set at three and a half feet, the top foot of
that made up of lightweight "bricks" that would dislodge easily

when bumped. Spencer had no doubt that the gelding could take the jump—it was his confidence that was in question. She was determined to try it, however, and lined him up with the fence steadily.

She felt his stride falter just a bit, a minute hesitation, saw his right ear flick back as she crooned softly, and then he gathered himself and easily cleared the fence.

Delighted, Spencer praised him, beginning to check his stride because the next fence was a bit higher and she wanted him to take it completely balanced. That was when she glanced aside, wanting to see Mike Bartlet's face at his horse's success.

Drew was standing beside him.

Spencer was never sure what happened then, although she blamed herself for it. Perhaps she tensed and jabbed at the gelding's sensitive mouth, or lost her balanced seat, or perhaps, with the peculiar ESP of horses, he sensed her sudden disturbance. In any case, the chestnut's stride broke awkwardly and he couldn't stabilize himself in time to attempt the jump looming in front of them. He tried to stop or shy away or both, and Spencer was unprepared for the sudden violent movements.

She went over his head and crashed into the fence.

chapter three

THE JUMP, LIKE all the others in the ring, had been designed with an eye to falling riders and horses. From the ground to a height of just over two feet the barrier was merely a line of neatly trimmed potted hedges, and above them two red-striped poles rested on pegs so that they'd be easily dislodged. If she had to fall, Spencer thought somewhat dizzily, this was one of the least dangerous jumps at which to do it.

However, she'd come off an unusually large horse moving at a fast gait, and even if bushes were relatively soft and wooden poles designed to give way when struck, the jarring contact with the ground was more than enough to knock the breath out of her. She had released the reins as she started to fall, partly because they were in a training ring where the chestnut would be confined and partly because she had a poor opinion of riders who dragged at the

mouths of their horses by throwing the whole weight of their
falling bodies against the reins.

It wasn't the first time she'd fallen, and it wouldn't be the last;
she had learned as a child how to fall with the least risk to herself.
Her jumping helmet protected her head, and though she was
vaguely aware that one of the poles had left its mark on the small
of her back, she was also reasonably sure that she hadn't broken or
seriously bruised anything. She didn't move right away, knowing
from experience that it was best to just remain still for a few moments and recover her breath and equilibrium.

She had turned a somersault in the air, landing flat on her back
on the far side of the jump with her head toward it, and found herself gazing up at a cloudless blue sky—and then a very worried
chestnut face. A slightly breathless laugh escaped her, and she
thought for perhaps the thousandth time that the animal experts
could say what they liked about people's tendency to accord horses
human emotions but anyone who knew a particular horse well was
convinced they felt emotions just like people. And any horse who
felt a bond with his chosen rider tended to get visibly upset when
he lost that rider. Spencer had known horses to express emotions
that varied from sheepish embarrassment to panicked anxiety
when they and their riders, from whatever cause, parted company.

The chestnut, Beau, was dismayed and anxious about her. She
would have tried to reassure him, but the involuntary laugh had
taken what little breath she could claim and she wasn't quite ready
to try moving yet. Though it felt like hours, only moments had
passed, and as she felt Beau's warm, grass-sweet breath and looked
up into his worried brown eyes, she heard quick steps approaching.
The horse was pushed back roughly, and Drew knelt beside her.

"Is she all right?" Mike Bartlet asked hoarsely as his face appeared on her other side.

Drew's long, powerful fingers, surprisingly gentle now, were methodically examining her arms and legs for injuries. Spencer gazed up at him and thought that he looked a little pale, but his voice was cool and steady when he replied to Mike.

"Nothing broken. I think she just had the wind knocked out of her."

"I'm fine," she managed, albeit in a breathless voice, as she struggled to sit up.

"Easy," Drew ordered, slipping an arm around her shoulders for support.

Spencer was glad of his assistance, because the motion of raising up made her head swim for a moment. "I'm fine," she repeated in a stronger voice, and then couldn't help but laugh. Beau, pushed back by Drew when the men reached her, kept trying to get his head down to her and was frustrated because Mike was holding the reins and trying to keep the horse away from her.

"Stay put," Drew said in a sharp voice, but she ignored that and got to her feet anyway. He rose with her, an arm still around her until he was sure she was steady.

Though she was honestly grateful for his aid, Spencer didn't waste any time moving away from him; she couldn't forget what had happened between them last night. So she stepped toward the horse, reaching out to stroke the velvety nose gently.

"It's all right, Beau, it was my fault," she murmured, taking the reins from Mike's relaxed grasp. "I threw you off balance, didn't I, boy?" She looked aside to Mike. "He didn't hit the fence, did he?"

Mike shook his head. "No, he went around. Spencer, are you sure you're all right? The way you hit that fence—"

Trying to reassure him, she said solemnly, "A forward one and a half out of the saddle. I'd give it a seven-point-six. At least two points off for not keeping my feet together."

He gave a short bark of a laugh, unwillingly amused. "And your arms were windmilling, too. Lousy form."

Spencer grinned at him. "Next time I'll try the forward pike position. Will you give me a leg up, please?"

"Hey, you don't have to—"

"Prove anything. I know. It's Beau I'm thinking about, Mike. I need to take him over a few jumps and then finish with this one, or he'll think it was his fault I came off." She kept her gaze determinedly on Mike. Drew wasn't saying a thing, and even though she was strongly aware of his presence just behind her, the last thing she wanted was to have her self-confidence threatened by his undoubted mockery.

Mike shook his head, but stepped up to give her a leg into the saddle. Spencer landed lightly and found her stirrups, gathering the reins as she settled into place.

"Put the bars back where they were," she said, still avoiding any glance at Drew. She waited for Mike's resigned nod, then turned the horse away from the jump.

She admitted honestly to herself that she was still shaken by the fall, and the stinging sensation across the small of her back told her there'd be a bruise there within hours, but Spencer also knew she had three more horses to ride today—and she quite literally couldn't afford to take time off just because she'd had a tumble. But it would have been much easier, she acknowledged silently, if Drew hadn't been watching. She knew he was, she could feel it, and it took all her concentration to block out the sensation of his eyes on her.

He owned horses, but kept none here, and she had the unnerving feeling he'd come here today only because someone—perhaps Tucker, she thought—had told him she was here. Was this how he meant to conduct his cat-and-mouse game? Showing up unexpectedly to remind her of his intentions? How could she cope with that tactic? And how could she keep her mind on her work when her eyes and her thoughts were continually drawn toward him?

She was too *aware* of him. Even though he was dressed to blend in here—a black leather jacket over a pale blue shirt and dark slacks—to her he still seemed to stand out vividly from everything around him. Despite ten years and everything that had happened to that eighteen-year-old girl, she still saw him as a man who was larger than life.

Spencer had to put it all out of her mind, at least for the moment. She rode the chestnut around the ring a couple of times to relax him, noting that Mike had replaced the bars of the jump as she'd asked and that both men had left the ring. Concentrating only on the horse beneath her and the jumps ahead, she put Beau to three low fences in succession, praising him softly when he took them in stride. Two more higher fences were jumped cleanly, and then she turned him smoothly to the jump where she'd fallen.

This time he was balanced perfectly, and his stride never faltered as he cleared the striped poles with a foot to spare.

She rode him around the ring a few more times, slowing him gradually. He was in superb condition and hadn't broken a sweat, but she wanted him completely relaxed when she dismounted. When she finally turned him toward the gate, he was moving in the easy, almost shambling walk of a naturally gifted hunter.

Drew opened the gate for her. Without looking at him, she said, "Where's Mike?"

"He had to leave to make an appointment," Drew said, cool and calm as usual. "He asked me to tell you that Traveler was running a light fever this morning, and the vet said to leave him stabled for the day."

Which meant she had two mounts left to ride today. Spencer nodded in acknowledgment and rode Beau toward one of the dozen spacious barns. She dismounted just inside the wide hallway, and cross-tied the horse to be unsaddled and groomed. Stable hands did that sort of work for some of the trainers, but Spencer preferred to do all the handling herself in order to build a stronger bond with her mounts.

She knew that Drew had followed her into the hall, and that he was leaning against the jamb of an open stable door as he watched her, but she still refused to look at him. She was afraid to look at him. She felt wary and threatened. Here at this farm, surrounded by horses and the people who worked with them, she was normally relaxed and confident; she counted on this place and her job for a much-needed note of success and triumph in her life. If she lost that, she wasn't sure she could recover from it.

He could take it away so easily. With his mockery, his deliberate cutting smiles, his contempt. Despite her decision after he had gone last night to simply do the best she could and stop pretending, she hadn't expected Drew to come here at all, much less so soon, and his presence disturbed her deeply.

"Bartlet said you'd been training for months now," Drew said suddenly as she carried her saddle past him to the tack room.

Spencer put the saddle on its stand and picked up a utility tray of brushes, waiting until she walked past him again to say simply, "That's right."

"Why?"

She pulled off her hard hat and riding gloves, setting both aside, then selected a brush and began grooming the big chestnut, vaguely aware that her entire back was now throbbing dully as a result of her fall. Ignoring the protesting twinges of bruised muscles, she brushed Beau in long, sweeping strokes and kept her attention fixed on the horse. "Why am I training? Because it's the only thing I'm good at. What are you doing here, Drew?"

"I came to return the emeralds," he said.

Spencer moved around to the other side of the horse so that the animal was between them; she couldn't look over his back and she was glad of that. "Not to me, you didn't. I sold them, you bought them—they're yours." A flicker of motion in the corner of her eye told her Drew had moved as well, obviously to watch her as they talked.

"A gesture of defiance, sweet?" he asked.

She paused in her work, one hand resting on Beau's relaxed shoulder and the other gripping the brush. She heard less mockery than there might have been in his voice, but the milder tone hardly made his question any better. And she couldn't help but wonder if this, too, was a part of his plan. Did he enjoy needling her? Did he derive some kind of satisfaction from her defensive denials even though he didn't believe a word she said?

Spencer's hesitation was brief. There was no way to convince him he was wrong about her, but she had decided last night never again to accept a role someone else wrapped around her and she clung to that determination even though she knew it left her terribly vulnerable where he was concerned. She began brushing the horse again, and said, "Not at all. The necklace doesn't belong to me anymore. Period." Her voice remained calm, and her grooming of the horse was firm and thorough.

"Not even as a gift?" More mockery this time.

"No." *Not from you.* "Now, if you don't mind, I have work to do."

There was a long silence, and then his voice came very softly. "Don't dismiss me, Spencer."

An alarm bell in her mind jangled warningly at the anger she heard, and she felt a dim surprise at how close to the surface his temper seemed to be. That was new, hardly part of the man she remembered, and it made her even more wary of him. She had the odd notion that from the moment he had touched her last night he had been just a bit out of control—as if some dam had cracked and the pressure of stormy floodwaters was widening the fissure. A fractured dam was dangerous.

So was a man who was a bit out of control.

Again she stopped grooming the horse, and this time she turned to face Drew. She met his flinty gaze steadily, and kept her voice calm, consciously trying to avoid anything that would sound like a challenge or provocation of any kind. "I'm sorry if I sounded autocratic. I didn't mean to. It's just that I have more than a day's work ahead of me. Work I'm paid to do."

"And you need the money," he said.

Spencer could detect no softening of his impassive features, but she hadn't expected to. "Yes," she said. "I need the money. I've run out of things to sell." Wishing she'd stopped herself before that last faintly bitter comment, she returned to grooming Beau.

Drew was silent while she continued with her work, and it wasn't until she set the brushes aside and started to untie the horse that he finally spoke. "How bad is it?"

There was no way she was going to tell him that, so she ignored the question totally. "You'd better stand back," she warned smoothly as she turned Beau toward the stable. "My next pupil isn't a gentleman."

She didn't look to see if Drew heeded the advice, but stabled the chestnut and then went on down the barn's wide hall to a stall at the far end. The horse she led out into the hall a moment later was a contrast to the placid Beau in almost every way. Formally named Intrepid Shadow on the papers listing his lengthy pedigree but fondly referred to as That Bloody Devil by all who knew him, the big stallion was pitch-black, rattlesnake mean, and hated everything that breathed with the exception of Spencer—whom he merely disliked.

He tried to bite her when she snapped the lead rope onto his halter but, inured to his ways, she evaded the wicked teeth and kept a wary eye on him as she led him out into the hall. As usual, he made a spirited attempt to bolt, rearing with a squeal of rage and lashing out with both forelegs, but she was ready for that as well and never lost control of him.

Spencer had learned a long time ago that in handling horses she could never hope to use physical strength in mastering half a ton of bundled nerves and muscle; what she depended on was quickness, skill and an intuitive understanding of how the equine mind worked. Devil was an angry creature, pure and simple, and to try either to contain that rage or to beat it into submission would have been a bad mistake. She did neither. She simply stayed out of his way when he lashed out, handled him quietly and firmly, and clung like a burr to his back once she was in the saddle.

By the time she had the big black horse cross-tied with relative safety in the hall, he had settled down a bit, but still presented the almost rigid, wild-eyed appearance of an animal on the fine edge of exploding. Drew had taken Spencer's advice, and was standing some feet away as he watched her begin grooming the horse.

"Are you out of your mind?" he asked, keeping his voice unusually soft. "That horse is a killer."

"Oh, you know him." She kept her own voice quiet, and her hands were steady as she brushed the glossy ebony neck. "It was never proven that he killed that trainer."

"Do you doubt it?"

"No," she replied somewhat wryly, very alert to Devil's tense stillness even as she appeared as relaxed as possible. "I don't doubt it."

"He should have been put down."

Spencer began humming softly, interrupting the soothing sound only to speak to Drew. "Maybe. His bloodline's priceless, and so far none of his foals have inherited his temper. Do you mind not talking for a little while? If I don't settle him down, he's going to erupt."

Drew forced himself to be silent, even though he badly wanted to swear good and loud. If Spencer had looked fragile beside the rawboned chestnut, the black made her look like a child—and a delicate one at that. One blow from the wicked animal could easily kill her, and it wouldn't take a fraction of a second for the horse to lash out.

She was humming, a soft, crooning sound that the stallion responded to with nervous flicks of his ears, her hands steady and relaxed as she groomed him. Drew wanted to yank her away, but he didn't dare move a step closer, because he knew that the horse hated men above all else and couldn't bear to have one near him. The white-rimmed eyes were fixed on the nearest man—Drew—now, and contained an almost palpable fury.

So Drew remained motionless, filled with the icy awareness that he was too far away to reach Spencer if anything were to happen. It was a helpless feeling, and he didn't like it. He didn't like anything he'd been feeling since arriving here a couple of hours before. First Bartlet, then Spencer's sudden fall and now this dangerous horse . . .

Drew knew Mike Bartlet by reputation—and he was reputed to be nobody's fool when it came to people. A hardheaded businessman who despised pretense and who could spot a phony across a crowded room, he had talked about Spencer in glowing terms. And not just regarding her expertise with his horses. Clearly, Bartlet had adopted her emotionally; he fretted over her apparent habit of skipping meals, her tendency to work long hours, her willingness to take on horses that other trainers wouldn't get near, and the strain he thought he saw in her eyes.

Drew had listened, increasingly disturbed by this picture of a woman he didn't know. He told himself that Bartlet had been deceived by Spencer, but the assurance held a hollow note. She was *here* after all, doing a relatively dirty and sweaty kind of work that demanded physical strength and endurance, considerable skill and endless patience. Hardly the sort of job for a spoiled, greedy hot-house flower reluctant to damage so much as a fingernail—espe-cially since Drew knew damned well her earnings here weren't a fraction of the allowance Allan had given her for years.

It didn't jibe, didn't fit his idea of her.

Then she had fallen, her slight body appearing terrifyingly fragile as it had catapulted from the big horse and crashed through the fence, and Drew didn't like to remember the sick feeling in his chest when he had watched that. The relief of finding out she was all right had been supplanted by surprise, because she had reacted to the fall with instant humor and self-blame, wasting no time in easing Bartlet's worry, soothing the horse and climbing back into the saddle.

Now she was just a few feet away, handling a deadly stallion that ninety-nine out of a hundred trainers wouldn't have taken on for any price, and she was doing such a good job that the animal was relaxing visibly, calming, becoming manageable. She even made it look easy, and Drew knew it wasn't.

Ten years ago, jilted without warning and left to make what sense he could, Drew had believed he'd figured her out. It had seemed to fit then, his idea of her. And if his conviction had been born in hurt and bitterness, it had still been based on the facts as he had seen them. Now . . . now he wasn't so sure. And he hated that uncertainty.

If he *was* wrong about her, there had to be things he didn't know—about her and about her motives in running away to marry another man. There had to be a *reason* she'd done it, and if not greed, then what? Love? Had she discovered that she'd loved Reece Cabot? The marriage hadn't lasted long, and several mem-bers of the Cabot family had heavily implied to friends and ac-quaintances that Reece had misjudged Spencer, foolish boy, and that they'd handled the problem for him.

A lie to save family pride? Had it been Spencer who had sought a divorce, bailing out of a bad situation and asking for nothing but her freedom?

Drew wasn't accustomed to feeling uncertain, and it had a gnawing effect on his temper. Wary of letting Spencer get to him and yet driven to find out for sure if he was right about her, he found himself examining every nuance of her voice and every fleeting expression he saw in her face.

He had needled her deliberately; she had reacted without either defensive venom or coldness. Her eyes were still unreadable, but he could see the strain as well as Bartlet had. And today there was none of the chin-in-the-air haughtiness that had the power to anger him so. She was subdued but not sulky, impersonal but not chilly. He thought she was wary of him even though there was no visible sign of it, and if she was disturbed by his expressed intention of taking what had been promised to him there was no indication of that, either.

As he watched her gradually calm the big black horse, Drew admitted to himself that he was the one who was disturbed—by her because she didn't seem to be what he had believed her to be, and by his own emotions and motives because both were tangled and unsure. The only thing he was absolutely certain of was that he wanted her, and that he intended to have her.

Even if she was a greedy little bitch.

THE MAN LOOKED like any other of the dozen or so owners who happened to be at the farm that day. He was casually dressed, and wandered from training ring to training ring intently watching the horses being worked. Everyone who saw him merely assumed that he belonged there, so his presence wasn't challenged.

Spencer probably wouldn't have noticed anything unusual about the watcher even if she'd seen him. She had focused her entire attention on Devil in an attempt to block out her unnerving awareness of Drew, and didn't notice the man or his covert interest. Drew was watching her too intently to realize that the two of them were under observation. If he had noticed the man at all, he would have been suspicious; with ten years spent in pursuit of antiquities in some very rough areas of the world, Drew had developed a keen sense of potential danger and could usually sense watching eyes.

This time, however, he sensed no threat.

The man continued to watch them unobtrusively, moving within the general area so that he didn't remain in any one place too long. From the shadowy interior of a barn hall, he saw Spencer ride the black stallion into one of the training rings, his gaze straying to Drew, who stood at the fence watching her. He studied Drew for long minutes, then checked his watch and eased away toward the parking area.

He used the phone in his car to place a call, and as soon as the connection was made said, "There may be a problem."

"What is it?"

"She has a visitor today—and I don't think he came here to see the horses."

"So? With her looks, it'd be a little strange if she *didn't* have men coming to see her."

The man in the car grimaced slightly. "There's no love lost between these two, believe me. I've seen blood enemies that were friendlier."

"What's your point?"

"My point is that her visitor is Drew Haviland."

There was a long silence, then a soft oath.

The man in the car nodded to himself. "Yeah. From what I've heard, he isn't a man to make a fool of himself over a woman, but he's gone a hell of a lot farther than Austria to pick up a nice new bauble for his collection."

"You think he knows about the cross?"

"Look, all I can tell you is what I've seen. He showed up late last night at the Wyatt house, and when he left I wouldn't have wanted to get in his way. Something had him ticked off plenty. He's been here for hours. He and the girl aren't saying much to each other, but he's watching her like a hawk. So you tell me."

"I don't know—but I don't think we can take any chances. It would have been easier and safer to let her find the cross for us and bring it back here, but if Haviland knows she's going after it he could complicate things."

"That's an understatement," the man in the car muttered. "You know his rep as well as I do—if he gets a good look at Wyatt's papers, you might as well kiss the cross goodbye. Even worse, if she won't let him see them and he decides to tag along after her, we won't be able to get close enough to grab the cross."

"You sound a bit intimidated, Clay."

The mockery had no effect on Clay, who merely said, "I count myself handy in a fight, but you aren't paying me enough to take on Haviland. I had it from somebody who knows—the man can handle himself and gets a bit touchy when you try to take things away from him."

"That's assuming he gets his hands on the cross before we do."

"You changing the plan?"

"I don't want to take any chances. We need Wyatt's papers. Can you get in and get them?"

"Piece of cake, I told you that before. But even if we can figure out where the cross is, getting it out of Europe is going to be hell. The girl has permission to bring it back here, but we certainly don't."

"You worry too much, Clay. We'll get the cross out. It'll take more time and effort, but we'll get it."

"What about the girl? When the papers come up missing, she'll know someone else is interested in the cross."

"Spencer Wyatt," his employer said contemptuously, "is no threat to us no matter what she knows. And Haviland won't be as long as we get to Austria ahead of him. Just get the papers, Clay. Tonight."

"Yeah, all right," Clay responded, then added, "but I think I'll make it look like a common robbery just to be a little safer."

"Suit yourself. Can you watch those two the rest of the afternoon?"

Clay frowned a little as he stared through the windshield. "Depends. The way Haviland's watching her, I doubt he's even seen me—but I could get real visible if he took a look around. I'll have to play it by ear."

"Stay there if you can. If not, come back here. She'll go straight home after she's finished for the day, won't she?"

"Always does. And she doesn't go out at night. Crying shame, if you ask me."

"I didn't ask you."

"Right."

"Check in later."

"Right," Clay repeated, and broke the connection. He sat in his car a few minutes longer, frowning, feeling a growing uneasiness. He didn't like wild cards, and from all he'd heard Drew Haviland was definitely that. And though his boss might have a poor opinion of Spencer Wyatt, Clay had his doubts about that, too. He'd watched the lady handle people and horses over the past weeks, and he thought there just might be both smarts and steel underneath her delicate exterior.

He was beginning to wish he'd never hired on for this job.

"IT'S PAST TWO," Drew said when Spencer had finally stabled a much more relaxed Devil. "Don't you eat lunch?"

Spencer automatically glanced at her watch, but she was already heading toward another stall when she answered. "I'm not hungry."

Drew took two long strides and caught her arm, pulling her around to face him. "According to Bartlet you've been here since seven this morning, and I haven't seen you take a break during the past five hours."

Very conscious of his grip on her arm, of the way he towered over her despite the high heels of her riding boots, and of her own weariness, Spencer found it very difficult to keep her voice steady and calm. But she tried. She did try. "I haven't taken a break because I haven't needed one."

"Are you lying out of habit, or do you just want me to feel sorry for you?" he snapped.

She jerked free of his grasp, wanting to back away from him but holding her ground. Ignoring the taunt, she said, "I have one more horse to ride today. Will you please let me do my job?"

"Answer my question," he ordered flatly, both his hands catching and holding her shoulders with a force that stopped just short of pain.

She could feel her control slipping. All during the hours he'd been there she had felt it diminish, seeping away from her relentlessly, until now it was not more than a thin veneer. He'd said very little, but she had felt his eyes on her, heard in her mind all the unspoken mockery and had waited with a kind of numb apprehension for him to start cutting at her.

Waiting for it had been worse, she thought, than coping with it would have been. The tension of being certain that he was going to start needling her any moment had destroyed her tenuous peace. She'd found no comfort in working with the horses today, no sense of achievement or triumph. She just felt sore all over from her fall earlier, unusually tired, and her nerves were so raw she was very afraid she'd burst into tears any moment.

But not in front of him. Please, God, not in front of him.

In a carefully steady voice that betrayed more than she knew, she said, "I'm not lying, Drew. I'm not hungry, and I don't want to take a break. I just want to get Corsair out of his stall and saddle him up and take him over the jumps. Please let go of me so I can do that."

A frown drew his brows together, and his eyes probed her face so sharply that she almost felt them cut her. "The horse can wait," he said, his tone a little rough. "You may not want to admit it, but you'd have a hard time lifting a saddle right now."

Spencer didn't hear concern in that statement; she heard criticism, and it easily pierced what was left of her self-control. "Don't," she murmured, hating the thready sound of her voice but unable to steady it. "You're entitled to your revenge—at least from your point of view—but not this, please."

"What are you talking about?" Drew demanded, his frown deepening.

"I need this. The horses, the people here . . . Don't ruin it for me." Spencer had the most peculiar feeling of distance, as if she were floating away from him. Light-headed. That was it, she decided vaguely. It had come over her all of a sudden and she was puzzled by the sensation. She also didn't understand why she couldn't stop talking, but her mouth seemed to have a mind of its own. "I have to have this, or I couldn't do the rest. It isn't much, you can let me have this, can't you? You don't have to destroy everything, I didn't do that to you . . ."

"Spencer, did you eat breakfast?"

She frowned up at him. "I wasn't hungry. Let go of me now. I have to get Corsair—"

Drew said something extremely violent under his breath, then put a hard arm around her and led her out of the barn. He was moving her along so rapidly that Spencer felt even more dizzy, and it wasn't until he put her in the passenger seat of a racy-looking sports car that she managed to protest.

"I can't leave now. I have to—"

"Be quiet," Drew said roughly, folding his length easily behind the wheel and starting the engine with a roar.

She thought maybe she'd better be quiet, because he looked very angry. For twelve years she had thought him an utterly calm, even unemotional man, and she wondered now how she could have believed that. Surely there'd been signs, indications that the unruffled surface of his was misleading? Why hadn't she seen that? Had Reece's bright, temperamental glitter blinded her to *everything?*

She was still thinking about that, her mind locked methodically in a single puzzling track, when Drew parked the car in the lot of a small restaurant. He got out and came around to open her door, then took her arm firmly when she rather carefully got out.

"I'm not dressed," she protested as he led her toward the entrance.

"Of course you're dressed." His voice was calm again, but curiously controlled, as if the composure was deceptive.

"I mean I'm not dressed right," she tried to explain. "You have to dress right, so people think you belong. I'm wearing riding clothes, not—" She broke off abruptly, finally hearing the little voice in her head that was telling her to shut up before she made a total fool of herself.

She didn't say another word while an attentive hostess conducted them to a booth in the back of the nearly deserted restaurant, and she didn't realize that Drew had ordered for both of them until a glass of milk was placed in front of her. She frowned at it.

"Drink it," he said quietly.

Spencer had never been very good at following autocratic orders—probably because of her father's indulgence—but every instinct now told her it would be safer to do as Drew ordered. She picked up the glass and began sipping the milk, watching him steadily. The light-headedness she'd been aware of faded by the time she finished the milk, and she slowly realized that skipping meals had finally caught up with her. No breakfast this morning, and she'd only picked at her dinner last night—no wonder she'd felt so peculiar.

He probably thought she was making a ploy for his sympathy. The way he was watching her, she couldn't be sure. Her gaze skittered away from his and fixed itself on the polished tabletop as she tried to fight the hot surge of embarrassment.

"Better?" he asked, still quiet.

She nodded. "Thanks. Sorry I made a fool of myself."

"You didn't. But you did say a few things you're going to have to explain."

Spencer glanced up at him fleetingly, then looked away again. "I don't think—"

"Not now," he interrupted. "After we've eaten."

She didn't have the energy to protest. Instead, she sat silently until the food arrived, then began eating. She couldn't have said later what she ate, and she still didn't feel at all hungry, but ate simply because her body and Drew thought she needed food. And she did feel better for it. He ate as well, watching her from time to time, but said nothing until they finished the meal.

Their waitress came to take the plates and offer dessert—which both Spencer and Drew refused—and coffee. They accepted the coffee, and Spencer was once more conscious of her worn and somewhat dusty riding clothes as she watched the pretty blond waitress smile at Drew. To be tall and blond like him, that's what she had wanted all those years ago. To have blue eyes instead of her indeterminate gray—

She cut the thoughts off sharply, determined to teach herself to stop thinking like that. Especially around Drew. "Now," he said as the waitress reluctantly went away with her coffeepot, "I think we have a few things to discuss."

Spencer shook her head a little. "Whatever I said back there at the farm isn't important. You were right. I needed a break and something to eat. I didn't know what I was saying."

He ignored that. "You said that you had to have this—meaning your work at the farm—or you couldn't do the rest. What did you mean by that, Spencer?"

She'd promised herself she wouldn't lie to him, wouldn't pretend to be anything she wasn't, but she didn't want him to know how bad things were. "Just—coping. Dad's illness. Having to take care of things. That's all."

"Financial problems?"

"Nothing I can't handle," she said stubbornly.

His eyes narrowed slightly, but instead of persisting he said, "You said you supposed I was entitled to my revenge. And the bit about me ruining your work, destroying everything? What did you mean?"

Spencer managed a shrug. "You made it pretty plain last night that you're out to . . . even the score. I just—I'm asking you not to mock me or belittle my work." Her gaze dropped to her coffee cup. "I know you probably think it's hilarious, to say nothing of trivial, but I—I enjoy working with horses, and I'm good at it. It's the only time I feel . . . Well, never mind."

"I never said it was hilarious or trivial."

She shrugged again. "When you showed up this morning, I expected you to say something like that."

"Because I want revenge?"

"It wasn't difficult to figure out. I can't—I can't fight you with words, Drew, you use them too well. I found that out last night."

chapter four

"SO I STRUCK a nerve or two," he said.

"Weren't you trying to do just that?" When he remained silent, she looked up at him suddenly. "Maybe I deserved it, maybe I deserved everything you said to me."

"Don't you know if you deserved it?" he asked with a trace of mockery in his voice.

Spencer wondered what she really thought about that, but shook her head a little and said, "It doesn't matter. The only thing that matters to me right now is finding the cross, and if you intend to interfere with that—"

"Wait a minute," he interrupted, frowning. "You aren't seriously planning to try to find the cross?"

"I know you thought it was a terrific joke," she said evenly, "but I wasn't kidding. My father believed the cross existed when no one else did, and I am *not* going to let him die without know-ing he was right."

"You don't know that he was right about it. And even grant-ing its existence, experts *have* looked for the thing without luck. For God's sake, Spencer, think a minute. Even if you had a hope in hell of finding the cross—which you don't—just how do you pro-pose to get it out of Austria? In case you don't know, it would be considered a national treasure."

She laughed softly, but it wasn't a sound of amusement. "I guess I'm not as stupid as you think I am. I have permission from the authorities in Austria to bring the cross back here for Dad to see. They'll arrange transport as soon as I can find the cross, and provide a courier to keep me honest. No matter what you believe, I don't intend to try to keep the thing for myself."

If anything, Drew's frown had deepened, and his gaze was very sharp. "What did you tell the authorities?"

Spencer wondered why it mattered, but shrugged and an-swered anyway. "I told them I'd gone over Dad's papers, and I thought I had a good chance of finding the cross. An old friend of Dad's works for the government over there, and he vouched for me. Like you, they don't believe I can do it, but they're willing to stand ready just in case."

After a moment Drew said, "According to your itinerary, you leave Monday morning."

She remembered then that the itinerary had been jotted down on the topmost sheet of the legal pad on her father's desk, and re-membered Drew studying it when she'd come into the study last night. From what he'd said then, she had decided that he hadn't seen anything important, but she wondered now if he'd seen all he needed to. He would know where she was going.

She tried to concentrate. Did he hate her enough that he would go after the cross himself, or somehow take it away from her if she found it, just for spite? If he found the cross it would certainly gild his already world-renowned reputation, and that success might appeal even more to him than the cross itself. And besting her would be revenge of a sort.

"Spencer?"

She didn't know what kind of game he was intent on playing. He had voiced a promise to take her, to make her surrender to him completely, yet today he seemed—what? Less forceful somehow, less definite in his intentions. He had even been kind in a sense, bringing her here and making certain she ate something. But had his motives changed, or was he simply playing a more subtle and ultimately more destructive game of cat and mouse?

"Yes," she said finally. "I leave Monday."

"And your contact in Austria knows that?"

What was he getting at? "Of course he knows."

"That may not have been a smart move, Spencer." For once, he seemed totally serious and not at all mocking. "The experts might have laughed at Allan, but I know a dozen collectors who've just been waiting for someone to find the cross, and more than one of them wouldn't hesitate to kill in order to get it."

It was a new idea to her, and she wondered if he was just trying to scare her enough that she wouldn't search for the cross. Still . . . this was far more his area of expertise, and perhaps it was a sincere warning. She just didn't know.

Managing a light tone, she said, "Even if those collectors somehow heard that I was going after the cross, I doubt they'd have any more faith in my ability to find it than you do."

After a long moment he said, "That does rankle, doesn't it?"

"Your opinion of my abilities?" Spencer pushed her empty coffee cup away and leaned back, wondering if her smile looked as strained as it felt. "If it gives you any sense of triumph to hear it, yes. I don't suppose anyone likes being considered a stupid and talentless fool."

Drew seemed to hesitate, then reached across the table suddenly and grasped one of her hands. "Why do you want to find the cross, Spencer?" he asked flatly.

She tried to pull her hand away, but abandoned the attempt when his grip tightened. The touch of him was instantly disturbing, and she answered his question automatically as she tried to cope with the response of her body to even so casual a contact with him. "For Dad. It's the only thing I can give him before he dies, and I have to . . . Please let go of me." The expression in his eyes bothered her. It was almost distant, as if he were listening to some far-off sound.

Somewhat to her surprise he did release her hand, and when his eyes focused on her face again they were almost angry.

"Damn you," he said softly.

Spencer nervously brushed at a strand of hair on her forehead that had come loose from the neat braid, and then laced her fingers tightly together in her lap. Why did she feel suddenly more threatened than ever? It was as if he was somehow closer than he'd been before, looming, and she couldn't hide from him. Damn her? Damn *him* for making her feel so vulnerable.

Holding her voice steady, she said, "I should be getting back to the farm. The horses are fed at six, and I need to work with Corsair before then."

"You should quit for the day." It wasn't an order, but a flat statement, and before she could say anything he went on in the same level tone. "Today's Friday. If you seriously intend to go to Europe on Monday, you need to rest, Spencer. Be sensible."

He was right, and that didn't make the knowledge any more palatable. She half nodded and slid from the booth. "Will you take me back to that farm, please? I need to get my car."

Drew didn't seem surprised by her acquiescence. If anything, he was matter-of-fact as he joined her. "Fine. Then I'll follow you back to the house. I'd like to see Allan."

"No!" She got a grip on herself, knowing her voice had been too sharp, the refusal too adamant; she was still wary of provoking him. "He—doesn't see anyone," she murmured, watching Drew toss a few bills onto the table.

Drew didn't say anything in response to that until they were in his car on the way back to the farm a few moments later, and when he did speak his voice was calm. "A lie to keep me away from him, Spencer?"

"I'm not a liar," she said, wondering if he would ever believe that. "Dad doesn't see anyone. He doesn't want anyone to see *him*, don't you understand? He's very thin and—and weak, and the stroke affected his speech. He'd hate it if you saw him. Especially you. He thought a lot of you."

After glancing at her briefly, Drew said, "Did you tell him I came to the house last night?"

"No."

"Does he know you're going after the cross?"

Spencer hesitated. "He knows."

Drew glanced at her again. "But?"

"But nothing. He knows, that's all." She wasn't about to tell Drew that a couple of weeks earlier her father had gotten it into his head that she would have help in her search for the cross, and that the help would be Drew. That was one reason he was confident she could find it. With Drew helping her, he'd said, she was sure to find the cross. After the first moment of shock, she had just assumed that her father's mind had drifted into the past, because it sometimes did that. Still, she'd been more unnerved than she might otherwise have been when Drew had shown up at the house last night.

"You can't go alone," Drew said.

She started slightly. "What? Of course I can. I've been to Europe before."

"That isn't the point. Spencer, weren't you listening when I talked about those collectors? If word gets out—and it will, it always does—that there's even a chance the cross could be located, things could get very nasty for you."

"I can take care of myself," she said stubbornly, even though she wasn't at all sure of that.

"Can you handle a gun?"

The flat question made a chill run down her spine. "If you're trying to scare me—"

His glance this time was impatient and something else, something she couldn't identify. "I hope to God it's working. You should be scared. That cross is worth millions—people have been murdered for a hell of a lot less."

Spencer didn't want to think about that; after all, what could she do except be cautious? But what he was saying caught her interest in another way. Curious, she said, "That sounds like the voice of experience. Surely you haven't had to deal with violent people in building your own collection?"

"Once or twice," he replied, definitely impatient now. "Spencer—"

"I can't imagine you in violent situations," she said. "You were always so cool and calm. I mean, I knew you went to some pretty out-of-the-way places looking for antiquities, but I never thought of you carrying a gun. Have you?"

"Yes, I've carried a gun. Quite often. And before you ask, I've had to use it a few times."

Spencer stared determinedly through the windshield, just stopping herself from wincing at the sharpness of his voice. "Sorry I asked. I know your life's none of my business."

Cool and calm, Drew thought, wondering what had happened

to those qualities. He sighed roughly. "No, I'm sorry. I didn't mean to bite your head off. But my past isn't important. Your immediate future is the point right now. You have to take this seriously, Spencer. Some of the people who collect antiquities are very dangerous. They'll stop at nothing to get what they want. You'll be a long way from home, in an unfamiliar situation, and you don't know the players. You could get hurt."

"If you're trying to demolish my confidence," she said a bit shakily, "congratulations on doing a good job."

Drew swore under his breath and abruptly pulled the car off the road just yards from the farm's driveway. He killed the engine and turned to face her, his expression a little tight. "We do seem to read the worst into each other's motives, don't we?"

The car was small, and with his entire attention focused on her it felt even smaller to Spencer. She was already unnerved by what he had said and done last night; his mercurial moods today had served only to confuse her further. She couldn't *not* suspect his motives. Very conscious that only the gear console separated them in the enclosed space of the car, she shrugged defensively and looked at him with wary eyes.

"Dammit, Spencer, I know what I'm talking about when it comes to collectors. Can you accept that?"

"Yes, I can accept it. I can even accept that you're probably right and I'm in over my head." She drew a short breath. "But that doesn't change a thing. I am going after the cross, and nothing you could say to me would make any difference. So why don't *you* accept that?"

"Because you're doomed to fail. You should spend Allan's last days with him, not haring off on a wild-goose chase."

She stared at him for a frozen moment, then said softly, "Thanks a lot. Add guilt to the rest. You really do know where to stick the knife, don't you?"

Drew looked at her white face, still seeing the flash of anguish that had briefly darkened her eyes, and for the first time didn't question his reading of her emotions. She was haunted by the fear that her father would die while she was far away in a foreign country searching for a myth.

"God, I'm sorry," he muttered, reaching over the console to grasp her shoulders. "I didn't mean—Spencer, I wasn't trying to hurt you."

"Sure." She shifted a little as if to dislodge his hands, then said in the same stiff voice, "If you'll let go of me, I'll get out here. You don't have to drive to the barns."

The past twenty-four hours had been unsettling ones for Drew. Stepping back into Spencer Wyatt's life had opened a Pandora's box of gnawing, unresolved emotions, and he hadn't been able to find a calm balance among them. Last night he had believed that simply taking what belonged to him—her—and making her surrender to him completely would satisfy him, but today he had faced the knowledge that it wouldn't be that simple.

He was angry, worried and frustrated, and talking was doing nothing except exacerbate the situation. Their mistrust made them both believe the worst no matter what was said.

"Dammit, Spencer . . ." Hating the withdrawn look in her eyes and the masklike stillness of her face, he pulled her toward him suddenly and covered her mouth with his.

Spencer wanted to fight him. She wanted to remain stiff and unresponsive, for the sake of her pride if nothing else. But she couldn't. At the first touch of his warm, hard mouth, a dizzying wave of pleasure washed over her with stunning force, and the hands that had lifted to push against his chest lingered instead to clutch the edges of his open jacket. She barely felt the steel teeth of the zipper bite into her fingers.

All her thoughts were submerged, drowned by physical and

emotional sensations so powerful they bordered on pain. It was as if he had opened a door to the part of her she had shut away long ago, releasing the wild storm of feelings she'd never been able to control. And couldn't now. Nothing mattered but him and what he made her feel, nothing at all. Every nerve and instinct her body could claim came alive, and the empty ache inside her was a hunger so vast it was like madness. Was madness.

She wondered later where it would have ended if there hadn't been an interruption. But the loud blaring of a car horn jerked them apart as a convertible filled with teenage boys roared past, and Spencer found herself staring dazedly through the wind-shield at the retreating car and the laughing faces turned back toward them.

Drew said something violent, his voice hoarse, then started the engine with a slightly jerky motion. He didn't say another word until he pulled the car into the lot near the barns and stopped, and when he did speak his voice was still a bit strained. "At least there's one thing we don't fight about."

Spencer reached for the door handle and had one foot out of the car when he caught her wrist.

"Admit it, Spencer."

Her breathing and heartbeat were just beginning to settle down to something approaching normal and she felt feverish from head to toe, and she did *not* want to say anything at all because she knew her voice would be treacherously unsteady. But she also knew he was determined for her to say what he wanted to hear. Without looking at him, she merely said, "Yes."

"It's just a matter of time. You know that."

"Yes," she repeated softly.

His fingers tightened around her wrist, then suddenly released her. She got out of his car and closed the door, then walked steadily to the barn where she'd left her hard hat and gloves. She didn't look back, even when she heard the sports car roar away with an angry sound.

Once inside the cool, shadowy barn hall, she leaned back against a closed stable door and shut her eyes. For the first time she understood why she had felt nervous and threatened around him all those years ago. It was because her deepest instincts had known then what her mind only now accepted as truth—and understanding made it no less frightening.

She was lost when he touched her, instantly his with no will to save herself. From the first time she had looked into his eyes she had been tied to him, had belonged to him on some deep, almost primitive level of herself. Perhaps it had happened because she had been so young, had fallen in love so desperately, or perhaps it had happened simply because it was meant to. For whatever reason, she had known she was his. It was a knowledge deeper than instinct or reason, a certainty that was ancient and without question. So simple. And so terrifying.

She had known it even ten years ago, even though his restraint had kept her from losing control then. With him her instinct was to give, whatever he asked, more than he asked, to relinquish even her own identity and let him take that as well. Her mind had rebelled ten years ago, too immature to understand except subconsciously that to give all that she was to him would destroy her unless he gave of himself as freely.

She hadn't believed he could—or would—do that. So cool and calm, so controlled, he had seemed untouchable to her, and the subconscious terror of being lost forever within his detachment had driven her to run from him. And she had run to another man, a man who had demanded nothing of her except that she be the focus of his tempestuous captivation.

She couldn't run again. Spencer knew that, knew the uselessness of it. Because this time he meant to have her. He was risking nothing, not even his pride, and that lack of any vulnerability would make him relentless. She knew he could be relentless now, and she knew she couldn't fight him.

As he had said, it was just a matter of time.

WHEN TUCKER WOKE her up very early Saturday morning with the news that the house had been robbed in the night, Spencer's first emotion was wry amusement. Robbed? There was nothing of value left, only copies of priceless things, and wouldn't the burglar be staggered to discover that?

"What did he take?" she asked Tucker as they walked down the hallway toward the stairs.

In a precise tone, Tucker replied, "Everything he could carry, I would say. Including the contents of your father's safe."

Spencer stopped at the head of the stairs and looked at him, her faint amusement vanishing. "You mean the papers? The set of copies I made of all Dad's papers?"

"Yes."

She began to feel just a little chilled. "How was the safe opened?"

"Professionally," Tucker replied without expression.

"And the security system?"

"None of the alarms were triggered, but the system's still active. I don't know how he got in."

Though it had been expensive to install, the security system of the house cost little to maintain and Spencer hadn't been forced to shut it down. Her father had once told her that no security system was foolproof, that if a burglar wanted to get in badly enough he would, but that both insurance companies and home owners slept better with the illusion that valuables were protected. Even though she had little to protect these days, Spencer had slept better thinking that at least a burglar would have to work at it to get into the house.

Now she knew what her father had meant about illusions.

But even that disturbed her less than the fact that the papers had been taken. Burglars who took artworks and emptied out the silver drawer seldom bothered with papers that were quite obviously without intrinsic value. Stock certificates or bonds were one thing—but handwritten notes, drawings and maps were something else again.

Spencer couldn't help but remember what Drew had warned her about, and a few moments later as she stood with Tucker in her father's study, a fatalistic certainty crept over her. The safe, on the wall at right angles to the desk, was cunningly and quite well hidden behind the face of a working clock. It was open, obviously empty, and nothing had been damaged through carelessness or inexperience. As Tucker had said, a professional job all the way.

Almost to herself, she murmured, "He didn't even try to open the trick safe behind the painting."

"No," Tucker agreed.

In a bit of sleight of hand meant hopefully to fool anyone looking for valuables, her father had installed a far more obvious or "trick" safe behind a hinged painting above his desk. The theory was that a thief would quickly discover that safe, find it empty and conclude that nothing of value was hidden in the room. But their night visitor had indicated contempt for the trick: the painting was pulled out away from the safe and no attempt to open it had been made.

Of course, he might have opened and then closed the safe—but Spencer didn't think so. Everything else he had opened remained open: the other safe, desk drawers, the silver drawer in the pantry and the few curio and collectible cabinets that had held mostly worthless figurines. No, he had wanted them to know that he saw through the trick.

Spencer was very glad he'd found nothing of value, and even

more glad that the originals of her father's papers were safely in a bank vault and that a second set of copies she'd made was upstairs in her bedroom. But she was very much afraid that whoever had broken into the house last night had been after only one thing. The papers. The cross.

Softly she said, "If he was professional enough to bypass the security system, find the safe and get into it without fuss, don't you think he would have known that the silver was plated, and the figurines and prints were worthless?"

Almost as quietly, Tucker answered, "I would think so."

"Then he was after Dad's papers, and the rest was just to cover up his real target." Spencer shivered a little, for the first time seriously wondering if she would risk more than simple failure in going after the cross. "Somebody could be a step ahead of me."

"Someone dangerous. Miss Spencer, some collectors are ruthless in acquiring what they desire. You have no experience of that kind of person—"

"Tucker." She half turned to stare at him. "Don't you start, please. I've already heard enough from Drew. This theft doesn't change anything except that I have to move faster." Very deliberately, she added, "If I fail, I fail. But I won't spend the rest of my life regretting that I never even tried."

After a moment Tucker said, "The cross isn't worth dying for. Your father would never forgive himself if that happened."

"It won't happen."

"I know you, Miss Spencer. I know how much this means to you. I believe you'll find the cross, where it's lain hidden all these years or in the hands of someone who got there first. But I also believe that it won't be easy, and it will be dangerous. I don't want you to forget that you mean more to your father than anything else in the world. He'd be the first to consign that cross to hell to spare you pain."

It was a long speech for Tucker, and it left Spencer without very much she could say. So she merely nodded and said, "I know that, believe me. Don't worry—I'll be careful." Since his face was expressionless as usual, she wasn't sure if he had any faith in that promise, but he half nodded before speaking again.

"I haven't called the police yet."

"Don't. Not until I've gone. I can't afford to be tied up here answering questions all day. And don't mention the papers to them, just the other stuff. I doubt they'll be much interested anyway, since we didn't lose anything of value."

Characteristically, Tucker picked up on the important part of what she'd said. "You'll leave today, then?"

"If I can get a flight to Paris." More money, she was thinking worriedly, and no guarantee that she wouldn't have to wait until Monday for the train to Austria. But what choice did she have? Even though the papers had been stolen, she still had an advantage—she hoped—if she moved quickly enough. It had taken her two months to piece the clues together, and even someone with expert knowledge would have to study all the papers carefully in order to figure it out. Her father had been too close, too familiar with his own work, to see the pattern. With luck it would take anyone else at least a little time to figure it out.

"What about Mr. Haviland?" Tucker asked.

"He isn't a part of this, I told you that."

After a moment Tucker said, "Can you afford pride?"

The quiet question was too pointed to ignore, and Spencer managed a twisted smile. "No. But it isn't just pride. What I did to him was unforgivable, and he has no reason to want to help me now. He has plenty of reason to want to hurt me—I won't let him use the cross as a weapon."

"Would he do that?"

Spencer shrugged a little, because she just wasn't sure, then said, "I'd better go start making phone calls and finish packing. If Dad asks for me, tell him I'll be up later to see him."

"Very well."

Luck was with Spencer, though by this point she wasn't sure if it was good luck or bad. In any case, she was able to book a seat on an early-afternoon flight to Paris. It meant a scramble to finish packing and take care of the other last-minute details that always accompany a trip, but at least the haste had kept her mind occupied and distracted her from thoughts of Drew and worries about who else was after the cross.

It was a little after noon when she went into her father's bedroom. There was less time to say goodbye than she would have liked, especially since his health was so precarious, and the guilt of leaving him for days at least and possibly weeks ate at her.

She slipped into the wingback chair by his bed, nodding to the nurse, who took the opportunity to slip out and take a break. Spencer sat silently for a few moments, looking at her father as he dozed, her heart wrung as always because of the change in him since the stroke.

Physically, Spencer had inherited more from her small-boned and delicate mother than from her father, but she had gotten his black hair and gray eyes. Allan Wyatt had been a big, bluff, hearty man, the strength of his very active youth remaining with him well into his sixties, but now he was a gaunt shadow of the man he had been. His thick hair, only lightly graying before the stroke, was now almost pure white, and flesh had melted from his big frame. The stroke had completely paralyzed his right side, dragging down the corners of his mouth and eye, slurring his speech, and both his concentration and memory were erratic from moment to moment.

He had been more alert during the past weeks, seemingly because Spencer had been making her plans to go after the cross, but his doctors had warned her that there was little chance of a recovery.

His eyes opened suddenly, fixing on her and gradually clearing of most of the fog. "Hi, Princess," he murmured, his deep voice so distorted that only Spencer, Tucker and the nurse would have understood him.

"Hi, Daddy." She smiled at him, reaching for his left hand as his fingers uncurled invitingly. "Did Tucker tell you? I'm leaving for Paris in just a little while."

The gray eyes brightened. "That's what he said. You're—going after the cross."

She nodded. "It's all arranged. A flight to Paris and then a train to Austria."

"Should fly—all the way," he muttered, a slight frown creasing his brow. "Into Vienna. Why train?"

Not wanting him to know that money was one of her biggest problems, she said soothingly, "I'll be able to see more from a train, you know. I've never been to Austria, and it's supposed to be so beautiful. But I promise not to spend too much time sight-seeing."

A ghost of a laugh escaped him. "See it while you're there. Never know when—there'll be another chance. Always—take advantage of your—opportunities, Princess. I remember—the first time I was there. . . ."

Spencer listened with a smile as he talked about a long-ago visit on the eve of a war, just before the borders had been closed. She knew the story well and was short on time, but wouldn't have interrupted him for anything, cherishing every moment she could spend with him now. But when his voice finally trailed off nearly ten minutes later, she knew she had to go.

"Daddy?" She lifted his wasted hand and cradled it against her cheek. "You be good, all right? Listen to Tucker and Mrs. Perry. I'll be home as soon as I can."

His gaze, very foggy now, drifted around the room briefly and then found her face. "Yes," he murmured. "Yes. You—be careful. The cross—isn't what you think. What you see. Something else. Didn't write it down. Tell Drew—they hid it inside. Like the clock . . ." His eyes closed heavily, and his breathing deepened in sleep.

Spencer held his hand for a moment longer, then gently tucked it beneath the blankets. His mind had drifted again, assuming Drew would be with her, but she didn't think he'd been rambling completely. Still, she didn't understand what he'd meant, and couldn't spare the time to think it through. She bent over to kiss her father's gaunt cheek gently, then left the room.

And it wasn't until she was sitting on the uncomfortable airplane seat and staring out the window at a grayish Atlantic far below that she wondered if her father had tried to tell her something that would turn out to be terribly important. It was just a feeling she had, vague and uneasy, a niggling sense of having missed something somewhere along the way.

What? What was it?

She was too tired to grapple with it just now. She was very conscious of the growing distance between her and her father. And between her and Drew. What would he think when he found out she'd gone? What would he do? She didn't know. But she wished he was with her now. She hated herself for that, but wished it all the same. She felt very much alone.

DREW SPENT ALL of Saturday morning on the phone. It wasn't an ideal day in which to seek the kind of information he was after, but that hardly deterred him. He called in favors, bribed, wheedled and badgered. Some might have said that what he was doing was wrong—some, in fact, *did* say it—but that didn't stop him, either, and he didn't take no for an answer. He had found out long ago that with enough nerve, connections, persistence and money, it was possible to get almost any kind of information any hour of the day or night.

Discretion went by the board. This time he wasn't probing carefully for hints, but digging for facts. And he got them. By noon he knew that Allan Wyatt had made a series of bad investments just before his stroke, had sold real estate at bargain prices and heavily mortgaged his house in an effort to recoup his losses, and had spent that money just as unwisely. He owed a staggering amount in back taxes, uninsured medical bills and various credit accounts.

And it had all fallen on Spencer's shoulders.

She had sold her car—buying a cheap rattletrap for transportation to and from the farm—her horses and her jewelry. The family silver was gone and she'd tried every means possible to break her trust fund, without success. Allan's car and collectibles had gone more slowly, the reluctance to sell them obvious. Much of the antique furnishings of the house had been sold piece by piece, quietly to private dealers. And there were other economies.

Drew got the whole story, more grim as each fact was revealed, and he knew his instinct hadn't been at fault. The woman he had believed her to be existed only in his bitter imagination.

That woman would not have accepted the burden of her father's debts with such quiet, uncomplaining grace. She wouldn't have negotiated fairly but shrewdly with creditors, earmarked her own trust fund income for debts, or sought a physically demanding job to pay household expenses. And she certainly wouldn't have withdrawn from the social scene in which she'd been brought up, particularly if marrying a rich man was something she considered an acceptable solution to her financial worries.

Drew had asked her how bad it was, and she had turned the

question aside. Wyatt pride? Maybe. But perhaps, Drew realized, that chin-in-the-air Wyatt pride that so angered him wasn't so much haughtiness as it was sheer bravado. Who was she really? What lay underneath that defiant show of courage? And how could he find the truth when his own words and actions had convinced her that he meant nothing but harm?

chapter five

THE PRIVATE SCHOOLS Spencer had attended had offered a wide range of foreign languages to their students. She had taken Spanish. Unfortunately, she was in France rather than Spain, and the taxi driver she had finally snagged at Orly understood neither English, Spanish, nor sign language.

The communication barrier was heightened by the fact that Spencer wasn't sure where she wanted to go. Practically any east-bound train would have satisfied her, but according to the schedule she had, nothing was heading east until morning, and she'd made no provisions for an overnight stay in Paris. It was late, and even though her system was still functioning on East Coast time, she was worn out from the travel and the hectic day behind her. All she wanted—and all she could afford—was some place with a bed and plain food, and she tried to communicate that to the taxi driver.

She was beginning to wonder if she'd ever be able to leave the airport tonight when a deep male voice spoke a couple of sentences sharply in flawless French. The taxi driver looked past her left shoulder, instantly bent to pick up the bags from the pavement at her feet and trotted around to put them in his trunk.

Spencer turned, conscious of feeling absurdly guilty.

"Running away from me again, Spencer?" Drew asked mildly.

Standing no more than two feet away from her and dressed almost as casually as she in dark slacks, a black leather jacket and a white shirt open at the throat, he seemed to her, even more than usual, larger than life. Appearing suddenly, and here, almost as if some supernatural force had spirited him across an ocean ahead of her. He shouldn't have *been* here; he was supposed to be thousands of miles away, and she wasn't prepared to face him. Not now. Not yet. He had the unnerving trick of knocking her off balance, and she spoke without thinking with far more emotion in her voice than she liked.

"No, I didn't run away from you. I won't do that again." His eyes narrowed swiftly, but Spencer managed to get hold of herself and added, "What did you do, leave D.C. last night?"

"I left just after you did."

"Then how—" Spencer realized even before she could finish the question, and answered it herself. "The Concorde."

Drew nodded, then stepped toward her as the driver came around to open the car door. "Get in, Spencer."

She found herself doing just that, which appalled her so much that she didn't trust her voice until Drew was sitting beside her and the taxi was fighting its way through the crush of traffic. God, was she going to meekly do *anything* the man ordered her to do? It was a terrifying thought.

"Where," she said at last, "are you taking me?"

"A hotel." He was half turned toward her, looking at her

steadily in the erratic illumination of passing cars and street-lights. "We're booked on a flight to Salzburg early tomorrow afternoon, with a connection to Innsbruck. There were no direct flights available."

Silently realizing that he'd apparently had enough time to memorize her itinerary—at least her ultimate destination—no matter how briefly he'd studied it, Spencer took a deep breath and tried to hold her voice steady. "Are you after the gold or the glory?"

It was his turn to take a breath, and his voice sounded as if patience was an effort. "Neither. Look, Spencer, whether you want to admit it or not, you're in over your head—and that's no insult to you. The black market for antiquities is a seller's market all the way, and antiquities are getting scarcer by the day. The players in *this* game break necks as easily as they break laws. The stakes are very high."

With the memory of a thief in the night fresh in her memory, Spencer found it hard to protest. But she didn't want to tell him that she was reasonably sure someone else was after the cross, so she had to at least try to protest. "You talk as if I took out a front-page ad in half the world's newspapers claiming I could find the cross. I haven't been that careless, Drew, or that stupid. And Dad's friend wouldn't have told anyone, I know he wouldn't have."

"What about the government officials who had to be consulted? What about their friends and coworkers? The secretaries who typed the paperwork and *their* friends? Spencer, the chances of someone saying the right thing to the wrong person may not be high, but they exist. And since I know for a fact that antiquities have been lost in the past because unscrupulous collectors had people on their payrolls inside government houses, I don't think it's paranoid to assume at least one wrong person knows you're going after the cross."

Spencer stared at him for a moment, then turned her head and gazed out past the driver at scenery she wouldn't have noticed even if it hadn't been dark. "All right," she said finally. "I'll grant that. You're probably right. I guess it would be naive of me to think otherwise. But it isn't your problem. I haven't asked for your help, or your protection, or—anything else."

"Why not?" He actually sounded a little amused. "I am considered to be pretty good at the game."

She sent him one disbelieving glance, then said stiffly, "That's a stupid question. I may not be terribly bright, but I have sense enough not to ask a shark for help while I'm treading water."

"Ouch," Drew murmured. "I suppose I deserved that." The words were uttered lightly, but there was something else underneath, something a little grim.

This time the look she gave him was a steady one, slightly puzzled and more than a little wary. She wished she could see his expression more clearly, but wasn't sure that would have helped in any case. "Which game are you playing now, Drew?"

He'd had ample time during the long trip to Paris in which to consider how to convince Spencer that his attitude toward her had changed. After the things he'd said to her, he doubted that she would believe so sudden a transformation, and besides that, he was still uncertain of just what he felt about her. There were still too many questions, and there was too much anger inside him.

As far as he could see, his only course of action lay in helping her to look for the cross. Firstly, because he didn't like to think of her facing possible danger alone, and secondly, because during that search he might find the answers to his questions. Still, he hadn't expected it to be easy.

"I'm not playing a game with you, Spencer," he replied after a moment. "In case you've forgotten, Allan and I were very close. I'd like to see his dream in his hands almost as much as you would.

Whatever else there is between us—well, that can wait." He wondered, silently, if it could. Or would.

"You said it was . . . just a matter of time," she said slowly. "You made me admit that."

"It is just a matter of time. But you and I have more of that than Allan does. I think I can help you find the cross. I know I can help if there's trouble."

"And I'm supposed to trust you? That's a lot to ask, don't you think?"

Drew glanced out of the taxi window, but without much interest, as if he simply needed a moment to gather his thoughts. Then, looking back at her, he said, "Maybe so. Offhand, I can't think of a good reason why you should trust me—except that you need help and I'm the best."

Spencer wished she could accuse him of vanity, but she knew that he *was* the best. Not only knowledgeable enough about art objects and antiquities, he was also quite famous for his instincts and intuition. And if that wasn't enough, he spoke a dozen languages fluently, was as familiar with most of the world as she was her backyard and no doubt knew by sight both the collectors and the black market dealers who could pose a threat.

Her instincts told her she *could* trust him, but she didn't trust her instincts. Not where he was concerned.

"Don't fight me on this," he said softly, watching her so intently that she could feel it.

After a moment Spencer said, "Would it do any good if I did?"

"No. A waste of time and energy." He reached over suddenly and took one of her hands in his, holding it lightly. She thought he was frowning just a bit as he gazed down at her hand, but wasn't sure of that. "A dangerous waste. You can't afford to fight me, Spencer, not while you're looking for the cross. Right now I'm the best ally you could have."

She knew, only too well, that she didn't really have a choice. It wasn't a defeatist thought, it was a logical one. If she said no, he'd only follow her—or get to Innsbruck before her and simply wait. Better to have him close, where she could keep an eye on him. That's what she told herself.

Besides that, she admitted at least silently that she wanted him here, with her. Not because of the possible danger and not even to help her find the cross, but because . . . She didn't let herself finish the thought. Wouldn't let herself. She tried to draw her hand away, but his long fingers tightened around it.

"I know you're finding it hard to trust me," he said evenly. "I know I've given you reason for that. If it helps, I'll give you my word that I don't want the cross or the credit for finding it. That's all I can do, Spencer."

She wanted to ask, *Can you give me your word you won't hurt me?* But she didn't ask.

She looked down, and in the erratic flashes of passing street-lights the clasp of their hands seemed strangely symbolic of what she was feeling. Her hand, pale in the light, almost unseen in the shadows, was lost in his larger, stronger one, held captive, unresisting. She hoped it was only because she was tired, because she hadn't slept much last night and could never sleep on planes and had never been a good traveler anyway.

She was tired. And she was glad he was here, with her. Never mind why. Why didn't matter, wouldn't matter, until he took what belonged to him and got her out of his system. Then it would matter. When he left her. Then she'd have to face it.

"Spencer?"

In a soft, careful voice, she said, "Finding the cross for Dad means everything to me. Promise—please promise me that you won't interfere with that."

His hand tightened around hers, curiously gentle. "I promise.

You have my word I won't do anything to hinder you, Spencer. I'll help all I can."

She nodded in the flickering darkness. "All right." She didn't know if she believed him, but she didn't try again to pull her hand away. She had a faint sense of bridges burning behind her, and it gave her an odd feeling of relief. She was going to do her best to find the cross. And whatever happened between her and Drew, she would do her best to emerge from it, if not whole, then at least with enough of herself left intact to go on.

There were worse things to be than a survivor.

Drew didn't release her hand even when they arrived at the hotel, helping her from the taxi after he'd paid the driver and leading her through the imposing lobby. A bellman trotted after them with Spencer's two bags, and she carried a smaller tote bag on her shoulder in lieu of a purse.

Detouring by the desk only long enough to speak briefly with the clerk—in French, so Spencer had no idea what he'd said to produce the smile on the man's face—Drew led her to the elevators, still holding her hand firmly. He said something to the bellman, which also drew a smile, then looked down at Spencer and explained that he always stayed in this hotel whenever he was in Paris, and that the staff knew him.

The information didn't surprise her.

There was no question that Drew was in charge; he was matter-of-fact about it without arrogance, but she had the feeling he wouldn't give way if she challenged that cool authority. He clearly believed that her acquiescence had given him this role, or else he simply intended to take it.

Oddly, Spencer wasn't tempted to protest—not yet, at any rate. She wasn't called on to make any decisions or choices, not even what floor she wanted a room on, and it was easy to simply accept. For a few minutes she even allowed herself to enjoy the feeling of being taken care of. She hadn't been conscious of wanting that during the past months, because there had been too much to do and too many other worries to think very much about shifting her burdens. Now, when it occurred to her that she was at ease with Drew's having taken charge, she wondered what that said about her.

Grappling with that unnerving question, she didn't pay much attention to her surroundings until Drew unlocked the door of his suite and led her inside. She pulled her hand gently from his grasp and went to stand near the window as she looked around the spacious sitting room. There were two bedrooms; she watched the bellman take her bags into one of them when Drew told him which one was hers, but said nothing until the man accepted his tip and left them alone in the suite.

"I'm surprised you got two bedrooms," she heard herself say in a slightly wry tone.

Drew shrugged out of his jacket and tossed it over the arm of a chair, smiling a little. "I could say it was all the hotel had available."

"You could. Would it be true?"

"No. I meant what I said, Spencer. The priority right now is the cross."

She half nodded, accepting that even though she couldn't help wondering if he was merely amusing himself by toying with her. "What time is the flight tomorrow?"

"Two. Earliest I could get."

Her watch was still on U.S. time and Spencer didn't bother to look at it. No matter what the local time was, she was tired and needed sleep. She'd cope better with jet lag—to say nothing of coping with Drew—after a good night's sleep. "I think I'll turn in, then," she murmured.

"Did you eat anything on the plane?"

Before she could stop it, a faint grimace pulled at her lips. "I hate airplane food. I'm not hungry though, so—"

"To hear you talk, you're never hungry. But I am, and you need to eat something. Why don't you get ready for bed while I order a light meal from room service. Then you can sleep late tomorrow and we'll both be ready for the hunt."

What he said made sense, and she shrugged an acceptance as she started toward her bedroom. "Okay, fine. Just don't order snails unless you like them."

"I don't." He seemed amused. "Anything else you'd like me to avoid?"

"Anything with alcohol." She paused in the doorway of her bedroom and offered a faint smile. "I'm allergic. Can't even take cold medicine unless it's alcohol free."

Drew was obviously surprised. "I didn't know that. How do you react to it?"

"Putting it as delicately as possible, I get rid of it. Quickly. The stuff makes me vilely sick."

"I suppose that includes wine in sauces?"

"Yes."

He nodded in understanding and watched her bedroom door close quietly behind her. He was more than a little worried about her. Knowing now what she'd gone through in the past months, he was hardly surprised that the trip from D.C. had left her pale with exhaustion. The emotional strain since her father's stroke had to be intense, had to be wearing away at her reserves of strength and will—and she was still on her feet, still determined to go on with this.

Wyatt pride, bred into her very bones? Or something else, an inner core of steel that kept her going when most would have given up the effort? He didn't know, not yet, but he was beginning to believe that she had more than her share of courage. That her seeming fragility was deceptive he already knew; watching her difficult and demanding work with the horses had told him that. But in a few short months she'd been burdened with overwhelming stresses on a level she could never have been prepared for, and there had to be a breaking point.

Only days ago the thought of her control in splinters had afforded Drew a savage pleasure. Now the very idea was something he didn't like to imagine. He wanted to know what was under the control, wanted to be able to read the emotions in her eyes, but he didn't want her broken. He wasn't sure, now, if he ever had wanted that.

He wanted to take care of her. That awareness had lurked in his mind since he had realized at the farm that she hadn't been taking care of herself, hadn't been eating right or resting enough, and he hadn't stopped to examine his own feelings. Now he pushed the matter aside, still too raw and unsettled emotionally to try to untangle what he felt about her.

He studied the room-service menu briefly and then called to place the order, double-checking to make certain there was no alcohol in anything. After that he killed time by pacing restlessly, too aware of the sound of the shower in the next room, of her nearness. His desire for her had only increased during the past days, and the protective feelings, his anxiety about her, had done nothing except turn what had been a bitter and almost savage need into something that was far less harsh and yet curiously more relentless, more imperative.

She wouldn't fight him, he knew that. She wanted him. But she didn't *want* to want him. He knew that, too. She would burn in his arms with an astonishing passion he'd had only a taste of, but she wouldn't be his. That certainty, more than anything, was responsible for his hesitation to take her now as he'd promised he would. It wouldn't be enough, just to take her, not if it was something she simply surrendered to because her body couldn't fight his. He wanted more. Not just a physical response but the pride and strength of her, the secrets her control hid so well, the emotions he could only guess at. He wanted it all.

Halting near the door to her bedroom, he stood listening unconsciously to the sound of the shower, his mind conjuring up an image of her with haunting ease. Remembering how she'd felt against him, the soft curves and delicate bones, the warm silk of her hair wrapped around his fingers, the electrifying way her body had molded itself to his, the hunger of her mouth beneath his.

In the shower there would be droplets of water clinging to her pale gold skin. Steam all around her. She'd be warm and slippery, her lips wet when he kissed her, her eyes dazed with pleasure as he touched her naked body. . . .

The sound of the shower stopped suddenly and, realizing what he was doing, Drew turned jerkily away from the closed door and paced over to the window. "God," he murmured, staring blindly out into the darkness.

Control. She had too much. And he had precious little.

The arrival of the room-service waiter a few minutes later was a welcome distraction, and by the time the food had been set out on the table near Drew's bedroom he had managed to pull on a mask of his own. When Spencer came out of her bedroom, covered from neck to ankles by one of the thick terry robes the hotel thoughtfully provided its guests, he was even able to greet her lightly.

"Perfect timing."

"Looks that way," she responded with equal casualness, taking her place at the table. She didn't appear quite so exhausted as she had, but with her hair loose around her face she seemed very young and almost heartbreakingly fragile.

Drew had never felt protective urges toward any woman in his life except Spencer, and he had never felt a desire for any woman so intense he wanted to make wild love to her until neither of them could walk without help—except Spencer.

He wondered if he was losing his mind.

Taking his own place across from her, he tried to think of something else, some casual topic that would distract his mind. But in the end it was Spencer who spoke first.

"I suppose you'll want to see Dad's papers." Her head was a little bent as she unfolded her napkin across her lap, and she didn't look at him.

He hesitated, then said, "I think I'd probably be more help to you if I saw them, and I'd like to try and find the clues you found. But it's up to you, Spencer."

She sent him a fleeting glance. "The originals are in a bank vault. I made copies of everything, even of some notes he scribbled on odd sheets of paper."

"Was that a yes or a no?" Drew asked wryly.

"It's a yes." She picked up her fork, meeting his gaze steadily this time. "I'm a little curious to see if you find what I did. After all, maybe I'm wrong. Maybe you'll be able to tell me without any doubt that this is a wild-goose chase."

"You have doubts?" he asked curiously, because she had seemed so sure.

"No. But what do I know, after all? You're the expert. I'm not even a talented amateur."

Drew was silent for a few moments, watching as she began eating, then said quietly, "I've said a few things you're not going to easily forgive, haven't I?"

She looked up, clearly surprised and, for an instant, puzzled. Then her slight frown cleared and she said, "I wasn't being sarcastic, if that's what you think. The truth is that any claim to knowledge I have is shaky at best. I went to college and I earned a degree, but I majored in history, not archaeology. I've listened to Dad, but he wasn't trying to teach me and I wasn't trying to learn."

He half nodded, but said, "Still, I've been pretty rough on you. For what it's worth, I'm sorry."

Spencer absently sipped the milk he'd ordered for her, wishing she could read his expression. Even in the light, she had no idea what he was thinking or feeling. "That sounds like an abrupt change of attitude. What brought it on?"

Drew hadn't meant to bring up the subject, but he was angry at himself for having misjudged her out of his own bitterness, and disliked the idea that he had added to her burdens. Flatly he said, "I spent the morning checking a few of my assumptions. You obviously didn't want me to know, but I found out anyway."

"Found out what?" she asked warily.

"That Allan as good as bankrupted himself before the stroke. And that you've been coping with the results for the last six months."

"That's none of your business," she said, chin lifting.

"You should have told me."

"Why? To give you another chance to call me a liar, or to accuse me of trying to drum up a little sympathy? No, thanks. Besides that, it isn't your concern."

Remembering that first night when he had torn at her mercilessly out of his own caustic anger, Drew could hardly blame her for believing that his reaction would have been disbelief or something worse. In fact, he knew it would have been. The realization left him with nothing to say. He finished eating, more automatically than out of any sense of hunger, and thought that she did the same.

"Do you want to have the papers tonight?" she asked somewhat stiffly as soon as she pushed her plate away.

"I can start on them tonight," he said. "I don't need much sleep."

Spencer got up and went into her room, leaving Drew to rise more slowly. He moved into the sitting area, even more restless than he'd been earlier, conscious of frustration and anxiety. He wasn't handling this well, and he knew it. Just when she seemed to have accepted his help, when she appeared to be almost at ease with him, he'd had to bring up something virtually guaranteed to make her retreat stiffly. He hadn't meant that to happen; more than anything, he'd just wanted to make amends for the way he'd treated her that first night. To try to tell her that he knew he'd been wrong about her and that he was sorry for the things he'd said.

Her chin had gone up, the flash in her eyes warning him that he'd trespassed on ground she had marked as off-limits. Wyatt pride again, maybe. Or perhaps it was just her pride, her determination to carry the burdens alone. Whatever the reason, she clearly wasn't willing to talk to him about her father's—and her—financial problems. And though that was understandable, it bothered him that there were things she couldn't tell him, places in her life that weren't open to him.

He told himself that he'd only come back into her life days ago—and acted like a bastard when he did—so he couldn't expect the path to be a smooth one. But the patience that had always come so easily to him seemed beyond reach now. He *needed*, and the hunger was as much emotional as physical, leaving him more vulnerable than he'd ever been in his life and urging him to hurry, to grab and hold on tight.

Before he lost her again.

He felt a shock and then a strange, cold tightness in his chest. It was fear, and he knew it. A fear of somehow making the same mistake he must have made ten years ago, the mistake that had driven her away from him.

"Here are the papers." She came into the sitting area and

dropped a thick manila envelope onto the coffee table, then immediately turned away.

Drew took three long steps and blocked her way out of the room, his hands lifting to rest on her shoulders. "Spencer, I was wrong about you, and I'm sorry. I want you to know that. To believe it."

"All right." She didn't meet his eyes, but looked fixedly at the top button of his shirt. Her voice was a little breathless, and she was very still.

Just thinking about her had his control on the fine edge of impossible; touching her was pushing him over the brink. Even through the thick terry of her robe he could feel warm flesh and delicate bones, feel how petite she was. Her hair smelled like sunshine and her skin looked so silky that he had to touch it. His hand moved before he was even aware of it, sliding beneath the dark curtain of her hair to touch her neck. Her skin was silky, and so fine he could feel her pulse thudding rapidly as he gently pushed her chin up.

"Have I made you hate me?" His voice was strained.

She looked up at him with huge eyes, the smoke gray of them disturbed and nervous. "I don't hate you. But . . . I don't understand you."

His thumb rhythmically stroked the clean line of her jaw, feeling the tension there. Gazing down at her, he was seeing the girl she'd been all those years ago—lovely, sweet, accepting the role of woman with grace and doubt. What had he done to push her away then? He didn't know, couldn't ask, and he wanted her so intensely he could hardly think. The distraction was reflected in his voice when he said, "I'm not so complicated."

"You are." She sounded a little bewildered. "You've changed so much since the night you came to the house. I don't know what to think, what to believe. Who are you? What do you want from me, Drew?"

He didn't have an answer, at least not one he could explain to her—or to himself. Except that he wanted her and was afraid of losing her. That was the only thing he was sure of.

Driven, he lowered his head and covered her slightly parted lips with his own, the hand at her shoulder moving down her back to pull her closer, until he could feel her against him. Hunger jolted through him, so abrupt and potent it was like a blow, and his mouth hardened fiercely on hers as his tongue probed deeply. She trembled, her delicate body molding itself to his and her arms lifting to slide around his waist. She made a soft, muffled sound of pleasure.

Even though desire had been tormenting him, Drew hadn't intended this to get out of hand. He was too aware of her exhaustion and her wariness not to know that the timing wasn't the best. But her response, so instant and total, tested his uncertain control to the limits, and he wasn't at all sure he'd be able to stop. His need for her was almost intolerable, burning and aching through his entire body until he nearly groaned aloud. Her mouth was so sweet and hot under his, and her body felt so good in his arms, against him. It felt so right.

He wanted to carry her into the bedroom and press her back into the softness of the bed, cover her slender body with his. Tortured by the erotic feel of her breasts against his chest, he wanted them naked in his hands, wanted to take her nipples into his mouth and stroke them with his tongue, taste them. He wanted to feel her satiny legs wrap around him as he settled between them, feel her soft heat sheathe his aching flesh.

He wanted her to belong to him.

Suddenly certain that if he didn't stop now he wouldn't be able to, Drew tore his mouth from hers. He held her against him, trying not to hold on too hard and hurt her, while he struggled to regain at least a fingertip grasp on his control. He wasn't at all sure he could do it; his heart was slamming in his chest, every rasping breath was like fire in his aching throat and his muscles were so rigid they quivered from the strain.

It was several long moments before he was able to slide his hands up to her shoulders and ease her trembling body away from him. Her arms fell to her sides as she stared up at him, and her eyes were wide, dazed, her lips a little swollen and reddened from his fervent passion. There was color in her face now, a soft flush of desire, and knowing he'd kindled that heat almost made him forget his good intentions.

But he managed, barely, to stop himself from yanking her back into his arms. "Go to bed, honey," he said in a thick voice. "I'll see you in the morning." He took his hands off her with an effort and moved away, crossing the room to stare once more out into the dark Paris night.

"Drew?" Her voice was husky.

He turned his head, looking at her as she stood hesitantly in the doorway to her bedroom. "Go to bed," he repeated, his voice more normal now.

She swallowed visibly. "Why? I wouldn't have said no." The admission was clearly difficult but honest.

"You wouldn't have said yes."

Spencer shook her head a little, bewildered. "I wouldn't have stopped you."

"I know. But it isn't the same thing." He managed a faint smile. "Get some rest. Tomorrow will probably be a long day."

After a moment she turned away and went into her bedroom, closing the door softly behind her.

Drew glanced toward his own bedroom, but knew without even thinking about it that he wouldn't be able to sleep. Luckily, he really didn't require much sleep, and was able to function quite well for days at a time with very little rest. He looked at the enve-

lope containing copies of Allan Wyatt's notes. At least he could occupy his mind and possibly distract his thoughts from Spencer's
presence in the next room.

His entire body ached dully, and when he moved toward the
phone it was slowly. He'd managed to contain his desire, but it was
like a storm trapped under glass, the fury restrained illusively but
not in the least diminished. God, he'd waited twelve years for her
and he didn't know how much longer he could stand it. The need
he felt intensified by the hour, and his control was wearing away
under the force of it.

And he hadn't yet been able to ask the one question that had
haunted him for years, the one question that, more than any other,
he needed to have answered. *Why?* Why had she run away from
him to marry another man?

He called room service, requesting that the remains of their
meal be removed and ordering a large pot of coffee. He had a long
night ahead of him, he knew.

A very long night.

SPENCER HADN'T EXPECTED to sleep well. The brief, passionate interlude between them had left her feverish, aching and more
than a little confused. It didn't make sense, *he* didn't make sense,
and she didn't know what to think.

In the end, she was too exhausted to think at all. She called
home to let Tucker know she'd arrived safely in Paris and to check
on her father. Her father was fine, Tucker told her, and seemed at
ease because, he'd said several times, Drew was with her.

"He is with me," she reported with more than a little wryness.

"He came to the house," Tucker said in his usual expressionless voice. "Upset, but not angry, I thought. He guessed you'd gone
to Paris."

"Umm. He got here before me. The Concorde."

"He can help you," Tucker said.

"It looks like he's going to." Spencer sighed. "Anyway, I'll call you tomorrow, from Austria."

She hung up after saying goodbye, wondering if her father was still lost in the past or merely psychic. She climbed into the big, lonely bed, turned out the lamp on the nightstand and was almost instantly asleep. She slept dreamlessly for more than eight hours, waking to a bright, quiet room that was briefly unfamiliar. Then she remembered. A hotel. She was in a hotel in Paris, and Drew was here, too.

Keeping her mind carefully blank on that point, Spencer slid from the bed, relieved to find that her weariness was gone and that she felt better physically than she had in a long time. She took a quick shower to finish waking up, then dressed as casually as she had the day before in white jeans and a pale blue sweater, putting her hair in a single braid to fall down her back and applying only a bare minimum of makeup.

It was only when she was sitting on her bed putting on her comfortable shoes that she caught herself listening intently for some sound of Drew in the next room. Awareness of what she was doing shattered the careful blankness of her mind, and she sighed a bit raggedly.

In the light of the morning it still didn't make sense. At her house, Drew had been cruel and scathing, promising to take her, to make certain she was in thrall to him. At the farm the next day he'd been cool and calm at first, then a little mocking, then angry, but not like before, not cruelly angry, and he'd talked to her without tearing her to shreds. Then, last night, he had been quiet and watchful, careful, it seemed to her, as if he were trying to guide their relationship in a new direction. He had begun taking care of her. He had even apologized for having misjudged her, and when he'd held her in his arms and kissed her so hungrily, when she'd been totally unable to resist the desire he'd ignited between them, he had pulled away.

Not saying no, he had said, wasn't the same as saying yes.

Spencer stared at the door leading out into the sitting room, wondering which man was out there. Complicated? The man was baffling. *Had* his opinion of her really changed? Or was he still bent on revenge? She didn't know.

And then there was the other matter, the cross. Unless he disagreed with her conclusions and could state flatly that there was no chance of finding it, they'd be searching for the cross together. She had to tell him about the stolen papers. He needed to know that.

Spencer rose to her feet and unconsciously squared her shoulders. There was nothing she could do except just go on, one step at a time, the way she'd learned to these past months. Whatever Drew intended, worrying about it wasn't going to help her a bit, and fretting over the cross wouldn't do her much good, either. She had to keep going, that was all. One step at a time.

She opened her door quietly and went out into the sitting room. The television near the window was on, tuned to a news program with the volume down low, and Drew was on the couch. The copies of her father's papers were spread out on the cushions beside him and on the coffee table, along with a large map of Austria. He was holding several sheets of paper in his hand, and looked up from them when she came in.

"Good morning," he offered quietly.

"Barely," she conceded, managing a smile. "I didn't mean to sleep so late."

"Do you good." He nodded toward the dining table. "The coffee's still hot, and there's fruit and rolls. If you'd rather have something more substantial—"

"No, that's fine." She went over to the table and sat down,

reaching for a cup. While she ate breakfast she watched him covertly. She had the feeling he hadn't gone to bed at all, and a glance into his room showed her a neatly made bed with no signs of having been occupied. His golden hair was still a little damp from a recent shower and he'd changed into jeans and a dark sweater. Like her, he was wearing comfortable running shoes.

He was intent on studying the papers, going through those in his hands slowly and methodically before setting them aside and reaching for more. He made several notes on a legal pad resting on the arm of the couch, and once leaned forward to study the map with a considering gaze.

Spencer couldn't guess what he thought. She finished her breakfast and carried her coffee over to the sitting area, taking the chair at right angles to him. Drew looked up to watch her for a moment, still without expression, then gathered the papers into a neat stack on the coffee table.

"Well?" she said finally, unable to stand it a moment longer.

His cool blue eyes warmed slowly, and a crooked smile curved his lips. "You're your father's daughter," he said softly.

chapter six

SHE FELT A jolt of relief, mixed with an unfamiliar feeling of ac-complishment. "You think I'm right?"

"I think you did a hell of a fine job." Drew's tone was very deliberate. "The only reason I found it was that I knew your desti-nation was Innsbruck. I sorted out the references to that area and backtracked. I never would have seen it otherwise. How did you figure it out, Spencer?"

"I didn't for a long time," she said a bit wryly. "I went over those papers every night for more than a month, and all I got was a headache. You've studied them. Because so many experts said it didn't even exist and never had, Dad had done most of his re-search trying to establish that Maximilian I did have the cross commissioned in 1496 when he arranged the marriage of his son to the daughter of the king of Spain. I decided to assume he was right, and to weed out all the references before 1618, when the cross was supposed to have vanished at the beginning of the Thirty Years' War."

He was listening intently, wondering if she had any idea how assured she sounded—and how expert. She may not have been trying to learn from Allan, but she had obviously absorbed much more than she'd realized. "So then you were left with about a quarter of Allan's original notes."

"Right. I started from the point where the Protestants in Bohemia revolted in 1618. There was one contemporary reference, a report to Rome written by a priest, that mentioned something about how the Protestants had stolen a cross—*the* cross, Dad believed—from the Hapsburgs. That didn't make sense to me. I mean, why would they? They were fighting for their rights, but I didn't see why they would have stolen a cross. It's a Protestant symbol, too.

"So I wondered if maybe somebody had had the bright idea to hide the cross—someplace safe—and claim it was stolen, just for personal gain. Or to fan the flames. It did seem to do that—the Protestants made a number of denials that they'd stolen anything, but the Hapsburgs' vague accusations seemed to carry more weight. Still, the priest was the only one who mentioned what, exactly, was supposed to have been stolen."

As far as Drew remembered, that theory had never been advanced by any of the so-called experts, and it showed, on Spencer's part, a direct and coolheaded understanding of human nature that was surprising in a woman who had been very sheltered for most of her life. It also caused his opinion of her intelligence, gaining ground rapidly, to take another leap forward. "And you focused on the priest, because his was the only contemporary reference that was specific."

"Yes, and because he'd mentioned the theft in a report to

Rome—it was like official notification that things were getting out of hand and something had to be done about it quickly. There was almost an air of smugness in the way he worded it, like he knew something, and I wondered if he did."

Allan Wyatt had never been known for his intuition, but his daughter was showing a definite flair for sensing undercurrents and reading between the lines, Drew thought. He had the feeling that if he commented on it, she'd shrug off any claim to talent and merely say it had been a lucky guess, but Drew knew only too well that inspired guesses came from intuition—and that hers had been inspired.

She went on in a matter-of-fact voice. "I managed to find the rest of the report—Dad didn't have it with his notes, but he had translated it—and saw that it had been sent from Innsbruck. That was a long way from Bohemia, *and* a long way from other areas that had been searched for the cross."

Slowly, Drew said, "Earlier researchers who accepted the existence of the cross also accepted the theft, so they'd searched the areas closer to Bohemia, where the revolt had taken place, and closer to the family seat." He nodded again. "Very good, Spencer. And then?"

She looked momentarily confused, as if the praise had surprised her, then went on. "Well, I doubted the original idea was the priest's, or that he had access to the cross even if he'd wanted to steal it, so there had to be at least one of the Hapsburgs who took it to Innsbruck and hid it. By using the date of the priest's report, and comparing it to the letters and journals that Dad had copied or collected over the years, I found out that one of the Hapsburgs— Kurt—was in Innsbruck visiting his sweetheart during the same time the priest was there. He'd written half a dozen letters to a friend of his, and since the friend was related to at least three royal families his letters turned up around the turn of this century in a

Vienna museum, where Dad had found them and made copies. He wanted anything mentioning any of the Hapsburgs, but hadn't connected those particular letters to the cross. Luckily for me, though, he had translated them verbatim, and that's how I found the clues."

Drew glanced at the legal pad beside him and said, "The trips Kurt took into the mountains with a friend."

Spencer nodded. "They were very chatty letters, weren't they? Very descriptive of the scenery. On the surface the details seemed almost casual, but when I studied them with the idea that Kurt and his friend—probably the priest—were searching for a place to hide the cross, they really stood out. Kurt had also asked his friend to keep the letters, which struck me as odd until I wondered if he'd used them to record where he'd hidden the cross on the chance that he might forget."

"If hiding the cross was just meant to be a temporary meas-ure," Drew said, "then why do you think it never turned up again?" His tone wasn't disbelieving, just curious, as if he wanted to hear her opinion.

Spencer had given that a lot of thought, and she'd found an an-swer that had satisfied her. "I think that Kurt never intended to re-turn it to the rest of the family," she said dryly. "He was from a junior branch of the Hapsburgs, and from his letters I'd say he was awfully ambitious. He'd tried several times to finagle more power within the family, without success. I think he took the cross to Innsbruck, planning to hide it purely for his own future need. He enlisted the priest's help—both in hiding the cross and in report-ing the 'theft' to Rome—because it was his idea and because *he*, not the Hapsburgs, wanted somebody to blame. The family wasn't likely to admit that one of their own had stolen it even if they knew. And *if* they knew, it would have been a good reason why they didn't make more of a fuss about a valuable family heirloom being stolen. Anyway, with so much going on just then, if they did know he'd taken it, they probably decided to deal with Kurt when he returned to Vienna."

"But the cross never surfaced again, and there's no mention of it in later letters or journals. Because something happened to him?" Drew said. "It wasn't in the notes."

"I was curious about that, and I found the answer in one of Dad's books about the Hapsburgs. It seems that Kurt's sweetheart fell ill a month or so after that last letter he wrote, and he nursed her. She survived, but he caught the fever and died. The priest, by the way, never made it back to Rome—notice of his death appears in the town records. It seems he had a bad fall shortly after his report to Rome and broke his neck. I'd like to think Kurt had nothing to do with it, but who knows?"

Drew was smiling slightly, and that look was in his eyes again, the warmth that had unsettled her before. "Allan didn't research Innsbruck specifically—how did you find the bit about the priest?"

Spencer wondered what he was thinking. "Well, I was curious, like I said. I called the university in Innsbruck and, luckily, their records were very complete."

After a moment, and in a very deliberate tone, Drew said, "Spencer, I hope I never again hear you question your own intelligence. I know I won't question it."

She had quivered under his insults, and Spencer found that his compliments affected her even more strongly. She didn't know what to say, and had to look away from the warmth of his eyes. Almost at random, she said, "So . . . you think we have a good chance of finding the cross?"

"I would have gone after it knowing a lot less than you've put together," he said. "Unless someone stumbled over it and moved it in the last three hundred years or so, I think you've found it."

Remembering suddenly, Spencer wondered if he would take

back his compliment on her intelligence. She cleared her throat and looked at him. "Somebody else could have found it already, or at least be ahead of us."

His eyes sharpened. "What makes you think so?"

"The reason I came over here ahead of schedule and in such a hurry was because someone broke into the house Friday night. It was a very professional job—except that he took a lot of worthless things."

"You believe he was looking for Allan's papers?"

"Do you remember Dad's trick safe? I know he showed it to you."

"I remember. The real safe was behind the clock."

"The thief ignored the trick safe behind the painting, which was empty, but he got the other one open easily enough. I'd made two sets of copies of Dad's papers, and one set was in the real safe. It was taken."

Drew's face was without expression, almost remote, but his eyes were curiously hard. "An ordinary thief wouldn't have bothered with handwritten papers. You're right—he was after the notes."

Spencer realized that he was angry, and it made her a little nervous. "That's not the worst of it," she confessed reluctantly. "My itinerary was lying on the desk. I had meant to leave it for Tucker, in case he needed to get in touch with me. The thief didn't take it, but if he noticed it . . . You figured out where the cross was in just a few hours, you said, because you knew the area was Innsbruck. If he knows that, too, then he could be ahead of us."

"Why didn't you tell me this sooner, Spencer?" Drew asked very softly.

"It wouldn't have mattered if—if you'd studied the notes and told me I was wrong—"

"No, I meant why didn't you tell me when it happened?" Then an odd laugh escaped him, and he shook his head. "Never mind. It was a stupid question. You wouldn't have come to me if I was the last hope between you and hell."

He was angry at himself, she realized in surprise. Because his behavior that first night had made her staunchly determined not to ask him for help? If she *had* asked him and he'd agreed, they might well have been in Austria by now. It was her limited funds that had brought her to Paris and prevented a more direct route. Was Drew angry because they might have lost the cross partly due to his earlier hostility?

"I'm sorry, Spencer," he said.

She looked at him, wondering what to say to that. "I probably wouldn't have asked you for help no matter what your attitude had been," she said finally, then went on immediately before he could comment on that. "The only thing that makes sense is that some collector or black market dealer somehow found out that I was close—or thought I was—and paid a professional thief to get the papers. We have to assume Dad's notes are in the hands of someone who knows what they're looking for, and how to look for it. Even if they aren't as good or as quick as you, they'll find the clues, given enough time."

Drew took a deep breath. "And if they were prepared to leave at a moment's notice, they may already be in Innsbruck."

"I wish I knew who they were," Spencer murmured, "and how they found out. . . ."

Rising abruptly to his feet, Drew went over to the phone and placed a call. He spoke in French, rapidly, and she had no idea who he was talking to or what he was saying. She glanced at her watch, which she'd reset to local time, and was vaguely surprised to see that it was barely noon. Drew's voice distracted her. He seemed to be arguing, but then his tone turned decisive, and when he hung up he was obviously satisfied.

Looking at Spencer, he said briefly, "Are you ready to leave?"

She nodded. She hadn't unpacked the night before, so all she had to do was pick up her bags and go.

Drew made another call, a short one this time. After cradling the receiver a second time, he said, "A bellman's coming up for the bags."

Spencer nodded again.

"If I read those clues correctly," he said, "the hiding place for the cross is miles outside Innsbruck in the mountains. Even bypassing Salzburg we won't have time to get started today, but we might be able to find out who our competition is."

"Bypassing Salzburg? I thought there were no direct flights available."

"I've chartered a plane," Drew said.

HE HAD, ACTUALLY, chartered a jet. A Lear jet. Spencer, sitting in the efficiently soundproofed and luxurious cabin, gazed around at plush carpeting and furnishings as they left Paris far behind. Her background was one of wealth and privilege, but she had never before flown in an aircraft like this one. She was less impressed by the luxury than by the convenience, speed and efficiency that were possible when there were no budget considerations.

Drew was still in charge, making arrangements with cool authority so that she hadn't had to even think, and she hadn't objected. She kept telling herself that he was doing this because of the cross and because of her father, not because he wanted to help her. To take care of her. It wasn't personal, she thought. He'd shown no protective impulses all those years ago, had given no sign that accepting a woman's burdens was something he desired or was even prepared to do.

But, then, she hadn't needed him in that way at the time. She wondered, now, what would have happened if she had. Would she have seen a less remote side of Drew, as she was seeing now, if she had turned to him with a problem? Were the changes she saw and sensed less his than her own? She needed his help now, and she knew it, needed his intelligence, his expertise and his knowledge. He'd been right in saying he was the best ally she could have.

Because of that, because his inner qualities were far more obvious and more imperative to her now than the elegant surface of him, she didn't feel so intimidated by his confidence and sophistication. Those traits were only part of him. Since he'd come back into her life, she had begun to understand that he was more complex than she'd known—and certainly not detached. She wasn't seeing him now as a schoolgirl's fairy-tale prince, but as a man a woman could count on for far more than handsomeness, courtesy and social composure.

Was that the difference? Ten years older and wiser, a woman instead of a child, she was more comfortable with both herself and him, less inclined to shy away like a frightened child from the terrors of uncertainty. He still had the power to unnerve her, and she still felt vaguely threatened by him sometimes, but there was less fear in that now and more . . . excitement. As if the woman she was now had some instinctive knowledge that the girl of ten years ago had lacked, some understanding that losing herself in him would be as exhilarating as it would be terrifying.

"You're very quiet," he said.

As the jet reached its cruising altitude and leveled off, she loosened her seat belt and looked at him. He was sitting across from her, his face still, the way it had been ever since he'd become angry—at himself?—at the hotel. He hadn't said very much and, grappling with her own thoughts, she had said very little to him.

Now she said the first thing she could think of. "The customs official at Orly certainly knew you."

"Most of the customs officials in Europe know me." He unfastened his seat belt and got up, going over to a wet bar placed toward the front of the plane. "Would you like something to drink? I see a variety of fruit juices here."

"Orange juice, please." She watched him, thinking of the laconic response that said a great deal. During the past ten years she had heard or read of dozens of spectacular finds Drew had made, as well as confrontations with black market dealers and transactions with other collectors for various antiquities and art objects. Customs officials all over the world probably knew him by sight and most, judging by the Frenchman's attitude, no doubt both liked and respected him.

Drew returned to hand her a glass, holding one for himself that also contained fruit juice and sitting down beside her this time. The seats in this jet ran lengthwise, more like plush couches than standard airline seating, so there was no armrest separating them. Very conscious of his closeness, she sipped her juice and then clung to what seemed like a casual topic.

"The official at Orly was very friendly. Are they all like that?"

Drew was half turned toward her, one arm along the back of the couch so that his hand was very close to her shoulder. His tone sounded a little absent when he replied, "No, not all of them. Most of them trust me, though, after all these years. They know they can be pretty sure I'm not carrying contraband, or trying to smuggle anything in or out of a country."

He couldn't stop looking at her. She was no longer pale as she'd been last night, her gray eyes clear and steady, and Drew wanted to touch her so badly that it was a constant ache inside him. She seemed to have no awareness of her effect on him and, despite her instant response to him last night, if she felt any urge to cast herself into his arms now she was hiding it well. He wondered again, with an odd blend of wry amusement and acute frustration, if he really was losing his mind. He was having trouble stringing two coherent thoughts together, and she seemed bent on keeping the conversation casual.

"You don't approve of black market trading, do you?" she asked.

He forced himself to concentrate. "When it comes to antiquities or art objects, no. But some things sold on the black markets of the world, especially where there's no free trade, are beneficial." He smiled suddenly. "I doubt that the invasion of blue jeans and stereos into communist countries had much to do with sparking a few revolutions, but you never know."

Looking at him curiously, she said, "I've heard that you've gone into some pretty rough places searching for antiquities. As much as you travel into and out of countries without free trade, have you ever been tempted to . . ."

After a moment Drew said, "I have a good reputation with most officials and border guards, and it isn't wise to abuse something like that. But there have been a few times in the past that I've helped to transport supplies into a country. Medical supplies, usually. Never guns, and never anything that a democratic government would consider contraband."

It didn't surprise Spencer, though she thought it would surprise some people who knew him. She had a feeling that even those who knew him well actually knew little about him and the things he'd done.

Smiling a little, she said, "No nerves to speak of?"

"Plenty of nerves." He returned the smile. "But, hell, what's the fun of trying if you're sure you'll win?" That philosophy applied to most things, he acknowledged silently, but he wasn't sure it applied to them. He felt as if he were walking a high wire without a net, and *fun* wasn't the word he would have chosen for that.

"Fun? Risking being thrown into some dark prison for the remainder of your natural life?" Her voice was still casual, and she appeared faintly amused.

"That possibility has given me a few bad moments," he admitted, still smiling. "But there's a sense of triumph in beating the odds, and even in just trying to. Think of Allan's search for the cross. A lifetime's work and plenty of disappointment—but you know he wouldn't have missed it for the world."

They were, Spencer realized, slipping out of the casual topic and into something more sensitive, despite her efforts. The cross. Always it came back to the cross. She wondered, had to wonder, if Drew was with her now only because of that.

"I know that," she said, pushing the question aside. "And I suppose if you have the triumph, it's worth it. But what if you fail?"

His smile faded a little, and Drew's eyes were intent on her face. "Failure isn't an ending, Spencer, it's just a place to stop for a while and consider your options. You try again, or try something else."

"Learn from your mistakes, you mean?" she asked lightly, staring at her glass.

"You can do everything right and still fail." In a deliberate tone, he went on. "Take you and the cross, for instance. You've done everything right—more than right, in fact. You found clues that have eluded experts for centuries, and pieced them together to find an answer. It wasn't your fault that someone stole Allan's papers, and it won't be your fault if they get to the cross before you do."

"It certainly won't be yours." She managed to hold on to the light tone. "You're spending a great deal of time and energy—to say nothing of money—to get us there as quickly as possible."

"Does that bother you?" Drew asked.

It had bothered her all along, but she'd managed not to think about it. Now she had no choice. "I don't like being indebted. Even if it's for Dad, I—"

"Spencer, there's no debt." His tone roughened suddenly. "And I won't claim one later, if that's what you think."

She had an almost painful urge to apologize, but couldn't form the words. Instead, still gazing into her glass as if it contained the secrets of the universe, she said, "Then it is for Dad that you're doing this?"

Drew took the glass away from her, setting both hers and his on a low snack table at his end of the couch. Then he reached over and made her look at him, his long-fingered hand gentle but firm against her face. "I want Allan to see the cross." His voice was low, still a little rough; his expression was grave and very intent. "But if you weren't hell-bent to find it, I wouldn't be here."

"You said—"

"I know what I said. I thought you'd fight me if I said I only wanted to help you. Either that or think the worst of my motives. So I said it was for Allan."

Spencer stared into his eyes, doubtful but conscious of her heart beating rapidly and of all her senses coming alive as a pulse of heat throbbed inside her. Something else, she realized, that it always came back to. This. This potent desire between them was never far away. It was difficult to think at all, but she tried, because she had a curiously certain idea that they were at a turning point of some kind. He was saying this was for her, that he wasn't with her because of the cross or her father—and she had to decide whether she believed him.

"Then how can I believe there's no debt?" she whispered. His eyes, she thought, were the color of blue topaz, a shade that wasn't light or dark but somewhere in between. There was heat in them, blue heat that melted something inside her.

"Because I say there's no debt. Spencer, I want to be with you. Is that so hard for you to believe? I just want to be with you."

It was difficult for her to accept, but his insistence and her own silent yearning made it impossible for her to say so. She had to believe him, and if it was a mistake, if she had to pay a price for trust, then she'd pay it.

"I guess I have to believe it," she murmured. "But . . . you're very confusing."

"Am I?" He was smiling again. His hand moved slightly, so that the fingers lay along her neck while his thumb brushed her cheek in a slow, stroking caress.

She'd been very conscious of his hand on her, but that little caress made her want to close her eyes and actually whimper out loud with the pleasure of it. It was increasingly difficult to think, but she tried. "Last night—"

"Last night, you were tired," he murmured. "And you didn't trust me. I want you to trust me. I want you to believe we'd be good for each other. This time."

His low voice was almost hypnotic, as acutely erotic as his touch, and Spencer wondered vaguely if this was what drowning felt like. She was sinking into something velvety soft and warm, and she had absolutely no urge to save herself. When his mouth touched hers, she was incapable of doing anything except sway toward him, an unconscious purr of pure sensual bliss vibrating in her throat. His tongue slid deeply into her mouth, the small possession so hungrily insistent that her response was instantaneous. The now-familiar but still astonishing burst of desire jolted through her body like an electrical shock, and her arms lifted to wreathe around his neck.

His arms were around her now, holding her as close as possible, but even that wasn't close enough for Spencer. The constriction of her seat belt kept her from turning completely toward him as she wanted to do, and the throbbing emptiness deep inside her was a torment. She could feel his hands burning through her sweater, feel the hardness of his chest flattening her breasts, and his thick hair was like silk under her fingers.

He kissed her as if he were starving for the taste of her, the intensity of his need overwhelming, and that fierce desire ignited an answering passion in her that had never been touched before. Spencer had never even imagined anything like this; the sheer raw power of it was stunning, and if she could have said anything at all she would have said yes, because she wanted him with every throbbing nerve in her body.

He finally pulled back with obvious reluctance, murmuring her name huskily, and she became vaguely aware of a scratchy voice on the jet's PA system announcing that they were nearing Innsbruck. The information sank into her numb brain, but she could only stare up at Drew's taut face with helpless longing.

He kissed her again, quickly this time, and gently pulled her arms from around his neck. He held her hands in both of his, darkened, heated eyes fixed on her face, and his voice was still a little thick when he spoke. "If we weren't twenty thousand feet up in a jet . . . I wouldn't have stopped this time. I've waited twelve years for you. I don't think I can wait much longer."

Twelve years? She was dimly puzzled by that, but it didn't seem important at the moment. Her entire body was filled with a pulsing ache, and she didn't even try to hide what she was feeling because that would have been impossible. "I don't want to wait," she whispered.

His eyes burned hotter, as if banked embers had suddenly burst into flame. "Don't say that unless you mean it." His voice was even thicker, rasping over the words.

Somewhat to her surprise, Spencer was utterly calm and certain about this. Her body was still throbbing, but slowly now, and what she felt most of all was anticipation. She already belonged to him; fighting that was like pitting her strength against a force of nature, a battle she could never win.

"I don't want to wait," she repeated steadily.

Drew leaned over to kiss her, the heat inside him banked again but searing her nonetheless, and muttered as he lifted his head, "Dammit, it'll take hours to find out anything in town, and it has to be done today."

She smiled slowly, understanding that the digression was made with extreme reluctance and not a little strain. "The cross is our priority. You said that."

His mouth twisted. "I may have already cost you the damned thing. I don't want to make another mistake."

"Drew, it won't be your fault if somebody gets there ahead of us. I couldn't have asked you for help—not because of anything you'd said or done, but because of what I'd done. Ten years ago."

"You know we're going to have to talk about that," he said, his hands tightening around hers.

Spencer half nodded, then glanced away as the altered sounds of the jet's engines indicated that they'd be landing soon. "Yes, but not now."

He didn't like the way she'd looked away from him, or the sudden wariness in her eyes. She hadn't withdrawn from him exactly, but there was a barrier he hadn't been conscious of only moments ago. It bothered him. He was certain she wanted him now, and both his usual judgment and his peculiar instincts kept assuring him that her words and her responses to him were completely honest. Why did she shy away from telling him her reasons for marrying another man? Were those reasons so painful that, even now, she couldn't bear to remember them?

SPENCER HAD NEVER been to Austria and, knowing that she probably wouldn't have time to do any sight-seeing, tried to see as much of Innsbruck as possible from the taxi as it conveyed them from the airport to their hotel. She immediately felt an affinity for the valley city, particularly the older sections with their narrow streets and tall Gothic buildings, and she loved the spectacular view of mountains that ringed the city.

Drew had told the driver where to take them—his German was as fluent as his French—and told Spencer that he'd chosen an inn for them in the section of the city nearest the area of mountains where they hoped to find the cross.

"You've been here before," she noted.

"A few times. I have at least a couple of contacts in the city, so we may be able to get some information."

Spencer looked at him curiously. "Wouldn't whoever's after the cross be cautious? I mean, how could your contacts know anything about it?"

Drew smiled and took one of her hands. He'd been touching her almost constantly since the interlude on the jet, and if the touches seemed casual and undemanding Spencer was still highly aware of them. "People who deal in antiquities," he said, "or even have knowledge of them are very adept at reading signs. They notice certain questions or actions, or an unusual preoccupation, and take note. After all, it could be something they'd be smart to go after themselves."

"Innsbruck is a big city," she commented, still looking at him.

"Yes, but the community of people interested in antiquities is relatively small, even worldwide. Most of us know each other, certainly by name and usually by sight. Aside from that, to find something hidden in the mountains, whoever's after the cross—including us—will need certain supplies and equipment the tourists don't bother with, and that's a signal which an expert would read quite accurately."

Spencer was fascinated. "You mean that if I had come here alone and didn't ask a single question of anybody, but just rented a horse and bought supplies—?"

He answered dryly, "At least two people that I know of in Innsbruck would hear of it within an hour. And once your name was known—which would be fairly quickly—there would be a dozen or so people across Europe speculating frantically that you were in search of the cross."

"I hadn't realized so many people knew about Dad's obsession," she mumbled somewhat dazedly.

"He hasn't exactly kept it a secret during the last fifty years," Drew reminded her. "Even the collectors who didn't believe it existed were interested, not only because of intrinsic and historical value, but because there are so few disputed relics left to find. Collectors want one-of-a-kind objects, Spencer, and the more elusive they are, the greater their value."

He should know, she thought, and said, "You're a collector."

"I enjoy the hunt as much as the find," he responded lightly.

Spencer didn't say anything else on the subject, because they arrived at the inn. It was a beautiful old building, Renaissance in style, with such a gracious, Old World atmosphere that Spencer was instantly enchanted. She followed Drew into the lobby, her hand still securely held in his, and stood looking around as the bellman brought their bags in.

"Are you up for a little sight-seeing?" Drew asked, gazing down at her.

Knowing that he intended to get in touch with his contacts, she didn't think he meant that literally. She was intensely curious about the procedures involved; her imagination conjured up images of furtive meetings in shadowy alleys, and she had to smile at herself even as she replied to his question.

"Of course I am."

Drew tried to remember what they were talking about. Those slow smiles of hers had a devastating effect on his mind, his pulse and his blood pressure. Granted, it didn't require much to upset his precarious control where she was concerned. After she had said on the jet that she didn't want to wait, he was dimly surprised he'd been able to talk at all. If he hadn't fiercely concentrated on the search for the cross . . .

"Drew?"

He looked at her upturned face and cleared his throat. He could hold on a few more hours. Couldn't he? "I'll get us checked in," he said with only a trace of hoarseness, "and have the bags taken up."

She nodded, then gestured toward a small gift shop tucked discreetly in one corner of the lobby. "I think I'll see if they have a guidebook and a more recent map of the area."

He released her hand with reluctance, conscious once again of a haunting fear that if he didn't keep hold of her she'd somehow vanish out of his life. It was a perfectly understandable and rational fear based on past mistakes and he knew it, but reminding himself of that was an ongoing battle. He was hardly given to flashes of foreboding, and certainly not precognition, but the fear of losing her was so strong inside him that it was almost like a premonition of actual danger.

For a moment, watching her gracefully cross the lobby toward the gift shop, Drew's mind went absolutely clear and cold. A premonition? Or years of experience whispering to him? Someone had broken into Spencer's house and stolen her father's notes. That indicated both haste and a disregard of the law, to say nothing of ruthlessness. What would happen if the search for the cross ended in a confrontation of some kind? Would the strange, elusive history of that relic end, as so many had, in violence and death?

Danger was not only possible, Drew admitted silently to himself, it had to be expected. He hadn't been so successful all these years by ignoring risk, and he knew he had to be prepared for anything.

Anything except losing Spencer.

He turned toward the desk, a last chill thought filtering

through his mind even as he automatically went through the procedure of registering for a suite. He was well-known to collectors and black market dealers alike. Was it a coincidence that the theft had occurred almost immediately after he had reappeared in Spencer's life?

chapter seven

DREW TOOK HER to lunch first, at an outdoor café that provided a splendid view of the Goldenes Dachl, which was the top tourist attraction in Spencer's guidebook and, judging by the crowds, was quite popular today. She knew the history of the beautiful Gothic building, which had been built to commemorate Maximilian's marriage, and could see how its name, "Golden Roof," had originated with the gilded copper tiles that shone brightly in the sunlight. She wished there was more time to just sit and look at it, or to go nearer, but she sensed a certain restlessness in Drew and she didn't protest when he rose as soon as they'd finished eating.

He seemed to be in a peculiar mood, as briskly informative as any tour guide, yet almost imperceptibly distracted, as if his mind were elsewhere. Despite that, though, he held her hand or tucked it into the crook of his arm constantly, making certain she never strayed more than a step away from him.

As they walked through the picturesque quarter, Spencer became so wrapped up in her fascination for the sights it took her some time to realize that Drew was already seeking information about the cross and their competitors for it. He'd been talking to her all along, casually pointing out this or that with far more knowledge than her guidebook displayed, but he'd also spoken to at least half a dozen people in German.

"I thought you had only a couple of contacts in Innsbruck," she said mildly as they stood looking at a museum that had once been a ducal palace.

Answering the implied question readily enough, Drew said, "They referred me to a few other people."

She would have sworn their casual walking had been just that, and was a little amused to realize that Drew had followed a definite but unobtrusive route from contact to contact. Looking up at him, she asked, "What have you found out?"

"Nothing yet. It may be tomorrow morning before the questions I've asked begin to produce answers—if they do."

Somewhat wryly, Spencer said, "I think I've been reading too many intrigue stories. I expected your contacts to look furtive and dangerous. The last man you spoke to looked like an ordinary street vendor to me."

"He is an ordinary street vendor." Drew tucked her hand into the crook of his arm and led her away from the museum. "People who work on the streets of any city tend to know what's going on around them. Besides, that man's brother-in-law happens to own a stable and rents horses for mountain rides."

It was like a network, she realized, a series of connections between people, each possessing a specific kind of information. Drew was obviously plugged in to that network.

"Is this how you work anywhere in the world?" she asked curiously. "Asking questions until they spread out like ripples in a pool?"

"That's a good description," he replied. "It doesn't always work that way, but if I go into a situation with more questions than answers it's an effective way to operate. The people I talk to may not know anything helpful, but the people *they* talk to just might."

"Why do they bother to help? Money?"

"Sometimes, but it's often a question of favors. Having someone owe you a favor may be worth more than money."

Spencer thought about that as they continued to wander almost lazily through Innsbruck. Drew pointed out various sights and she responded appropriately, but she noticed that he spoke to three more people as casually as he had the others. As far as she could tell from her almost nonexistent German, two of those responded with negative answers and one appeared doubtful.

She didn't ask Drew to confirm her impressions. The sense of urgency she'd felt since the thief had stolen her father's papers was still with her, but there was also—though she was reluctant to admit it to him—a very strong feeling of confidence in Drew. She had little doubt that her chances of locating the cross had increased tenfold once he had joined her in the search. And for the first time, she truly felt that her certainty in his abilities did nothing to diminish *her*.

This was his world, his area of expertise, and she could accept that now with no loss of her own hard-won confidence. She no longer felt so inadequate, uncertain, or even in awe of him. She respected his knowledge and abilities, and found both fascinating rather than threatening.

What a difference ten years could make.

There was something else, Spencer admitted silently, which had pushed her urgency regarding the cross out of the forefront of her mind. She had fallen in love with Drew with all the wild desperation of a teenager, had run from him in an equally intense panic two years later, and had realized only when he reappeared in her life days ago that all these years, in some deeply buried part of herself, she had been waiting for him to claim what belonged to him.

Now he was going to. Though she hadn't asked, she was certain that he had chosen a one-bedroom suite for them this time. Since her arrival in Paris he had taken charge with cool authority, and after what she had said on the jet she had little doubt that he expected to be in her bed tonight and that he had arranged the accommodations accordingly.

It was difficult to think of anything but that waiting bedroom, even though she had tried to. A part of her was filled with a sense of expectation she'd never known before—heart thudding unevenly, a vague weakness in her knees and vivid memories of earlier kisses and touches rising up with no warning to catch at her breath. But she was nervous, too, and more than once she glanced up at the tall man by her side and felt a pang of alarm.

Those fleeting sensations of anxiety were the hardest to push away because they came from her own awareness of vulnerability. She knew that whatever Drew's intentions were—to scratch an old itch, to get her out of his system or to begin some kind of new relationship between them—she had committed herself to him. From now on, and particularly after tonight, she would be vulnerable to him as she'd never been before.

If anything had been needed to prove to her that her marriage had been a mistake, that was certainly proof enough. She had never committed herself to Reece or to their marriage; the divorce had brought pain only in her realization that she'd been a fool to marry him. She would never be able to say goodbye to Drew so painlessly, she knew.

"You've gone quiet on me again," Drew said.

"Have I? I'm sorry." She looked around to find that they were heading back toward the inn, and wondered just how long she'd been silent.

"Tired?"

She glanced up, encountered the warm concern in his eyes and immediately forgot whatever she'd been about to say.

"Don't look at me like that," he murmured. "We're on a public sidewalk."

They were stopped on a public sidewalk, she realized, and tried to think of something to say. It was ridiculously difficult. He was holding her hand now. She liked that. "I'm not tired," she managed finally.

He took a deep breath, looked away from her with an obvious effort and said, "It's getting late. I know a good restaurant just around the corner from the inn. Why don't we have dinner before we go back."

Years before, that nearly toneless voice would have made her believe he was indifferent, and the remoteness of his handsome face would have further unnerved her. Now, what she saw and heard was an almost rigid mask of control over emotions a long way from detached. For the first time, she wondered if that stern self-command would desert him in bed, and the possibility that it would sent a warm shiver through her body.

What kind of a lover would he be? Would he be gentle? Rough and urgent? Impetuous, or slow and deliberate? A considerate lover or a selfish one? She didn't think he'd be selfish. She knew he was skilled. He had to be. From what she'd heard and seen herself, he'd had women chasing him since his teens, and during the past ten years there had been a number of stories circulating in D.C., where he made his home base, about women he was involved with in various corners of the globe.

Spencer hated those women. She hated them with a wave of emotion so sudden and so powerful it shocked her. The feelings were raw and primitive, churning inside her until she could hardly bear it. Jealous. That was it, that was what she was feeling. She was painfully, furiously jealous of every woman he had held in his arms.

He must have felt the intensity of her gaze, because his voice had changed when he murmured her name.

"Spencer . . ."

He wasn't looking at her, and she could hear the strain now, the faint tremor of something stretched so tightly it was in danger of snapping. It was a quality that seemed alien to his deep, low voice, and it was strangely moving.

She cleared her throat in an uncertain little sound and tried to remember what he had said. Dinner, that was it. "Fine," she said huskily. "Dinner's fine."

Dinner was fine, though neither of them had much to say and Spencer, at least, had no idea what she ate. It occurred to her that Drew always seemed to be feeding her, and she wasn't quite sure how she felt about that; no one had ever taken care of her before, not the way Drew did. Her father, though she had no doubt of his love, had always been absentminded when it came to the practical-ities of life, and during their short-lived marriage, Reece had been concerned, first and foremost, with himself—his needs, his pleas-ures, his emotions.

Drew, it seemed, was very different. Some might have called him domineering, but Spencer didn't think that was it. Though she couldn't be sure, she doubted that it was his nature to be autocratic. The feeling she got from his matter-of-fact attitude was that he was just doing everything he could to make this trip easier for her. At the farm in D.C. he had been angry that she refused to take a break and hadn't eaten, and he'd promptly made certain she did both. In Paris she had been conscious of her exhaustion and had probably showed it—he had even commented on it later. Again, he'd made certain she ate something and got enough rest.

Was that why she hadn't felt a desire to fight it when he took charge of all the travel arrangements? Because her instincts told her his motive was concern? Whatever the reason, she decided to stop worrying about her own acquiescence. It hardly seemed important compared to everything else.

They finished eating and left the restaurant, both still relatively silent. She thought Drew seemed a bit tense, and thought she knew why—until he stopped in the lobby of their inn and handed her a room key.

"The suite's on the second floor," he said.

Spencer looked at the key, then at him. "That sounds sort of like 'see you later,' " she noted a bit dryly.

In a voice that held reluctance he said, "Unfortunately, that's what it is. Spencer, there are a couple of men I have to locate, men who might be able to help us, and they won't talk to me unless I'm alone."

"More contacts?" She stared down at the room key in her hand.

"Yes. I should be back within a few hours."

"I see," she murmured.

Drew had released her hand when he'd stopped, and now reached up to brush a strand of shining raven hair away from her cheek. His hand lingered, thumb brushing her cheekbone. "I don't want to leave you," he said a bit roughly.

A little embarrassed by the intensity of her own disappointment, Spencer managed, with an effort, to meet his steady gaze, and was immediately reassured. Her cheeks remained unusually warm, but at least she was able to smile at him. "I see that, too," she said softly.

He bent her head and kissed her swiftly and briefly, then

looked at her, a muscle leaping in his tightly held jaw. "When this is over and Allan's seen the cross," he said, "I'm taking you to Wales."

She blinked. "Wales? What's in Wales?"

"A castle. With a moat and a drawbridge. It kept out invaders a few centuries ago. I think it can keep the world at bay long enough for you and I to have a little unhurried time alone." He kissed her again, just as briefly as before. "Do me a favor and stay in the suite while I'm gone, all right?"

"All right," she agreed, a bit dazed. It wasn't until she was in the suite a few minutes later that she wondered why he'd asked her to stay put, and by then she was thinking clearly enough to know the answer.

He had warned her, more than once, that by going after the cross she was entering a dangerous world where the rules were different and the stakes were high enough to spark violence. All afternoon, she realized now, Drew had been unusually alert. That was why she'd sensed a distraction in him—and partly why he'd made certain she never strayed from his side. Despite his almost lazy attitude and the casual questions to his contacts, he had been extremely wary and watchful.

She didn't know if he expected trouble or was merely cautious enough to be vigilant, but it was clear that Drew was readying himself for whatever might come.

Spencer frowned as she pushed herself away from the door she'd been leaning against since coming into the suite and walked slowly into the sitting room, dropping her tote bag absently onto a chair. She wondered about the contacts he was trying to locate now, the ones he'd said wouldn't talk to him unless he was alone. She doubted that was because they were shy. Maybe her imagination hadn't been so far off when she'd envisioned furtive meetings in dangerous places.

"He knows what he's doing," she said, startling herself with the sound of her own voice in the silent room. She blinked and looked around, seeing that she'd been right in thinking he would get a one-bedroom suite. The realization distracted her mind from anxious thoughts that, if not entirely leaving her, at least retreated a bit so that they were shadows in the back of her awareness.

She went into the bedroom, turning on a lamp since it was getting dark outside. The king-size bed had been readied for the night, covers turned back invitingly. It was odd, she thought, the things that got to you: her bags and Drew's had been brought up by a bellman and were now neatly on luggage racks near the bed. The sight of them made her throat ache for some reason.

Before she could ponder that, she looked at the phone on the nightstand and noticed that the message light was blinking, and a pang of fear shot through her. Had Tucker called about her father? Had he—

Then she remembered that she hadn't known where they'd be staying, so Tucker couldn't know, either, or at least it wasn't likely that he could know, and her racing heart slowed. She went over and sat on the bed, then lifted the receiver and called down to the desk. The message turned out to be for Drew, and she wrote it on a notepad she found in the top drawer of the nightstand.

It was a simple message, though it made little sense to Spencer. Someone named Pendleton had called and said that they were in Madrid if Drew needed them. They? Who were they? Friends, or at least allies, from the sound of it. Were they, she wondered, some of the people Drew had gotten in touch with early this morning in Paris? Or had one of his questions today sent a ripple all the way to Spain? The terse message seemed to presuppose that he'd know where in Madrid he could find them. Spencer had no idea if he would, but made a mental note to ask because she was curious.

While she was sitting on the edge of the bed, she called home to let Tucker know where she was staying and to check on her father. Unexpressive as always, Tucker told her that her father seemed to be stronger physically, but that he'd been fretting over her.

"Why?" she asked.

"Unfortunately, he's been muttering in German, a language I've never been comfortable in, but I gather he's saying something about a journal you haven't seen."

Spencer frowned to herself. "I saw all the journals that related to his notes. Didn't I?"

"I thought so." Tucker paused, then continued slowly. "Just before he had the stroke he received a package from a man who had been doing research for him. It could have held a journal."

She knew that her father had hired researchers during the past few years, because his doctors had forbidden him to do any globe-trotting, but she wasn't certain what information they'd been instructed to search for. A journal she hadn't seen?

"Tucker . . . without upsetting Dad, try to get him to tell you what he means, all right? If there is a journal, try to find it. I need to at least know who wrote it, especially if Dad thinks it's important."

"He may be rambling, you realize that?"

"Yes. But try, anyway."

"I'll see what I can do."

"Thanks." Tucker was a storehouse of information, especially when it came to the people with whom Allan Wyatt had associated throughout his life, and Spencer wondered . . . She hesitated, feeling a bit foolish, then said, "Tucker? Does Drew have a castle?"

There was a moment of silence and then Tucker's voice came over the line calmly. "In Wales, I believe."

"Oh." What else was there to say in response to that, she wondered. How would she have reacted at eighteen, discovering that her prince had an honest-to-God castle? For heaven's sake. . . . "I was . . . just wondering. I'll try to call tomorrow, but we may be up in the mountains most of the day so don't worry if you don't hear from me."

"Take care."

Her laugh was a little shaky. "Drew's doing that. 'Bye, Tucker."

After hanging up the phone she went into the sitting room to turn on a couple of lamps and the television set, which she tuned to an international news program in English, more for the sound of voices than because there was anything in particular she wanted to know about. Deciding once again not to unpack except what was necessary, she chose a change of clothing for the following day— anticipating a ride into the mountains—and sleepwear.

The last gave her something of a problem. She'd packed for practicality and comfort on this trip, and her bedtime choices consisted of a couple of overlarge sleep shirts. They were dandy for sleeping when one slept alone, but hardly what any self-respecting woman would call sexy. Last night a thick hotel robe had hidden the sight of a football-jersey-type shirt from Drew's gaze.

What about tonight? Spencer wasn't a vain woman, but she was certainly feminine enough to want to look her best tonight of all nights. After debating with herself briefly, she left the sleep shirts packed, got her room key and tote bag and left the suite. She'd told Drew she would stay in the suite, but surely going down to that little shop off the lobby wouldn't hurt.

Luckily, it didn't. Spencer was able to get down there and back in fifteen minutes without incident. She didn't know whether to be amused or distressed by the pride that had sent her in search of a nightgown. Here she was, in Innsbruck, Austria, engaged in a kind of treasure hunt for a centuries-old cross, with possible enemies lurking about, and the goal uppermost in her mind had been to buy a sexy nightgown.

In the end, she had to laugh at herself, and that wry amuse-

ment turned out to be a blessing. Without it she probably would
have been forced to cope with ragged nerves much sooner.

It wasn't so bad at first. She took a long shower, washed and
dried her hair, then put on the shimmering lavender nightgown
and negligee. She ordered some fruit juice to be sent up before
room service closed down for the night—the inn didn't keep chain-
hotel hours—and sipped a glass of that as she watched the cover-
age of a competition at the Olympic Ice Stadium on television.

Sometime around nine she found herself staring at her
hands, vaguely bothered. Her nails were still long and perfectly
polished. She kept them that way, requiring a conscious effort
considering her rough work with horses, because her mother had
had beautiful hands. But Drew had said something that first
night, she remembered now. Something about hands that had
never done any work.

Frowning, she dug out her travel manicure set, stripped off the
pale polish and ruthlessly filed her nails down to neat, short ovals.
She told herself it was because they'd probably have to do some
digging or the like tomorrow and long nails would only get in her
way. It wasn't, of course, because of anything Drew had said.

As time passed, things began nagging at her. All kinds of
things. Where was Drew? Was he all right? That journal . . . A journal her father thought she hadn't read, and why was it important?
She'd run from Drew ten years ago—what made her think she
could handle him now? Furtive meetings in dangerous places. She
was asking for heartache, just *asking* for it, and he'd been so angry
that first night, a man couldn't change that much in such a short
time. Could he? Was he all right? He was the threat to their competitors for the cross, not her, so he'd be the target if someone
wanted to . . . Reece had been the glitter; was Drew the gold? He'd
been gone a long time, but surely he knew what he was doing.
Surely. Would she please him as a lover? She felt so nervous about

that. She lost control when he kissed her, touched her, and maybe . . . The intensity of her response to him was something she'd never felt before, something overwhelming . . . Was that wrong?

The jumble of questions and thoughts went on and on, becoming more tangled as the minutes ticked past. A small, rational voice in her head told her it was just nerves, that she was worried about Drew, about them and what they might be after tonight, about her father and the cross, but the whisper of reason didn't help. Uncertainties were chasing her like tiny, snapping demons, and her earlier confidence began to desert her. There was too much she couldn't control, and she'd fought so hard for at least the illusion of control in the past months.

An illusion. That's what it was. Or a delusion. Yes, she was deluding herself. Falling in love with him all over again despite the mess she'd made of things the first time—

The realization had barely risen in her mind when the sound of a key in the door cut through the silence. She had turned off the television and had been pacing. When she heard the door being unlocked she stopped near the bedroom door and swung around to face the short hallway.

When Drew stepped inside and closed the door, what he saw made him forget everything except her. She had obviously just turned toward him, the full skirts of her long nightgown and negligee sweeping out around her, and the silky material shimmered with the movement. Her black hair tumbled around her shoulders, and wide gray eyes met his with a disturbed intensity he could feel as well as see.

He came slowly into the room, shrugging out of his jacket, and dropping it carelessly onto a chair. He stopped a few feet away from her, trying and failing to read the emotions stirring in her eyes. The light was too dim or she was too wary—he didn't know which. Wary himself, he said, "I'm sorry—I didn't mean to startle you."

She took a quick breath, almost as if she'd forgotten to breathe for a moment, and when she spoke her voice was husky. "Did you find out anything?"

"No, but there's a good chance we'll know something by morning."

Spencer moved away from the bedroom doorway and away from him, toward a window. "I called home. Tucker says Dad's fretting. Something about a journal I haven't seen." Her voice sounded nervous to her own ears, and she tried to steady it. "I don't even know if it's important, but Tucker's promised to try and get Dad to explain. If he can. Sometimes Dad gets an idea into his head and just won't let go, even if it doesn't make sense to anyone else. It may not mean anything—"

"Spencer."

She felt herself tense even more, and a sudden wave of panic swept over her. No, it was a mistake, another mistake. She wasn't ready for this, she couldn't handle him, he was too much and she'd be lost in him. She swung around to voice the wild protest, but it tangled in her throat when she found him too close. He'd crossed the space between them in silence, and she couldn't back away because there was nowhere for her to go.

Drew didn't give her a chance to try to move, or to say anything at all. He pulled her stiff body into his arms, bent his head and covered her parted lips with his. He kissed her with a hunger so intense it seared through her like a brand, his mouth hard and greedy, his tongue sliding into her mouth with the certain intimacy of a lover.

Her rigidity melted away instantly, her body molding itself pliantly to his. She lifted her arms to slide them around his lean waist, holding on to him, her panic replaced by a wave of sharp pleasure and urgent need every bit as uncontrollable. As always, she was his the moment he touched her, doubts and questions scattered to the winds, the familiar desire spreading through her like wildfire.

She murmured a faint, wordless protest when his mouth left hers, opening her eyes reluctantly. She wondered with only vague interest why she had wanted to protest this. She belonged here, in his arms. She belonged to him.

"I left you alone too long," he said thickly, one hand sliding down her back to press her even closer. The topaz heat in his eyes intensified when she caught her breath, and a muscle leaped in his taut jaw. "Maybe that was the mistake I made before."

"Mistake?" She felt so dazed and feverish that she could hardly think.

"I should have ignored the rules." His lips feathered along her jaw, and when her head fell back helplessly he explored the vulnerable flesh of her throat. "I shouldn't have given you time enough to think."

Spencer didn't want to think now—she only wanted to feel. Her whole body was hot and aching, her heart was racing and she couldn't seem to breathe. Her body moved against his, instinctively seeking, and the instant response of his hard body sent a shudder of need rippling through her.

Drew made a low, rough sound and kissed her again, the intensity of his desire already so much greater that it was as if he touched her with a live wire. She moaned into his mouth, her fingers digging into his back, and all the strength drained out of her legs in a rush.

Still kissing her urgently, he gently broke the death grip of her arms and swept her up, carrying her into the bedroom. She was dimly aware of the movement, conscious of a feeling of lightness in his arms as if she were floating. Then she was on her feet again, beside the bed and still enveloped in his heat. The negligee was tugged from her shoulders, and her hands blindly pushed his sweater up until he paused long enough to yank it off and throw it aside.

He hadn't worn a shirt under the sweater, and when her hands encountered his bare skin she made an unconscious sound of pleasure. The hard muscles of his back rippled under her seeking fingers, his flesh smooth and heated, and she loved the way he felt beneath her touch. And the way his touch felt. She could feel his mouth moving down her throat, feel the hot darts of his tongue touching her skin. His elegant, powerful hands cupped her buttocks, moving sensuously as the silk of her nightgown provided a slippery friction, and he began drawing the long skirt up slowly as his fingers caressed her.

"You feel so good," he muttered hoarsely, strong fingers kneading her firm flesh and slowly, very slowly, gathering the material of her skirt into his hands as he pulled it up.

Spencer got her own hands between them and touched his hard stomach that was ridged with muscle, then moved higher to explore the hair-roughened expanse of his chest. Unlike most blond men, Drew possessed a literal pelt of golden hair covering his chest, so soft and thick to the touch that she wanted to purr at the erotic feel of it. Her breasts seemed to swell, her nipples tighten in anticipation, and she was suddenly wild to press herself against him.

Then she felt his hands on her bare bottom, the skin of his palms a little rough, and a jolt of pleasure caught at her breath. "Drew," she whispered, unconsciously pleading, her short nails digging into his chest. She couldn't bear much more; the intensity of sensation was so sharp it was a bittersweet pain.

He raised his head and looked down at her, his hands still moving over her silky flesh. He was so hungry for her that the slow caresses were torture, but it was a torture he had to endure. For ten years she had haunted his dreams, thoughts and memories of her shut up in his subconscious because his waking mind had been too bitter to accept them, and touching her now was as necessary to him as every beat of his heart.

She was here, in his arms, her smoke-gray eyes dazed and lovely face soft with wanting him, reality instead of a dream, and he wanted to prolong the loving no matter what it cost him. He wanted to explore all the textures of her body, touch and taste and sate himself in her. Even more, he wanted to please her, and needed to forge a bond between them that would leave them connected when morning and all its potential problems intruded.

"I want you so much," he said in a thickened, rasping voice, merging all the wants and needs into a single, overwhelmingly simple statement.

"Yes," she murmured, her eyes fixed on his face. "Yes, please."

He kissed her parted lips again and again, feeling her hands moving restlessly against his chest, and when she kissed him back wildly the threads of his self-control began snapping. What his mind wanted and his body could stand were two different things. Desire spiraled inside him, hot and greedy, and a ragged sound escaped him.

He pulled the nightgown up and off her, tossing it aside, then lifted her in almost the same motion and bent to lay her on the bed. Reluctant to stop touching her even for a moment, he swiftly discarded the remainder of his clothing, unable to take his eyes off her. She was beautiful, slender and perfectly formed, her breasts surprisingly round and firm, her waist tiny and hips curved gently. He'd always thought her beautiful clothed, but naked she was magnificent. Her black hair spread out on the pillow in a cloud of gleaming darkness around her face, and she was looking at him with gray eyes so bottomless he knew he could lose himself in them.

Naked, he eased down beside her, moving slowly because he was fighting to control himself. His need for her had grown so intense it edged into savagery, and the delicacy of her slight body was a vivid reminder of how easily he could hurt her. He kissed her deeply, exploring the warm sweetness of her mouth, and her arms lifted around his neck.

She made a little sound when his lips left hers, and he concentrated fiercely to hold on to his threadbare control. That sound . . . It was a soft, throaty purr of pleasure, and it drove his desire impossibly higher. He braced himself on an elbow beside her, brushing his lips over the warm, satiny skin of her face, her throat, then drifting lower to her breastbone. He slid a hand slowly up over her narrow rib cage and surrounded one swollen breast, his thumb circling the nipple rhythmically as his mouth closed over the other one.

Spencer caught her breath and jerked slightly, his hand and mouth on her breasts affecting her like nothing she'd ever felt before. She had thought she'd reached the absolute limits of what she could bear, but the hot, sweet tension coiled even more tightly inside her, tormenting her, as he caressed her breasts. When his hand moved down her quivering belly and his fingers probed gently between her thighs, she jerked again and moaned. The most exquisitely sensitive nerves in her body throbbed wildly at his touch, and she felt a strange, panicky sensation well up inside her.

"Drew . . . don't . . . I can't—"

He lifted his head, burning eyes fixed on her face. His expression was so fierce, so utterly male and primitive that it made her pounding heart skip a beat, and in that flashing instant she realized with utter clarity that Drew was capable of depths of emotion she had never suspected.

"Please," she whispered, and some part of her knew that it wasn't just an end to the physical torment she pleaded for, but something far more elusive.

He kissed her hungrily, shifting his weight until he rose above her and between her trembling thighs. His powerful body was so much larger than hers, so much harder and more forceful, and the feverish need in him was a primal male demand that called out commandingly to everything in her that was female. She could have refused him nothing. Her eyes locked with his and the breath caught in her throat as her body slowly accepted him.

It had been a long time for her and he was a big man; she could feel the taut stretching of her flesh and the brief, instinctively shocked feminine awareness of an intruder. But then, in a curious melding she'd never known before, he seemed to become part of her, filling an emptiness she hadn't been conscious of and making her feel, for the first time in her life, complete.

A single tear slid from the corner of her eye and a shuddering breath left her as he settled fully into the cradle of her thighs. She could feel him pulsing deep inside her, and the hovering tension of desire began winding tightly again. His eyes were burning down at her and his mouth was hard as it covered hers. He was heavy, wonderfully heavy. Then he began moving.

I love you. She didn't say the words aloud, at least she didn't think she did, but Spencer heard them echoing in her mind even as her body went totally out of her control. She had few clear memories of that first joining, except for sensations and the certain, dimly shocking realization that her need for him was so overwhelming that nothing else mattered.

She was virtually untaught in the art of giving or receiving pleasure, but with Drew either her instincts or her love for him made knowledge unimportant. Her body knew how to respond to him, and she was incapable of controlling or even tempering her acute desire. Even as he claimed what belonged to him, his own urgent hunger had, in some way, set her free.

She barely heard the sounds she made, or realized how wildly her body writhed beneath his. All she was conscious of was the maddening tension, the frantic straining and striving to reach something just beyond her grasp. She wasn't aware of crying, of clinging to him desperately and pleading with him in a voice she would never have recognized as her own.

Until, finally, the pressure increased beyond bearing and snapped with a shock that was waves and waves of burning, pulsing ecstasy. The heat washed over her, consumed her, and she held him with all the strength left to her when it consumed him, too.

chapter eight

"YOU CRIED," HE said.

Spencer had felt him lift his head and ease the weight of his upper body onto his elbows, but she'd kept her eyes closed. Her arms were still around his neck, her legs coiled limply with his. She felt utterly drained, almost boneless, and she didn't know if she could look him in the eye. She'd gone crazy in his arms, and her own lack of control embarrassed her. In fact, it appalled her. That had never happened to her before, and she was half afraid that it was somehow wrong. Even though he hadn't seemed to notice anything to complain about, and even though it had certainly *felt* amazingly wonderful—

"Sweetheart, did I hurt you?"

She looked at him then, startled by the question as much as the troubled undertone in his low voice. She hadn't known his mouth could curve so tenderly or that his eyes could hold such a glow. Her heart turned over with a lurch, and she had to clear her throat before she could say huskily, "No, you didn't hurt me."

He brushed a strand of hair back from her temple, his thumb stroking the soft skin there as if he could feel the wetness of her tears. "You cried," he said again.

That wasn't all she'd done, Spencer thought. How many times had she pleaded with him? She didn't remember, but heat rose in her face and her eyes skittered away from his. "I didn't know I could feel that way." She had to admit it, if only to ease his concern. "I guess that was why."

Drew seemed to hesitate, a brief look of indecision on his face, then kissed her gently. "I knew you were having second thoughts when I came back, but I couldn't wait. I'd waited so long for you already. Even now . . . I don't want to leave you. Am I too heavy?"

"No." She focused her gaze on his chin, still unable to meet his eyes except fleetingly. She hadn't realized that the lamplight was so bright, but it was, and they were lying on top of the covers, naked bodies still entwined. Still joined. So close and starkly intimate. He wasn't too heavy, she wasn't physically uncomfortable, but . . . His weight and much greater size held her easily beneath him in an unnervingly primitive way, and with memories of her wild pleas and frantic, passionate sounds becoming more and more vivid in her mind, her embarrassment was intensifying rapidly.

Her wanton behavior was all the more shocking to her because it was so vastly different from the way she'd been with Reece. He'd been obsessed with her during the first short months of their marriage, so much so that he'd been gentle with her and concerned about her pleasure—even if his own had come first. But she had never lost control with Reece, and she'd never felt anything more than mild pleasure in their bed.

With Drew, what she'd felt had been so acute it was a kind of sensual madness, so utterly overwhelming that she'd had no hope of controlling it—or herself. She had given herself to him as if some ancient instinct had demanded it, with passionate intensity and total abandon. One difference, of course, was that she loved Drew as she'd never come close to loving Reece. She belonged to Drew in a way that was basic and primitive, touching all her deepest emotions. But knowledge of that didn't help ease her anxiety now. She was so vulnerable to him, and her mindless abandonment with him made her feel even more defenseless.

His hands surrounded her face warmly, and he moved subtly against her and inside her. She caught her breath and looked into his eyes helplessly.

They were a little narrowed as he gazed down at her, veiled so that she couldn't guess what he was thinking. And when he spoke his voice was lower, rougher, something implacable in the words. "You're trying to hide from me. I won't let you do that, Spencer. What is it? What's wrong?"

She didn't want to answer, but refusing him anything was still beyond her, and she couldn't look away now because his eyes held her trapped. "I couldn't . . . control myself," she whispered.

Drew brushed one thumb across a delicate cheekbone, feeling the heat of embarrassment burning in her skin. He could see it in her smoky eyes as well, along with anxiety and uncertainty. Was that why she seemed so far away from him now despite their physical closeness, because she was worried about the intensity of her response?

He thought that was it, and it gave him a strong sense of both pleasure and triumph to know that no other man had felt the fire of her passion, but he had no intention of allowing her to try to temper that response in any way. He wanted her to be certain that nothing she felt in his arms, nothing she said or did, could ever be wrong.

He kissed one corner of her trembling lips and then the other, his lower body moving again subtly so that she could feel his renewing desire. "Do you know what you do to me?" he murmured against her soft skin. "You make me so crazy I can't even think, so hot with need that nothing else matters. I love the way you feel, soft and warm against me, the way your body fits mine so perfectly. I love the passion in you, the wild, sweet way you respond when I touch you."

Spencer felt his mouth on her throat, the slight vibrations of his words an added caress, and she closed her eyes as dizzying pleasure began welling up inside her. He was moving just enough to make her aware of it, and her breathing quickened as her body responded wildly to the erotic sensations. She felt feverish, and exhaustion was forgotten as her legs lifted to wrap around his hips and her hands wandered restlessly over the taut muscles of his back and shoulders.

He lifted his head to gaze down at her. "Look at me," he murmured, and when her eyes flickered open dazedly he held them with his own. His voice grew rougher and more strained, the slow, deliberate movements against her combined with the tight heat of her flesh sheathing his so erotically charged that every nerve in his body was screaming with pleasure.

"That night at your house . . . you looked so cool, so distant. Untouchable. It drove me mad. I wanted to see you like this, naked and burning for me." She made a tiny sound and he kissed her deeply, taking it into his mouth. "I wanted to make you go crazy, just the way I go crazy when my hands are on you. You feel so good, so tight and silky . . ."

Spencer whimpered a little, her body beginning to move instinctively beneath him. She couldn't be still, because he was torturing her and she couldn't bear it. Her short nails dug into his back, the hot, sweet tension coiling, stealing her breath. She couldn't control herself, just like before, her body writhing, desperate pleas and wordless sounds winging free of her.

He held her securely, his hands stroking her heated flesh as his body seduced hers. His voice encouraged her to let herself feel, to let herself go completely, as he hoarsely muttered bluntly sexual words of passionate need. Until finally Spencer's restless shifting beneath him became the lithe, graceful undulations of essential female desire, an imperative hunger that could no longer be denied or resisted.

Drew groaned and tangled his fingers in her thick hair, kissing her urgently, and his subtle movements abruptly became deep thrusts as his control shattered. He knew he was going to explode, the pressure building so violently that he was conscious of nothing but the torturing fire of that and the woman who cradled his straining body, urging him on with her own frantic need. He drove into her again and again, barely hearing her soft moans and cries or his own hoarse sounds, the primitive drive toward completion so overwhelming that if he had known release meant death, he wouldn't—couldn't—have stopped.

He was deep inside her when the hot, rhythmic contractions of her pleasure caught him in an unbelievably sensual caress, and her gasping cry was trapped in his mouth as he kissed her with an unconscious, ancient possessiveness. She was crying again—he could taste the salt of her tears—and his own release shuddered through him with a force so intense it bordered on agony, leaving him drained.

Spencer didn't think at all during the following hours. She slept for a while, held warmly in his arms, not even aware when he got them under the covers and turned out the lamp. She woke once in the darkness, his hands and mouth bringing her body vividly alive again, the pleasure so acute that she lost herself in it without even trying to resist. Lost herself in him. And it was still terrifying and exhilarating and something she had no will to withstand. Even if his words and his own intense passion hadn't reassured her, she couldn't have held back, couldn't have tempered her response to him. If she didn't cry out her love it was only because she was convinced he wouldn't want it.

IT WAS THE chill of being alone that woke Spencer the second time, and even before she opened her eyes she knew that if he'd left her without a word she wouldn't be able to bear it. As soon as she opened her eyes she saw him, standing by the window. Moonlight spilled through the panes to show her a stark profile that was too beautiful to belong to a man and yet was utterly masculine. She lay there for a moment watching him, vaguely conscious that her body felt different but far more aware of him than of herself.

His body was in shadow, the darkness hiding his nakedness, and the expression on his face was remote. Knowing him better now, Spencer recognized that remoteness and understood that it was his mask of control. He was disturbed about something, his disquiet strong enough to have driven him from their bed in the cold, lonely hours before dawn.

With a vivid memory of the lover he had been in this bed stamped deeply in her mind and body, Spencer felt a chill touch of fear. Demons of uncertainty snapping at her heels. He'd said he would teach her what it felt like to be in thrall to someone else; now she knew. Had that been his goal all along, to have the satisfaction of knowing that her desire for him was like an addiction, a craving in her blood?

If he wanted to hurt her, there would never be a better time. A few cutting words or merely a cool goodbye, and she'd be devastated. She wanted to close her eyes and pretend she hadn't awakened, pretend that nothing was wrong. Morning was soon enough, she thought painfully, to face whatever he'd say.

She couldn't pretend. There had already been too much pretense in her life. Feeling so vulnerable that it was terrifying, she sat up slowly in the bed and wrapped her arms around her upraised knees.

He didn't turn his head to look at her, but obviously knew she was awake. His voice was soft when he spoke. "Why, Spencer?"

She waited, not sure what he was questioning.

"Why did you marry him?"

Not an easy question to answer, but at least it wasn't—yet—goodbye. She drew a breath and held her voice steady. "Because I was afraid."

He did turn his head then, his eyes sharply probing the dimness of the room. "Afraid of me?" His surprise was obvious, and there was more, something she couldn't identify.

Spencer managed the ghost of a laugh. "You. Me. So many things. It was nothing you'd done. I was just afraid. I think I knew even then—"

"What?"

She hesitated, but just couldn't bring herself to say, *I knew I was lost even then, knew I belonged to you.* Instead, she explained another part of the truth. "I knew that I could never measure up. That I was . . . inadequate."

"What are you talking about?" He left the window and crossed the room to the bed, sitting down on the edge. When he reached toward the lamp on the nightstand, she spoke quickly.

"We don't really need the light, do we?"

Drew hesitated, but then allowed his arm to relax. The room wasn't totally dark, so they were vaguely visible to each other. Blurred features and the colorless dark shine of eyes. "Do we need the dark?" he asked finally, quietly.

She was silent, and after a moment he seemed to accept the tacit reply. "Spencer, why did you think you were inadequate? In what way inadequate?"

"I was pretending." Her voice was so low it was only a murmur of sound, but perfectly clear and audible in the hushed room. "Pretending that I was someone else. Being . . . assured and confident, and always in control. As if that was the real me, as if I belonged. But I didn't. It was all a sham. I was just pretending. And there you were, the real thing."

"Spencer—"

She cut him off, going on in the same soft, deliberate tone, almost without expression. "That first time you came to the house, when I was sixteen, I knew who you were. I'd heard Dad and other people talk about you. About all the things you'd done—and you were barely out of college. The way they talked, about summer digs and trips to dangerous, exotic places, about your uncanny instincts and how brilliant you were, it made me picture you as something larger than life.

"Then I—I looked up that night and saw you." Spencer was lost in memories, the night she had first seen him so vivid in her mind that the clarity of the image was almost painful. "You came through the door, and maybe it was the light falling a certain way or—or something, but whatever it was, you seemed to be . . . all gold. Something so bright it made my eyes hurt and stole my breath. People made way for you, as if they knew it, too, as if they knew you were apart from the rest."

She blinked, looked at him. She was unable to read his expression in the dimness, but was grateful that he said nothing. It gave her the chance to get hold of herself, so that she was able to manage an almost impersonal voice. "Larger than life. Not only that, but you were everything I wanted to be. Elegant. Sophisticated. Confident and assured. Always calm and in control. I had . . . polished up myself, and the gloss fooled just about everybody. But you were the genuine article. Something I could never be."

Still unmoving, he said in an odd voice, "That was why you ran? Because I made you feel inadequate?"

Spencer was too honest to say yes and let it go at that. "It was partly that. I didn't know what you saw in me, but I knew I was pretending. I felt like a phony." A humorless breath of a laugh escaped, and she shrugged a little. "I was afraid. Confused. I didn't understand you or myself, and both of us scared me. Drew, I was eighteen, and not a very mature eighteen at that, not inside. If I was thinking clearly at all, the only thing I was sure of was that there was . . . too much of you and not enough of me. I was afraid of getting lost. That was the most terrifying thing of all. So I ran."

"To Cabot." Drew's voice had an edge now, a curiously ragged edge. "Why him, Spencer? Why did you run to him?"

She shook her head slightly, almost helplessly. "It seemed so clear then. The only answer. Now . . . I don't know. Because he was uncomplicated, I guess. Because he was brash instead of controlled. Because he wasn't larger than life. Everything that he was lay on the surface of him, easily seen and touched and understood. He had no secrets or shadows, no complexities, and I thought he was—safer. I'd known him for years, and for years he'd been saying he was going to marry me. Even after I got engaged to you, he sent me flowers and called me, and he kept saying he was going to marry me."

"You didn't love him." It wasn't a question, and yet there was a question in it.

Spencer hesitated, then shook her head again. "No. But I thought I could learn to love him. He—he didn't expect anything of me, Drew, ask anything except that I *be*. I didn't feel as if there was something I had to live up to with him, some image of myself that wasn't real. I didn't know what you wanted of me, but I was afraid that whatever you wanted I didn't have. He just wanted to love me, I thought, and I believed it would be better to be loved— without complications."

Drew was silent for a moment, still motionless, then said flatly, "What happened?"

This time her soft laugh was wry. "If I'd been older or wiser maybe I would have realized that any love with no depth couldn't possibly last, any more than a man with no depth could feel anything except fleetingly. Reece was like a child with a bright, shiny new toy. Intense, passionate, almost obsessed. Until the next toy caught his attention. Once I was no longer out of his reach I became less . . . desirable, I think. He couldn't love me forever. He couldn't even love me for long."

"Who asked for the divorce?"

She wondered at the question, but answered it honestly. "I did. I wasn't as hurt as I probably deserved to be when I realized Reece was habitually unfaithful, but I was more than a little humiliated by my own stupidity. There were no big fights between us, I just said I was leaving."

"He didn't contest the divorce?"

Spencer's voice held real, if rueful, amusement. "He barely noticed it. He had a new toy he was trying to entice away from her husband, and that was occupying all of his attention." Then her amusement faded, and she said, "His family didn't like it. I think they were afraid I'd drag all the dirty linen through the courts. Before I could file the papers, their lawyer did. So, officially, Reece divorced me on the grounds of irreconcilable differences. I didn't care. I just wanted out."

She drew a deep breath and held her voice steady. "I wish I could make it all sound more dramatic somehow, or at least more compelling. I wish I could make my motives sound less vague and selfish. But I can't. I can't, Drew. I never meant to hurt anyone. I was just afraid."

There was a long silence, and then he said, "You were so afraid of me you couldn't tell me any of this."

Anxious that he had misunderstood, she said, "I wasn't afraid you'd hurt me or—or anything like that. I was just—oh, in awe of you, I guess. I didn't feel close to you, or understand you at all."

"Then why in God's name did you say yes when I asked you to marry me?" he demanded with suppressed violence.

Spencer wanted badly to reach out and touch him, wanted to crawl into his arms and hold on to him with all the desperate love churning inside her. But she held herself still and kept her voice quiet and steady. "Because I was in love with you."

"What? Spencer—"

"Drew, I don't expect you to understand. I don't understand myself. Everything I felt then was so damn confusing. When you asked me to marry you, I'd been mooning over you like a silly little girl for two years, building fantasies around you. I had no idea you wanted to marry me until you said so. Then I didn't know *why* you wanted me."

"I told you I loved you," he said roughly.

"Yes, but . . . I didn't believe that. I couldn't, even though I wanted to. You were always so calm and you never seemed to feel very much except amusement. You were polite and kind, and sometimes I saw you watching me, but you seemed detached. What I felt was so—wild, and I never saw anything like that in you."

He was silent.

Spencer took a deep breath. "I said yes because it was like a dream falling into my lap, and it was only later that I started wondering if there was anything real in the dream. I was sure you wanted a wife as assured and sophisticated as you were—and I *wasn't.* I thought you'd been fooled by me like everyone else, and it was terrifying for me to imagine what you'd think when you discovered the truth."

"What truth?" Drew demanded almost harshly. "What is it you think you were hiding?"

"Me." She felt very tired now, and the room seemed colder than it had been only minutes before. "The real me. Always uneasy and unsure and frightened. I wasn't woman enough for a man like you, and I knew it."

When he moved suddenly it caught her off guard, and before she could say a word she found herself lying back on the bed with Drew leaning over her. "Just for the record," he said in a taut voice, "I'm not made of gold, Spencer. I'm not a schoolgirl's fairy-tale prince and I'm sure as hell not larger than life. I'm just a man, like any other."

"Drew—"

"You were the one who was fooled," he continued in the same taut, relentless voice. "About me and about yourself. The mask you wore was almost transparent—everyone saw through it, including me. We could see the shyness and uncertainty and sweetness, even the fear sometimes. But there was something so . . . graceful about the way you tried, so gentle and gallant. We all saw that, too. Spencer, why do you think I handled you so carefully? Why I was such a bloody gentleman instead of carrying you off over my shoulder as I wanted to? If I'd believed you were the assured, confident woman you tried so hard to be I'd have married you out of the schoolroom instead of waiting for more than two long years to even ask you."

Staring up at him, all she could think of to say was, "I didn't know you wanted to marry me then."

"I made up my mind to marry you that first night," he said, his voice still tight. "But you were too young, and I knew it. So I waited. I knew you were wary, nervous of me, that you were more comfortable with all the damned polite social rules and I tried to be patient and not overwhelm you. You were like a shy little bird, so beautiful and sweet, and so fragile I was almost afraid to touch you."

She lifted a hand to his face almost unconsciously, feeling the hard tension there, and her heart was pounding, aching. If he had felt so much then, and she hadn't hurt him too badly, then maybe there was a chance . . . But he went on speaking before she could complete that thought, and hope died a silent, agonizing death inside her.

"When Allan called me to the house, I knew there was something wrong," he said, his voice as hard as his face now. "I'd never seen him so upset. He didn't know much, he said. He didn't know why. All he knew was that you'd gone, and you'd eloped with Reece Cabot. He gave me the ring, the one I'd given you, and I wanted to throw the damned thing across the room. I wanted to go after you, tear you away from Cabot and carry you off somewhere."

He laughed suddenly, a strange, harsh sound. "Of course, I didn't do that. It wouldn't have been civilized. I told Allan very quietly that I hoped you'd be happy, and I left. I left the country, getting as far away as I could, because I knew if I saw you with his ring on your finger, I wouldn't be able to be civilized about it. I didn't come back until I thought I could. When was that, Spencer, when did we see each other again?"

She swallowed with difficulty, and whispered, "More than two years."

"Twenty-six months, almost to the day. It was at the opening of a gallery. You were divorced by then. You were with Allan, and he was the one who spoke to me first. All three of us were polite and civilized."

Spencer was biting her bottom lip so hard that she tasted

blood, staring up at him. Her hand fell away from him, because she couldn't bear to go on feeling the granite stillness of his face. "I'm sorry," she said almost inaudibly.

"Do you think that helps?" His voice was suddenly quieter, not so harsh as before.

She drew a ragged breath. "Nothing I can say is going to help. It's too late for that."

"Is it?" He bent his head, his mouth brushing hers very lightly, almost absently, again and again. "This helps. Knowing I can make you want me. Knowing he never found the fire in you. Knowing you belong to me now. You do belong to me, don't you, sweetheart?"

She would have denied it if she could have, but he had to know by now. And what did it matter, after all? She'd already given him all she was; admitting it aloud wouldn't change anything, and keeping it to herself wouldn't protect her from hurt. There was still nothing she could deny him, nothing at all.

"Yes," she admitted softly.

His arms gathered her closer, pushing the covers away, and his mouth hardened slowly with desire as he kissed her. Spencer clung to him, and even as her body responded wildly to his passion she was filled with the painful knowledge that she had given her heart and soul to a man who could never love her again—because he had loved her once.

A long time later, as she lay close to his side almost too pleasantly exhausted to think, she murmured, "Drew?"

"Hmm?"

"You said I'd been fooled by you. What did you mean?"

His arms tightened around her. "We all wear masks. Some of us have just had more experience at it than others. Go to sleep, honey. We have to be up in a few hours."

Spencer closed her eyes, but it was a long time before she

drifted off to sleep. Where would they go from here? She no longer feared that Drew would be cruel to her, even though she had a better understanding now of just how badly she'd hurt him, but it was clear to her that all he wanted from her was passion. He'd as good as said it himself. She belonged to him now, and that in some way helped ease his bitterness.

Maybe she owed him that, no matter what it cost her. In any case, it wouldn't be her who walked—or ran—away this time. She loved him too much to end this even if she could summon the strength and will to do it, and she didn't know what she would do when he ended it. All she could do now was to go on a step at a time. A day at a time.

She slept deeply and dreamlessly, waking to the delightful, drowsily sensual feeling of warm kisses. She opened her eyes and smiled when she saw him sitting on the edge of the bed. Her embarrassment of the night was forgotten. He'd been convincing when he'd said he loved her passionate response to him, and since the heat of their desire was a tie between them—the only possible tie—she couldn't feel it was in any way wrong.

"Good morning," he said, smiling just a little.

Spencer realized that he must have been up a while. He was dressed in jeans and a sweater, was freshly shaved and his golden hair was still damp from the shower. "Good morning," she murmured, stretching slightly and wincing at a few twinges.

Drew's intent gaze never missed much, and his smile faded. "Was I too rough?"

She pushed herself into a sitting position and absently held the covers to her breasts as she looked at him. "No, of course not. I'm just not used to . . ." She felt a touch of heat in her face, and shrugged a bit defensively.

He looked at her a moment longer with probing eyes, then

cupped her warm cheek with one hand and leaned over to kiss her slowly and thoroughly. When he straightened, she was a little breathless and he was smiling again.

"Why don't you take a hot shower while I order breakfast," he said. "That should help."

Spencer felt self-conscious about getting out of the bed naked even though, heaven knew, she had no secrets from him, but she pushed the covers back and slid from the bed when he stood up, telling herself not to be an idiot. She was so intent on not being embarrassed that she was startled when Drew's hand grasped her wrist with a sudden hard strength that wasn't quite painful.

She had taken a step toward a chair where she'd left fresh clothing the night before, but was stopped abruptly by his grip. Before she could say anything he turned her around and his free hand lifted to touch her back.

"What the hell is this?"

Spencer couldn't see his face, but his voice was so harsh that for a moment she couldn't think and had no idea what he was talking about. Then, as his fingers very gently touched her, she remembered. It had been a few days since her tumble off the horse, and she'd more or less forgotten about it. Unfortunately, she bruised very easily, and though she hadn't bothered to examine herself, she realized that the mark of the wooden jump pole was probably a multicolored band across her back by now.

"When I hit the jump Friday," she explained, trying to look back over her shoulder at him but still unable to see his face. "It doesn't hurt. I just bruise easily."

His touch brushed across her skin, halfway between her shoulder blades and the small of her back. The grip on her wrist finally relaxed and he bent his head to kiss her bare shoulder as he released her. "Go take your shower," he said in an odd, gruff voice.

Before she could turn toward him or respond, he had gone

quickly from the bedroom and into the sitting room. Spencer stood there for a moment staring after him, then gathered her clothing and went into the bathroom. She put her tumbled hair up carelessly, and before getting into the shower paused a moment to look at her back in the big mirror over the vanity.

It looked as if someone had been beating her. The mark of the pole she'd hit was most obvious, a solid line of bluish yellow from one side of her back to the other and more than two inches thick. But there was another, fainter bruise running diagonally across her back—the second pole, she supposed, although she didn't remember feeling it hit her—and a number of lavender splotches of various sizes. From rocks on the ground where she'd landed, presumably.

A bit ruefully, Spencer realized now why she'd been so uncomfortable on the plane from D.C. No wonder Drew had been so startled to see the marks on her. They looked vicious. But they really weren't painful now, and she didn't think any more about them as she got into the shower.

Drew heard the water running, and though it distracted him from the note he'd just found pushed underneath the door, his thoughts this time were less sensual than worried. The bruises on her back had been another reminder of how fragile she was, how susceptible to hurt. He'd been vividly conscious of how delicate her slender body was as she lay beneath him in their bed, and even though he knew she was both stronger and tougher than she looked, she seemed to him terrifyingly defenseless.

All she had to shield her was a steely core of will, and though that had brought her through the past difficult months he was worried that more pressure would shatter her. She'd already endured so much stress and she doubted her own strength, her own ability to cope. He knew that—he'd seen the moments of uncertainty in her eyes.

She was very vulnerable right now, risking a great deal of herself in the attempt to find her father's dream and put it into his hands. Failure might destroy her; even a setback or a delay could be too much for her. Drew tapped the note against one hand, staring at the message he didn't have to read again. What would this do to her?

And what would it do to her if he forced her to stop, if he ended it here and now? It was something he would have done in an instant if he hadn't been so certain that the action might well do her more harm than going on. But the haunting fear of losing her was cold and tight inside him now, because there was a very real danger. If she went on. If she got anywhere near the man who had beaten them to the cross.

He could stop it now, he knew, by refusing to go any farther. Spencer lacked the experience necessary to find elusive information in this dangerous game, and when he told her their competitor had already beaten them to the cross, she would be unable to follow the trail without his help. But she would try, he knew, unless he could somehow stop her, and that kind of failure would surely mark her. The cross meant more than a last gift to her father; right or wrong, consciously or unconsciously, to Spencer it represented a vital test of her own self-confidence.

She wouldn't be willing to call off the hunt; she wouldn't stay put here or return to the States without a fight. And even if she trusted him now, he didn't think she'd let him continue alone.

What she had told him in the dark hours of the night had stunned him in more ways than one, but what he remembered most clearly was the pain in her soft voice when she had talked of her feelings of inadequacy. She seemed to see herself in a distorted mirror, where the reflection was always lacking. He thought she had a great deal more quiet confidence now than she'd had ten years ago, but it was a fragile assurance she had little faith in.

If she failed in her quest for the cross, it could damage that shaky confidence beyond repair, and if he forced her to go home so that he could search alone it would be even worse.

Drew hesitated a moment, checked his watch briefly, then sat on the couch and reached for the phone. He'd seen the message on the nightstand when he'd gotten up, and though it took him a moment's consideration, he did indeed know where in Madrid to call. He was a little impatient as he waited for the connections to be made, because he didn't want Spencer learning his news by listening to him tell someone else. He heard the shower cut off just as a very irritated voice in Spain demanded to know what the hell he wanted.

"Help," Drew responded mildly.

"Oh, it's you." Kane Pendleton's aggravated tone smoothed somewhat, though he still sounded rather like a bear that had been prodded with a sharp stick a few times too many. "You don't happen to know a crazy sheik with a suicide wish and a lust for redheads, do you? "

"I can think of one or two," Drew murmured, amused despite the dark thoughts and emotions churning inside him. "Are you ready to trade her in so soon?"

"Trade, hell, I'm ready to give her away."

Since at least one sheik Drew knew of had already attempted to steal the lady in question years before and had barely escaped with his life when Kane got a bit upset about it, Drew didn't make the mistake of believing the threat. And since he could hear Tyler laughing in the background, it was clear that she didn't believe it, either.

They had an interesting relationship, those two. Both fierce, temperamental and passionate, they'd fought for years as violently as two cats tied up in a bag. They'd fought as bitter rivals, as enemies, as unwilling partners and finally as lovers. Like the two of them—separately and, especially, together—their fights were rather magnificent, and had earned them a worldwide reputation among the community of people interested in antiquities. They were also well-known for their abilities and knowledge when it came to antiquities, and for their solid integrity and honor.

Drew knew them very well, despite the fact that he'd met them face-to-face less than a year before. He trusted both of them implicitly—and he couldn't say that about many.

Now, rightly guessing the reason for Kane's temper with his spirited wife, Drew said, "Are you in Spain because of Tyler's doing?"

Kane grunted, sounding as annoyed as a man could when he absolutely adored the woman he wanted to strangle. "We were *supposed* to be going back to Montana, but then that asinine curator in London had to mention a rumor he'd heard about a jeweled dagger. And here we are. Tangling with crooks, as usual. Ty just had a run-in with a smuggler who would have killed her as soon as spit, and she just won't—"

He broke off, there was an unidentifiable sound or two and then Tyler's cheerful voice came over the line.

"Hi, Drew. Pay no attention to Kane, he's just grouchy because a donkey kicked him yesterday."

Since Drew could hear an exasperated sigh, he gathered that Kane was on an extension. "I thought he got along with donkeys," he commented.

"I should," Kane growled. "I married one."

Not at all offended, Tyler merely said, "This one—I mean *that* one—was possessed of a fiend. Anyway, we found the dagger and handed it over to a museum here in Madrid, so we're pretty much at loose ends."

"What about Montana?" Drew questioned, knowing that Tyler had just endorsed Kane's earlier offer of help.

"The world's round," Kane replied, his temper fading. "Any news on the cross?"

If Drew had believed that Kane really was hell-bent to get back home to Montana, he wouldn't have asked them for help. But he knew very well that even though Tyler's frequent close brushes with danger shook Kane so much that he invariably stated his determination to take her home where she'd be safe, he could no more resist the lure of elusive antiquities than she could.

"Yeah, there's news," Drew said. "Bad news. One of my sources just confirmed that Lon Stanton went up into the mountains before dawn yesterday. He was back within hours, and he didn't waste any time leaving Innsbruck."

chapter nine

"STANTON?" KANE MUTTERED something about Mr. Stanton's ancestry, which that individual would have found more than a little offensive.

"If he was that quick," Tyler said, obviously thinking along more practical lines, "he must have found the cross."

"Even worse," Kane said. "He must know you're no more than a step behind him."

"I have to assume that, even though my being after the cross is a very recent development," Drew said, looking at the note in his hand and certain that it was more than an assumption. Stanton knew. Drew had no doubt now that it had been his own sudden presence in Spencer's life that had caused Stanton to steal Allan Wyatt's notes and then race to Austria with no loss of time. Stanton would expect to be followed.

Some enemies knew you more intimately than a best friend ever could.

Holding his voice steady and quiet, Drew said, "The problem is that I can't afford the time for him to relax his guard. I have to go on the offensive, and that means finding him before he's crossed too many borders."

"Okay, then," Kane said briskly, "we'll start getting in touch with our contacts and see what we can turn up. The bastard isn't invisible—he has to show up somewhere."

"Will you be on the move right away?" Tyler asked. "Or stay in Innsbruck?"

"We'll be here at least long enough to go up into the mountains and make sure he did find it."

Tyler didn't question the plural. "All right, then. We'll call you by tonight, one way or the other."

When Drew cradled the receiver, a sudden awareness made him look toward the doorway to the bedroom. Spencer was standing there, one small hand gripping the doorjamb tightly, and she was very pale.

"It's all right," he said involuntarily, dropping the note on the coffee table and rising to his feet.

She was looking at him in an odd, probing way, as if she were puzzled but didn't know why. "Is it?"

Before he could answer, a knock at the door signaled the arrival of breakfast, and Drew had to deal with that. By the time the waiter had gone, Spencer had obviously gotten herself under control. She wasn't as pale, and she even managed a small smile when he went to her.

"Even though I knew someone else was after the cross," she murmured, "I kept thinking it would be there, waiting. Pretty stupid, huh?"

He put his hands gently on her shoulders, unable to resist kissing her, then led her to her chair at the table. He was still worried about her, still trying to decide how to handle the situation without risking her in any way, and made his voice matter-of-fact as he responded to what she'd said. "No, not stupid. There was every reason to suppose we could get to it first. I'm just sorry you had to hear about it like that."

She poured coffee for them both and then sipped hers as she looked at him gravely. "I don't think I heard it all. You know who did get there first? His name, I mean?"

Drew told her about the note he'd gotten, just mentioning Stanton's name without description, and about whom he'd been talking to on the phone and why. He explained that Kane and Tyler Pendleton not only were expert hunters with good instincts and solid contacts, but also were unusually quick when it came to finding information.

"Quicker than you?" she asked, surprised by that.

"We've never had a contest," he replied, pleased when that brought a smile. He loved her slow smiles, and they were still rare enough that they speeded up his heartbeat. Or maybe, he thought, it wasn't because they were rare. Maybe it was just because he loved her smiles.

"So they're going to help?"

"If they can. Stanton has an edge if he knows he's being hunted. He'll avoid the obvious routes and keep out of sight, and that won't make it easy for us. But he has to get the cross out of Europe and back to the States, so he has to move, and he can't afford to risk too many cute tricks. He'll want to move fast at least out of Austria, because he has to assume the first thing we'll do is sound the alarm, and that means every border guard will be on the alert and half of Interpol will be sniffing out his trail."

"Will we sound the alarm?"

Drew sipped his coffee as he considered that, still trying to decide. "I have a few friends in Interpol who'd take my word for it that Stanton got his hands on the cross, but they couldn't move against him without proof. He doesn't panic easily, but too much attention could make him go to ground, and we don't have time to wait him out. I think we should find out which way he's gone and then decide."

Frowning a little, Drew went on. "If he's following his usual methods, he's over here with his own passport, big as life, with a hired gun in case there's trouble. He isn't likely to move the cross via one of the airlines, at least unless he's willing to risk it crossing the Atlantic, because of customs and because even checked luggage is X-rayed. He could charter a plane, but not out of Innsbruck because too few are available and that's a sign anyone on his trail would be able to read."

Spencer was so fascinated she'd forgotten to continue eating as she listened.

"He won't go to Vienna," Drew said slowly, obviously working it out in his mind. "Trying to get out of the capital city with an Austrian treasure would be a bit too reckless, and heading east just makes the route home longer. Germany to the north—there's a lot going on there right now, and I wouldn't risk it. Switzerland to the west—maybe, but doubtful unless you're trying to move or safeguard cash. The safest bet would be to go overland and head south, through Italy to the Mediterranean. The border wouldn't be too risky, and once he reached the coast there are any number of vessels he could book passage on without having to go through customs. Once he's at sea he can pick a nice, safe, out-of-the-way port where smugglers will take him anywhere he wants for the right price."

Spencer had the feeling her mouth was open. She reached for her coffee hastily and took a sip, then murmured, "God help the world if you take to crime."

Drew looked at her, smiling slightly. "You can learn a lot about your enemies—and their methods—in ten years," he said dryly.

"He is an enemy, isn't he? Stanton, I mean. The way you talk about him, you must know him very well."

A part of Drew's mind had been occupied by that very certain knowledge even as he'd mentally traced Stanton's possible route, and now, as he looked at Spencer, the coldness he was becoming familiar with was heavy in his chest. "I know him," he said.

Spencer frowned a little at the tone, which was curiously bleak and hard. "Is he . . . dangerous?" she asked slowly.

So dangerous that I don't want you anywhere hear him. Drew pushed his plate away, his appetite gone. "Spencer . . . would you consider going back to the States—or waiting here—and letting me find the cross for you?" He saw the instant flash of some strong emotion in her eyes, but forced himself to hold her gaze steadily.

"No," she said.

Very softly, he said, "I don't want you to get hurt."

She hesitated, but even though it was almost painful to refuse him anything, she had to, and shook her head in response. It wasn't only because she still felt driven to find the cross for her father. There was something else now, something she'd been aware of ever since she'd walked into the room and heard Drew talking on the phone. Maybe it was just because she loved him, but she had the strongest, strangest feeling that if she didn't go with him, if she didn't stay as close to him as possible, something terrible would happen to him.

In a way, it was absurd to believe that her presence would keep him safe; she certainly couldn't protect him physically and he'd proven himself adept at surviving dangerous situations in the past. But what she felt was a conviction too deep to be questioned or ignored, and she had to accept it even if she didn't understand why.

"No," she said quietly. "I have to go with you."

"Because you don't trust me?" His voice was taut now, his face very still.

"I trust you." It was the truth, and one she had to admit. "I know you'd get the cross and bring it back to me if you could. It's just . . ." She couldn't tell him that, it sounded too senseless. "I have to go with you. Please, Drew, it's very important to me."

They both knew that he could keep her from going with him, by trickery or by force if there was no other way. But after a long moment Drew muttered an oath and looked away from her, and she knew she'd won. She wasn't sure why she'd won, and she was too relieved to ask. Instead, she asked another question.

"Why is Stanton so dangerous?"

Flatly, Drew said, "Because he cares about nothing on this earth except his collection, and his only emotion about that is cold, ruthless greed. He has plenty of money, but the things he wants money can't buy, so he just takes them. It doesn't matter who they belong to, and it doesn't matter what he has to do to get them. He doesn't give a damn about anything but his own gluttony, and he's completely soulless." Drew hesitated, then added in a voice that was stony with control, "I once saw him cut a woman's throat."

Spencer was so shocked that for a long moment she couldn't say anything at all. She had no experience of violence, no understanding of how any human could commit such an act. A wave of nausea passed over her and she had to swallow hard before she could speak. "He—he wasn't punished for that?"

"Not the way he deserved to be."

Something about that grim reply made Spencer's heart turn over with a lurch. What other unbearable things had Drew seen? And what kind of strength did it require of him to show a composed face to the world with memories like that haunting him?

"What happened?" she asked.

Drew half shrugged, his gaze fixed on something only he could see. "It was in Central America years ago in the middle of some cockeyed revolution. Stanton had gone down there after a gold idol that had been stolen from a museum. I was—I was just there. Our paths crossed by accident. I was too far away to see all of what happened, but I found out later that the thief wasn't willing to part with the idol even though Stanton had paid him to steal it. Stanton grabbed the thief's wife and held a knife to her throat. The man immediately handed the idol over—but Stanton killed her anyway.

"There was fighting going on all around. Stanton was shot, wounded, but not fatally. He managed to get away. There was no government to speak of, and if the thief reported his wife's murder, no one cared."

Spencer thought that someone had cared. Someone still remembered the brutal, senseless waste of a life. But she couldn't say anything because her throat was aching so badly.

Drew looked at her, focused on her face. His eyes were very dark, and his voice was so low it seemed to come from deep inside his chest. "The cross isn't worth a life, Spencer. Allan would be the first to say so."

She swallowed hard. "I know."

"We'll track Stanton if we can, but we won't get close. As soon as we have something solid, we'll alert the Austrian authorities and Interpol, and let them handle it."

Spencer nodded. "Yes. All right."

He reached over and grasped one of her hands. "It could take more time than Allan has," he warned quietly. "Once the authorities are involved in investigating the theft of a national treasure, things will get complicated in a hurry. You may not be able to take the cross back to the States for months."

She turned her hand so that her fingers twined with his, and smiled. "I know that. But it seems to be the only way."

Drew sighed a bit roughly, almost as if he'd been holding his breath, and squeezed her hand before releasing it. "Okay. I need to make a few calls, and then we should ride up into the mountains and make sure Stanton got what he came for."

Spencer agreed to that, and while he made his calls she finished her cool coffee and thought about everything he had told her. Now she knew why she had to stay with him. It was because she loved him, but it was also because her presence did have the power to keep him safe.

When she had come into the room and heard him on the phone, something in his voice had touched an alarm bell deep in her subconscious. Though she hadn't understood it then, she did now. Alone, Drew would have gone after Lon Stanton without hesitation, not just for the cross but for that cruelly murdered woman— and perhaps even others he hadn't told her about. He would have hunted Stanton, and finding him wouldn't have been enough, turning him over to the authorities wouldn't have been enough.

What Spencer had heard in Drew's voice had been the soft echo of an emotion so primitive only her deepest instincts had recognized it for what it was: the utter loathing of a man of conscience for something evil.

Alone, Drew would have confronted that evil, risking his life without a second thought. But he wouldn't risk her life. She knew that. As long as she was with him, he would take care of her. He would keep his distance from Stanton to protect her, and that would keep him safe.

THEY FOUND THE cave midway through the afternoon. Miles from Innsbruck, and carved into a cliff face so steep they'd had to leave the horses below and climb, it had been hidden from sight by a cunning arrangement of boulders that looked natural. Or at least had looked natural before Stanton had found it. Now, two of the huge rocks were scarred by marks of pickaxes and a third had been broken into pieces, leaving a thin opening that gaped darkly in the sunlight.

Drew helped her up the last couple of feet so they were standing on a narrow ledge and, glancing back down the way they'd come, he said almost idly, "How much mountain climbing have you done?"

Spencer, who was carefully not looking down, replied with the truth. "None. Why?"

He smiled slightly. "Do you know what courage is, Spencer?"

Puzzled by the seemingly oblique question, she frowned up at him. "The dictionary's definition?"

"No, the true definition. Courage is doing what you have to do, even if it scares you silly." He leaned over and kissed her, so deeply and thoroughly that she was shaking when he finally raised his head.

She was glad he was holding her hand, because she was so dizzy she might easily have tumbled off the ledge. Blinking up at him as the dizziness cleared, and wondering why he'd said that about courage, she said, "Um—shouldn't we go into the cave?"

Drew turned his head to study the opening with a considering gaze. "You stay put a minute, all right?"

She nodded as he unclipped the big flashlight he carried from his belt. She could still feel the warmth of his mouth on hers, and though a night of intense passion had left her feeling wonderfully sated, she was conscious of desire stirring deep inside her now as she looked at him.

The sunlight gleamed in his golden hair and made his blue eyes seem even brighter than usual. The sweater he wore set off his broad shoulders, just as the snug jeans complemented lean hips and long, powerful legs. He'd been graceful on horseback and now, as he went toward the cave opening, she admired the lithe, catlike suppleness of his movements. She felt amazingly primitive when she looked at him, her body heated, her emotions fierce, and it was a struggle to contain that.

But she managed to. Barely. She didn't know why he wanted her to wait outside the opening, but remained there and watched as he disappeared into the darkness of the cave. It was only when he came back out less than five minutes later that his absent comment told her why.

"I didn't think he'd had time to rig anything, but it never hurts to be sure," Drew murmured, taking her hand and leading her to the opening.

"Rig—you mean a booby trap?" As soon as the words were out, Spencer reminded herself yet again that he'd warned her from the beginning how dangerous this could be. Still, she was shaken—and not only by the threat of that. She had stood there, wrapped in sensual thoughts and feeling absolutely no sense of danger, and had calmly watched Drew walk into what might very well have been a deadly trap.

Before he could answer her question, she snapped, "Don't do that again, dammit."

Drew looked down at her in surprise. "Do what?"

"Just—just walk in when you know it could be a trap. What if it had been?"

"Worried about my hide?" he murmured, smiling a little.

Spencer felt herself flush, but met his eyes very steadily. "Yes."

He looked at her for a long moment, his face curiously still, then smiled again. "Sweetheart, I've been doing this kind of thing for half my life. I've probably studied every kind of device ever used to defend anything of value, from the state-of-the-art technology smugglers use to guard their shipments to the traps the pharaohs' engineers designed to protect their tombs. And I'm never careless."

It reassured her—but only a little. Yes, he did know what he was doing; she didn't doubt that. But she had sensed the depth of his loathing for Stanton, and she had a very strong feeling that the hatred was a mutual one. Enemies could be vicious. If Stanton knew who was tracking him . . .

Abruptly, she said, "Does he know? Does Stanton know it's you who's after him?"

Drew hesitated, then said, "Probably." His hand squeezed hers gently and he pointed his flashlight ahead to show them the way as he led her into the cave.

As they went in and the thick stillness of immense weight above their heads closed about them, Spencer told herself with steely determination that she'd be alert to possible danger from now on and not just meekly expect Drew to do everything. Unlike him, she hadn't been exposed to the kinds of danger that would have sharpened her instincts, but fear for him was a very strong and primitive spur to learn what she had to in a hurry.

The passage they walked through was wide enough for them to go side by side, with smooth stone curving above them several inches higher than the top of Drew's head, and turned gently in a slow arc to the west of the point where they'd entered. Beneath them the floor was stone with a thin, grainy top coat. The air was heavy and very dry, with no circulation at all.

In a low voice that nonetheless echoed softly, Drew said, "Only one opening to the outside, and that was blocked off. This place was airtight until Stanton broke in. With no oxygen or moisture, it was a perfect place to hide something valuable. Spencer, if you start to feel dizzy, tell me. There hasn't been time for much fresh air to get in here."

"All right." She kept her eyes fixed on the circle of his flashlight ahead of them, aware of the thickness of the air but not troubled by it. Not yet, at least. "I wonder how long Kurt searched before he found this place? When he sent those letters to his friend, I think he'd been in Innsbruck for a couple of months already."

"I'll bet it took him that long, at least," Drew said.

Spencer opened her mouth to say something else, but whatever it was remained unsaid. The passage had taken a sharp left-hand turn and abruptly dead-ended, and in the glow of Drew's flashlight a life-size figure of a man stood squarely before them with his back against the wall. He stood as if at attention, straight and proud, with both hands held out together at his waist, palms up. Lying on his hands was a lidless box made of the same grayish material he was constructed of, and it was empty.

Standing beside Drew in silence, Spencer watched him reach out and touch the statue, rubbing a thumb consideringly along the edge of the empty box. "A kind of plaster," he said. "Heavy enough so it wouldn't be easily moved. And it definitely dates from the early sixteen hundreds."

"The box is the right size to hold the cross," she said softly. "The Hapsburgs supposedly kept it in a carved wooden box a little smaller than that plaster one. All Stanton had to do was pry the wooden box out and carry it away."

"Funny," Drew mused, "that Kurt went to all this trouble when he intended to get the cross later. He could have just left the box on the floor here—why the statue?"

Spencer, who had been studying the face of the statue, was frowning to herself, and answered absently. "Maybe it was vanity. That's him, Drew. It's Kurt. In that book about the Hapsburgs, there was a painting of him, and the face of this statue looks just like . . ." Her voice trailed off.

"What?" Drew asked, looking at her in the dim backwash of light from his flashlight.

She was concentrating so hard on trying to figure out what was bothering her about the plaster face that Spencer was hardly aware of how difficult breathing had become. "I don't know. It looks like Kurt Hapsburg, even to the little scar bisecting his left eyebrow, but it isn't quite right."

"Portraiture isn't an exact art," Drew reminded her. "Different artists interpret subjects in different ways."

The comment seemed to ring in Spencer's ears, and she thought with total clarity, *That's it.* But she didn't know why she thought that, or what it meant, and she had no idea why a little voice in her head kept insisting in an annoyingly repetitive way that there was something important she knew if she could only remember what it was.

"Spencer?" Drew reached out to her quickly, then swore softly and lifted her into his arms. He turned away from the statue and carried her back along the passageway, not pausing until be slipped through the narrow opening and out onto the sunny ledge.

She blinked at the bright light, vaguely surprised to find herself sitting on the ledge. Drew was supporting her as he knelt beside her, and as the dizziness began to recede she felt like an absolute fool. A lot of help she'd be in case of danger—she couldn't even stay alert enough to know when she was running out of oxygen!

"Take deep breaths," he urged.

Spencer obeyed, breathing slowly and deeply until the scenery stopped dancing, then looked up at him. "I'm sorry, I should have realized."

"It usually creeps up on you the first couple of times," he said in a reassuring tone, though his eyes remained watchful. "After that you learn to be wary. Better now?"

"Much better, thanks."

Drew eased back onto his heels, but one hand remained on her thigh as he turned off the flashlight and clipped it to his belt. "Something was bothering you about the statue."

She frowned "Yes, but I can't remember what it was."

He half nodded. "You probably will eventually. If we have time, we can come back up here later on. Once the wind shifts, it should clear out all the bad air in the cave. In any case, it's a pretty good bet the statue will end up in a museum as soon as the authorities know about it."

The little voice Spencer had been hearing was only a whisper now, maddeningly indistinct, and she felt frustrated because she was sure there was something . . . She glanced down at Drew's hand on her leg, and all thoughts of the statue faded away.

His hand, elegant and powerful, lay over her upper thigh in a light, casually possessive gesture. It was a very simple thing, but intimate as well, the unthinking, familiar touch of a lover. Vivid memories rose in her mind with suddenness that stole her breath, memories of how those strong hands had touched and caressed her, how they had held her beneath him. Her body responded to the mental images so instantly that she felt overwhelmed, and she could only look up at him in helpless longing.

Drew went very still, blue heat flaring in his topaz eyes. His hand tightened, then began to slowly stroke her thigh as if obeying a compulsion. "One of these days," he said a bit thickly, "you're going to look at me like that, and I won't give a damn if we're on a public sidewalk—or a narrow ledge on the side of a mountain."

"I can't help it," she murmured, his rough voice sending an even stronger wave of desire through her.

He leaned over to kiss her with a hard brevity that made strained control obvious, then rose to his feet and grasped her hands to pull her gently up. "Just hold the thought long enough for us to get off this bloody mountain," he told her.

Spencer followed him to the rim of the ledge, her hand held firmly in his, and she didn't even look back at the cave. Nor did she hesitate to start down the cliff despite her fear of heights. All her attention, all her awareness, was focused on Drew. Everything else in her world had shrunk to a dim, distant unimportance.

Drew went first, staying close behind her as they picked their way slowly down the cliff face. It wasn't a particularly dangerous climb since there were numerous solid handholds and sturdy granite outcroppings, but he'd seen the flicker of nervousness in her eyes before they'd gone up and knew that the trip down would test her courage even more.

It was a test he knew she would pass with flying colors. She had guts—and she didn't even know it. She also had a trick of looking at him in a way that was so intensely erotic it sent a jolt of urgent, almost primal need through him.

If he had ever really believed that possessing her would be enough, he knew now he'd been wrong. He wanted her even more fiercely, despite a night of passion so incredibly fiery and satisfying he'd felt raw with the pleasure of it. The pleasure of her. Yet desire was like a tide inside him, ebbing with completion and then almost immediately surging again. She had only to look at him in that intimate way, her eyes soft and dreamy, lips slightly parted, and he could hardly think for wanting her.

He had been able to concentrate for a while today, his mind grappling with the potential danger of Stanton, his own determination to get the cross for Spencer and the surprising and unsettling things she'd told him in the night. But his concentration was shaky at best where she was concerned, and more than anything else he wished it could be just the two of them with no outside pressures.

Drew wanted time with Spencer. He'd hated leaving her in bed alone this morning. What he'd wanted was to keep her in bed, to

wake her by making love to her slowly, to watch her body come
alive under his touch, her eyes glow with desire. Looking down at
her as she lay curled on her side sleeping, he had felt fascination
and desire and an aching in his chest. She was such a delicate thing
to hold so many varied emotions, from the muted pain of self-
doubt to the astonishing force of her passion. She was so beautiful,
and she'd worked her way under his skin a second time until he
could barely think of anything but her.

He had wondered then if she loved him, because her response in bed was so sweetly wild and giving, and because she
had softly agreed that she belonged to him. Belonged to him. . . .
What did that mean? She had loved him once—he believed
that—and yet had run from him in a panic to marry a man she
hadn't loved, a man with whom she'd felt safer. That had been
ten years ago, yes; she'd been a schoolgirl frightened of trying to
live up to the image of him she'd fixed in her mind, and the
image of herself she believed was in his mind. It was different
now. Her self-confidence was tenuous, but she was no schoolgirl
dreaming of princes and she wasn't wary or nervous of him as
she'd been then.

But love? She hadn't said it, and he thought that if she had
loved him she would have said it last night. It had been a night of
honesty, after all, and she hadn't flinched from showing him her
vulnerability. He wondered if, between them, he and Reece Cabot
had cured her of the desire to love anyone. One man had hidden
his feelings so completely that she'd thought him remote, while
the other had run off with her in a violent tempest of emotion that
had barely outlasted the honeymoon.

Perhaps this time Spencer had opted for uncomplicated passion.

As for his own feelings, Drew avoided defining them. She was
under his skin, yes, and his hunger for her seemed stronger with
every passing hour, but he couldn't forget what he'd felt when

Allan had handed him the ring and told him Spencer had eloped with another man, even though it had been ten years ago. It had been like a hot knife in his gut, the pain so bad it had taken him months to stop hurting. He never wanted to feel that again, never wanted to be so vulnerable to someone else that the loss of them was devastating.

He wanted her, though, with a desire he couldn't control. He needed her. In his bed, her mouth lifting for his kisses, her silky heat sheathing him. He wanted more of her slow smiles, her sensual gazes, her sweet passion.

Now, one hand on her hip guiding her as they climbed slowly down the cliff face, he watched her supple movements and every muscle in his body slowly tightened. He'd never have believed that climbing down a rocky cliff could be erotic, but he was coming apart just watching her, his attention so fixed on her that it must have been blind instinct that kept him from putting a foot wrong and falling. That look of hers before they'd started down had inflamed his senses, but he'd thought he could keep his hands off her at least until they returned to Innsbruck.

It would take a couple of hours, less time than had been needed to find the cave—but more time than he could stand. His control was splintering even now, his heart pounding, breath rasping in his throat, his body heavy with an ache that would only grow and grow until it became unbearable, until he had to lose himself in her or go mad.

Drew felt solid ground beneath his feet not a moment too soon, and put both his hands on Spencer's hips to guide her the rest of the way. She took a step away from him, but he immediately pulled her back against him.

"The horses—" she began, then broke off with a gasp when she felt him behind her. "Drew?"

He wrapped his arms around her, his mouth nuzzling her hair

aside to seek the warmth of her neck. "I want you," he muttered in a thick, rasping voice.

Spencer went weak, all the strength draining out of her legs as if a dam had burst. Even through the barrier of their jeans she could feel the pulsing hardness of his arousal, and the hands that closed over her breasts were shaking a little, almost rough, urgent with need.

When he'd told her to hold the thought until they got off the mountain, she'd assumed he meant back to Innsbruck. He'd seemed perfectly in control, and though her own desire had been feverish it hadn't occurred to her to suggest anything else. Even if she'd considered what making love out under the open sky with him would be like—which she hadn't—her imagination would have balked at the idea of a man as calm and elegant as Drew so overcome by desire that he was unwilling to wait for the comfort of a bed or the privacy of a locked door. She would have shied away from the idea herself if she'd been given a moment to think.

He didn't give her a moment. His hands and mouth seduced her, the hunger in him so strong and immediate that it kindled an instant, answering fire in her. She was trembling, breathless, aching with a desire so imperative she didn't care where they were or anything else. She was barely aware of being turned and lifted into his arms, of being carried, because his mouth was hard and fierce on hers, and if he'd put her down on solid rock she wouldn't have murmured a protest.

They were in a kind of valley, a relatively small area where several mountains shouldered against one another in a series of tumbling hills. Clumps of tall trees gave way to rocky outcroppings and patches of thick green grass. Drew put her down on one of the grassy places and immediately began stripping her clothing off.

If she'd been thinking at all by that point, she would have expected him to remove only as much as necessary, because his face was a primitive mask of passion and the look in his burning eyes was almost wild. But Drew wanted them both naked, and their clothing was flung aside carelessly.

Spencer wasn't aware of the faint chill of the mountain air. The summer sun warmed the ground beneath her and when his body covered hers she was conscious of nothing else. She was as frantic as he was, so desperate to feel him inside her that she was writhing and whimpering beneath him, her arms tight around his neck and her legs lifting to wrap around his hips. Wildfire was racing through her veins, searing her senses, and she moaned into his mouth when she felt the burning hardness of him sink deeply into her body.

Whether it was the primitive influence of the musty earth beneath them and the wide sky above or something equally ancient in them, this time they mated. It was hasty and a little rough, their bodies straining together in an almost silent conflict as old as the mountains that cradled them.

SPENCER WAS SO drained she didn't want to move. The ground beneath her was hard, but surprisingly cushioned by the thick grass. Drew was heavy, but her body seemed perfectly designed to bear his weight without strain or discomfort, and this time the starkly intimate sensations caused her no shyness or embarrassment at all. She didn't even think about the fact that they were lying naked on a sunny patch of grass in an area where the odd tourist might well ride or hike through.

She felt his mouth moving against her neck, and then he raised his head to gaze down at her. His forearms were under her shoulders, his fingers tangled in her hair, and there was an expression in his darkened eyes she'd never seen before, almost a look of awe.

"Spencer," he murmured, and kissed her very gently.

Spencer felt blissfully happy. She wasn't thinking beyond this moment, and for this moment there were no problems or doubts or questions. She nuzzled her face into his warm throat briefly, then smiled up at him. "We'd better move," she said, "or you're going to get sunburned in a very painful place."

chapter ten

ALL THE WAY back to Innsbruck Spencer could feel herself smiling. She couldn't seem to help herself, and whenever her glance caught and held Drew's he smiled as well. They were able to ride abreast occasionally as they made their way toward the city, and each time he reached for her hand as if touching her was a compulsion.

She felt oddly serene, the frantic, primitive mating having given her something she couldn't even define. All she was certain of was that, for the first time in her life, she felt entirely comfortable with herself. Comfortable enough to tease Drew, predicting that he would indeed be sunburned, and laughing when he reminded her that, as easily as she bruised, she'd probably have a black-and-blue rear end by morning.

"Then we'll both sit on pillows," she said, unworried by the prospect.

He glanced at her again, unable to stop looking at her. She had laughed a moment ago, the sound as clear and sweet as the mountain breeze, and it was only when he felt the shock of it that he realized he'd never heard her laugh. Not really, not like that, her lovely face alight with amusement, her eyes bright with simple enjoyment.

For the first time, she was utterly tranquil in his company, the little smile curving her lips so secret and feminine, her glances warm with an intimacy that was without obvious sensuality and yet held the glowing embers of passion. The promise of what he'd seen in her all those years ago was realized now: beauty, grace, intelligence, humor, an inner poise, strength she had no awareness of—and a depth of passion he had never expected to find.

He reached for her hand as they came abreast again, and as her fingers twined with his, his curious instinct for detecting the genuine sounded inside him. Over the past days, the tone of that inner intuition had grown clearer and clearer with each touch, and now the single note was so perfect in its distinct, sweet sound that it was haunting.

The real thing.

This was Spencer. This was the woman she was meant to be.

His instinct only confirmed what other feelings had told him, and after that compulsive joining on a patch of sunny grass he could no longer avoid facing another truth. He loved her. He had loved her since she was sixteen years old.

He should have known from the moment he came back into her life, because it had been the uneasy suspicion that she was in trouble that had drawn him back to her. Even then, even believing he no longer felt anything for her, he had acted almost instinctively by going to her despite everything that had happened between them. The shock of realizing he still wanted her had collided with all the gnawing, unresolved emotions he'd thought long dead—and that was when he'd begun reaching for excuses, for rationalizations, even for lies he could tell himself, to avoid the truth.

Not love, lust. That was all it was, he'd told himself. He couldn't love her—she was a greedy little gold digger. He just wanted her, that was all, wanted to purge himself of the bitter desire. He'd be a fool to trust her, a fool to let her get to him a second time, he'd reminded himself harshly. Besides that, he couldn't love her again, it wasn't even possible; he'd learned his lesson too well, and would never again leave himself so vulnerable to her that she could destroy him.

Lies. All lies. It was love, and it had always been love. He had been able to lie to himself about it only because it was possible to grow accustomed to anything, even pain, until it was so familiar it went almost without notice. But now she was here, with him, tranquil by his side, eager in his arms, and what he felt for her was an emotion so vast it filled his entire being. This time the roots of love were sunk so deeply inside him that tearing them out would cost him his soul.

It was terrifying to love so much, to know without doubt or question that his life would be hollow and unbearable without her. He wasn't a man who had known much uncertainty in his life, but it was tormenting him now. She had loved him once, but that had been a girl in awe of a man she saw as something larger than life. She knew better now. She'd seen him at his worst, knew how anger and bitter hostility could make him cruel, how scornful and cutting and implacable he could be.

Could she love that very human and flawed man? He was afraid to ask. They'd been together for such a short time and so much had happened. Though she seemed happy now, he couldn't forget the stresses and strains she had withstood during the past months, and he was afraid that her peace was a fragile thing. He couldn't put more pressure on her, demand a commitment when

she'd barely had time to think. All he could do was love her and try
to be patient, try not to hold on to her too hard out of his own terror of losing her.

"Drew?"

He looked at her, his throat aching, knowing that his patience
was threadbare with anxiety, and that he wouldn't be able to be
civilized about it if she left him again. Not this time. This time he'd
kill any man who dared try to take her away from him. And if
there was no other man, if she just left him, he'd go after her and
he'd spend the rest of his life trying to convince her that they belonged together.

"Are you all right?" she asked, reining her horse a bit closer
and studying him with a slight frown.

It was easy to smile at her even though what he felt was savage.
It was even easy to find a mild, wry voice when he answered her, because he would have cut his throat rather than disturb her happy
serenity. "Sunburned and exhausted, but otherwise flourshing."

She lifted an eyebrow at him in a quizzical expression that was
adorable. "Exhausted? I haven't noticed you having problems with
energy so far."

"You may notice tonight," he murmured, knowing she
wouldn't but enjoying the way her eyes widened slightly and her
secret little feminine smile returned.

"Are we going to stay in Innsbruck tonight?" The question
was casual, and Drew answered in the same tone.

"That depends on Stanton." He wished it didn't, wished that
very dangerous man was on the other side of the world or, better
yet, in hell where he belonged. Where he would have been, Drew
thought viciously, if only his own aim had been better.

She glanced at him again, not upset by his return to silence but
wondering at the cause. She thought it was Stanton, thought that
the man's very name had the power to disturb Drew. She ac-

knowledged that, thought about it, but it didn't break her serene mood. She felt incredibly optimistic about everything. As long as she stayed with Drew he was safe, and she had faith that they'd get the cross eventually. She was also certain that it would be in time, that her father would wait for them.

Still casual, she said, "I wish I could figure out what bothered me about the statue. It's the most peculiar feeling, like hearing a song and *knowing* the words are in your head somewhere."

"It'll come to you."

"I guess." She pushed the question out of her mind, knowing that if she tried to remember it would only be more elusive. They reached the outskirts of Innsbruck about then, anyway, and by the time they'd returned the horses to the stable and taken a taxi back to the inn she'd forgotten the matter completely.

They were crossing the lobby when Spencer became aware of a great deal of noise coming from the veranda at the rear of the building. It sounded like a roar from a wounded bear, followed immediately by other, less identifiable sounds a bit lower in volume but still impressive.

"What on earth?" she murmured, halting when Drew did.

He cocked his head to one side briefly, then smiled and squeezed her hand. "I had a feeling they'd be showing up."

"Who?"

"Kane and Tyler Pendleton."

Spencer glanced up at him as they headed toward the wide hallway that led to the veranda. "Your friends from Madrid? They sound as if they're about to murder each other."

"They've sounded that way for years," he explained a bit dryly. "In countless places all over the world. I've seen them fight with each other when most people would have been making peace with their Creator."

She felt a spurt of amusement, and the feeling grew when

they stepped out onto the veranda. The wide, tiled porch boasted a splendid view of the Alps, with scattered groupings of chairs and tables placed so that guests could take advantage of the scenery. All the chairs tended to be occupied at this time in the late afternoon but, even as Spencer watched, one couple retreated into the inn and another opted for the relative peace of the garden off to one side.

Only a lone man, casually dressed and seemingly either tired or just a little sleepy, remained near the combatants. He was slouched back in his chair with a drink on the table before him, watching them with an air of lazy interest.

Spencer heard Drew chuckle softly, but most of her fascinated attention was fixed on the man and woman who stood a few feet away near the low balustrade.

The man was about Drew's height, but he was heavier through the shoulders and a great deal more rugged looking, especially wearing jeans and a black sweatshirt that emphasized the sheer, raw strength of his large body. He had shaggy black hair and vivid green eyes that were almost literally shooting sparks at the woman who was confronting him. She was a tall and strikingly beautiful redhead with a figure, Spencer noted enviously, that no doubt caused traffic jams whenever she walked down the street and that was obvious even beneath the khaki slacks and loose blouse she wore. Her voice was as fiery as his, and since they were both yelling at the same time it was impossible to understand what the blistering argument was even about.

Drew led her over to the watching man, who immediately climbed to his feet with a faint grin of welcome on his thin face. "Don't mind them," he said over the roar of battle. "They should be winding down any minute now."

Spencer was introduced to Burke Corbett and found herself sitting at the table between him and Drew, still conscious of amusement. "Interpol?" she asked, questioning that part of the introduction.

"For my sins, yes." He smiled at her, and Spencer acknowledged to herself that she'd never seen a more exotically handsome man. He had eyes of a peculiarly vivid and unusual shade of gray, so pale they looked almost silver, with perfectly shaped bat-wing brows flying above them. His thick black hair grew in a widow's peak atop his high forehead, his smile was singularly charming and his voice was low and pleasant.

"Did you just happen to be in Austria," Drew asked, "or did you tail along with those two?"

"I came with them," Burke answered. "I was working on a case involving a smuggling ring in Madrid when they crashed the party. After the dust settled they told me about the cross, and since my usual bailiwick is Italy, Kane thought I might be of some use to you here."

Drew lifted an eyebrow. "Did he get confirmation that Stanton crossed the border into Italy?"

"No, not yet." Burke shrugged. "He just thinks—like you do, I imagine—that Stanton will aim for the Med and pick the shortest route."

Spencer was so interested in the conversation that she only then noticed the abrupt cessation of noise. She turned her head to see the Pendletons glaring at each other in total silence. Then the redhead grinned suddenly and stood on tiptoe to kiss her scowling husband. His fierce expression didn't change very much, but it was easy to see he kissed her back even as one big hand lifted to gently encircle her throat.

"One of these days," he growled warningly.

"You and what army?" she retorted, grasping his hand and holding it in her own as she turned toward their audience.

Neither of them was at all self-conscious as more introductions were made and they took their seats at the table. Both seemed to recognize Spencer's name, or at least appeared to know who she was, either because Drew had mentioned her to them or else because of her father's reputation.

Tyler was cheerful, Kane somewhat morose, and only Burke had the temerity to ask dryly, "Who won?"

"I did, of course," Tyler said cheerfully.

"She makes me crazy," Kane grumbled.

Her amber eyes laughed at him, and after a moment Kane's scowl faded and he grinned. "Drew, keep the name of that sheik in mind, will you? Maybe I could get a tasseled saddle or a couple of camels for her."

Spencer had realized quickly that the Pendletons were quite deeply and securely in love—it was as openly obvious and without constraint as one of their fights—so she wasn't very surprised when Tyler's only response to that was a soft chuckle.

Drew obviously knew it as well, since he ignored Kane's request and said, "I expected you to turn up here sooner or later, but not this soon. Why the rush?"

"Madrid was very hot," Tyler said solemnly. "And Kane wanted to hunt down that poor donkey."

Kane gave her a look, then answered Drew's question. "We didn't expect any word from our contacts until tonight anyway, and since Innsbruck was closer to the action we decided to come ahead."

"I hope there won't be any action," Drew told them. "Not the violent kind, anyway."

Burke was looking at Drew very steadily, and his voice was quiet when he said, "In the past five years you haven't missed a chance to go after Stanton, and the three times that I know of when you caught up with him, you cost him plenty. Do you expect it to be different this time?"

Somewhat grimly, Drew said, "I thought you were just a bit too casual about why you were here. Come to keep an eye on me, Burke?"

"I'm just on my way back to Milan," Burke replied in an unruffled tone. "Stopped by to see an old friend. Are you going to answer the question, or aren't you?"

"It's not Stanton I'm after," Drew replied. "Not this time. Just the cross."

Spencer, listening silently, was very much alert as she looked between the two men, and a glance showed her that Kane and Tyler were also deadly serious now. There were undercurrents, ripples of meaning in what was being said, and she listened even more intently as she tried to figure it out.

"How can he know that?" Burke asked, his voice becoming flat and hard. "You've always gone after him before. The last time he ventured out of the States you were on his trail within days, and he was damn near killed before he got away."

Drew's expressionless eyes met Spencer's briefly, then returned to Burke's face. "Past history."

"History he hasn't forgotten. Drew, I was there, remember? I saw his face. Hate's a mild word for what he feels for you, and you can't expect—" The Interpol agent's voice broke off abruptly as a waiter approached and spoke briefly to Drew in German.

Drew nodded in acknowledgment to the waiter, then looked at Spencer. "I have a call—it might be news about the cross."

"I'll wait here," she said quietly. She said nothing more until he left, then looked at Burke. "Why does Stanton hate Drew so much?"

Burke was frowning a little, and it was Tyler who said softly, "I think she has a right to know, Burke."

"Then he should tell her," the agent snapped.

"He won't. You know that."

Spencer kept her clear, steady gaze on Burke. "Drew's after the cross because of me," she said, and there was a world of emotion in that statement.

After a long moment Burke sighed explosively. "A few years ago we got word that a gold idol stolen from a museum in Mexico was about to change hands in Central America. Drew was in Colombia on business of his own, but we got in touch and unofficially requested that he try and find out who the buyer was."

"Why Drew?" Spencer asked, guessing the answer but wanting it confirmed.

"Because he knows most of the world like the back of his hand and can get into and out of places where we wouldn't stand a chance. It wasn't the first time we'd asked a favor. He's done work for us off and on since he was in college."

She nodded. "I see. So—he went to Central America?" Drew, she thought, hadn't told her why he was there. She wondered what else he'd left out of his brief retelling.

"Yeah, he went. It was hell down there. The country was in the middle of a revolution, and foreigners were considered fair targets by both sides." Burke's pleasant voice became impersonal in the way that some men learn to speak, in order to save their sanity, when they've seen too many unendurable things in their lives. "We'd heard rumors about a rabid collector, but we didn't have a name then. That was all we wanted, just a name. Drew knew that. His instructions were to try and observe the exchange if he could, to try and identify the buyer.

"He managed to locate the meet, God knows how. He had to stay well back, out of sight. When Stanton got there the thief decided he wanted more money, or the idol. Stanton grabbed a woman who was there, the thief's wife, and held a knife to her throat. The thief gave in without hesitating, but Stanton killed his wife. She was several months pregnant."

Spencer caught her breath and half closed her eyes briefly. He hadn't told her that part, she thought, and she wondered suddenly if it had occurred to Drew that she might well have conceived his child. He had said nothing about birth control, and they hadn't used any kind of protection despite the fact that both of them had had the time to consider that and decide. She had said nothing because, she realized only now, she wanted his baby. But his silence seemed uncharacteristic to her, given his responsible nature, and she wondered about that.

They'd been lovers so briefly, and so much else was going on around them—perhaps he just hadn't thought about it. She hadn't, not until now. And there wasn't time to consider, to untangle what she was feeling; she had to push the disturbing emotions aside and concentrate on what Burke was saying.

He had hesitated for a moment, bothered by the fleeting intensity of emotion on her face, then went on in the same remote tone. "Drew didn't know Stanton then, and he couldn't believe the man would actually murder that woman. When it happened he blamed himself, because he could probably have taken Stanton out if he hadn't hesitated. Stanton ran almost immediately and Drew got off one shot. Considering the terrain and the distance, it was remarkable that he hit his target. Unfortunately, it wasn't a fatal wound. Drew tracked him as far as possible, but in the chaos down there he lost him within a couple of days."

Clearing her throat, Spencer said, "So that's why Stanton hates Drew? Because Drew shot him?"

"He didn't know who was after him then," Burke said. "But since then, whenever Stanton left the safety of the States—where he's a taxpaying, law-abiding citizen—Drew was on his trail. We couldn't touch the man legally, because we've never been able to get any solid proof against him, and Drew isn't a man who could kill in cold blood, although God knows he wanted to kill Stanton.

So he kept pushing. If Stanton was after something, Drew got there first. If there was a corner, Drew backed him into it. If there was a chance in hell he could ruin Stanton's plans, he did it. He alerted everyone he could, made it so hot for Stanton that the man could hardly maneuver outside the States—and by then he knew who to blame for it.

"A few months ago things finally came to a head. Working with us, Drew helped arrange a setup to nail Stanton. We still don't know what went wrong. There was a mix-up, somebody jumped the gun, I don't know. Stanton got away again, but this time the man was . . . disfigured. He blamed Drew, of course. The last thing we heard him say was that he'd make Drew suffer."

Fiercely, Spencer said, "You can't get him for that? You can't stop him?"

"Threats aren't against the law," Burke replied stonily. "And as far as the international police are concerned, Stanton hasn't done a thing to be arrested for. We have no proof. The only witness we have to an illegal act is Drew, and what he saw took place in a country that was coming apart at the seams."

Spencer stared at him for a moment, then said, "I'm sorry."

The strange silvery eyes lost their metallic sheen and he smiled faintly. "So am I."

Tyler looked at both of them, then said mildy, "As soon as Drew told us it was Stanton, we grabbed Burke and hustled him on a plane. He'd told us the story a while ago—Burke, not Drew—and we figured there could be trouble. But it looks like Drew means to stay back this time."

There was a tacit question in the words, and Spencer looked at the redhead, half nodding. "Because of me. I won't let him go without me and—and he doesn't want me near Stanton."

Tyler smiled at her. "Sounds like a good reason to me."

"And me," Burke said definitely. "As a matter of fact, I'd already made up my mind that if Drew tried to cross the border into Italy—assuming Stanton went that route—I'd throw him in jail the moment he set foot on Italian soil."

Sliding into his chair beside Spencer, Drew said calmly, "I'd like to see you try."

Burke looked at him with very steady eyes. "Watch me."

After a moment Drew smiled. "No need. Not this time." He spread open a map on the table, studied it for a moment, then indicated a spot along the Austrian-Italian border. "According to a border guard who's always been straight with me, Stanton crossed over into Italy right here, at about noon today."

Kane frowned over the map. "He isn't making very good time."

"No, he isn't," Drew agreed. "I would have expected him to be halfway to Milan by noon."

Burke looked at Drew from under his flying brows. "I don't suppose it occurred to you to alert us as soon as you knew it was Stanton so we could catch him at the border?"

"It occurred to me," Drew replied, meeting the stare squarely. "But unless he left Austria with the cross, there wouldn't be much of a charge you could hang on him. This way, he's transported a stolen national treasure into another country. With any luck at all, you can nail him this time."

"If we can catch him before he reaches the Med."

"You'd better get busy," Drew suggested, pushing the map toward him.

Spencer could almost feel Burke relax suddenly, and she realized that until that moment he hadn't been entirely certain that Drew really intended to leave the matter of Stanton's capture to the authorities.

"I've been busy all day," the Interpol agent said. "I have half a dozen men stationed between the Austrian border and Milan, and a few more making certain we have the coast covered. Every police agency in Italy has been quietly alerted, as well as the relevant Austrian authorities—who are, by the way, biting their nails and going nuts."

Drew looked at him. "You do realize that we have absolutely no proof that Stanton stole the cross? Or even that he found it if it comes to that. Spencer and I located what we both believe was the hiding place for the cross, and an empty box seems to indicate the cross was stolen, but everything else is based on hearsay."

"Yeah, I know. Sometimes I scare myself." Burke shrugged with a faint grin. "But since your hearsay seems to be on par with other people's facts, I'll risk embarrassment and disgrace, to say nothing of the loss of my pension."

"If you wind up needing a job," Kane said, "I could use another hand at the ranch. Mucking out stalls or something."

"I'll keep that in mind," Burke told him politely.

LATE THAT NIGHT, cuddled close to Drew's side in their bed and feeling utterly sated in the peaceful aftermath of lovemaking, yet oddly wide awake, Spencer murmured, "You didn't protest when Kane and Tyler decided to fly to Milan first thing in the morning. I thought you would."

He rubbed his chin in her soft hair. "I don't think Stanton will risk going through Milan, and I don't think Kane believes it, either. He just wanted to distract Tyler before she got impatient and decided to try and track down the cross herself."

"Would she?"

"Sure she would. And could. Kane calls her a lightning rod for trouble, and he's right. Of course, he's just the same."

"But he doesn't want to go after the cross?"

"The cross, yes. Stanton, no. He's encountered Stanton at least once that I know of, and he doesn't want Tyler anywhere near the man. Like you, she wouldn't let him go alone." Drew was silent for a moment, then said quietly, "Burke told you, didn't he?"

"Yes." She could feel the steady beat of his heart beneath the hand resting on his chest, and a chill of fear went through her as she thought of how quickly and ruthlessly a life could be snuffed out. "Why didn't you tell me?"

His arms tightened around her. "Because I didn't want you to look at me and know how easily I could kill."

Without hesitation Spencer said, "You could never kill easily, I know that."

"I could kill Stanton."

"Yes. But not easily. Not without it costing you."

Drew was vividly aware of the silk of her skin touching his, the warm aliveness of her body pressed against him, and thought that if Stanton in any way threatened her, killing him would be a very easy thing. He wondered if Spencer had yet realized that his mask of civilization—that any man's—was only a thin veneer of polish over savage instincts that two million years of evolution had failed to tame.

No man was civilized when he loved a woman. Once her brand marked his heart—once her unique scent and taste filled his senses, her eyes looked at him in passion and her body accepted his—all the instincts of the cave were reborn in him. She was his, to be protected and cherished, and he belonged to her body and soul.

Drew wanted to tell her that, wanted to tell her that he loved her. Talking about Stanton had reminded him again of how vulnerable he was to her. Like that thief who had instantly handed over a gold idol and had begged for the lives of his wife and unborn child, Drew knew that if a knife was held to Spencer's throat, he'd do anything. Anything.

Patience was wearing away under the strain of uncertainty. He wanted—needed—to bind her to him with all the words a man could utter, all the hopes and promises and dreams, all the tenderness and potential pain that came with love and need, and life.

She moved against him just then, snuggling closer, and he felt the softness of her belly pressed against his hip. Life, he thought, and a strange sensation that was both yearning and alarm welled up inside him. His child growing inside her delicate body. . . . It was possible, he knew. They might already be connected in the most basic and primitive way possible, their very cells merged to form a new life.

Drew made a rough sound, shifting on the bed so that he could kiss her. She responded to his tenderness as instantly as she did to his passion, her lips clinging softly to his, her hands lifting to stroke his face gently. His heart was hammering and he knew his voice was too harsh when he spoke, but he couldn't rein in the surging emotions that forced the words out of him.

"I just realized . . . you could be pregnant."

Spencer went utterly still, her hands motionless against his cheeks, and in the dimness of the room the dark shine of her eyes told him nothing. But she didn't flinch from the abrupt words and harsh tone, and her reply was very soft.

"Yes, I could be." She drew a quick breath, not quite nervously but a little wary, and added even more softly, "As a matter of fact, I think the timing is right. Or wrong, depending on—on how you feel about it. So much has been happening so fast, and— It wasn't deliberate, Drew."

He lowered his head and kissed her deeply, until her hands slid to his neck and the tension drained from her body. Even then he couldn't stop kissing her, brushing his lips over her face, her throat, and his voice was still rough when he muttered, "We're getting married as soon as we get back to D.C."

She tensed again and whispered, "Because I might be pregnant?"

"No," he said against her throat, and raised his head to look down at her with burning eyes. "Because we belong together. Because I love you so much I'm half out of my mind with it." His own body was rigid, and he went through silent agony in the few seconds it took her to respond.

Spencer made a choked little sound and lifted her head from the pillow, kissing him with warm, trembling lips. "I was afraid to hope you could love me again after what I did to you, and I didn't think you'd want me to love you . . . but I do. I love you, Drew, I love you. . . ."

The relief was staggering, and fierce satisfaction filled him. He held her tightly against him, burying his face in the soft curve of her neck. "I kept telling myself I wasn't going to push you any more than I already had," he said huskily. "You'd been through so much, and I was such a bastard at first that I couldn't expect you to trust me. But I needed to hold on to you because I was so terrified of losing you again. God, sweetheart, I've loved you for twelve years."

She'd been right, Spencer thought in a daze of happiness as his hungry mouth and urgent hands brought her body alive. Losing herself in him was exhilarating when he gave of himself as well. And he did. She had no doubts, now, about what he was feeling. There was nothing coolly detached about him, nothing dispassionate or remote.

He loved her as if this would be his one and only chance, so fiercely tender it made her throat ache. His powerful body trembled with the force of his desire, and the heat of it burned in his eyes even in the darkness. He touched her as if she were infinitely precious and desperately needed, his hands shaking, and his voice was choked with intense emotion when he murmured words of love against her skin.

As always, it was frantic and almost wild, but this time openly expressed love made it even more profound, and the hot, sweet tension that built inside their straining bodies was so acute in its power that when it finally snapped they were hurled into a shattering culmination.

She refused to let him leave her afterward, her arms and legs clinging with what strength was left to them. She was so blissfully happy, so gloriously content that she never wanted to move again. It seemed to her a miracle that he could love her, and she almost held her breath for fear of having imagined it.

Drew brushed his lips tenderly across her closed eyelids and, catching the faint trace of salt at the corners, murmured deeply, "You always cry."

Spencer opened her eyes slowly and smiled up at him. "I can't seem to control that," she admitted. "Does it bother you?"

"It's a little unnerving. Scared the hell out of me the first time. I thought I'd hurt you."

Softly, she said, "I feel so much when you love me that it's almost frightening."

"You aren't alone in that," he said, kissing her. "I love you so much, Spencer. I made the mistake of hiding that before, but I never will again."

She didn't doubt that. Curled up at his side as sleep finally claimed them, she didn't doubt anything at all.

But she had peculiar dreams. Unsettling dreams. In them, Drew was holding her hand and telling her how much he loved her while another voice, a distant voice, kept saying, *"The painting and the statue—I did them both, don't you remember? But years later, when I was old and he was gone. You have to remember, it's very important. And I was English, not Austrian. That's important, too."*

Something had her other hand, pulling it as if trying to get her away from Drew, and she was staring at the face of a clock with huge, crooked numbers and wildly spinning hands. She wanted to look at the clock and think about it, because she had the feeling there was something she should have remembered about it. But that other thing was tugging hard, trying to pull her away from Drew, and the grip of it was cold and cruel.

Then her father's voice, strong and clear as it had been before the stroke, said, *"Behind the clock, Princess. Look behind the clock."*

Spencer pulled her hand free of the cruel grip and turned to Drew, wanting to tell him that she knew now, that she remembered everything, but he kissed her with so much warm tenderness that she forgot again. . . .

chapter eleven

SPENCER MURMURED DROWSILY and opened her eyes with definite reluctance. The room was bright with morning, and Drew was leaning over her.

"Go back to sleep, sweetheart," he said. "It's early."

She looked at him, waking up instantly and feeling her heart turn over with so much emotion that all she could say was, "I love you."

He kissed her again, his face so transformed by tenderness that it moved her almost unbearably. "I love you, too." His voice was husky, topaz eyes glowing.

She had heard the love in his voice in the night, had felt it in his touch, but now she saw it in the light of day and it was a naked thing. She had a curious certainty that Drew's mask of detachment was gone forever now, shattered by the power of the feelings between them. He would never again hide what he felt from her, and he would never again be able to hide what he felt from others.

When he straightened, smiling down at her, she tried to think of something casual to say and found it when she realized he'd been up for some time. "You're dressed."

His mouth twisted slightly. "Not because I want to be. I wouldn't leave you willingly, believe me. Burke called, damn him. He wants me to meet him for coffee downstairs."

Uneasiness stirred in her, a reminder of problems even in happiness. "Trouble?"

Drew shook his head. "He's expecting his men to check in with him in the next hour or so. I should be there, so we'll know what's happening."

"I didn't hear the phone," she commented, and glanced at the clock on the nightstand as she sat up, absently holding the covers to her breasts. "I might as well get up, too."

"What you should do is rest," he told her.

"I don't feel at all tired. Besides, I want to have breakfast with you." She smiled at him. "Why don't you meet Burke, and I'll join you when I've had a shower."

He hated leaving her so much that the thought of spending even a couple of hours out of her presence was almost unbearable, but he was also determined to never again see the painful white exhaustion her delicate face had held in Paris. He'd thought a few extra hours of sleep would be good for her, and it hadn't been his intention to wake her at all. But she was glowing, contentment and love shining in her eyes, and it would have taken a much harder heart and far stronger will than his to refuse her anything.

"All right." He rose to his feet. "We'll be on the terrace. Take your time. Burke needs at least half a pot of coffee before he's reasonably human."

Her soft chuckle followed him out of the room, and he was

smiling to himself quite unconsciously as he left the suite and went downstairs. He'd been awake since dawn, just lying there watching her sleep and feeling incredibly lucky. God knew the path had been a rocky one, but they'd made it, and there was a sense of wonder in that. He'd thought of all the future mornings and waking up beside her, feeling her warm body against his, and he was so damned grateful.

He walked through the early-morning quiet of the lobby and went out into the terrace, thinking absently that if the chill in the air was still present when Spencer joined them, they'd go inside for breakfast.

Burke, seated at one of the tables with a pot of coffee and a phone, looked up with a scowl and said sourly, "I hate people who're cheerful at the crack of dawn."

Drew sat down and poured a cup of coffee for himself. "Dawn cracked a couple of hours ago, friend. Are you sitting out here in the cold to stay awake?"

"More or less," Burke admitted, smothering a huge yawn with one hand.

Knowing that the agent tended to go weeks at a time short on sleep and that he'd had little chance to rest since completing the investigation in Madrid, Drew merely said, "If that was your first cup of coffee, drink another one. You're still half asleep."

"Three-quarters," Burke muttered, pouring more coffee. "But awake enough. I got two calls during the night," he added abruptly.

Drew felt tension steal over him. "You didn't tell me that. Trouble?"

"Hell, I don't know." Slouched in his chair, the collar of his black leather jacket standing up to frame a hard jaw and his flying brows drawn together in a frown, Burke looked more like a ruffian than a cop in an international police agency. "One of my guys knows the border as well as his own face, and he got antsy. Said the place Stanton supposedly crossed over into Italy was all wrong, too obvious, nobody on the run would pick it if there was an easier way—and there is, a few miles east. I told him to go check it out if he wasn't happy."

"Did he?"

"He went. I haven't heard from him yet."

"What about the second call?"

"From a cop on this side of the border. He said he wasn't sure he should be calling me at such an ungodly hour, but something had been bothering him. He stopped a car for speeding yesterday—before the bulletin on Stanton went out—and gave the driver a ticket. He didn't think any more about it until he heard the bulletin, and realized from the description that Stanton had been his racing driver."

"So?" Drew stared at his friend. "Stanton was in a hurry."

"Yeah," Burke said softly. "An almighty hurry, according to the cop. But he wasn't making tracks for the border. He was heading for Innsbruck."

Drew frowned. "The cop must have been mistaken."

"Don't think so. I recognized the type even though I was barely awake. Very painstaking and thorough, and he's been patrolling those roads a lot of years. He also described Stanton perfectly, right down to the scars on his face."

"What time yesterday?" Drew asked slowly.

"Eleven-thirty," Burke answered. "The cop gave me the precise location, and I checked it on the map. There's no way Stanton could have crossed the border at noon, at least not where your informant said he crossed. Could your man have been bribed to lie about it?"

"I don't think so—but I don't know for sure."

"In that case, we'd better assume the cop was right. Stanton was still in Austria at eleven-thirty yesterday morning, and he was heading toward Innsbruck."

"That doesn't make sense," Drew objected. "He might want to lie low for a while, but not in Austria."

"Maybe he meant to get out and had some kind of trouble. Or maybe he just meant for us to think he'd gotten out."

After a moment Drew said, "He usually has a hired gun. I suppose he could have sent him over the border, looking the part, in the hope that we'd follow a false trail. But to head back toward Innsbruck . . . Why would he?"

"I can think of one reason," Burke said flatly.

Drew immediately shook his head. "He didn't come back to get me, not with the cross in his hands."

"Are you sure about that?"

"Burke, if there's anything I know, it's that Stanton would never risk something as valuable to him as the cross for the sake of revenge. No matter how much he hates me. And he wouldn't trust a flunky to carry it over the border for him. That means he still has the cross."

Burke looked at him for a long moment, then sighed. "That was my reading. So—the question is, what's the bastard up to?"

Drew was silent, conscious of an itchy sensation between his shoulder blades. It was a feeling he recognized. If you could pinpoint an enemy's location, or at least his direction, you could make certain he wasn't coming up behind to blindside you. Stanton could be anywhere.

Absently, he said, "Kane and Tyler get off all right?"

"Yeah, they left about an hour ago. One of their contacts checked in around midnight, after you and Spencer had gone to your room, but he didn't have anything."

"So we wait," Drew said.

BITS AND PIECES of her dream came back to Spencer as she stood under the shower, but she could make no sense of them.

Something about the statue and a painting and a clock. The images wouldn't come clear in her mind.

Shrugging to herself, she decided to forget about it for the moment. She dried off and got dressed, thinking instead about the night before. In a way, she didn't regret the twelve years behind her and Drew. She *had* been too young for him then, too immature to understand him, too timid to love him as she'd longed to do. If he had married her then, she might never have found any certainty in herself, and he might well have ended up with a woman who was too blinded by the gloss of gold to notice the enduring strength of the metal itself.

Now everything was right between them. In a few short days, it seemed that her entire life had changed. Even with the worries about her father, she had never been happier, and the future looked wonderful.

She was smiling to herself as she went into the bedroom to put her shoes on, humming a little. But when she stepped into the sitting room, a cold shock like nothing she'd ever felt before stopped her in her tracks, and a gasp left her lips.

"Don't do anything stupid," he said softly.

He might, at one time, have been a fairly ordinary-looking man. He was a little above medium height, with exceptionally wide shoulders and a light way of standing that suggested both grace and agility. He was dressed casually. But all semblance of normality ended at his neck. From the collar of his plaid shirt, ugly, angry scars twisted upward, puckering the flesh and virtually covering the right side of his face all the way up to his hairline. A dull black patch angled over his missing right eye, and the left eye that was fixed on her face was as colorless as a glacier and just as icy.

"I once saw him cut a woman's throat."

Spencer swallowed hard, tearing her gaze from his ruined face to look at the gun in his hand. It was pointed squarely between her breasts. She had never imagined anything like the primitive terror that held her immobile as she looked at that deadly weapon, and knew without a shadow of a doubt that the man holding it was entirely capable of killing her as easily and unfeelingly as he'd swat a fly.

"What do you want?" she whispered.

His head cocked to one side and an empty little smile curved his lips. "You know who I am?"

"Yes. You—you're Stanton."

He half bowed in a mockery of courtesy, but the gun never wavered. His voice was utterly without inflection. "I suppose that bastard Haviland told you. Well, no matter. I want what I came here for, Miss Wyatt. The cross."

That surprised her so much that fear was overlaid with confusion. "The cross? But you got to it first."

Stanton laughed shortly. The free hand that had been behind his back moved, and he held up a cross. "I got this."

Spencer looked at it blindly for a moment, seeing only a cross shape roughly twelve by eight inches in size. Then she focused on it, saw that it looked like gold and was encrusted with drab, colored stones. *That's wrong. There are too many stones and the ruby's off center.* The thought came from nowhere, and she accepted it numbly. This wasn't the Hapsburg Cross, not the one her father had described.

"I was in such a hurry I barely looked at it," Stanton said flatly. "For a while. Then I looked. It's a damned fake, and not a very good one at that." With a sudden, vicious fury, he flung it across the room, and it thudded against the wall before dropping to the floor. "I want the real one—and you're going to take me to it."

She'd flinched when he threw the cross, and stared at him in total bewilderment as his demand sunk into her brain. "Take you to it? I thought it was in the cave. That's all I knew, to find the cave. I don't know where the cross is."

"You must know," he said, his tone reasonable now. "You still have Wyatt's original notes. What I had were copies. You kept something to yourself, didn't you? Something about why there was a fake cross instead of the real one. You know how to find the real cross, don't you?"

"No, I . . ." Her voice trailed off as the softly insistent voice in her head said that there *was* something she knew, something she just couldn't remember. Her face must have given her away, because Stanton's empty, colorless eye narrowed.

"I thought so." He cocked the pistol and very matter-of-factly said, "Tell me, or I'll kill you."

Whatever she knew was still elusively trapped in her memory, but Spencer was certain of one thing. Stanton would kill her whether or not she gave him an answer. He'd killed that other woman when he no longer needed her, without hesitation or mercy, and he'd probably killed others as well.

The only hope she had was to stall for time, to keep herself alive long enough to try to escape him, or long enough for Drew to realize something was wrong—

No. No, she didn't want Drew coming after them. He'd said he was never careless, but this would make him careless, she knew. Careless of his own life. He'd do whatever it took to get her away from Stanton safely, and if that meant offering himself as a target the other man wouldn't be able to resist, then that's what he'd do.

She couldn't bear the thought of that. The memory of Stanton killing another woman years ago still haunted Drew; what would it do to him to see it happen all over again, this time to the woman he loved—and perhaps the seed of life inside her?

Spencer looked at Stanton, and though the terror was still cold in her mind, another emotion overpowered it. She wouldn't let this animal hurt Drew like that. She wouldn't. And she wouldn't be another helpless victim sacrificed to his greed. There had to be a way, there *would* be a way to defeat him.

"Tell me!" Stanton barked harshly.

Only seconds had passed, she realized, and her mind worked with the clarity of desperation. Time, she needed time. Clearing her throat, she said, "I don't know where the cross is, but I might be able to figure it out. Something about the statue bothered me when—when I looked at it. I don't know what it was, but I think if I could see the statue again, I might remember."

"You're lying." His finger tightened on the trigger.

Spencer held her voice steady with an effort. "Don't you think if I'd found the cross—or knew for sure where it was—I'd have gotten it and gone back home right away? It's for my father that I came after it, and he's dying. I don't have much time."

A frown made his face even more hideous as he considered her words. "*Was* there something in the notes I didn't see, or are you just stalling?" he demanded.

She swallowed hard. "Dad got a journal. Just recently. And there were some books I found on my own. There's something about the statue I can't remember. I need to see it."

It would take at least two hours and probably three to reach the cave, she thought. They'd have to go by horseback, and one horse could never carry them both—they'd have to take two. That would put at least some distance between them. She didn't know what advantage it would give her, but she was determined to think of something.

"All right," Stanton said, smiling in a way that made nausea rise in her throat. "We'll go up to the cave, just the two of us. I don't want company. So you're going to write a note to your lover, in case he realizes you're gone. Tell him something he'll believe."

The phone in there was on the end table beside the couch, and there was a notepad and pen beside it. Spencer glanced at it, then looked back at Stanton a little helplessly. She couldn't think of a single reason she would have left the inn without Drew, even though she tried to.

Impatiently, Stanton said, "Tell him you went off to buy a gift for your father. And be convincing about it."

She moved slowly and carefully as she got the notepad and wrote a brief message, very conscious of the gun trained unwaveringly on her. Stanton told her to put the pad on the coffee table when she was through, then ordered her to step back and went over to read the note himself.

"Touching," he mocked.

She'd had to tell Drew she loved him, though she kept it simple and without undue emphasis. Looking at Stanton, she understood at least a part of what Drew felt for the man, because she was conscious of utter loathing for the first time in her life. It was a horrible feeling.

"Listen carefully," Stanton said in a flat, hard voice. "We're going down the back stairs, and out the side door to the street. I have a car waiting there, which you will drive to the stable. If you say a word, or indicate to anyone at all that you might be in trouble, I'll kill you. Understand?"

"Yes."

She didn't remember the fake cross lying on the floor until they were well on their way, and by then there was nothing she could do about it.

THE PHONE RANG, and Burke picked it up with a quickness that belied his air of sleepy exhaustion. They'd been sitting there, more or less silent, for nearly an hour, drinking coffee and waiting for some word of what was going on. Both men were accustomed to such waits and neither was given to restless gestures or movements; anyone watching would have assumed they were merely contemplating the view, with nothing on their minds more serious than idle interest in the scenery.

Burke just said hello into the receiver and then listened, his narrowing eyes fixed on Drew's face. The silvery sheen of them was unreadable at first, then slowly took on the cold gray of polished steel. When he hung up a few moments later, he was scowling.

"Well?" Drew's voice was very calm, almost unnaturally so.

"We just picked up the man who presumably crossed the border yesterday," Burke reported flatly. "Got him near Milan. He still had the fake scars on his face, and an eye patch stuffed in his pocket. Name's Roger Clay. The computer has a rap sheet on him half a mile long from the States. Mostly small stuff, burglary and forgery."

Drew waited a beat, then said softly, "What else?"

Burke cursed roughly, the words angry and a little baffled. "Clay talked—not willingly, but he talked. Said that he and Stanton were halfway to the border before Stanton took a good look at the cross—and went berserk."

"Why?"

"It was a fake, according to Stanton. He seemed pretty damned sure about it."

Drew stared at his friend, his mind moving with a peculiar sluggishness. A fake? That didn't make sense. Unless someone had found the cave long ago and stolen the real cross. But why go to the trouble of substituting a fake cross after the real one had been taken?

"I don't get it," Burke was saying. "There's no reason why anyone would want to *hide* a fake, especially as carefully and securely as you say this one was hidden."

"I know." Coldness was spreading through Drew's body slowly as a more important realization hit him, and his voice sounded hollow to his own ears when he said, "But that does explain why Stanton would come back here. He'd know it wasn't a trap for him—we couldn't have gotten into that cave before him without leaving evidence that we'd been there. He found a fake cross where the real one should have been, hidden hundreds of years ago. If I were him, I'd suspect that the real cross could still be there, somewhere."

Burke half nodded, frowning. "So, obsessed bastard that he is, he sent his hired thug across the border to buy him some time, and comes tearing back here to look again. But he must figure you're here by now—" Breaking off abruptly, Burke saw Drew's still face drain of blood as if a savage wound had opened up his veins.

"Not me," Drew said. "I didn't grow up listening to Allan Wyatt's stories."

Even as Burke was shoving back his chair and following Drew into the building, he was drawing his gun from the shoulder holster and swearing softly in a bitter monotone. They'd missed it, both of them. Drew had said Stanton wouldn't have come back to Innsbruck with the cross in his hand, but he had come back and that should have warned them to be more alert. It should have told them something was wrong. Once his mind was set on possessing something, Stanton would risk anything, even an attempt to slip past his worst enemy, with his soulless gaze fixed on the one person who might have heard more than she realized about the whereabouts of the cross.

They went up the stairs to the second floor, reaching the suite no more than a couple of minutes after they'd left the veranda. Drew used his key and shoved the door open, calling her name hoarsely. There was no reply. When he stepped into the bedroom, the bed was empty, the covers tumbled. A faint moisture in the air and the scent of Spencer's perfume hinted that she'd had time to shower. Drew checked the bathroom and found it as empty as the rest of the suite.

"Drew?"

He went quickly back into the sitting room, fear winding so tightly in his chest that it felt as if it were crushing him to death. Burke held out a notepad to him and Drew took it, reading the short message. His heart clenched at the final three words, remembering her soft voice speaking them.

"What do you think?" Burke asked.

"No. She wouldn't have left—on her own." Drew looked at him. "He's got her."

Burke had to look away from those suffering eyes. He'd known Drew Haviland a long time, had seen him in brutal situations and dangerous ones. He'd seen him amused, furious, charming, exhausted, deadly quiet, and remote with the iron control that was always a mask over unusually powerful instincts and emotions. Until now, he'd never seen his naked soul, or the clawing terror that only a man who loved a woman could ever feel.

Lon Stanton was a dead man. He'd done the one thing capable of shattering Drew's reluctance to kill. Burke had no doubt of that at all.

He looked around the room, trying to think. The cave, of course, and from Drew's description it was a bitch of a place for any kind of confrontation. His eyes sharpened, focused on a dull object lying on the floor, and he swiftly crossed over to pick it up. "Drew, look at this."

In a moment Drew was turning the cross in his hands. His hands were rock steady, and when he spoke it was mildly. "A fake, all right."

Burke studied his friend worriedly, fully aware that the quiet voice and seeming calm came, not from control, but from the paralyzing grip of emotions too violent to be mastered. It was just a matter of time before they blew, a matter of time before Drew exploded with a force that would leave everything between him and the man he wanted to kill in a shambles.

God, let her be alive, Burke thought.

He made his own voice even. "They're less than an hour ahead of us. Think, Drew. Is there any way we can get up there before them? There's no time to get a helicopter, even if we could find a spot to land it near the cave. Is horseback the only way?"

Drew nodded slowly, then set the cross on a table near the window and started for the door. "The only way," he murmured. "But I know a faster way."

That didn't make much sense to Burke then, but within an hour he understood. They'd gotten horses—and a rifle, handed to Drew instantly upon request from the stable owner—and made straight for the mountains. Drew rode fast and Burke, less experienced on horseback, clung to his own mount grimly as he kept up. He thought he was doing pretty well, too. Until the horse ahead of his own turned suddenly to begin a suicidal climb up a jagged, rock-strewn ridge.

Burke realized then what Drew intended to do, and though it appalled him he didn't waste breath or energy trying to dissuade his friend. He was too busy just hanging on.

There was only one way to the cave, a winding route among the high peaks and narrow valleys. No sane man would have attempted any other path. But Drew wasn't sane at the moment, and he wasn't attempting—he was doing.

AS SOON AS they left Innsbruck behind, Spencer knew what her edge was. She just wasn't sure how to use it.

Stanton was a lousy rider. He made her ride ahead of him and kept the gun trained on her constantly, but she'd seen enough to know that he was, at best, a Sunday rider. Experienced enough to be able to stay in the saddle under normal conditions, he swayed unsteadily on the uneven terrain and muttered curses to himself as they began the winding climb up into the mountains.

Spencer had never been more grateful for her own skills, allowing her body to relax into the horse's movements automatically while her mind worked desperately. The gun he held was no longer cocked. At some point he must have eased the hammer down though she hadn't seen him do it. She didn't know very much about guns, but she thought that might give her an extra fraction of a second before he could shoot her.

Little enough.

Could she spook his horse? The instinct of an inexperienced rider was to hold on tight at any sudden movement; would he drop the gun, or at least grab for the saddle horn, wasting a few precious seconds? If he was unable to control his mount, the horse would behave as startled horses tended to and quite likely bolt. Firing a gun accurately from a racing horse looked easy in the old cowboy movies, but in real life it would be sheer luck if he hit anything.

Like her.

She chewed on her bottom lip as they wound deeper into the mountains, closer and closer to the cave. She kept her shoulders a little hunched, trying her best to convey a beaten, submissive posture that might cause his guard to drop a bit. She tried not to think about Drew, because it hurt so badly to think she might never see him again.

The cave. She had to act before they reached the cave. Once Stanton was on his feet, her chances of getting away from him were virtually nil, and the thought of going into that dark, close place with him at her back was terrifying. In all likelihood she would be walking into her own grave.

Don't think about that, either.

A plan, she needed a plan. She could spook his horse easily enough, and she trusted her ability to control her own mount. But she needed to be able to put distance as well as obstacles between herself and him very quickly. Very, very quickly. Looking around without turning her head, she tried to remember if this was the way she and Drew had come yesterday. It seemed to be.

There was, she remembered, a short, level stretch just before they'd reach the cave. Lots of obstacles all around, between the huge boulders and clumps of trees, and if Stanton could even stay on a bolting horse in that kind of terrain he certainly wouldn't be able to fire a gun accurately.

She hoped.

LYING FLAT ON a rocky knoll, Drew sighted down the barrel of the rifle, scanning from the mouth of the cave above and to his right where he expected to see the riders. His mind was focused totally on the crucial need to hit his target precisely. This time. He wasn't even aware of the man beside him, except with some tiny part of his attention.

"You won't get a second chance," Burke said.

Drew barely heard him, but responded anyway. "I know."

"His track record with hostages . . ." Burke didn't complete that thought, just added in a very grim voice, "Don't let him get his hands on her."

"No," Drew said in a chillingly mild tone, "I won't let him do that."

Burke had just gotten his breathing under control. Going up the side of a mountain had been bad enough; coming down the other side was something that was going to give him nightmares for years to come. He wasn't just surprised they'd survived, he was utterly incredulous.

Drew must have infected both horses with his fury, because they'd bounded down inclines so steep they'd been practically sliding on their rumps, skidding on rock and loose gravel, snorting and grunting with the effort of remaining upright—or some reasonable facsimile of it. There'd been a couple of times Burke could have sworn his own horse had actually been airborne, and he knew there'd been daylight showing between him and the saddle on more than one occasion.

By the time they'd made it down, the horses had been covered with lathered sweat and looked both exhausted and wild-eyed, which wasn't, Burke thought, all that surprising.

Drew's attention had appeared to be fixed only on getting here in time, but as soon as he'd dismounted he had thrust his horse's reins into Burke's hands and said, "Walk them."

Burke walked them. He wasn't a man who took orders easily, but he wouldn't have protested that one even if he'd had the breath to do so. He cooled the horses, muttering to himself and to them, glancing up occasionally to make certain Drew was still there, still waiting on the knoll.

When the horses were reasonably cool and a little calmer, Burke tied them in a small grove of trees as far from the cave as he dared to go, and joined Drew in waiting.

"Any sign of them?" he ventured, not even sure Drew would respond to the question, because the other man's tension was building visibly.

"Not yet." Drew's voice was strained now, and the blue eyes that scanned the area below were like windows to hell.

Burke knew all too well that he had no business letting Drew do this. Aside from the legalities, the man was quite simply in no shape to make reasoning decisions right now. But there were some decisions that would always be made with the heart and the instincts, not the mind. Burke knew that, too.

Besides, Drew was a much better shot.

"There." The strain had intensified in his voice, but there was relief as well, because Spencer was alive.

She was riding ahead of Stanton, Burke saw. They were too far away to allow any reading of their expressions, but she was slumped a bit and appeared both very small and utterly defenseless in the saddle. Any man with half a soul would be angry seeing her like that; it must have gone through Drew like a knife.

He tensed even more, and Burke glanced aside to see one long finger curl over the trigger of his rifle and tighten gently. Because of the winding path the riders were taking, Stanton didn't present a solid target. More often than not, Spencer's body shielded his.

Very softly, Burke said, "First clear shot you have—take him."

Drew didn't respond. He was completely motionless and didn't appear to be breathing at all, his unblinking eyes fixed on the riders coming toward them.

Several things happened very quickly then. In a violent movement, Spencer's horse whirled around on his haunches, half rearing so that his forelegs jarred Stanton's horse—which immediately shied away in an equally violent movement. Stanton didn't drop the pistol he held, but he used the same hand to grab for the saddle horn as his other hand hauled at the reins in an attempt to control his mount.

Without hesitation Spencer reined her horse around hard so that he turned full circle, and dug her heels into the surprised animal's flanks. The horse leaped forward, coming straight toward the knoll at a dead run far too dangerous for the uneven terrain. She was crouched low over his neck, obviously trying to make the smallest possible target of herself as she attempted to reach the nearest stand of trees.

It might have worked, except that Stanton's fury was as great as Spencer's need to escape. With raw strength instead of finesse he held his sidling horse under control, and the hand gripping the pistol raised it with almost blinding speed.

The crack of a rifle preceded the more hollow sound of the pistol by less than a heartbeat.

chapter twelve

SPENCER WAS DIMLY conscious of a crack of sound ahead of her and above, but the blast of the pistol behind her was closer and louder, and she knew she hadn't gotten far enough away to be safe. Something tugged at her sweater and she instinctively flinched to one side, but before she could think about what must have happened, her horse somehow got both front hooves into a ridiculously narrow little rut that he should have taken in stride.

Sometimes, Spencer thought in the instant granted to her, there was just no fairness in the world.

With a squeal, her big gelding pitched forward. There was no possible way to remain on a cartwheeling horse, and it would have been suicidal to try. Spencer's feet kicked free of the stirrups, her hands released the reins and she automatically allowed the horse's momentum to throw her as far away as possible so that he wouldn't fall on top of her. Astonishingly, she landed on her feet.

It had all happened so fast that the echoes of gunfire had barely died, and all Spencer's instincts were screaming at her to run. Still, she couldn't help glancing back over her shoulder, and what she saw surprised her so much that she froze.

Stanton's riderless horse was trotting back the way they'd come, reins trailing. The scarred man was draped over a big boulder, limp and motionless, his gun on the ground.

She stared, vaguely aware of her horse climbing to his feet with a snort. She barely had time to wonder what on earth had happened when a sound jerked her head back around, and she instantly forgot about Stanton. Drew was coming toward her, racing down a rocky slope in reckless haste, a rifle held in one hand. She ran to meet him.

Drew didn't realize that he dropped the rifle as soon as he reached her. All he was conscious of was the warmth and life of her in his arms. He lifted her completely off her feet, both his arms wrapped tightly around her, his face buried in her soft neck. In a hoarse, ragged voice, he murmured her name over and over.

Spencer could barely breathe, but it didn't seem important. She held on to him just as tightly, her arms around his neck, feeling too much to be able to say anything at all. His big, powerful body was shaking as he held her, and she could feel the wetness of his tears on her skin.

"I love you," she said, finally able to speak and saying the only thing that mattered.

"God, Spencer, I thought I'd lost you," he groaned, holding her even tighter. "I was terrified when I realized he had you."

He must have shot Stanton, she realized vaguely. He'd gotten here ahead of them—how had he done that?—and had lain in wait at the top of the knoll. She remembered, now, the sound she'd heard when Stanton had fired his gun—that must have been Drew's shot. She had no doubt that the scarred man was dead, and the only thing she felt about that was relief.

"I love you," Drew whispered, lifting his head to kiss her almost roughly.

She kissed him back, her response fervent, and when she could she said, "He thought I could take him to the cross, and all I could think of to do was stall and hope I could get away from him. I didn't know you'd be here—"

He kissed her again, then eased her down until her feet touched the ground. A faint smile curved his mouth, though he was still pale and strained. "You did a good job of shaking him up long enough for me to get a clear shot."

"I wasn't going to let him win if I could help it," she said intensely. "He'd already hurt you too much."

"If he'd hurt you . . ." Drew held her for a moment longer, still so shaken by how nearly he'd come to losing her that he knew he wouldn't be able to let her out of his sight for a long time to come. He had thought losing her ten years ago had been hell, but that was nothing compared to the mind-shattering terror of knowing she was in the hands of a man who would have killed her.

Of the two of them, it was Spencer who'd come through the past few hours in the best shape. She was smiling up at him, a little pale but calm. God, she'd taken a hellish chance by trying to escape Stanton, but the attempt had shown both courage and steely determination. She was far from being a helpless woman despite her slight delicacy, not waiting to be rescued by anyone or anything except her own skills.

And when she loved, it was clear that she loved with everything inside her. In her resolve to protect *him* from further hurt, she'd apparently thought little about her own safety.

Drew kept an arm around her as Burke approached them, realizing that the other man had picked up the rifle and gone to check on Stanton. The slight nod he gave was a definite answer to Drew's inquiring look.

"How did you get here ahead of us?" Spencer asked, both her arms around Drew's waist as she gazed up at him.

Burke snorted before Drew could reply. "Remind me to answer that—in great detail—when you've got a few hours to listen. Doesn't matter when—that's one trip I won't forget if I live to be a hundred."

"What do you mean?" she asked, puzzled.

Burke glanced at Drew, who was frowning a little, then said a bit dryly, "We came over the mountain." He went to get his and Drew's horses, muttering to himself.

"Over—" Spencer stared after him, then looked up at Drew. "You came over the mountain. *That* mountain?"

"I guess we did," Drew said, not looking around at the mountain in question. He honestly didn't remember getting here.

"You could have been killed!"

"No," he said. "I had to get to you."

Spencer gazed up at him for a long moment, then buried her face against his chest. Her throat was aching, and in her mind was a kind of numb wonder. She held on to him tightly, feeling his arms close around her and his cheek rub gently against her temple. She wanted to say, *You can't love me that much!* but she knew that he did, and the miracle of that held her speechless.

Burke returned to find them standing just that way, motionless, and even though he was a sympathetic man he was also trying to think of how he was going to explain all this to his superiors, so his voice was a bit wry when he spoke.

"Since Stanton's horse ran off and we can't double up going back to Innsbruck, I vote we leave now so I can send somebody back up here before dark."

Spencer turned her head toward him a little blindly. "I should look at the statue," she murmured. "Something about it is still bothering me, and since he didn't get the real cross—"

Drew shook his head. "We can come back up here tomorrow if you want."

She agreed to that, partly because she couldn't face the thought of climbing up the cliff after everything that had happened today. Reaction was setting in. She felt shaky and, more than anything else, just wanted to spend quiet time with Drew.

Her horse turned out to be uninjured from the fall, and since the other two horses were weary they rode slowly back down from the mountain to Innsbruck. The stable owner—whose other horse had come home some time before—accepted Burke's brief statement that the rifle, which he was holding, would be returned to him later. It wasn't until then that Spencer considered the possible legal problems of what had happened in the mountains.

It was Drew who mentioned the subject as they entered the inn. "Are you going to have trouble because of this?" he asked Burke quietly.

The Interpol agent smiled. "Nothing I won't be able to handle. Of course, it would have been easier if we'd been able to get our hands on the real cross."

Spencer looked at him steadily. "Will there be any charges against Drew?"

"No. I'm a witness to the fact that Stanton was trying to kill you. Don't worry, nobody's going to waste any pity on the likes of him." He looked back at Drew. "I'll take care of the questions, at least for today."

"I'd appreciate that," Drew said. "I'm taking Spencer up to the suite, and if anybody other than room service knocks on the door before tomorrow morning, they'd better have a damned good reason."

His voice had been quite mild, but Burke thought as he went looking for a phone that he'd make certain he didn't disturb them, at least. He wasn't a fool.

Drew wanted to take care of Spencer. It was early afternoon; she hadn't eaten today, and even though she was still calm he knew that everything was catching up with her. He wanted to baby her, to keep her close and fuss over her, and just delight in cherishing her. So when he led her into their suite, that's what his mind was fixed on. Taking care of her.

"Why don't you change into something comfortable, while I order some food?" he suggested.

She stood on tiptoe to kiss his chin, smiling. "I think I'll take a shower, too. Wash away the dirt."

A sudden thought made Drew's fingers tighten around hers. She didn't look as if she'd been hurt and there were no marks on her that he could see, but he was too familiar with Stanton's ruthless methods to rule out the possibility.

"Sweetheart, he didn't hurt you, did he?"

"No, he never even touched me. I'm fine, Drew, really." She squeezed his hand and then released it, going into the bedroom to undress for her shower.

He went and got the room-service menu, but because she was out of his sight and he couldn't bear it, he went to the doorway of the bedroom thinking that he'd ask her what she felt like eating. He stopped there, a shock jolting through him.

Spencer was standing by the bed, neatly made now since housekeeping had been and gone hours before. She'd pulled her sweater off and was holding it in her hands, looking down at it in faint surprise. As he watched she slowly put one slender finger through a ragged bullet hole.

"My God," Drew breathed.

She looked up quickly and started to cover the hole with her hand as if to hide it from him. Then, in a voice that was trying hard to be light, she said, "He missed, after all. Close only counts in horseshoes."

Drew threw the menu aside and went to her, pulling her into his arms frantically. She was *here*, he told himself, safe and unharmed, but the visible evidence of how terribly close that bullet had come to hitting her was like a knife inside him. He had to hold and touch her, to feel the reality of her warm body against his and the fiery, astonishing strength of her passion. As always, she was instantly responsive, her mouth lifting for his, arms wreathing around his neck as she pressed herself even closer.

The bullet-torn sweater fell to the floor and was soon hidden from sight beneath the jumble of clothing that followed it.

"I'M GOING TO get fat if you keep feeding me like this," Spencer remarked nearly two hours later as she finished the very belated lunch Drew had ordered.

"You barely eat enough to keep a bird alive," he retorted, smiling at her.

She chuckled, but pushed herself back from the table and wandered over to pick up the fake cross. He turned his chair to watch her, knowing that, despite her contentment with him, the loss of the cross was a painful disappointment. She hadn't said anything about it, but he knew her well enough by now to be able to read her smoky eyes.

Right now, they were distracted.

"Something's bothering you about that cross," he said.

"Yes. And, like the statue, I don't know what. I keep thinking there's something I should remember." She paused, turning the cross slowly in her hands, then said, "Why would anyone hide a fake?"

"They wouldn't. It doesn't make sense." Drew might have said

more, but the phone rang and he went to answer it. He spoke absently in German, watching her, then switched to English and said,
"She's right here, Tucker. Is everything all right?"

Spencer went to him quickly, reassured by his smile as he listened to whatever Tucker had to say. He handed her the phone a
moment later, and her relief intensified when she heard that her
father was fine—stronger, in fact—and that his doctor was cautiously optimistic.

"Your father hasn't said anything more about it, but I found
the journal, Miss Spencer," Tucker said.

"I suppose it's in German," she said dryly.

"No. English."

She felt tension steal over her. "Whose journal is it, Tucker?"

"A lady by the name of Theresa Garland. The entries cover
the years from 1648 to 1650. I've had no chance to read it yet,
but I can tell you that she lived in Innsbruck, at least during
those years."

Garland. Theresa Garland. It sounded familiar. "Oh—she was
Kurt's sweetheart. And she—" Staring at Drew, Spencer suddenly
remembered. "She did that painting of him. Tucker, when you get
a moment, start reading the journal, would you, please?"

"What am I looking for?" Tucker asked.

"Anything about the cross. She knew about it, knew Kurt had
taken it. She had to. Let me know if you find anything."

"I will."

Spencer hung up the phone and then sat down on the couch,
frowning. She put the fake cross on the coffee table before her and
stared at it. When Drew came to sit beside her, she told him what
Tucker had found, repeating her realization that Theresa Garland
had been Kurt's portraitist.

"I've never heard of a female artist during that era," Drew
commented slowly.

"I hadn't, either. I guess that was why it stuck in my mind. She painted his portrait—and she sculpted that statue."

"Are you sure?"

"That's what was bothering me. When we were in the cave you said something about different artists interpreting subjects in different ways. What I'd been thinking was that the statue was the image of that painting I'd seen—and it is. Two different artists working in different mediums could never have gotten the statue and painting so precisely alike."

Drew nodded. "Okay, you've sold me. What does it mean?"

Spencer laughed a little. "I was hoping you could tell me." She thought about it. "Theresa painted the portrait sometime around 1650. The journal Tucker found covers 1648 to 1650. But that was years after Kurt died."

"And after the Thirty Years' War," Drew noted. "Didn't it end around 1648?"

"Yes." Spencer brooded, frowning at the fake cross lying before her.

Trying to help her, Drew said, "You thought the journal might be important because Allan seemed to be fretting about it. But Tucker didn't understand him because he was speaking German."

Absently, Spencer said, "Yes, and if you talk in your sleep it'll probably drive me crazy. If Dad's any example, multilingual people run the gamut of their languages whenever their conscious mind isn't in control."

"I don't talk in my sleep."

She sent him a glance that was a little amused. "We'll see, won't we?"

"Never mind," Drew murmured, hoping his subconscious could keep its mouth shut. "The point is that Allan must have read the journal. So what could he have found in Theresa Garland's writings to tell him something about the cross?"

Spencer went very still suddenly. "Wait a minute. Before I left home Dad said something I didn't understand. I thought he was rambling, so I didn't really pay attention."

"What did he say?"

She closed her eyes, concentrating. "It was so disjointed. Something about . . . the cross not being what I thought. Something about them hiding it—like the clock." Her eyes snapped open, and she looked at Drew.

"The clock? What clock?"

Spencer had the strangest feeling. It was like that song she couldn't remember, only now the tune was getting louder, and the words were falling gently into place. "That's what he meant," she murmured. "Drew, he knew we'd find a fake. He knew it was a deception—just like his trick safe."

"The real thing was behind the clock," Drew said, realizing. "A little sleight of hand, to fool would-be thieves. But why would Kurt have gone to all that trouble? The cave alone would have kept the cross secure, certainly long enough for him to go back and retrieve it later."

"Yes, but . . . what was bothering Dad must have been written in that journal thirty years after Kurt died." Her mind was working rapidly now, considering possibilities. "Suppose that Kurt did just put the box holding the real cross in the cave, and told Theresa where he'd hidden it."

"That makes more sense," Drew agreed, watching her. "Since he planned to get it later, he wouldn't have bothered with anything fancy."

"Right. But then the priest was killed, and Kurt died after nursing Theresa. She was the only one left who knew where the cross was hidden."

Drew nodded slowly. "It wouldn't have been wise to go and get it since it was stolen property."

"And she might not have wanted anyone else to know for sure that Kurt had stolen it. Whatever else he was, it seems clear he was devoted to her. She certainly loved him—that comes across in the painting. So she has this worrying knowledge of the cross, just lying there in the cave. It belongs to the Hapsburgs, and it should get back to them—eventually, at least. But she can't bear to brand Kurt a thief, not while she's alive and able to see it happen, anyway."

Drew, who had discovered many such tragic stories while unearthing antiquities over the years, didn't find it at all farfetched. He did find it fascinating, and even more so to watch Spencer work it all out. "I wonder who helped her get the statue up there?" he mused. "Allan did say 'they' had hidden it, didn't he?"

Spencer nodded. "I remember that distinctly. It had to be someone she trusted. I'm not sure why she would have thought up the trick, though. To keep casual thieves from getting the cross if they found the cave?"

"That sounds likely. Maybe her journal will tell us."

It hit Spencer then. The cross. The elusive relic her father had spent his life in pursuit of—and they'd found it. Together, her father, Drew and herself, each of them supplying bits and pieces of fact and intuition, had located a priceless object nearly five hundred years old.

She held her hands out before her as if holding something on her palms, and murmured, "Behind the clock. Behind the deception." Slowly, one of her hands turned, and a finger pointed at her middle.

"In the statue," Drew said softly.

Spencer laughed unsteadily and looked at him with glowing eyes. "We found it. Drew, we found it!"

"You found it," he said, drawing her into his arms. "You and Allan." He had no doubt that the cross would be there, where it had waited for centuries.

"Dad did most of the work, but you—if you hadn't been with me, it never would have happened." Her delicate face changed, and one hand lifted to touch his cheek. "So much never would have happened. I love you."

"I love you, too, sweetheart," he said, holding her next to his heart where she belonged.

THE AUSTRIAN AUTHORITIES were delighted the following afternoon when Spencer and Drew returned from a final trip into the mountains with a solid-gold cross studded with rubies and diamonds. The Hapsburg Cross.

Since Spencer already had permission to take the cross to the States for her father to see, and since she and Drew asked nothing more than that, they were able to leave Innsbruck the next day. The authorities had decided not to announce the find publicly just yet, so that Spencer and Drew could transport the cross quietly without being bothered by collectors or the media.

One week to the day after Spencer had flown away from D.C. strained, miserable, lonely and afraid, she quietly entered her father's bedroom. Drew was behind her, and in her hands she carried a heavy wooden box.

"Daddy?" she said softly. "We have something to show you."

SHE LEANED AGAINST the parapet and looked out on the lush green Welsh countryside, taking advantage of the bright sunlight and still-warm breeze. The weather could change, Drew had warned her, and probably would since it was early fall. They'd feel the chill of stone walls then, he had said wryly.

Spencer was rather looking forward to that, even though unobtrusive central heating would no doubt preserve only the illusion of the hardships of an earlier age. In any case, her surroundings suited her very well.

It had been two months since she and Drew had left Innsbruck, and six weeks since their quiet wedding. Her father had been present—in a wheelchair. Holding his dream in his hands had done more for his health than any amount of medical care, and though he was still frail, his doctors were confident.

So was Spencer. Allan Wyatt had stood off the grim reaper long enough to see the cross, and he'd continue to battle, she believed, in order to hold his first grandchild. In fact, if she had anything to say about it, he might well hang on a good many years yet, if only to see how many grandchildren he eventually ended up with.

Spencer wanted four children, at least. Drew had suggested two and Allan, chuckling, had advised them to split the difference. But Spencer was determined. She had discovered just how determined she could be—and so had Drew. Not that he appeared to mind her stubbornness.

Strong arms closed around her from behind, and warm lips briefly kissed the nape of her neck. "Here you are," Drew said in a chiding tone. "I've been looking for you nearly an hour."

She leaned back against him, smiling. "You should have tried here first," she told him.

"I should have—especially since I specifically told you not to come here alone because half these stones are crumbling."

"I was careful," she said serenely. "Besides, I needed some fresh air."

Drew hugged her, then slid one hand down over her still-flat belly. "How's she doing?"

Though morning sickness hadn't troubled Spencer very much, there were occasional bouts of nausea—and a tendency to get sleepy, which was another reason Drew worried about her being up here alone.

Spencer tilted her head back and looked up at him, amused. "She? You're convinced this one's a girl, aren't you?"

"Absolutely positive," he said.

"What makes you so sure?"

He smiled. "Just a feeling."

"Umm. Well, then, *she* is doing just fine. In fact, she's very impressed at being in a real castle. With a real moat and drawbridge. She's already spoiled rotten."

Drew laughed.

"I'm serious," Spencer said severely, trying not to laugh. "How on earth is any other man ever going to be able to live up to her father? Talk about a Cinderella complex!"

"Princess?" Drew was still smiling. "I thought I'd cured you of that nonsense, sweetheart."

She turned in his arms and reached up to touch his face, her eyes suddenly tender. "It isn't nonsense. The problem is that girls get silly ideas of what a prince is. But if they're lucky—very, very lucky—they grow up and find the real thing."

Drew kissed her, then kept an arm around her as he led her back into the castle. He wasn't a prince, but he no longer minded if Spencer thought he was. With a woman like her by his side, loving and loved, being a man was all that counted.

author's note

TO MY KNOWLEDGE, there exists no Hapsburg Cross. All historical characters mentioned in connection with this mythical object are either figments of my imagination or else—like Maximilian I—merely recognizable names with which I wove the threads of my story.